# THE TURKISH MIRROR

## LISA C. MURPHY

Denny
Creek
Press

The Turkish Mirror
2nd Edition
Copyright 2018 by Lisa C. Murphy

ISBN Paperback: 978-1-946832-05-4
ISBN Kindle: 978-1-946832-07-8
LCCN 2nd edition: 2018900484

Denny
Creek
Press

Kirkland, Washington

Originally published by
Crispin Hammer Publishing Company
Copyright 2011 by Lisa C. Murphy



This is a work of fiction. Names, characters, places, brands, media, and incidents are either the product of the author's imagination or are used fictitiously. The author acknowledges the trademarked status and trademark owners of various products referenced in this work of fiction, which have been used without permission. The publication/use of these trademarks is not authorized, associated with, or sponsored by the trademark owners.

# DEDICATION

*To my parents, O.T. and Carolyn Murphy, who dared to take our family beyond where tourists go. You taught me to love adventure.*

# ACKNOWLEDGEMENTS

This book touches on a transformative time in my life: a summer spent in Turkey when I was twelve years old. Heartfelt thanks to my husband Mark, who helped me find the buried seeds of that summer and grow them into fiction. And thanks, too, to my son Devin, who is ever my wise advisor on all things magical.

Many thanks to the critical readers of manuscript drafts who gave excellent feedback; Karen MacLeod, Craig Danner, Mark Jensen, O.T. Murphy, Carolyn Murphy, Dr. Jim Macon, Dr. Anita Peñuelas, Michael Peñuelas, Dr. Michael Martin, Dr. Adam Hirsh, and Betty Krier. Jiè's London dialect would have suffered terribly without the generous help of James Willcox; may he never get caught in porkies or lose his dosh. I am grateful to my father, O.T. Murphy, for his advice on French grammar; *tu est un vrai mec.* And a warm *Teşekkür ederim!* to my Turkish consultant (who asks to be unnamed) for help with language and cultural questions.

Every Monday I found myself in love again with my writing group, Kay Morison, Karen MacLeod, Cindy Wyckoff, and Pam Binder. Dear friends, honest hearts, and ruthless editors; thank you for helping me untangle the knots.

Though the characters invented here exist only in my novel, generosity, kindness, and the love of a good story were alive and well, 1970 on the Turkish Mediterranean. Thank you Turkey, for unsurpassed hospitality.

# ONE

mut's brown, callused toes touched lightly from rock to rock, graceful with excitement. Foamy hands from the Mediterranean grabbed his ankles, shocking blue green, frothing too white against his skin. That far out the jetty waves thundered from deep below, their curls surging higher, up his calves, hindered by boulders as he scrambled around to where the path was flat. Overhead gulls drifted, screeching harsh calls as inarticulate as the boy's. I never understood Umut's garbled Turkish, but I knew what he was saying: they were coming. From my place on the cliff I could see them. Around the thick jaw of rocky teeth that protected Incir's bay came small wooden boats, painted blue and trimmed with red and white, diamonds of green and yellow on their cabins. Behind the boats, the sun descended into the sea, pouring blood red on the agitated waves. The fishermen were coming; spared by the sea one more day. *Maşallah.*

Children on the beach—digging holes with branches, tossing bulbs of seaweed like balls—glanced up. They saw Umut's stick-thin arms waving and his tattered flapping trousers and they dropped their wood and seaweed. In a dash to be first they ran for the village, taking the goat path up the cliff, going home. Like so many crows, they took up the call: their fathers were coming.

Xiao Lian sat high on a rock at the root of the jetty that pushed into the bay. Xiao had been writing. A letter home. I knew because Mizou told me. His curled hand dipped brush into ink, forming character after character of elegant Chinese calligraphy, an inkstone balanced on the uneven rock by his knee. He took his eyes off the wind-ruffled page and peered down at Umut, leaping below him on the slippery boulders.

"Umut!" He waved, and the child looked up. Just *un petit instant*. Umut took his mind off his feet *un petit instant*— and he was gone. Slipped into the sea without a sound. Swallowed. *Mon Dieu!*

Xiao stood and dove: a fluid, singular gesture from sitting to swimming. He plunged without hesitation into brilliant Mediterranean blue, unconcerned for rocks that shattered the waves, or undertow, or the menace of that dreadful mirror.

His hands were the last that I ever saw of him. They thrust out of foam, gripping the boy's waist. With a heave they threw the child onto black, wet rock: battered, frightened, bleeding. We never found any trace of Xiao Lian, though Incir's boats searched coast and open sea, and the fishermen threw their nets where currents might carry him. I paced the jetty where he disappeared a hundred times in the next few days, wishing I had the courage to throw myself in after him.

But I didn't. Because of you, my girl. Xiao's death marked the beginning of your life, sweet daughter, and the end of my childhood.

～

"And now you know what became of your father, *ma petite*," says my Maman. Maman is parked in her sumptuous armchair by the window, the gray light of Paris buffing color off her blonde hair. She closes thin lips and sucks in a stiff inhale, exquisite in her hoity-toity suffering. I stand over her, a towering six feet, too much of a biffa to ever come across so frail. Her porcelain skin, same white as mine, looks cold. I am so disappointed. Of all the things I dreamed my real mum might be, I never imagined such a ghostly aristocrat.

I'm not in a warm-hearted mood, having just stolen, lied, and done a runner from London with the police on my arse and this effing mirror in my rucksack. No mood to be sweet to this snooty nonstarter of a mum, even if it is the first time I've ever laid eyes on her. I yank out the mirror by its handle. It's swathed in a snippet of silk the color of dead goldfish. Much as I fear that mirror, I love that red orange silk—royal orange in the sunlight, an eerie stain of red in the dark.

"Right then," I say, "Dad died. But that doesn't explain *this* bit of trouble, does it?" I chuck the mirror in her lap. She jerks away her hands, avoiding what just landed in the folds of her wool dress. The silk slides apart. Painted waves wash up the mirror's handle and reach for the monster sculpted in mosaic tile on the back. "I want a full account, Maman. You owe me."

She raises her eyes: fearless. Wealth is always fearless—Emma, George, the whole upper crust. Maman is as confident as her antique *fauteuil,* from which she can glance out the window, clock the spring buds on the trees of posh Square Barye. No matter how seriously I give it a go, I can't rattle them. But I haven't finished trying yet.

Her eyes lock onto mine and I dare her to hate me. Sixteen years after she abandoned me, let her tell me to my face that she doesn't want me. Let her demand to know how I found her, and threaten to punish the lot who snitched. But she smiles with well-bred restraint and contends with the silk, righting the mirror's handle under the cloth. She tops off her demitasse with coffee, then lounges back in the armchair's crewel upholstery. I see that I've inherited my stubbornness from her—that steel that drives Emma into a dark room to suffer migraines.

"*Eh bien*, I can tell you only half the story, as much of it took place in China." She raises her cup, sips, and swallows. "China's revolutions shaped your father, Xiao Lian Chin, scarred and raised him to the hero he was. Patriotism, sacrifice, torture…these were not things that made sense to me at the time. *Mon Dieu*, I was an artist, obsessed with beauty, a mere girl of twenty! I was lost, spoiled, furious…well, perhaps a bit like you, *non*?"

*Non,* I think, you don't know a bloody thing about me. But I keep my gob shut. She sips again delicately, as if each taste in her mouth were a meal to be savored start to finish. So absoeffinglutely French, my Maman.

"And you will judge what I did, *n'est pas*? That is why you have come." She laughs. I can't tell if she's having a laugh at me, or if I make her sad. Either way, it's not a cheerful wheeze. Her gaze travels from the fine scar above my left eye, across my cheek to my ear where the cartilage thickens, having re-healed poorly after one of my fights. She studies my hacked off hair, dyed blue.

"Sit down, *chérie.* You look uncomfortable, standing there in those heavy field boots. This is a long story, so you may as well enjoy some coffee as I tell it."

Then, as though the mirror were harmless, Maman scoops up the handle and lets silk fall away. She gazes at the inlaid tile on the mirror's back, not a bit intimidated by the horrid three-headed beast who glares back at her, dog jaws slobbering. She sets the mirror in her lap. "I know how hard a child can be on a parent," she says. "When I was young, I laid full blame on my father, your grandfather, the formidable Boris Trotoskov. Because of Boris I fled to the tiny Turkish fishing village of Incir, where I met Xiao."

She leans back and closes her eyes. For a minute I worry she will have a kip, leave me wondering what she's on about. Finally someone who knows my Chinese half—a hero of some sort, no less—and she's ready for an afternoon snooze. But then she continues in a voice soft as a misty spray of golden paint.

# TWO

ncir. Now, of course, it is a famous tourist *rendezvous* on what they call the "Turkish Riviera." But seventeen years ago in 1988, the first morning I woke in Incir, I opened my eyes to the sound of a braying donkey. I lay three rickety stories up in the only hotel in town: a tired, cheap *pension*. The wooden beams smelled of Lebanon Cedar. The boards of the roof bowed over my head under the weight of tile. Beyond the hoarse *braiment* of the donkey I could hear the sea, rustling like silk.

I turned my head on the pillow to look out the window and two black beads of eyes stared back into mine. Two antennae, long and finely segmented, bent towards my nose with a quiver of curiosity. Two gangly, folded back legs sprung delicately backwards.

*Mon Dieu!* I bellowed in fright and leaped off the bed. The cricket, startled by my unsociable reaction, took wing for the open window. Within a minute Mizou was knocking on my door.

"*Ça va ici?* Are you all right, Mademoiselle?" She pushed open the door and peered through the crack that the loose chain lock allowed.

"It was a cricket. Right on my pillow. It startled me." I leaned against the wall, buzzing with adrenaline.

"*Eh alors*, a cricket. The last poor survivor of summer. You screamed as though barbarians from the Taurus Mountains had invaded."

When Mizou had introduced herself the night before, she had claimed she was French. There is no doubt that her accent was flawless, but she made an error of gender—a female cricket, *une grillon*. Even you, Jiè, raised in London but tutored by Emma, would know that *grillon* takes the masculine gender.

"It was as big as my finger!" I stood trembling, thinking about the bizarrely large insect, humiliated by her scoffing.

"But still, she is smaller than you, *non*?" When I didn't answer, Mizou took a softer tone. "Breakfast is on the table. Please come, the family wants to meet you."

"I'll eat it here. You will bring it to me." *Tu va me l'emporter.*

*Tu.* It was out of my mouth without a moment's thought. *Tu* is for children, familiars, servants, and inferiors.

You, my daughter, given the example of gracious and tactful Emma, you would not have said *tu*. You stand as big and defiant as your courageous father. You convince yourself that your teenage antics strike the world in the face. But when you smile—and you do smile, Jiè, despite yourself—you have Emma's charm.

I, however, was raised by Boris Trotoskov.

Behind the semi-locked door, Mizou rested a beat in stony stillness. In my innocence, I interpreted her silence as a servant's defiance. *Imbécile!* I should have feared an evil-eye curse to make my hair fall out and my teeth grow holes. Mercifully, she was merely rude.

"Then we will see you at lunch." She used *tu*.

"Send someone to search my room for insects."

"If you don't like insects, close your window. It's too cold to have the window open, *quand même*." She turned, shuffling slightly as she padded down the creaky staircase that spiraled in the heart of the *pension*.

Though I waited expectantly, breakfast never came. Neither did lunch.

Late in the afternoon I grew tired of observing charcoal clouds rolling over the ocean. Without paint, brushes, or vellum, the intriguing, ever-changing light became a taunt. An empty expanse of beach spread beyond the cliff beneath my window, too cold to entice a single person to walk in the crystalline waves. A southern wind blew bursts of rain onto shore, blackening rocks and turning yellow sand to a deep ochre. As far as I could tell, brooding out my window, when I ran from my father in Paris I left behind every living human soul.

Around dinner time a thin, ragged boy made his way out the slippery rocks of the jetty. He stood on the point, seemingly immune to the November wind. Still, as if frozen there, he watched the irritable turmoil of the sea. When the first boat showed a mast, a toothpick of a line plunging and heaving in the blue, he took up his cry. Toward the desolate beach he ran, calling, croaking, seeming to tug the boats after him off the wild water and into the safety of port. A ritual I would see a hundred times over the next year.

Finally hunger overcame pride and drove me downstairs. I remember feeling imperious as I strode into the small dining room, nose up, as if I stood tall enough to see over everyone's head. I must have looked ridiculous.

The room was small and warm, lit by bulbs overhead that flickered when the electricity surged. Some clever hand had woven loose baskets to encase the bulbs, fracturing the light into an impressionist painting of tiny dots. The rugs on the floor were thick Turkish masterpieces, so old that they had faded to only a gentle reminder of color. The dominant piece of furniture was the dining room table, hacked from cedar planks, built to feed a fisherman's family, not to grace a hotel. People on wooden chairs clustered around this crude giant. Boris' housekeeper, Mme. Groseille, would have approved of the care to the wood—the table's lumpy surface was polished to an oily shine. But she and my father would have agreed that the atmosphere was distastefully intimate.

The family gathered around the table stopped chatting, turning to me with cautious small-town curiosity. Suat Bey, old features crimped with amused wrinkles; Kemal's frank, crass, fisherman's appraisal; and little Damad, who merely looked surprised, as though I were a friendly *fantôme*. How do you say in English? Ghost.

Mizou rose, a stack of gold bracelets clacking around her tanned forearm, pendulous jewels swinging at her earlobes, and yards of a red orange silk rippling toward the ground. Aphrodite rising from the waves must have caused a similar undulation.

"We may not be in Paris, but we do ask that you dress for dinner." She was cool and polite, this time using *vous* instead of *tu*. "Do you have an evening gown?"

At two am, escaping my father's house, I had considered packing many things. I ran my fingers longingly over heavy tubes of watercolors. I weighed in my hands my album of Monet's Giverny reproductions. I ached to bring my vellum sketch book. But my satin debutante gown had never crossed my mind. I was, I thought, running from ball gowns.

"*Non,* I don't."

Mizou switched to English. "Della, take the child and put her in something more appropriate."

I hadn't noticed Della. The big American woman sat in the shadows, so eclipsed by Mizou's presence that she seemed invisible. Until she smiled.

Della had a smile like the Nile River, running its lazy course over a huge continent, whole civilizations buried in her mud. When she stood, she carried shadows with her. A black velvet dress rolled over her ample hips and flaunted an Italian taste for cleavage. Without comment she swayed out of the room and led me up the scantily-lit staircase.

She paused at her door. "You speak English, honey?" Her words were heated and stretched in the style of the American South.

It is an old diplomatic instinct, well instilled by Boris' training, to conceal one's language skills until alliances and enemies were evident. "A little. You have no French?"

She put her bare shoulder to the door and pushed, her black gown strap spilling down her arm. The door scraped open. "Not much use to me, French. Charming, but useless. I don't suppose you speak Turkish?"

"*Non.*" My father didn't consider Turkish a language of

diplomacy, therefore it was not suited to a future head of state's wife. "The Ottoman will not rise again," he once said, "especially if they teeter-totter forever on the razor edge of civil war." So I was tutored in English, Spanish, and German.

"Well, we'll get by." Della turned on what passed for a light and waved me into her thinly whitewashed room. Her bedroom was stark, facing towards the expansive bowl of a ruined Roman arena. A spare metal bed frame with a thin mattress was tucked against the wall. Her rickety desk and chair stood as empty as my own. And her window, with two large panes that could be thrown open like arms in the summer, was fastened tight as if expecting winter storms. While I had a *petit* backpack of jeans, shorts, and T-shirts flung on the floor of my bedroom, Della had dropped a monstrous blue suitcase upright in the middle of hers. And there it stood. Luggage that, by the look of it, had been tossed from trains and jammed into taxi trunks for fifteen of her thirty-odd years. Della laid this granddame of a suitcase flat on the floor and snapped open the lid.

"What colors do you wear? You're so white, child. Yellow won't suit you. Rose, burgundy, or dark blue?" Her large hands rifled swaths of folded cloth until she found the colors of a Renoir nude. "Try this, honey." With a yank she pulled free several meters of magnificent silk, printed with blotches of rich pink. I took the fabric, wondering if she expected that I could miraculously transform it into a dress.

"Hold it to your face, now. Yes. Perfect. Take off those jeans. I'll show you how to wrap it." She stood waiting, as if to strip in front of her was normal.

I didn't move. Mme. Groseille, who had waited on me my whole life, had the decency to turn her back after I was ten.

"*Offff.* Don't be ridiculous," Della said. "I know you French answer the front door in your underwear. Hurry now, they're waiting dinner on us, and the *kapuska* is getting cold."

Embarrassed, I turned around and yanked my sweater and shirt over my head. Then I dropped my jeans, unnerved by her unabashed consideration.

"Here," she said when I turned back around. "Hold this." In case the American English wasn't getting through, she shoved a corner of the slippery fabric into my fist and squeezed my fingers. Then she began to wrap. Several turns around my waist, then a turn that she hung loosely, pulling little pleats into a pretty gather. Under the skill of her fingers the fabric draped in concentric swoops, like so many necklaces below the small crescent of my bellybutton. She brought the fabric around back and bound my upper half; tight around my chest, soft over one shoulder, tucked and secured under an arm, back over the other shoulder. I could not have reproduced the gown for any gift on Earth. When she was done I was so smothered in drapes I was sure I'd never get the dress off. My severe, white satin debutante gown had made me feel like an ice sculpture. In Della's dress I felt lush as a rose.

She backed up to look at me. "Well, hon, the face won't win any beauty contests, but the body takes to silk like a catfish to grasshoppers. I wish I had a mirror, I'd show you." She considered me a moment, then asked, "Child, why are you here?"

It took me a beat to translate the question because she said 'here' in two syllables: he-yah. When it dawned on me what she asked, I shook my head, pretending that I didn't understand.

"Well, no matter. No one comes to Incir: they run from somewhere else." She ushered me out her door and followed me downstairs.

Despite the gowns, Mizou's dinner was hardly a formal occasion. I knew the difference between wealthy starch and middle class pretension; I'd been raised a Trotoskov. In the prime of his manhood, my father became the French ambassador to China. He went to Shanghai during Mao's Great Leap Forward, to throw a weighty *politique de balancier* against the hefty Soviet gift of steel furnaces. My mother, Fleur, comfortable in her *salon*, stayed in Paris. My sister, Emma, was born Christmas, 1962, and never saw Boris until she was six.

～

I choke on Maman's fabulous coffee. "Emma is your sister?" I splutter. What an unfair load; Emma, warm as cooked mush, pretty beyond decency, every wealthy man's wet dream with her puddin'-pie eyes and her dark curls so long they cuddle her thighs. And there sits Maman, plain and thin as a trickle of white paint, dried and tough to her core. For a moment, I pity her.

If Maman cares, she hides it well. With regal dignity, she lifts the mirror and secures the silk firmly around it. When every inch of its horror is frocked in that dead-goldfish silk, she sets it on her swish coffee table. "Of course Emma is my sister. Do you think I would entrust you to a stranger?"

I blink in the chill of her smile. How in the effing hell should I know? She gave me away; what's the difference if Emma was my aunt? I'm too gutted to say anything. Maman brushes flat the folds of her dress, then kicks off her shoes and tucks her slender legs up underneath her. She looks content, which stings all the more.

"When the Cultural Revolution came your grandfather was driven from his *château de luxe* in Shanghai, sacrificing his famous Chinese chef and several concubines to the bloody chaos of Mao's reforms. I was born in July, 1968 a year after he barely escaped alive. *Alors chérie,*" her eyes train on me like a torch, "do you wonder how these convulsions of great nations came to burden you?" Right. I give a nod, cautiously. "Then I shall continue my story."

~

I was allowed at my first diplomatic dinner when I was ten. It was the year my flawless sister turned sixteen, and my father insisted that she return from my mother's home in Marseille to make her debutante. He had great plans for Emma. She was beautiful enough to marry a prince, gracious enough to hold warring kings to good table manners, and smart enough to never openly cross him. He put out feelers among the sisters and mothers of great men; Emma Trotoskov was available. She might found another Hapsburg dynasty, or go east and marry an emperor.

I sat stiff and insignificant at my sister's debutante *soirée,* and it prepared me well for my first supper in tiny Incir. When Mizou's hands, heavy with rings, broke a pinch of bread and sopped up cabbage and lamb stew, I did likewise. When she halved a stuffed pepper and offered it, I held out my plate. When she scooped *pilav*, neatly containing every slippery grain of rice on her serving spoon, I tried not to shame myself by spilling on Della's silk. I drank water, because when Kemal tried to pour me Raki I put a hand over my glass as Mizou did, refusing the absinthe. Having established that Mizou was not a servant, I treated her like a head of state. That was how the world was divided, *n'est pas*? Servant and master. I ran from my father, but I could not leave him behind.

I had crossed the line with Mizou, but she was too Turkish (no matter how French she claimed to be) to abuse a guest. My father's well-traveled friends had told me stories of Turkish hospitality: sick travelers, stranded in small towns and aided by passing strangers; expatriates, alone in empty apartments in Istanbul and plied with gifts by neighbors. So Mizou smiled at me charitably, served me first, and conducted at least half of her conversation in French. The rest of my conversation she left to Suat Bey.

Suat Bey was a wrinkled little hot pepper of a man. His hair was white except for two patches of eyebrow, square and rusty red, shaped like Charlie Chaplin's. He never stopped moving, nervous energy shaving him as thin as a julienne strip. His mustache tips, scraping his chest, had worn into points. He could have been any age from seventy to one hundred and five. He spoke fluent French, heavily accented, a cross between the guttural *rs* of a Russian special envoy and the musical smoothness of an Arab prince. With effort and leaning forward, I could understand what he said. It was well worth the struggle.

Seeing my unease at this family gathering, Suat Bey fired up his protective gaze and spread it over me. "Let me tell you about my renowned ride into battle," he said, patting my hand with his wrinkled skinny one, lower eyelids damp with emotion.

Kemal, across the table, scoffed and rolled his eyes.

"Don't let my elder son fool you, *Princess*. I was decorated by the Sultan himself." His French pronunciation of *Prrrincessss* was a hearty kiss; he growled the *r* and hissed the *ss* as an old bear might. I felt, under his chivalrous care, more like a princess than I'd ever felt in a ballroom. Entranced, I surrendered my full attention.

"You think I'm not that old? What does a *gamine* like you know about old? It was in 1913, the year the godless Balkans torched Viero and burned all of her blessed villagers. I was a *cavalier* in the Turkish 10th division." He poured himself another three fingers of Raki, clear and pure from the bottle, white and poisonous as it mixed with water in his glass.

Damad, whose French was rudimentary, smelled a story nonetheless. He was a tiny child with eyes that belonged on a beautiful woman. Supple as an octopus, he slipped out of his chair and stood at Suat Bey's side.

"Out of the Rhodope Mountains poured ten thousand Bulgarian soldiers, like hands sliding over dark breasts. *Oh la,* Mademoiselle, you should see the curves of the Rhodope mountains!" Suat Bey put his nose to his squat glass and sucked in licorice vapor, then sat back and closed his eyes. A moment later, his eyes popped open and skimmed sideways to see if I was watching. It had always been difficult to raise my gaze to Boris; he wanted nothing from me but submission. But I couldn't take my eyes off of Suat Bey.

"*Eh alors?*" I prompted.

"We waited on our horses, telling ribald jokes, pokes at each other's manhood, military swagger, and such. Not things I would repeat to a lady." He took a drink, rolling pungent liquor around on his tongue.

"Don't be an old fool, Papa," growled Kemal. "There were no cavalry on horses in the First Balkan War." Kemal had clearly baked on a fishing boat under the hot Mediterranean sun for years. He gave the impression of tanned leather, stretched over powerful and practical muscles, and a mind that was used to tricky currents.

"What do you know, you potato of a fisherman? In 1913, you were not even a throb in my manly parts."

Kemal jerked his chin toward the ceiling and turned away, pretending to listen to Mizou and Della talk about shopping in Manavgat.

Damad gripped Suat Bey's skinny arm and shook. "Go on, Papa."

Suat Bey, apparently satisfied that Kemal no longer eavesdropped, began again. "The Bulgarians were better armed by far, and magnificent they were, too, in their red capes and embroidered boots. When they waved their silver Kiliji, blades drawn and bloody—"

Kemal obviously couldn't stand it. He gave up his pretense of listening to the women and rounded on his father. "That war was fought with manually loaded rifles, not swords. What a load of fish guts you're feeding the child!"

"Hush, boy. Don't interrupt your father." Suat Bey punctuated this with several words in Turkish that caused Kemal to rise, gather up his dishes, and skulk out of the room.

"Now, you can hear the story in peace, *Princess.*" Suat Bey lifted shrewd, sparkly eyes to the door Kemal had slammed, and gave it a final, exaggerated glower. "Where was I? *Ah, oui,* the Bulgarians were coming, engraved swords bloody and nicked from hacking bones and loping heads. Have you seen a Kiliji, Mademoiselle?"

I shook my head. Damad shook his head.

"A sword, long as a man's arm, and curved at the end to bring width and force to the fatal *crack.*" Suat Bey swung his arm and dropped forward his chin; the *crack* was a head, separating with a startled shiver from its neck. I shivered. Damad shivered. "They shine silver in the sun, with gold at the handle where the holy carving lies. Not that the Bulgarians are capable of being holy." He spat on the ground. Damad spat, too. I suppressed the urge to spit. "As they thundered down upon us, our courage wavered. Our joking sputtered and choked, our manhood withdrew. It was going to be a rout." He measured out the gravity of their situation, the certainty of their doom, with three solemn bangs of his glass on the wooden table. Damad's gorgeous eyes grew wide with fear. I gripped my hands together in my lap; I couldn't bear to think of him defeated.

"And then—" he took a long, slow drink and swallowed hard, tears pooling in his watery rims. He shook his head, clearly expecting me to beg him to continue.

"*Courage,* Monsieur, go on, go on," I pleaded.

"It gets worse!" He threw up his arms to heaven, his cry a sharp bark of anguish. "My horse, restless in the summer heat—" he waved his hands like a tail, "—was bitten in a most unfortunate place by a horsefly. The poor creature bolted straight into the oncoming thunder. *Oh la la la la,* what a dilemma, Mademoiselle." One hand reached to tug pensively at a scrap of moustache. "To retreat in the face of the enemy would bring shame upon all Turks. But I was saddle-sore, you see, from a night of passionate love with a shepherdess. To sit on a galloping horse was excruciating, more than a man could bear." He looked at me mournfully, entreating me to understand. "I did the only thing a man could do: I stood in the saddle, raised my sword, and charged!"

With this he sprung to his feet. One hand waving and the other hand whacking the rump of his imaginary steed, he bounced on his old knees into battle. "My regiment followed me, to a man, and what a battle we won. To Turkish honor!" He swooped up his drink and raised it high. In his enthusiasm, a splash of Raki slopped on the wooden table. The liquid beaded up, and white clouded its surface. All around the table, conversation stopped, and everyone waited, silent. I grabbed my water and clinked rims with him enthusiastically.

Suat Bey recoiled into his chair, wiry and bent, grinning. "And thus I became a hero of the First Balkan War, decorated by the Sultan and honored by the ladies. Here's to The Republic of Turkey!" He drained the rest of his Raki in one swallow.

Damad reached for Suat Bey's arm, tugging on his pressed, white sleeve, begging in Turkish for something. Suat Bey shook his head. "*Non, mon petit*," and he finished his refusal in Turkish. He stooped and lifted the child by the arms, handing him off to his wife.

"It's late. My youngest son must go to bed," he said.

His son? Damad was five at the most. And Mizou was at least sixty, *en fin*, closer to seventy! Mizou took her child in her arms, his head resting against the silk of her gray braid, and carried him from the room.

Suat Bey turned glistening, watchful, eyes on me. "Would you like more olives? Do you care for dessert?"

"*Non.* I've eaten well, thank you."

"*Mais non*, you have hardly eaten at all." He pressed the plate of olives into my hands. "Now, you must tell me how you came to our little town of Incir." He leaned forward, ears peeking between strands of the white hair flowing to his shoulders.

The glow of Suat Bey's story faded, and I looked away.

"*Non?* No matter. You bestow honor on our poverty stricken house." He stretched even closer and whispered, "All secrets are safe in Incir, *Princess.*"

When I look back, nothing in Incir generated more warmth than Suat Bey. Not the sun, when the depression of clouds finally lifted and the baking began. Not the sand where the old women warmed their arthritis. Not the curry Yurda made, that even Suat Bey could not eat without a gasp after each bite.

I lay in bed that November night, my window shuttered against frost and insects (the crickets were, in fact, gone until spring). In my chest I felt a hole, filling my ribs to bursting. A chest wrenched empty by the final battle with my father. A hole darkened by my fearful escape. A heart near frozen from the loneliness of hiding in a place too small to be on the map.

I was desperate for warmth; a hundred years of one hundred degrees in the roasting sun would not have been enough. You must understand, *ma fille*, that one by one my family defied and abandoned Boris Trotoskov. Even my mother Fleur, as insubstantial as vapor, managed to slip through his fingers. I alone stayed by him, twenty lonely years. But we must all find something to love, you see; it is the human way. We choose, and commit; a heart without passion is merely beating. I? I loved no one. Nothing gave life meaning but my art. Have you ever felt so alone, Jiè? I hope not.

# THREE

I've not told anyone; not Emma or George, who still come along presently, after I've gone to bed, and dim the Tiffany light. Not Chander, who squeezed my ribs in a drowning clutch that last night we had a sleep in his storage container. And certainly not Maman, because she would be chuffed if she knew and have another laugh at my expense. So no one knows that even at sixteen I won't sleep without *Little Cricket*. There is no one to read to me, now that I'm six foot or more, so I keep it in my rucksack and most nights I read to myself.

Tonight, after Maman has knackered herself telling stories, she snaps off the light in her drawing room, and the ceiling is lit only by the wobbly lights of passing lorries. I sneak to my rucksack and find my shabby little book, frayed and gummy from a child's fingers. I curl in the dark under the blanket on her settee and whisper to myself, holding the book's thick cardboard binding to my heart.

## Little Cricket and the Terribly Hungry Cat
## By T. Chin

Chinese calligraphy trails down the right border of the title page. When I was small and trying so hard to be Chinese, I translated it. *I will always love you.* It took me four flippin' weeks to suss out the characters with a Chinese dictionary. How do I learn to be Chinese? Chinese class. That's kiddie logic. I thought Emma—Mum—must have written the characters, because no one else loved me no matter what. And there was a fair bit of *no matter what* to loving me, even before I started graffing. Back then I called Emma 'Mum' because she ruffled my hair, kissed me good-night, and made lunches, so that made her my mum. More kiddie logic.

Then, at around ten, I puzzled out that she was five foot, Caucasian, and as breakable as her Louis XV china. Dad— George—was five-nine and thickly blonde. And I was hugely, aggressively, Chinese. Without question I was pale as milk, but my features looked like I should get off the underground at Leicester Square and slog home to a flat above some chinky bun shop south of Soho. Which meant that I was not only adopted, but that Emma was not really my mum. Somehow I hadn't gotten it into my kid-sized loaf that *adopted* meant *they are not your parents.* Brilliant. Nothing dafter than a bit of kiddie logic. Fast on the heels of this revelation, I began to muck about with serious trouble.

> Little Cricket poked her nose out of cozy hole. She liked the hot sun and the frisky smell of spring. "Mum, I want to go out and see the world."
>
> Mum wrapped three fat wheat seeds and an acorn of water in her handkerchief, and snuggled the corners together in a knot. "Then you must take your lunch," she said.

"Thanks, Mum."

Mum stood in the doorway and watched Little
Cricket spring from grass blade to grass blade.
"Be back before dark," she called over the wide
green field.

Crackle said the new grass as Little Cricket
landed, clickity-sproing went Little Cricket's legs
as she leaped.

The sunshine was as warm as sand.

"I think I'll touch the sun." Little Cricket
jumped as high as she could.

Crackle clickity-sproing, crackle clickity-
sproing sang out over the grass. Crackle clickity-
sproing all the way to the edge of the field,
which could have been the edge of the world.

Once I doubted that Emma was Mum and George was
Dad, I doubted everything. Maybe they were wide of the mark
about bedtime. Maybe I shouldn't wear that vomit-colored
school uniform. Maybe my hair looked super when I cut it
myself with George's straight razor. A wide crack of
possibilities opened under my feet.

Funnily enough, there was nothing Mum or Dad could do
about it. As far as I was concerned, life was cushdy. I skived
off school. I smoked ciggies (Pekelo put a stop to that). I took
a five-finger discount on anything I liked in stores. I learned
words that were not in Dad's city vocabulary. Emma and
George were just so *sweet* I could tell them all kinds of
porkies, cry when I got caught out, and then do it all over

again. After awhile making trouble was easier to tuck into than hot fish and chips.

Little Cricket was hot and tired. She stopped in the shade of an oak tree and found a cool nook between two roots.

"A fine place to eat," she told herself. She untied Mum's handkerchief and took out a wheat seed. She was about to take a nibble when she heard a nasty purr.

"What have we here, then? Lunch." Two slit yellow eyes glared down at her, and a paw-full of claws crept toward her nook.

"Good day, Mr. Cat." Little Cricket backed closer to the roots. "Would you like to share my wheat seed?"

"No, I'm looking for a fine, crunchy cricket. Have you seen any about?"

Now, Little Cricket's mum once told her that cats think they know everything. So she sidled out into the open and gathered her legs underneath her. "I heard one singing in the field a while ago...singing a secret."

The cat settled onto his belly and licked his lips. His slit eyes followed Little Cricket with interest.

"I'll wager you don't know her secret," said Little Cricket.

"What did this delicious cricket say?" asked
the cat.
"Close your eyes and I'll sing it for you."
The cat twitched and fur lifted around a claw.
"No. If I close my eyes you will hop away, and
then I won't have lunch or a secret."
"Then turn your ear toward me, because I'm
just a little thing and I can't sing very loud."
The cat twisted one ear toward Little
Cricket, and in that instant Little Cricket leaped.

It was this book that made me fancy being a graffiti artist.
The cricket had me at the outset, because she's drawn in such
detail that she quivers: one antenna bent like a scar she'll
always carry; the hairs on her legs shift with updraft and
undertow; and her triangular face keeps a canny smile, as if
clued up on something we'd all like to know. And she gets on
anywhere—even under the glistening saliva on a cat's teeth,
she's ready to have a go. She clickity-sproings through those
slashes of oriental grass so spare and simple they take my
breath away. Now that was my caliber of Chinese. The whole
grimy lump of London would stop and gawp, gobs hanging
open, when I splashed that cricket against the brick and
brownstone walls. Maybe the author of *Little Cricket*, T. Chin,
would even notice. But paint is expensive; I needed financing.

Emma had in excess of ninety necklaces, thirty bracelets,
and a shedload of earrings. It's really not on to have so many;
even if she went to one formal dinner a week, or entertained
George's banker friends every night, she'd be knackered

under the strain of wearing them all. And George collects the most worthless gubbins I ever saw: a snow globe from every city he ever opened a bank branch in, antique fishing rods that he won't notice again until the summer holidays. And the undertaker will be knocking closed the nails on George's coffin before anyone misses the silver clock he mislaid in the back of his wardrobe. So at about twelve years of age I started nicking Emma and George's stuff, and peddling it to Alton at his eBay brick and mortar.

I bought my first spray paint by mail order. I tried Doluxo: perfect junk. No coverage, the white is as bright as a police torch, and glare destroys the picture with highlights. I wasn't even hacked off when someone tagged over those pieces. I tried White Bishop: junk with bells on. Pressure's so high you feel like you're blowing a hole in the concrete instead of painting, and the whine of the nozzle can be heard by any interested fella from two blocks away. A girl alone in an alley at two am doesn't want any interested fellas. Threw those cans away. Somewhere about a year into it and one hundred walls later, I discovered Belton Molotow—hands down the best paint ever made. About then, I was good enough that taggers started respecting my work.

> Sproing. The cat snarled and swiped a killing blow, but Little Cricket was gone.
>
> Crackle clickity-sproing, crackle clickity-sproing trilled Little Cricket's legs. Crackle clickity-sproing, bounding towards Cozy Hole where Mum waited.

"I never tell my secrets," sang Little Cricket.

"And someone else will have to be your lunch."

But by then the cat was too far away to enjoy Cricket's joke.

Little Cricket skipped and soared home in a rush.

"Back so soon?" asked Mum.

"Yes, I've seen enough of the world for today."

"I'm glad you're home." Mum hugged her Little Cricket close. "But wherever you are, Little Cricket…"

"*…I will always love you.*" I finish the last words, roll onto my tum, and close the book. A heavy ache settles with the blankets on my back. Maman thinks she stands guard over the world's stockpile of loneliness, as if she managed to hoard it all in her childhood and there wasn't a shred left for the rest of us. But years ago, when that crack opened under my feet, I realized: I had always fancied T. Chin was my mum, and that she waited for me in Cozy Hole. Not on your nelly was anyone, anywhere, going to stand in for that. I had quite the loyal little heart. It hid as the rest of me ran off to pretend about Emma and George. Someday, that little heart whispered, I'll leap into the wide world and I'll find my real mum: T. Chin.

Instead, I'd found Maman.

Were you even more disappointed than I was, Maman? Bloody unlikely. Hands down, I got the worst of this flogging.

Fair enough, Maman gave me away and looks none too pleased to have me back again. But I always, always wanted T. Chin to come home to, and in my fantasy she wanted me, too.

My *Little Cricket* book is imprinted with the artist's Chinese chop. The stamp skids, a smudge down the page, as though pressed with emotion. Possibly with regret. Maybe T. Chin knew that there comes a day when you do something so outrageous that you can't go back to Cozy Hole. Society has another kind of hole they want to put you in, one with a lock and key. Then's when you need mates. Loyal mates, like Alton, who don't care what you've done for God knows they've done worse. They may not love you no matter what, or even love you at all for that matter, but they can track down a French *maman*, even a disappointing one.

It's the next morning, and even though I wake early, Maman is gone. She's left a bowl of apples on the coffee table, and tossed a velvet duvet over me as I slept. As if I need her mothering now, having done without, all of these years. I throw off the cover and ignore the fruit, even though the apple is beautiful, a ray of sun slicing across its red roundness like a blade. I need air, so I step onto her balcony and look down on the view from Ile St. Louis. Old women pull wheeled shopping bags down the sidewalk like donkeys with little carts. High rent, tan stone buildings stare down the rest of the city from behind the moat of the Seine. Black filigree balconies supervise the long blank concrete wall that squeezes the river. The *quai* is miraculously clear of graffiti; not a single tag scrawls across that virginal expanse of concrete. How best to piece that wall, given a moonless night? Hanging from rope off the railing? No, too difficult to bolt. I'd nick a rowboat, and plan on swimming if the police turn up.

If I knew for sure that Chander was safe, I'd just run. I could steal some of the expensive rubbish cluttering Maman's flat to pay my train fare. Alton said Maman was the best artist in Paris. He hopes I'll nick Maman's drawings to sell on eBay. Like as not that's why he gave me her address. It's a dead cert he'll be disappointed; I'll not take a thing from her, ever. I'll not even give her the satisfaction of stealing from her. She owes me more than a few odds and ends. Then again, who am I to fancy that I have ethics and morals, while the police search for my brilliant arse? Maman could never turn round my disappointment anyway, so why not take what I want and go? I'd be to Spain by tea time. Stop in Barcelona and hang around Las Ramblas, see if I could find a fight, make some Euros. Even down there they've heard of Cricket, trained by Jaxon Pekelo; worth betting on even when she fights a bloke. Maybe I could earn enough to get to Mumbai, to Chander. I hope Chander's mum was well enough to travel and wasn't harmed by their trip home. I hope Chander will think ever so hard when he arrives in Mumbai—remember what he stands to lose by leaving London.

No, I won't go, because I'm worried about that mirror. And that means staying to hear Maman out. I don't need her otherwise. Maman was lonely because granddad was a bastard. Bullocks. Lots of kids don't get the parents they mail ordered—a royal screw-up, for example, when they replaced T. Chin with Maman! Emma and George aren't a bad lot, really, just a bit baffled by it all. They're useless, when you get down to it. At least Maman tells a hell of a story, so I'll give her one chance to make it up. Everyone deserves one chance.

I start to spit off the balcony railing, and then I see it, same as on the back of the mirror. Same as when I came round the corner at Alton's eBay. But it's grown since I saw it in London—bigger than me now, likely outweighs me by a few heavy punches. A foul creature, and this time instead of slouching in a doorway, it suns its hideous backside in Square Barye, serpent tail curling and uncurling. Its doggy gut is in the dust. Tufts of hair grow out its holes-for-ears, feeling in my direction, as if listening for my heartbeat. One furry head rests on sleek brown paws, eyes closed; one head dangles on an arched neck, staring west out over the water; and one head has two red eyes, trained bang on me.

Bloody hell. I step back and my fists go up. I've got tingling in my armpits and a dizzy fear. I'm already panting, anticipating a drubbing. Anything that ugly is vicious, like as not. I size up the park for bystanders, see if anyone else is in for a bit of trouble. The old ladies with shopping carts must have legged it for the *boulangerie*; the pavement under Maman's balcony is empty. No kiddies with au pairs romp under Square Barye's trees. As I stare over the balcony the creature dissolves, melts into wind, nothing left but a salty damp smell. Have I gone round the twist? I rub my eyes, then check carefully; it's not slouching against an iron railing or lurking in the cedar shrubs. Flippin' spooky. I retreat inside and lock the balcony doors.

Emma was right, just this once: I should never have nicked that mirror. I can still picture Emma collapsed in the foyer, all that dark hair plastered by tears to her cheeks. *Why in bloody hell did you go and steal your mother's mirror? Why not just take the best silver?* All of those years stealing from Emma, and I never considered the silver! And Alton could have fenced it so easily. Bad luck to take that vile mirror instead. But I needed the money. A feeling like too much brown paint swirls in my middle, as if some darling backed me up against the ropes and threw a solid elbow into my guts. I needed to prove to Chander how much I loved him. I just couldn't let him go. I still can't. We've stuck our heads in the plastic bag of love, and we're fast running out of air. Now I worry something horrid might happen to him, like what happened to Xiao. I turn round and scan the room but can't suss out where she's put the nasty thing. Locked it up, I imagine. Brilliant. Lock and key won't stop it.

Maman comes home and slams the door and I jump like a rabbit. She steps out of ugly, ankle-length black bloomers, hangs them in the closet, then lifts off a black head covering and lays it, folded, on the hall table. She clocks my face for a moment, then says, "You saw it, *oui*?"

"*Oui*." I try to look as stouthearted as she does.

"He is playing with us, *le connard*." Swear words sound official when Maman hisses them, as if the beast were condemned to be a son of a bitch by international decree.

"What in friggin' hell *is* it?" I ask.

"Don't they teach Greek mythology in your fancy London school?"

I narrow my eyes. "I don't spend a good deal of time in class."

She turns her back to me. "It's Cerberus, Hades' creature." She takes a fat, leather-bound tome off her bookshelf and plops it in my lap. Without another word she goes to the kitchen and rattles around in a ferocious din, making breakfast as if giant, misshapen hounds were an ordinary, if unpleasant, part of her day.

The book's as worn as my *Little Cricket*, and I wonder if she spent her childhood with it, maybe still takes it to bed. The inside is annotated in French with a pencil, the writing nothing a kid would do: straight upright, and as skinny as a teacher who expects you to pay attention. The whole book is on the Greek gods, and the colored plate of Hades shows a muscular, bearded man, dragging a screaming girl into the split-open earth.

Bloody hell: that crack. For a moment I can feel it opening under my feet. Sheer panic as I'm yanked by an arm into bleak eternity. No second chance. No, "Wait a bit, luv, I'm not yet done here." My moment in the light is gone and I don't even know who I am yet. I wail with the ghosts by the river that forever separates the living from the dead, and a three headed dog with a serpent's tail stalks the banks; there's no getting round him. But he's not *real.* Not panting by the Seine. Not scaring me witless in 2006 while lorries rumble by and pigeons scratch on the windowsill. I slam closed the book.

Maman carries in a tray: a bowl of hot milk and coffee with slices of bread. Lots of good plum jam in a crystal bowl. Silver butter knife. I watch her with my heart racing. She sits in her *fauteuil* by the windows that face the park.

"What do you paint?" she asks.

I take a breath. I would have thought, given that she's asking questions, she'd go for the obvious one: What in effing hell is Cerberus *doing* here? I spar with fear, trying to collect myself. Finally I say, "Explain about the god, the dog, and the mirror."

Maman butters her bread. "I've been telling you. It's a long story, you'll have to be patient."

"Don't you think we should hurry it up a bit?"

"It's me he's after, not you," she says sharply.

That's a relief, felt all the way to my toes. She's calm for a woman with a dismal future chasing her. You have to admire her self-possession. She doesn't look like she could fend off a toy poodle; I wonder what holds the beast at bay.

Have it your way, then, Maman: we ignore the mirror until a three-headed dog sinks its bloody teeth in your knickers. So I ask, "How do you know I paint?"

"I saw sketch books in your knapsack, spattered with drips of color." She sees my expression and adds, "The sac was open *quand même*, I didn't dig in it."

Sure she didn't. Emma and George had their faults, but they didn't poke about in my things.

I make her wait a few sips of my *café au lait* before I answer. "I paint sidewalks, roads, garbage cans. Walls when I can get them, but in London most of the mint places are all pieced."

"And you write on these walks and walls?"

"No, I don't tag. Only a flippin' idiot scrawls their name on things. I paint hope, dreams: what neighborhoods long for. I'm an artist, not a homie."

"*Ah oui,* I see."

She rises from her armchair. With her first ever hint of nervousness, she paces to the window—a view she could have seen sitting—and stares out. She has a remarkably stiff spine as she studies the shadows flickering over bare dirt in the park. Then she turns, backlit by the pale spring sun.

"It's your turn to tell me a story," she says.

"Take a hike, Maman." The phrase pops out of my mouth in Alton's American slang, so she either doesn't understand, or she doesn't care that I refused her.

She says, "Painting under threat of arrest must have interesting moments. Tell me a story about creating your art."

I never talk about graff with anyone (except Chander, of course). Not in person, not online. Graff chat rooms are full of cack, and photos of men's hard-ons. Who wants to see that? Even the site that's supposed to be for girls is tagged with a shedload of male trash. And most blokes think graff is just vandalism. But I want to ruffle her up, put a crease in that meticulous wool dress she's worn two days in a row, flat and curve-less, as though it's still on the hanger.

"I will, then. Sit down. You're giving me a blooming headache standing against the sun like that."

# FOUR

Chander's family owned a Paki shop in Covent Garden's market arcade. Just a storage container, really, with two umbrellas in front and a tent at the back. Underneath, they set out tables with cow bells on ropes, incense, and cotton dresses in colors that ran and stained your legs if you got caught in the rain.

Well, it wasn't really a Paki shop, because they're from Mumbai, but I was eleven when I first met them and I didn't know the difference. His sister, Parul, cooked cuzzer in the back on a charcoal stove, the filmy silk of her sari waving dangerously close to the fire when she stooped to ladle hot bowlfuls. Parul ran the store, did the heavy work, and wiped Chander's nose for him until he was big enough to wipe it for himself. Chander's dad is dead; no one ever talks about how. Chander's mum, Ashra, had some sort of stroke when Chander was born; just walking gives her a rough ride of it.

Parul's cuzzer smelled so good that I'd stop on my way home from school and buy a bowl off her, days when I decided to walk and not waste my tube fare. It miffed Emma when I'd come home smelling like curry and too full to eat her cuisine.

So that's how I recognized Chander at three am in the dark; I'd seen him loads of times over that last three years, leaning just like that—feet crossed, bony arse against the wall, hands in his pockets, black eyes sunk so far back they were probably still in Mumbai. He'd never spoken, just studied me, like as not trying to work out how a girl two years younger could be as tall as him. But now he wasn't watching me spoon up his sister's nosh. He was watching me stencil graff on the western courtyard of Covent Garden, something I could be banged up for if he identified me to the police. But he didn't act like a bloke about to snitch on me. He looked…interested, and not the kind of interested I'd have to kick him in the goolies for.

So I ignored him. With four million CCTV cameras in the UK, I had five minutes to paint my piece before I had to be off. I yanked the next set of stencils out of my plastic bag and sprayed a second layer onto the cobblestones. Green, but not merely green—my color was a mix between exuberant and crazy. I couldn't see it in the dark, naturally, unless I shone my torch on the road, but I sussed it like the taste of my own mouth. The Belton Molotow paint sprayed on smoothly and smelled of ginger and nail polish. The finished piece would stretch fifteen feet, so I worked across the cobblestones, repeating at different angles: yellow, streaks of brown, tiny touches of blue, one stencil after another getting slippery with paint. I picked up my torch and directed the beam on the final stack of stencils, one at a time, painting the focus of the piece. I could hear a siren, but then, when can't you hear sirens in London? I was too chuffed with how well the piece was turning out to give it a thought.

Finished! A little Smart car with a blue Metropolitan Police tag pulled up under a street light on King Street.

Flippin' hell. I stuffed the last wet stencil in my plastic bin bag and threw the paint in my rucksack. Leg it quick, then, before they came to investigate. But other rozzers arrived from Henrietta Street, coming at me from the south. I didn't fancy a ruck with the police. A citation for public nuisance and jail time would be hard to lie about to Emma and George.

I legged like a frightened plonker to the arcade, toward stacks of folded umbrellas and locked storage boxes. Someone behind me was gaining, so I sped up. The bloke panted over my right shoulder, feet pounding with mine. I whirled to hit him in the gob, but he slipped the sack off my shoulder, grabbed the bin bag out of my hand, and pulled ahead of me: Chander, long legs stretching like rubber.

"Follow me, luv," he panted, sounding more upper class than Dad; none of that sing-songy accent for Chander. We loped between the two rows of metal storage containers, leaped over folded umbrellas and collapsed tables, and dodged into a crevice behind stacked boxes. He dropped the rucksack and bin bag and dug in the pocket of his tight trousers, tugging out keys.

"Two storage containers down. Climb in, lock the door, and shut your gob," he said.

"What about you?" I asked.

"I'll give them a chase. Go on then, they're gaining."

I snatched keys off his sweating palm, scooped up my paints and stencils, and scuttled to the container. As I locked the door behind me I could hear his footsteps echoing off the high ceiling of the arcade, banging against shrill whistles and cries to stop. I gasped in turmeric and cumin dust, working to find room for my head and neck among folded stacks of cotton.

"Run, you diamond," I whispered. "Run, run, run."

It was ten minutes before my heart stopped pounding.

Maman listens to my tale leaning forward, pale eyes open, gob pressed closed. When I stop speaking I expect her to ask the customary questions: "Did he get away?" and "What happened to you?" But Maman doesn't seem to have a Scooby about standard responses. As usual, she's way off the typical mark.

"What did you paint?" she asks.

I start giggling like a piece of fluff. Most people don't care *what* you write on their city, they just care *that* you wrote on their city. But Maman collars it; it's the *what* that speaks. No idiot tag lines, outlined in colors and scripted so that they're impossible to read. No death threats on territorial boundaries. That's all posturing; boys giving themselves hand jobs and calling it art. If you are going to deface a fifteen-foot swath of Covent Garden Market, make sure you do something that every bloody tourist will stop to gawk at. Something hundreds of people will catch the tube and drag kiddies ten miles to see. Something nobody will petition the city to buff off. Something to lift a knackered heart into a better world.

I reach in my rucksack and pull out a folded copy of the London Times, the copy Chander gave me three years ago, two days after he ran like the clappers. He'd tossed it on my lap, puffed and breathless as though he was still running.

"Didn't you see?" he'd asked, collapsing beside me onto a Covent Garden café chair.

"Do what?" I'd answered, because I never read the paper.

"The Times! Flippin' hell, Jiè, you're famous!"

I take this same paper from my rucksack and I lay it folded in Maman's lap. Maman unfolds the pages and there she is; sprayed on in Technicolor. Little Cricket with her one drooping antennae, and other antennae straight up, giving the world a gander with bangin' gusto. She's practically leaping off the cobblestones, streaks of grass suggesting the whole meadow with a few superb sprays. It wasn't as good as T. Chin. I couldn't pretend to even come close. But the city didn't buff it off, either. Parents brought their kiddies from Shoreditch, Kilburn, and Brixton. Some bloke put a fence around it so no one could walk there. It was months before the rain made it unrecognizable.

Maman is speechless. Even her diplomatic ancestry fails her. I watch her eyes, the crinkle and wetness, something to give away her emotions. The newspaper lies in her lap like a rag. I wait to be embraced (what Emma would have done), or lectured (what George would have done) or whacked (what Boris might have done?). But she just sits there.

Finally, after a pause worse than a headache she says, "You have talent—more than I. You have drive, the zeal to risk anything for the sake of your canvas. Inspiring. Bravo, *chérie*."

Her smile is thin, and for a moment its faint warmth thaws a bit of frost off my heart.

"The question is, do you have discipline? You've lost control of the boundaries, so the eye doesn't travel the whole piece smoothly."

"Bugger off, Maman. I did it in the dark."

"Isn't that the nature of your work?"

"Yes, but—"

"Then master it. Or don't. It's up to you." She folds the paper and hands it back to me.

What a load of rot. Anyone can see how free and expressive the painting is. Lacks discipline—well that's the point then, isn't it? I look away from her ice blue eyes.

"Emma kept mum about you because you've made a muck of your life."

"*Très bien.* Emma keeps her promises well."

"Why not let her tell me? I've a right to decide for myself."

"Ah, well…you are ready to listen to more of the story, then? It's a long one. Perhaps too long for modern patience?"

"Just get on with it, Maman."

"As you wish, Cricket."

Cricket. She knows my fighting name; I don't like her using it. It implies that Emma rung her up over the years, and that I was the topic. I sprawl on the floor and smolder, painting my toenails 'royal azure' as Maman narrates from her armchair.

# FIVE

The sun found cracks between the shutter slats, and crept along the floor. A November sun, pale as despair. By early morning a stripe lay across my pillow and turned the dark behind my eyelids misleadingly rosy. The donkey brayed a raucous protest. Then the *muezzin's* call to prayer floated out from the minaret on the harbor; a meandering song that found the citizens of Incir, wrapped about their lives, and pulled them to the heart of God. After the *ezan* ended, the hotel was silent. I could not have been further from everything I had ever known.

I sat up in bed that next morning, heart twisting with anxiety, and took groggy account of my life. My few clothes, unattended by any maid, lay ignored in a heap on the floor. Della's yards of silk were tangled over the desk chair. My passport hid on the windowsill under an art gum eraser, a charcoal pencil, and a thick wad of traveler's checks. It was a short inventory. From this, I was to reconstruct a life.

Trotoskovs have been running away for generations. Do you think we are unique, you and I? My French grandmother eloped to marry a Russian. She gave birth to Boris in Soviet Moscow, September 3, 1930. The First World War was over. You know nothing of war, do you, Jiè? Neither do I. While Boris mastered gravity with his toddler legs, the world stumbled under the weight of treaties. As he grew old enough to dominate the schoolyard, the countries on Russia's border began to squabble like so many *fourmis*—ants you say in English, *n'est pas*? Austrian banks collapsed, bringing economic famine. Everyone itched to crawl on their neighbors: Spain erupted into civil war, Hitler consolidated his power, Poland tried to take bites from Czechoslovakia's border. *Oh, la.* In August, the year Boris turned nine, the Nazis announced a nonaggression pact with the Soviets, then promptly invaded Poland. *Et puis* September 3rd, 1939 Britain and France declared war on Germany. Boris' father disappeared into the gruesome engine of World War II. Boris' mother, fearing for her life, fled to her family in Paris, taking *mon petit papa* with her.

*Eh bien*, it was a good thing they left, too. Little Boris was better suited for Tsarist extravagance than for Soviet austerity. He had a genetic inclination for gourmet food, fine clothes, and servants. He lived here in Paris. Look around you, Jiè. He grew up in this apartment, Ile St. Louis. They tried to smother him in this old wealth you make such fishy lips at. But he brooded out of that window just as you do, across the park to the Quai D'Anjou, and he became a man.

And so, Trotoskov that I am, after the *ezan* died away I got out of bed. I showered and dressed in jeans and my warmest shirt, then went looking for a maid to bring me breakfast. The dining room was swept clean, the table oiled, the hutch dusted, the chairs arranged in place and empty. From the other rooms I heard no calls, no flushing toilets, no conversations. I appeared to be the only *pension* guest besides Della. Even odder, there didn't seem to be any servants.

I wandered until I found the kitchen, where a dark lump of a woman sat at a table, chopping chicken livers. As I stood in the door, she looked up, startled, and pulled black fabric over her face, leaving only her green, thickly-lashed eyes exposed. When she saw it was me, she let the tail of cotton go and gave me a far too friendly grin-full of rotting teeth. From her smooth skin I guessed she was not yet forty. She had a warm expression in her eyes, as though life, and the mistress of the house, indulged her. I couldn't see much else; she was covered by a *kara çarşaf* that was pinned under her chin and draped over her whole body.

She stood and lumbered to the sink. Puffs of black trousers, gathered at the ankle, swayed out from under the black hem of her traditional robe. She washed her hands and filled a tea kettle, setting it on the stove. She waved me into a chair and set a bowl of sugar in front of me. It appeared that I was invited to tea. I would have much preferred coffee.

I sat down, uneasy, imagining my father's disapproval as I took tea with the hotel cook. He never spoke to the help, any more than he would talk to the starched hem on his pants or the wax on his shoes. They appeared and disappeared on schedule, under the direction of Mme. Groseille, the housekeeper. If the help ever did anything to bring attention to themselves, it was usually the last thing they ever did in Boris Trotoskov's house: Mme. Groseille fired them forthwith.

This cook's brown hands, patient from years of service, poured boiling water into an etched, brass teapot. She nested the pot onto the open top of a second teapot, and then placed the stack in front of me on a folded towel. I sat smelling the brewing tea, stronger than the onions she started to slice. I had an urge to sketch her hands: muscles hidden under plump softness, always in the shadow of her heavy body. Odd, because I avoided drawing people; landscapes and plants were my *forté*. But looking at her hands, so sure of themselves as they prepared my food, made me reconsider.

With rapid scrapes and shakes of the pan, she fried up a portion of liver and onions and slid it onto a plate, which she laid before me. Her nail beds were very pink under the shell of her nail. She offered me salt. Then she found a glass and sat down heavily. She poured very dark, fragrant tea from the upper pot, and then thinned the dense liquid with water from the lower pot. With a solicitous smile, she put the glass of tea in front of me and nudged the sugar bowl my way.

I never liked tea, but I was thirsty. I sipped reluctantly at the potent drink, looking around the kitchen. Stacks of perhaps a hundred plates tilted in the open hutch; a pan that could make soup for forty bubbled on the stove; small bunches of dry herbs tied with hemp rope dangled over a cupboard door; the red clay tile under our feet shone, swept and scrubbed; a still life of three cabbages, green as the cook's eyes, leaned against each other on the counter.

I reached in my pocket and took out a charcoal pencil, carried all the way from Paris. "Do you have paper?" I asked, pantomiming a sketch on my palm.

She gave an upward toss of her head, which I gathered meant no, and gestured for me to wait. She stood and shuffled out of the room. As I waited, I ate liver and onions. They were silky, tender, and she'd added lots of black pepper.

She came back with a child's school *cahier* and pressed it into my hands. The corners were dog-eared, and the first two pages had been torn out. The rest of the *cahier* was empty. The previous owner had spent more time rolling the book's corners between his fingers than writing.

"Do you have anything without lines?" I asked, underlining the blue rules with a finger, and then rubbing across the page as though to erase them. She clicked with her tongue and raised an eyebrow.

"No lines," I repeated, not sure what clicks and an eyebrow intended. She tutted again, this time with an upward toss of her head.

This was far from the smooth vellum I was used to and I wasn't happy. My exile was going to be hell indeed if I couldn't even get decent drawing paper. I tried once more to explain but she rose and went to the sink, where she began washing cabbages.

Annoyed and ungrateful, I stepped out the back kitchen door with the ragged notebook tucked under an arm. I was that kind of a child, Cricket. Do you feel annoyed and ungrateful sometimes? I wonder.

I paused on the stone stoop, breathing in sharp air. Brush clumped around the hotel, smelling of crushed sage. Scraps of old Roman columns lay about. Bare footprints sank in the yellow dirt, dark wells of dew at the toes where the pads pushed deep. Morning frost melted and everything in the sun glistened wet. I lingered on the doorstep, soothing my irritation. Then I wandered down the goat path, picking my way around hunks of marble and low bushes until I stood in a small clearing. *Mon Dieu!* I inhaled and held it, afraid the mist of my breath might tarnish the beauty. Apollo's Temple.

After two thousand years, all that remained for Apollo was a brief stand of impossibly tall pillars: a soaring half circle, pristine with peace, poised on the edge of a twenty-meter cliff that dropped to the ocean. In the circle's center squatted a twisted laurel, its waxy leaves dull in the winter sun. Intoxicating laurel, normally grown in rings around Apollo's sacred spaces, the leaves chewed by Apollo's priestesses for divine hallucination so they could enounce the oracle. But this rootling had dug its way into the center of the ring and survived as an unpruned weed, shedding mottled shadows on a marble altar. Carved marble stubs that had once been columns, arches, and walls had tumbled into chaos and were now washed painfully white by melting ice. In the fat blue shade made by the hunks of stone, frost shriveled and dried.

The steep bank of the cliff had eroded to within a meter of the temple, the sea creeping up on what the wind could not topple. The ridge fell steeply into the Mediterranean, the waves that seductive blue that requires green, white, and gold to paint. Not like any blue you are wearing, *ma fille.* Somewhere between the soft blue green on your finger nails, and the dangerous cobalt streaks in your hair.

Apollo: the god of art and healing, who embodies pitiless, perfect artistry. And here was unbelievable beauty. I wanted my water color paints with such intensity that my eyes filled with tears. I should never have left them in Paris, no matter what they weighed. No matter if Boris was closing in on my door. You understand that, don't you Cricket? I see the way you watch the light, gauge the hues and tints. You, too, are compelled by a gift that you cannot run from.

I found a lopped off stump of marble and sat. Like a school girl, I took out my lined *cahier* and charcoal. Nothing about this scene was black and white, but that was all I had. I worked on perspective, the crack lines in the aged marble, and the grace of Apollo's circle, until eight pages of the little notebook were full.

As winter sun settled on the horizon, I realized that I was chilled to the bone, stiff, and numb. I rose to go and a strangled cry startled me. I whirled around. The same painfully thin boy who had run out the jetty now crouched behind me, dressed in torn-off pants and a filthy sweater, bare footed in the rocky sand. He hopped backwards a few steps, a rabbit's posture, all round eyes and gangly legs, his small mouth in an 'o'.

I held out the notebook. "Come here, if you want to see." But he bolted, tearing off through the brush and to the edge of the cliff, then down the path that led to the beach.

That night, as Della wrapped me in silk for dinner, my thoughts were bound to Apollo. When the sun shone, the radiance of Incir's winter was washed, nervous, and young. But under cloud cover, innocence evaporated and a silver sheen soaked hungrily into every object it touched. The two moods of an Olympian god: breathtaking grace and lustful craving. My charcoal pencil had no words for the light I saw in Apollo's temple.

At dinner, I sat again between Mizou and Suat Bey. The cook with the generous hands brought small, tight cabbage rolls, bulgur cooked with parsley and butter, and a monkfish, stuffed with bread and herbs. I had taken only a few bites when Suat Bey took a sip from his Raki glass, rolled the liquor around in his mouth, and jutted his pointed chin in my direction.

"Have I told you, Mademoiselle, of my famous fight with the sultan's eunuch?" He helped himself to a wedge of fish and spooned yellow dabs of roasted garlic and cumin on top.

Had Suat Bey sat at my father's diplomatic dinners,

I might have learned to love the heroes of the world. It occurred to me, feeling the warmth of Suat Bey's attention, that heroes were kinder than the world's leaders. I shook my head, willing him to go on.

"*Oh la*, that's too rich to miss." He toyed with his fish head, delicately removing the cheek meat with his fork. When I didn't speak, he glanced at me coyly.

"Since you are too shy to beg me, I shall be a gentleman and tell you." He popped the fish cheeks in his mouth and chewed in a deliberate show. Then he said, "It was when I went to collect my tribute from the Sultan, after my bravery in battle. I was a fine sight that day in my polished metal breast plate, a swath of silver silk twisted in a turban on my handsome head." He gave me a charming grin, from which a few upper teeth were missing.

"As a Turkish man, I have nothing but the highest respect for the Sultan's harem, and would never have thought, under any circumstances, that I would be forced to breach those walls. But you must understand that I, too, have honor!" He gave a significant nod. The accompanying waggle of his long moustache looked more devilish than honorable, and I suppressed a laugh.

"I was walking among the pomegranates and lemons of the Sultan's splendid garden when I heard a gentle dove's voice, a delicate coo of distress that could wrench a sensitive man's heart from his chest. The precious sound rose over a Jasmine covered wall, pleading for help, as moving as poetry. Oh, *Princess*, her cries were piteous. You, yourself a young woman, must feel for such desperation."

"It must have been terrible," I murmured.

Across the table, Kemal stabbed a serving of fish with his fork and dragged it across the serving platter as though he meant to kill it a second time. Suat Bey pointedly ignored him.

"But what to do? I looked about for a guard or servant that I could send for help. Where were the lazy bastards? No doubt cracking sunflower seeds between their teeth and cleaning their grubby nails with their Cossack daggers." With great disgust he threw the fish head, picked clean, onto the bone plate.

"Kemal, pass the cabbage rolls." Father challenged son: slight and claiming one hundred years old against the muscular fifty-year-old who pulled sharks from the sea with a spear. Kemal scowled and passed the platter.

"So, I must rescue this troubled beauty myself, *non*?" Suat Bey selected a cabbage roll, unraveled the skin, and popped the lump of current and rice stuffing in his mouth. "How to proceed? I couldn't scale the fortress that held her, dressed as I was in military armor and silver-toed boots." He shook his head at his gutted roll. "I tried! I gripped the trunks of Jasmine vine, shaking down a storm of fragrant flowers. But heavy as I was, the plants came off in my hands, and my metal toes could get no purchase in the cracks between the stones. Oh, *ma Princess*, her pleading cries shredded my heart to ribbons, and there was nothing to be done." He shrugged with forlorn helplessness and eyed his plate as though it were his last meal. Then he took another bite, troweling up limp cabbage with a triangle of bread. "Perhaps an old man's tales bore you?" Suat Bey modestly dabbed stains of yellow cumin off his mustache.

"Please, Monsieur," I begged, longing to see the maiden rescued.

"Yes, what happened, Papa?" Damad, always a light eater, had finished his meal long before and crept to Suat Bey's chair. For the first half of the story he sat under the table at Suat Bey's feet. But when valiant Suat Bey was thwarted by the fiendish Jasmine vine, Damad scrambled to his father's side. "Tell us, Papa."

"Ah, well then, if you insist." He leaned forward with renewed enthusiasm. "Foiled by the delicate Jasmine vine, and unable to bear her cries of despair any longer, I did what any man would do. I stripped to the skin Allah blessed me with and scaled the wall in a fury, naked, with my dagger between my teeth." He swiped his hand across his mouth to indicate the dagger, sharp blade perilously pressed against his lips.

"*Mais non*, Monsieur!" I gasped. In my mind I saw Rodin's famous sculpture of the naked damned, muscular and desperate, scaling the gates of Hell.

"*Ah oui.*" His moustache twitched with anticipation. "And what was on the other side? *Ah la la la la la la!* Before me stood a monstrous eunuch, bare except for the token shorts he wore to cover what remained of his manhood. They must have taken his Gems of God late, because he was as muscled as a gladiator, his Yataghan gripped in a hand that could crush a head. Do you know the Yataghan, *Princess*?"

"*Non.*" There was no end to fantastic swords in a hero's life.

Damad jumped up and down, little feet wild with excitement. "I know, I know, Papa. It's a sword of silver, great and curved like a Minotaur's spine."

"*Exactement.*" Suat Bey toasted his youngest son with a swig of Raki. "Cowering at this brute's feet was a maiden of the harem, swathed from head to toe in golden cloth, with her bowed head modestly covered. I could guess by the lithe shape of her back that she was an exquisite tulip, about to be cut in the prime of her bloom. Nothing but I and my little dagger stood between her and the beast about to send her to the archangel Azrael." His hands trembled as he poured more Raki, and he set down the bottle a little too close to the table edge.

"I could see her situation was *á la minute*. If I didn't act quickly, she would be answering the three questions to pass into heaven. Unable to reach the monster's chest, I stabbed at what was closest—his knee! My dagger plunged through the cap and out the other side like the arrow through Achilles heel."

Suat Bey stabbed. Beside him, Damad stabbed. Together they almost knocked over the Raki bottle. I thrilled with delight as Kemal bellowed and lunged across the table, grabbing the teetering flask and setting it right.

"Bone-headed as an old sea cucumber," Kemal grumbled. Suat Bey ignored him.

"As the monster buckled, I swooped the golden beauty into my arms, out from under his toppling body. I set my precious flower on her feet and turned to finish the beast off with a stab to the heart. I yanked my dagger free and raised the gory tip. But the maiden cried, '*No! You are an angel sent by God. You must know it is a sin to kill.*' Ah, such piety. Such charity. You will do the same yourself, *Princess*, if you are ever forced to threaten a life. " He nodded slowly, weighted down with the wonder of a woman's compassion.

Perhaps in Suat Bey's presence, I, too, would be moved to spare a fiend. Looking into his eyes, I wanted to believe that I could be that kind.

Suat Bey rose unsteadily, lifting his Raki glass as though it weighed two stone. "The monster groaned and struggled to rise. But I put my bare heel in the center of his chest—," he put a foot on the seat of his chair, barely balancing, "—and I said to him, '*If you ever seek to harm this maiden again I will drop from heaven and send your soul to Jahannam.*' The maiden, recovering from her shock, did not linger to admire my naked triumph. She fled, calling over her shoulder, '*Goodbye God's angel. I will see you in heaven.*' Her voice was breathtaking, an aria. Beneath her golden veil were two almond eyes, roasted brown and shaped with more of God's love than Cleopatra's eyes."

He reached a hand to my face, and laid his wrinkled, bony

fingertips on my cheek. For a moment, for the first time in my life, I felt beautiful. A beautiful, protected child.

His hand dropped, and he sat down hard enough to cause his chair to squeak. "She ran away, of course. The guards were coming, clamoring down the maze of halls, sending screaming women running for cover. The *bêlement* was like a market-full of goats." Suat Bey laughed, a chortle reminiscent of an old rooster, warming up to wake the day.

"As naked as I was, the injured eunuch at my feet, I decided not to stay." He rested his hand on Damad's head. "Exits are important, Son, especially when it comes to other men's women." He ruffled the boy's dark hair. "So I climbed back over the wall and hid in the bushes to put my armor on. Here's to beautiful women!" He raised his glass. "French ones—," he toasted me and Mizou, "American—," he toasted Della, "—and Turkish," he toasted the cook. "May the angels of God watch over you."

And for a little while, God's angels kept Boris and his merciless tyranny at bay. Basking in their divine protection, a tentative happiness crept from its hiding place in the dark corners of my soul, cautiously seeking the sunshine. Every day for December, January, and February I drew the ruins, until I filled all the pages, front and back, of the little *cahier*. The light grew heavier as the rains lessened, and dust began to dance in the beams.

I announced several times that I wanted water colors, or at least good drawing paper. That would have been sufficient, in Paris, to send Mme. Groseille scurrying to the art store for supplies, which I would then find laid discreetly on my bed.

My requests didn't move Mizou, and I had no further luck communicating to the cook. Della just tilted her head in that patronizing way of Americans and said, "Can't help you there, honey."

So I took to drawing with Damad's crayons on his three-holed school paper. The perspective of cliffs falling into the ocean, the rise and twist of Roman columns, the bend of the brittle, frozen lavender: all improved until I could almost call my drawings art. But the Mediterranean light eluded Damad's crayons as easily as it had escaped my charcoal pencil. Until Xiao Lian came.

# SIX

Your grandfather, Boris, loved Greek myths; that is his book that lies in your lap. Immortals arranging the lives of lesser beings was his idea of a good social order. Olympian gods fought and squabbled over the fates of mortals with the same ferocity as diplomats. Therefore I read the classics, and I knew Apollo.

As spring came and the days grew warmer, I sprawled on my back on the altar in Apollo's semicircle, looking up through the laurel branches, marveling at the pale, tender sky that winter had hidden for the last three months. The white marble columns extended far, far into that gentle sky, making a bridge between Olympus and Earth. And down that bridge strode my memories of the legendary Apollo.

There were three brothers who conquered the Titans, and they divided the world between them. Zeus took Olympus and lived in the heavens, Poseidon took the sea, and Hades sunk into the darkest depths of the underworld. Apollo was the son of a union between Leto and Zeus. Hera, Zeus' wife, was furious, and forbid Leto to give birth on solid ground. Leto fled to a floating island and had twins; Apollo, the god of the arts and healing, and Atemis, the goddess of the hunt.

For all of his ability to heal, Apollo was a cruel god who would tolerate no rivalry; he flayed Marsyas alive for daring to challenge his supremacy as a musician, and nailed the satyr's shaggy pelt to a tree. He was fierce in defending those he loved, killing the dragon Python and the giant Tityos to protect his mother. Apollo's son resurrected a man from Hades' realm, infuriating Hades—who insisted that Zeus kill the boy—which incited the gods of Olympus into a feud of revenge and counter revenge. Hence, there was little love between Apollo and his uncle Hades. Built like Michelangelo's *David* and hairless except for his golden head of curls, Apollo had many lovers, male and female. Most of his affairs ended in bloodshed, banishment, or curses, or transformation of his lovers into plants.

I was not at all sure that Apollo had a happy immortality, but he certainly had a magnificent temple. Lying in the sun, it was warm enough that I shed the long jeans and heavy sweater of winter. The thick cotton headscarf that the cook (I now knew that her name was Yurda) insisted on tying on my head every time I walked through her kitchen, lay discarded in the yellow sand. Lavender bloomed, and mint, and sage, filling the semicircle with the smells of Yurda's cooking. The sun was hot, burning my bare skin beyond my shorts and sleeveless T-shirt. But I didn't care. A few entrancing brush strokes of cloud streaked across the sky and caught the early afternoon sun, filling my heart with wonder.

The sun spread a soft lemon blush over those feathery strands, and I knew I could capture their beauty if I only had paint. I daydreamed, yearning for water colors: blotted, flowing, washing. My eyes half closed, I tried to decide if an elusive shade I saw was pink or lavender. In the tiniest dabs, my mystery color flowed exquisitely over the edge of the clouds, blending with yellow, fading to white.

A dark spot appeared between me and the sky. Long shadows crossed my body. I blinked and sat up. Three teenagers stood around me, one at the head of the slab, and one on either side. They held themselves with juvenile jauntiness, and they were barely bigger than I: boys who should be drinking sodas at the corner store. Had they not been standing within feet of me I would have been inclined to ignore them. As it was, I had no choice but to look them awkwardly in the eye.

They leered at me. It took a moment to be afraid: after all, the kitchen was within screaming distance, and this was my sanctuary. Apollo was cruel to those who insulted him.

I scampered off the altar and backed up against a column, trying to gauge their intent. They spoke Turkish, smirking, relaxed. One young man reclined on the altar I had just vacated and unbuttoned his pants, beaconing for me to come over. He spread his legs like an offering, dark hair curling out from the 'v' of his open front. The other two took a few steps backwards, giggling, studying my face, as though they hoped for something other than shock and disgust.

I snatched a broken laurel branch off the ground and snapped it to make a weapon. It wasn't much, but it could poke and whack. Backing around the circle I glared at the boy's manhood swelling on the altar. He grinned at me, his hand gestures a rhythmic wave: inviting, mocking, demanding.

I doggedly backed around the circle, the stick squeezed painfully tight in my fist, heading for the goat path that led to the hotel. His friends guessed what I was doing and pressed forward to cut me off.

"Move aside, *connards!*" I commanded. Unfortunately, I am just an average sized woman, and Boris didn't waste time on self-defense classes—attacks at a diplomatic dinner are never physical. But I was genetically adept at snarling. I lifted the stick to make it clear that I was telling the bastards to get out of my way.

The stupid grins faded and they took a step backwards, clearly confused. I swung the stick, barely missing their thin, shirtless bellies. We jousted this way for several paces; me clearing a step forward with my stick, them leaping backward to avoid my blows.

The boy on the altar pulled up his pants and sprung to his feet. Like a hunting jackal, he padded around behind me, closing in. His friends took heart and lunged forward, trying to grab my stick. Cornered, my thoughts overran with fear and fury. I spun around and caught the jackal on the cheek, swiping a long nasty gash from ear to chin. He screamed and staggered backward, his hand over the cut. His friends cried out in astonishment and retreated. I was insane with rage. Thrashing with my jagged branch, I went after them. I would have killed them, Cricket, if I could have gotten to them.

But they were light on their feet and they ran, the jackal leading the way. Leaping over brush, they dashed for the path that wove back and forth, down the treacherous cliff to the beach.

I stood in Apollo's temple, stick raised and whole body shaking, screaming curses. I screamed and screamed. I could no longer see the white marble columns towering around me, the baby blue sky, the soft lavender flowers. All I could see was Boris, pounding his fist on his desk, face red as fire.

"You will do as I tell you, child," he bellowed, "or I will snap you in two. Don't defy me as your sister did, I won't stand for it. Not even London will be far enough away if I come after you. Get out of my sight, *salope.*" And he slapped me.

That night, four months before, I had backed out of the drawing room and closed the door, my palm pressed against my burning cheek. Even as furious as I made him, Boris had never before laid a hand on me. But then, in twenty years I had never challenged him. In the face of my independence, he was splitting at the seams.

Dizzy with fear, I ran the lushly carpeted halls to my room. I threw myself on my bed and lay panting. This was it. *C'est le moment ou jamais.* Now or never. I could stay and be pushed about like so much modeling clay, or I could run.

I don't know, Cricket, where I found the presence of mind, the raw courage. Perhaps from that grandmother who fled first from France, then again from Russia so long ago, believing that somewhere she could find peace. Hours later, while my father slept, I stole that grandmother's jewels, the ones she'd smuggled through a war zone in her bodice. I packed my passport in frantic haste, listening for the sound of Boris' tread in the hall. With a few clothes in my grade school knapsack, I left by the servant's entrance, terrified by every creak and crack in the apartment behind me.

The Metro closes at midnight, so I walked the streets all night, arriving at the Marais early in the morning. I slept on the doorstep of the first jewelry shop I found. The old *juif* who owned the shop recognized a desperate refugee and took pity on me, giving me an excellent price for the pearls, diamonds, and cloisonné that had been in my family for generations. I bought traveler's checks as soon as the nearest bank opened, and then caught Metro line B3 from Châtelet les Halles to Charles de Gaulle airport.

Why Incir? Because the Ambassador to England had once said the Turks were kind to his daughter when she lost her way in Istanbul. Because the lady at the travel desk at Charles de Gaulle said that staying in rural Turkey was dirt cheap. And because the plane to Istanbul left in twenty minutes.

Twenty excruciating minutes. He might already be in his limousine, on the way to the airport. He might have already called friends among the police. It was a very, very long twenty minutes.

Four months later, I fell to my knees in the sand at Apollo's altar, under the generous umbrella of laurel. Apollo caused plagues and murdered ruthlessly, but he had loved, and he had healed. Laying my hands on the warm, pure marble, I prayed.

I may not be beautiful, like Apollo's human lover Leucothea. I may not be powerful like the Spartan athlete Hyacinth, whom Apollo loved enough to want to die for. But I reverently laid my soul in Apollo's care.

Protect me Apollo. Raise your famous bow that Eros was so jealous of, and drive back my enemies. Well up a spring of sacred water in this dry sand that I can wash in. I cannot make music, as you can, but I promise that I will learn to draw with such beauty that I will warrant your love. Help me Apollo. Heal me. I have no one else.

I heard a crunch of gravel behind me and staggered to my feet, ready to fight. My heart, racing from fear, skipped once or twice and then slowed down, mute with awe.

He was a huge shadow. With his back to the glaring noon sun, his silhouette looked Olympian: solid torso, long hair braided to his waist, hands gripped into fists. This was no boy I could chase away with a stick. He stood breathing hard from running. Barefoot and bare-chested, he wore nothing but pants, as if he had dressed in a hurry. With the glaring sun over his shoulder, I couldn't see his face or guess his age.

"*Ça va*, Tatyana? Are you all right?"

He knew my name! His French carried an accent that I vaguely recognized, a musical interpretation of French that I'd heard many times in my childhood, but couldn't quite place.

"*Oui, ça va merci.*" I wished I could see his face, but shading my eyes didn't help. "Who are you?"

"My name is Xiao Lian Chin. I heard you yelling and saw you from my window. I came to help, but you obviously don't need it." He squatted, dropping onto his heels, his thick knees bending with flexible ease.

"How do you know my name?"

"Mizou told me. Do you need to sit down? You look pretty shaken."

His voice sounded younger than I expected for a big man. His accent danced about in my ears, then settled down to be recognized: Chinese. After my father left China, we had visitors every few years, serious men in plain, well-cut suits who sequestered themselves with my father in the drawing room for an afternoon and then left by the back door. "Amazingly clever young men," Boris often said after they'd gone. "Such a waste of talent." So like Boris, to see clever people as resources to be used, or squandered.

"I think I'll go to my room." I hurried toward the goat path, but some instinct made me twist around for one more look. Xiao Lian stood, and the sun no longer backlit his face.

Ah, Cricket, your father was magnificent. He turned my twenty-year-old heart inside out and handed it back to me, fibrillating. Fleur de Lyon never loved Boris Trotoskov, and Boris never loved anyone, but I loved your father from the moment I laid eyes on his face. Later I needed his strength, that could have lifted Boris one handed, and I came to adopt his posture, resolute through whatever life hammered us with. But first and foremost I loved the kindness of his face. So like yours, my beautiful daughter, though you go to great lengths to scar and hide it. So magnificent that it brings pain to gaze on you.

And I knew that face. In some other context, far in the past, I had seen an older, grizzled likeness of this man, middle-aged instead of youthful. Then, too, I had been awed. And perhaps, though I had been too young to know it, I had felt the tentative edges of a love that I could not escape.

My eyes wandered down to where thick, red scars, cut deep and bubbled with defective healing, scrawled like a warning across Xiao's upper chest. Then I turned on the goat path and stumbled to the *pension*.

That night, during the soothing ritual of Della's hands wrapping my silk gown, I brooded. Where had I seen those amazing deep set eyes with sockets that swoop upward? The eyebrows had been captured in two fierce strokes, conveying ruthlessness instead of humility and concern. Somewhere, similar black eyes sized up the world. Somewhere I had seen those lips, the lower one dominating the upper in its full softness. But the lips had been scowling, outlined with a graying moustache, the beard blown to one side by a brutal wind. I'd seen that face and I had involuntarily stepped away, putting my back flat against a wall, unable to either name or bear the emotion that flooded me. Boris had taken my hand and insisted that I look. Where was it?

"What's on your mind, hon? You're cloudy as buttermilk." Della gave the dark red silk a tug, tight around my waist.

"Have you met Xiao Lian?" I forgot, in my absorption, to pretend poor English.

She tucked a few pleats over my belly, her smile spreading thick and sweet. "Saw him on the front patio. He's worth a second look, too. Looks like Yue Fei."

*Oui!* That was who. Yue Fei. Xiao Lian Chin looked like a young Yue Fei. "How do you know Yue Fei?" I asked.

From her crouch in front of me, Della glanced up, clearly amused. "I'm a silk trader, and silk comes from China, doesn't it? Better I should ask how you know him. Yue Fei isn't exactly a French schoolgirl crush."

"My father, Boris, was—" I pretended to struggle for words, "— taken with great men in history. There is *un ancien rouleau*—" I gestured opening a roll of paper and flattening it on the wall.

"A scroll?"

"*Oui.* An old scroll in the Louvre. Yue Fei rides a horse that—" I gestured for rearing. "He is as big as two men, with a spear in one hand and a bow…." In my mind, I lay the bow across his saddle. "When I had twelve or thirteen years my father took me to see this painting." My words stuttered to a stop, daunted by further description of my emotions in the face of this ferocious Jin Dynasty warrior.

How my father admired Yue Fei. Departing from his usual, dry lecture style, Boris told me his story with dramatic animation. Yue Fei was born in 1103, surviving a flood as an infant by floating down the Yellow River in a clay jar. As a young man he clawed his way up the army ranks, and through intrigue and perseverance became the general centuries couldn't forget. Chinese school children (and the rare French one, like me) heard tales of his strict discipline, unbendable morals, and poetic soul. No one would hang that scroll over their coffee table; his monstrous chest clanged with armor, and the blood stained tassel on his helmet would sour the cream. But, my beautiful child, he dominated that expansive museum chamber as easily as he once dominated the Jurchen armies. Striking. Terrifying. Magnificent. And now a young man with the same noble face shook me like war shakes a nation.

Della brought the silk up around my chest, tucked and pleated, then draped my shoulder. She stood and made final adjustments to the folds. "There, that's as pretty as you get. Perhaps tonight it will be worth the effort, with Xiao Lian at the table, you think?"

She waited for me to answer, and when I didn't deign to

reply she leaned down and unfurled wads of silk she'd yanked from her suitcase, working to refold them.

"Della?"

"Yes, hon?" She kept her gaze on her mundane chore.

"Some boys tried to—" I considered the English word, and changed tactics. "I was *attaqué* today, in the temple."

"Attacked?" Della's hands stopped moving and rested, poised in a bed of silk.

"*Oui*. Some boys from the village. I hit them with a stick."

"Oooeee. Local Muslim boys?"

I nodded.

"Well, I guess it was bound to come to this sooner or later." Her eyes meandered over my face, assessing for emotional damage. "You look like you survived, but we'd best tell Mizou." She stood and put an arm around me. "Come on, dinner's waiting."

As we proceeded downstairs, she said, "Don't mention your problem at the table. We don't want Suat Bey waving a rusty ole sword and decapitating anyone. Someone could get hurt—probably Suat Bey." She smiled at me, dark and sticky as molasses. "This is something us women should deal with."

Xiao Lian was seated at Suat Bey's right hand. Xiao nodded to me as I took my place, and I felt my face tingle. Then he went back to conversation with Kemal.

They spoke French, so I understood, but the content was painfully dry. It never would have occurred to me to ask how the villagers fed themselves in the winter, and what proportion of their income came from farming, herding, and fishing respectively. I longed for Xiao to turn and ask me something about my life. Ask with the same intent fascination in those wonderful deep set eyes, now fixed on Kemal's face as Kemal spoke of Incir's woes. But he didn't. Having sought out my name, and having arrived at the altar like a gift from Apollo, Xiao promptly forgot me.

I half listened to Mizou and Della talk about the silk market in Istanbul. I picked distractedly at my lamb kebabs. I dipped eggplant strips in yoghurt and forced myself to concentrate on the tale of the three legged camel who aided Suat Bey's escape over the Taurus Mountains when he was pursued by Syrian bandits. I turned down, four times, Yurda's polite request (in Turkish) that I eat dessert, and then ate it anyway because she set it at my place while I stared at Xiao's profile. Dizzy with emotion, I straddled the chasm of first love: one foot in heaven's rapture, and one foot in love's hell. To glance at him was enough to give me vertiginous pleasure. To be ignored by him was enough to darken my heart with the tortures of The Furies.

I had never had a love, not even an infatuation. I remembered Emma, mooning over George the night she met him at my father's dinner for the American vice president. She lay on my bed in her lace slip, endlessly repeating, "I fancy you, George Galt," in her best imitation of an English accent. How absurd to feel that way about a perfect stranger. If this was love, it was more akin to *la grippe*, the common flu, than it was to profound sentiment. It had flushing fevers, delirious fantasies, and messy runny noses. I would never be so foolish, my thirteen-year-old heart had decided.

By the end of Mizou's dinner in Incir I was vexed with

myself for thinking such romantic *bêtises*—sheer stupidities. My heart twisted into a tattered rag over a man who looked like a twelfth century painting! Hidden underneath my internal self-reprimand, I was furious at Xiao for having successfully eaten a two hour dinner without addressing another word, or even a smile, to me.

It was with this aching misery and wounded Trotoskov pride that I went into the kitchen when Mizou called me. It was with this same puffed-up self-absorption that I told Mizou—in French—the story of the village teens' clumsy attempt at seduction and frightened retreat. As bold as Suat Bey, I exaggerated everything, from the ridiculous scrawniness of their manly parts to their cowardly fear of my stick. I imitated, with my best French sarcasm, their pitiful boyish swaggers. I was ferocious as I drove them to the cliff. I did not play the terrified girl, fighting for my virginity: I was Tatyana Trotoskov, banishing my inferiors with an imperial lion's roar.

Mizou's eyes glowed as she heard the tale. She giggled and chuckled as she translated it into Turkish for Yurda, and was howling with laughter by the time she had translated the more savory and complicated bits into English for Della. Overcome with mirth, the three of them laughed until the corners of their cotton scarves and silk robes were wet from wiping their eyes. Each time the laughter subsided, Yurda would choke out a brief comment in Turkish, and the hoots and guffaws would begin again.

I sat at Yurda's kitchen table, dinner dishes piled all around us, and watched their hilarity with self-righteous indignation. I shouldn't have expected sympathy, after all I had presented myself as a victor, not a victim. All the same, I wasn't expecting to be the butt of a joke.

Finally the laughter abated one last time, and an earnest conversation ensued. Yurda clucked and tossed her head, adjusting her head piece with irritated tugs as she spoke. Della crossed her arms over her chest, pushed up her significant cleavage, and nodded gravely at what Yurda said. Mizou sat as still as a statue at the oracle, looking down and smiling mysteriously into her hands.

After some back and forth discussion, Mizou turned to me. "We think the boys mistook you for a whore, perhaps one of the Russian whores from Manavgat," she said in English, presumably so Della could understand.

"Why do they think I am a *putain*?"

"Because of your exposed skin, and the way you lounge about with your legs open. It was a misunderstanding. They meant you no harm."

"No harm? How can you say this thing? They would have *me violer,* had I not defended."

Mizou tossed her head. "Perhaps. But you must wear the headscarf that Yurda gives to you. And you must cover your legs and arms."

My jaw dropped, dumbfounded. I had been attacked, and it was somehow my fault! I sputtered for a response.

Perhaps thinking that I was struggling with English, Mizou switched to French. "Yurda will put out the word in the village about who you are. You will be under her protection. You will have a chaperone now, if you wander from the *pension.*"

A chaperone. As I was watched over by Mme. Groseille and Boris, tended like pedigree breeding stock? *Elles ne manques pas de culot.* These women had a hell of a lot of nerve.

Yurda stood and lumbered to a drawer, where she took out a headscarf. She unfolded it and came to stand behind me. Her strong hands pulled the cloth across my forehead, tucked it under my hair, and pinned it. She pleated the folds around my ears and pinned it again under my chin. I felt stifled, hidden from the world as though I had something to be ashamed of. I wanted to rip off the scarf and toss it, but Yurda looked so pleased that I hesitated. Nodding with approval Yurda kissed me on the cheek. Then she said something in Turkish.

"What did she say?" I asked.

"She says this is a devout Muslim village, where girls cover their heads out of respect for God. And she wants to know why you're not married," said Della.

"I...I have only twenty years," I stammered in English.

Della translated, and Yurda began to chuckle. Whatever Yurda answered in Turkish caused Mizou and Della to double over laughing again.

I stood up, encased from head to toe in cloth someone else had applied. "What did she say?" I demanded.

Mizou rolled her eyes to the ceiling and said nothing.

"What did she say?" I insisted, stomping a heavy Trotoskov foot.

Della rose and leaned both palms on the table. "She said you are an old maid by village standards, and plain as a goat to boot." She smelled of clove perfume and Raki as she inclined toward me. "Yurda likes you, hon. God knows why, you're an arrogant little Napoleon. Don't be a fool. Put aside your haughty Western self-importance and wear the scarf. And try not to kill any of her neighbors as you wander around."

Yurda stood too, and lifted a rolling pin. With bold swipes and parries she imitated my defense, fending off an imaginary attack, the hem of her *kara çarşaf* flapping. Then she dropped the pin and pantomimed the boys, scurrying for cover, faces terrified and hands over their manhood. With a whoop she collapsed into a chair, hysterical with laughter.

It was then I knew that more than just the request for protection would spread among the six hundred inhabitants of Incir. This story, in all of its dramatic glory, would be whispered from giggling wife to giggling wife on laundry day. It would be told by old man to old man over Turkish coffee. It would be re-enacted by small boys in the market square. With a flood of satisfaction I realized that Yurda would tell my story with gusto, humiliating the boys in front of the whole village.

I am a diplomat's daughter; I knew exactly what I had done. Like many a spiteful politician, I had seized upon a misunderstanding and fashioned it into a war. A war I was smug enough to believe I would win, and foolish enough to think would be easy.

# SEVEN

mut was my chaperone.

Starting the very next morning, he slept at the base of the stairs. When I went out, he tailed me like a mosquito, singing to himself in a barely audible drone. When I came in, he sat under the kitchen table, skinny, dusty legs crossed, ankle over ankle, little fingers dancing some game on the slick, polished floor.

Umut, according to Della, was the orphan of a local family. Two years after his father never returned from the sea, his mother came up pregnant. Della didn't know whether she bore a child of illicit passion, or whether her pregnancy endured from violent shame. Either way, as soon as Umut was born, the villagers stoned her to death.

For the last ten years Umut had been raised by the village, eating at whatever door he knocked on, sleeping wherever he laid his head. With unwavering charity they fed and clothed him, hanging strings of blue and yellow beads shaped like eyes around his neck to protect him from evil. They welcomed him in the mosque, and gave him odd jobs in the market. Whatever hunger or cold he knew, he knew in the same proportion as the other villagers.

Umut, as much as he could speak, spoke Turkish. According to Della, his garbled language was a challenge. She suspected that he was somewhat brain damaged. But he was sharp enough to understand that I was his responsibility.

At first he irritated me, crashing through the brush, watching me rip off the *başörtüsü* (which is what they called the headscarf) and shake out my hair as soon as I was out of sight of Yurda's kitchen. He'd squat on his heels in the dirt, chin in his hands, tiny nose wiggling, eyes big as a rabbit's. I wondered: which village family would he join for dinner tonight? Could he tell them that I used the crumpled ball of a headscarf to swipe sweat off my forehead, and rolled up my long pants to get some sun on my shins? I assumed his inarticulate Turkish was to my advantage.

After a few days, I forgot him. In my growing agony over Xiao Lian, anything else seemed just an itch. During the day, Xiao disappeared. At dinner, he spoke with Kemal and Suat Bey, conversations that quickly became peppered with phrases in Turkish. Long discussions over topics like spear fishing and goat diseases. Their exclusive male *camaraderie*— the way they poured each other Raki, the way Kemal leaned forward and blocked my view, the way Suat Bey forgot me and sat entranced by Xiao's softly spoken tales—all of this conspired to wall me off. I sat sullenly, wrapped in Della's silk, thinking that I had finally become my mother: decorative.

A week later I was glad Umut was there. Prowling shadows began to haunt my daily trips to the ruins. Whispered Turkish drifted behind columns of marble. Eyes, veiled by shrubs, watched me. A brief sighting of the back of three young men's heads, bobbing rapidly down the trail to the beach, caused me to snatch up my headscarf and tie it on. I kept my broken laurel branch within arm's reach. But in my lonely suffering, the temple was my only sanctuary, so despite uneasy feelings that enemy troops were massing at my borders, I continued to lie on the altar, drawing for Apollo.

After another week, I despaired of ever attracting Xiao's attention. I went to the ruins as early in the morning as the faint dawn would permit, and stayed, suffering my loneliness until dinner, sketching and daydreaming in the shade.

Then one day in mid-March, I lay on my belly on the marble altar. I had mastered the perspective of the interrupted arch of columns, the faint wipes of white cloud beyond the laurel's branches, the cracks in the marble. I was bored and frustrated; unrequited love and the two hundredth drawing of a deteriorating temple were bringing Tatyana Trotoskov to her knees. Beyond my fury at Xiao's indifference, beyond my sniveling tears, I simply ached for him. Using my charcoal pencil, I began to draw his face. Having given up on the desire that he should know me, I poured out, instead, what little I knew about him.

With careful strokes, I tried to capture his squint, worried over the village's fresh water problem; the light in his pupils when he spoke of the engineering in the ancient Roman aqueducts; the pensive, inward gaze that overtook him, silenced him sometimes mid-sentence as though something strange and terrible had spoken in his ear. Perhaps it was the ghost of Yue Fei, come to haunt him.

With caresses from my fingertip, I smeared gray charcoal dust to form his lips, puckered in a kiss as he spoke French. With that same devoted finger I formed the amused curl at the left corner of his mouth, lifting, too, the left naris of his nose as he laughed at Suat Bey's stories, his expression as gentle as Yue Fei's was ferocious. Using brown, rose, and white crayons, I tried to capture the perfection of his skin, glowing with earnestness on his cheek bones and down his face. Until the gentle colors met that horrifying scar, where some appalling, red secret bled from his past and screamed across his breast just below the collarbone.

When I got to the expanse of his chest, thick as a bull's, I drew no lower. I spent as many summers as my father would allow in École des Beaux-Arts, sketching nudes. I knew the firm twist of the wrist that would draw a male buttock, and the slanting lines of a muscular abdomen and ribs. But Xiao Lian had not offered any hope to me, so I left these curves that heated my dreams alone.

When I was done with the drawing I held it at arm's length. It was a good likeness, capturing both Xiao's kindness and the dark secrets he hid. As mysterious as the Mona Lisa.

De Vinci painted the Mona Lisa in layers, a blending technique called *sfumato*. This blending of colors leaves no lines to stop the eye from wandering, wandering in endless, hypnotic circles over her radiant eyes and mouth. Light appears to come from her face alone; all else fades to vague darkness. Her veils of pregnancy, her hairstyle of a whore, her hand gripping the armrest of the chair: all of this is obscured by dab after dab of paint. I suspect that De Vinci knew: love adds layers that blind the viewer, sometimes hiding someone's true nature for five hundred years. As good as my likeness was, it only convinced me of all I didn't know about

Xiao Lian. Perhaps that made my drawing an even better offering to Apollo.

Umut, who had been watching me from a perch overlooking the sea, stood and loped over. As he always did when I finished a drawing, he took the notebook paper from my hands and brought it to within inches of his face, his little nose twitching as though the drawing had a scent. Usually he set the page in my knapsack amongst the *cahiers* and loose papers I'd amassed over the months. This time he looked up with a shy grin, stretching his small slit of a mouth to its limit. Croaking in his guttural tongue, he seized my hand and tugged me toward a path that led into the brush, away from the *pension*. I snatched up my knapsack and abandoned headscarf, and not sure why I trusted this deficient ten-year-old, I let him lead me.

# EIGHT

Maman stops speaking. My nail polish had dried an hour ago, and caught in the trance of her story, I'd neglected to return the brush to the bottle and screw on the cap. I lift the ruined bottle off the rug and use my fingernail to torment the rubbery polish that had dripped down the side.

"Well, on with it," I say.

"*Non*, I'm tired. Maybe later."

I toss aside the useless bottle. "I was promised the full monty. Get on with it."

Maman laughs, the first full belly laugh of our relationship. Perhaps the first one in a decade. "*Mon Dieu*, child, what makes you so entitled? You must have eaten dear Emma and George for appetizers. Do they even know you are here?"

I shake my head, no.

She leans back in her fauteuil and stares up at the plaster carvings—cupids and fleurs-de-lis—on her expensive ceiling. "So, now you will tell me why you left London."

"It's complicated."

"I'm sure it is. That will make the story all the better."

I figure the ins and outs, and decide this might be worth a go. "Will you tell me more about Turkey then, and about Xiao?"

I particularly like Xiao, who sounds like a hell of a bloke. A Chinese dissident is much more my idea of a father than a London banker. Poor George, his imagination is missing in action.

"You will hear, in the end, your full monty," Maman says.

"Right, then." I take a skittish breath. To keep from showing my nerviness, I find the bottle and badger the dry polish again. "I left because I fell in love," I say.

~

I didn't set about to fall in love with Chander. I was thirteen to his fifteen when he saved me from the police. He wasn't quite as thin as the string that held up his trousers, but it was close.

For a few weeks after my sweet victory with the cricket, I hung about Covent Garden, my back pressed to the last concrete pillar of the main market building. From there I could see in one go the mob gathered around my graff, Chander's family shop, and the policeman on his bike. I'd bunked off school again, so I particularly watched the rozzer, who was busy ogling the skirts and therefore wasn't likely to arrest me. As soon as school was out, Chander came twisting through the crowd with a barmy grin on his face. He was a head taller than everyone, which I liked. I get tired of looking down on boy's heads.

He'd eased down into a bony pile beside me. "Skived off school?"

I nodded.

"You sure have a right good time," he said. "What do you do for seconds, rob The Tower?"

I laughed. I liked Chander's face: shadowed Bollywood eyes and a long, elegant, East Indian nose. But then they forgot which continent they were on and gave him the big cheekbones of a Sioux. His asymmetry made me want to consider him from different angles.

"I should rob something, I'm completely out of dosh," I said.

"What do you need money for?" he asked.

"Paint."

"Should have guessed."

I liked the smell of Chander, too: his sister's cuzzer, clean ironed cotton, and strong black tea.

"Don't you worry about cutting it so close? I imagine it's not only plod you have to bomb from."

I didn't answer. So far I'd stayed clear of aggro by running, outrunning, any crew that caught me marking their walls. But it was a matter of time, and I knew it.

"You should learn to fight, Jiè. You shouldn't arse about with your virginity."

He just out and said it, thinking he was family, if you please. I turned full-round and stared at him like he was totally daft.

Chander nodded. He didn't have a vague head waggle like his sister—nodded straight up and down, like a Brit. "I know a bloke who might train you. You're a big biffa, you could throw a wicked punch."

Eventually I came to expect that from Chander; he just dived right in, no testing the waters. He decided he liked you, it was as if he'd known you all his life. But this first time, it made me fume. "Do you always mete out personal advice?" I asked.

He grinned, wide across his whole face and happy as a bite of ice cream. "It's a sort of hobby, if you like."

"Well, keep it to your effing self."

He shook his head, a sharp, single 'no', then stood up and grabbed my arm. No "excuse me for barging in," or, "I suppose you should have your say," he just lifted me to my feet. "Don't be a bloomin' idiot," he said, and pleasant as pie he hauled me down the street.

～

I'd wager that everyone who meets Jaxon Pekelo, remembers him. It was years before it struck me *why* he stands out—he's just a little bloke, stretching for 5'4", and you're hard pressed to see much of him under his baggy black sweatshirt and trousers. And he's old—already shoved open the door to sixty and pootled halfway down the hall. Sure, he has that scar center face, like someone tried to split him in two with a hatchet, but it's mostly faded, and at the scar's tip is that innocent smile, angelic, really. Mild brown eyes. And in the back of my mind I'm asking, "What is it about this bloke?"

I didn't sort it out until the day he put me in the ring for money, fifteen years old and in my first professional fight.

"Remember, Jiè, you're a cricket. He'll take one look and expect you to fight like a bull. Use your speed and those fast legs. Get him by the back of the neck before he can land the first blow."

Looking down at the whirl in Professor Pekelo's dense silver hair I'd thought to myself, "What's Professor's fighting style?" Then I'd understood: shark. Pekelo moves like liquid death.

But that was years later. That first day when he unlocked the door—his door was always, always kept locked—I instinctively stepped behind Chander, even though Pekelo came up to my shoulder.

"Hello," said Chander, and he curled one hand over a fist and bowed.

Pekelo didn't ask why we were there. He scanned behind us to be sure we were alone, clocked the couple walking across the road and the dog by the rubbish bin, then let us in. The door locked three times behind us.

We walked down a dark hall. I could have dragged my fingers over the ceiling it was so low. At the end was a row of shoes, neat in a line like Sunday school, only giant foot-sizes bigger. The room was a hair grander than two drawing rooms, if you count one drawing room as the fight cage and the other as rubber mats. Boxing mitts, combat pads, and padded punch shields hung on hooks about the walls. Battered mannequins of male heads stood on poles, their chins and temples taped to repair the damage. All the posts in the room were wrapped in tight coils of rope. One bruiser was rubbing his knuckles with brown oil, then punching a wrapped post with rash indifference. The oil smelled like sweet dried Chinese plums, the kind that come in rice paper and have salty pits. That, and greasy sweat. Chander kicked off his shoes and lined them up, so I did, too.

"Sit," whispered Chander, and we found a place out of the way.

The fighters in the room were having at each other in a bare-fisted ruck as if this were the pub, Catholic Irish against the Protestants. Full grown and hidden in head gear, they grappled in pairs and threes, letting out the occasional goose-pimpling *keeiiii*. Several eyebrows were bleeding. One bloke had another on the ground and had pinned his head in a complex tangle of legs and arms that looked like it might well crush his loaf right off.

Pekelo wandered around watching, periodically tapping a shoulder, interrupting to say something too soft for my ears. He'd demonstrate, his sleeves whooshing as his blurred fists flew. One knuckle bent, a blow too fast to see, and the bloke he fought was down. Then he'd quietly point out all the pressure points that could kill the man sprawled at his feet. I pressed against the wall and kept my ears flat, wishing to go home, shaking in my gut like too much pudding.

After a while the blokes lined up. They bowed to Pekelo with one fist covered, as Chander had, collected their shoes, and left. Pekelo went to a bureau against the wall and sat, opening his ledger book as if he'd forgotten us.

I was all for tiptoeing out of there, but Chander stood and crept over, keeping a respectful distance. "Sir?"

Pekelo jerked his head up, listening behind him as if he could hear us breathe. "No. She's too big," he said. His voice was as high as a crushed larynx, scratchy and muted.

"She's fast, I promise," pleaded Chander.

Pekelo turned round and looked me once over, every blink and hair accounted for. Then he stood and walked to the wall. He lifted two black knives off hooks and slid under the ropes, into the fight cage. He waited in the center of the ring, eyes on me like pretending I was vicious.

"Go on then," hissed Chander, bobbing his head toward the ring.

"Not on your bloody life, cabbage brain."

"What? You'd rather be gang raped some night on Broadwick?"

I didn't take long to think it over. "Yes, I would." Rape was off in some vague maybe-never, and they'd have to catch me first. But sharky Pekelo looked mean and *now*.

"You think that tonight, but you wait 'till tomorrow." Chander stood breathing in irritated puffs through his long nose, and when I didn't move he rolled those Bollywood eyes to the metal beams that crossed the ceiling. "Give us an effort, Jiè, they're *rubber* training knives, for God's sake."

I didn't move. Finally Chander did something I almost killed him for. He walked over, heaved me by the elbows as if I were some little sister, and with me struggling with all but my teeth, he tossed me into the ring.

I stood up as fast as knees could push, afraid Pekelo would stab me before I was upright. I had a good deal to learn about Pekelo; he stashed the knives in his waistband and bowed like a gentleman, both eyes on me, one hand over his fist. I approximated a curtsy.

"Don't get hit," Pekelo rasped. He slid the knives out of his waistband. "You follow me? Don't get hit." I stared at him.

I'm not perfectly clear on what happened next. One minute I was gazing into those mild brown eyes, and the next minute there was a blur, a cloud with teeth, poking at my arms, legs, face, moving too fast to be human. I'd never seen anyone stir his stumps that fast. I screamed. Pekelo stopped. He bowed again and glided toward the ropes, headed out of the ring as I stood trembling and rubbing at bruised spots.

"Hold on!" Chander rushed to the ringside and wrapped long fingers about the steel ropes. "Please, Professor. She graffs, she's brilliant. She's the bird who painted the cricket in Covent Garden. She's only thirteen, out at all hours of the night."

Pekelo turned round. "Pleased to meet you, Miss." He inclined his head. "Come back when you're lookin' for a fight."

~

Two weeks later Chander's vague maybe-never arrived. There's a neighborhood greengrocer on Greek St. where some balls-for-brains tagged their big, filthy name on the roll-down blinds. It gave graffers a bad reputation and made the neighborhood ugly at night when the grocer put the blinds down. Stupid, really, but it annoyed me.

Chander and I bought oranges from that grocer and he was a kind old geezer, always threw in something extra—like a box of Pocky Sticks—for free. So I set about to piece his roll-downs for him, add a few crickets, bring in some business. Crickets munching oranges, so he might suss out that it was me.

I had my mind on my stencils and didn't feel them closing in—two blokes, not boys like your attackers Maman, but big men, savvy enough to stay in the shadows. They were pissed on sour smelling lager, so they staggered as they collared me.

Don't grab a girl with a spray can in her hand.

I'd painted both their faces before their knives were out, but bloody hell, who wears *sunglasses* at night? One knocked the can out of my hand as the other went for my wrists. They got in a few sharp pokes at my face and chest, making me frantic. That was before my work boots, so all I had to sink into their groins were little light trainers. They doubled over and I ran, leaving fifty effing quid worth of paint and my favorite stencils lying underneath their arses.

It was early, not much past eleven, so Emma and George weren't home from their *soirée* yet. I had time for a wash and a heavy application of plasters, then spent an hour lying in bed dreaming up some porky pie about the cuts on my face, cussing myself for being such a divvy. Emma got it right; I step right off the cushy path and learn everything the hard way—blow by blow.

I was no toy graffer; at thirteen I was fast becoming the most up writer in London. But if I was going to make it in a bloke's world, I needed to be as mean as the next git. Women doing their own thing causes war, doesn't it, Maman? Funny, that. You'd think men had all they needed in the world, wouldn't need to grub after every corner of the earth.

Since I didn't have your wily Trotoskov diplomacy, I fancied shock and awe. Chander had been spot on when he took me to Pekelo. It galled me, for he was going to be major chuffed to hear me say it, but tomorrow I would gag down my pride and go back into the ring.

Pekelo's entrance exam is simple in theory; he pokes until you pass out. If you last one minute in the cage with him, he'll train you. There are between 202 and 372 fighting pressure points (depending on who you ask), but Professor Pekelo is easy on newcomers and restricts himself to the deadliest forty-eight. I lasted a minute and a half—both arms numb and dangling, hearing gone, reeling and nauseated, neck burning with that sickening pain of a pinched nerve—but he couldn't knock me out for ninety seconds. I had the combination he liked; fast reflexes and sturdy skin. Lucky me.

Chander became my sparring partner, because fighting a thirteen-year-old girl was beneath the likes of the mercenaries, bodyguards, and professional fighters Pekelo trained. Then there was the minor problem of payment. A teacher like Pekelo is not bargain basement, and as far as George and Emma were concerned, girls don't frequent sweaty gyms full of questionable men; they flat refused to hand over the necessary dosh. Dear souls, they do put a foot down now and then. But such a feeble foot! Emma clearly inherited nothing from the Trotoskovs. In any event, I was forced to nick a pair of Lapis Lazuli earrings Emma had hidden in the back of her jewelry cabinet. She'd never worn them, ever, Maman, so don't make such sad-puppy eyes at me. War is expensive, after all, and these were lovely hunks of stone. Pekelo's knobby fist closed tight when I laid them in his palm. Those earrings still pay my way.

So for three years, week after week, Chander threw himself on top of me, twisted my arms, tangled in my legs, and punched at my pressure points. Positively romantic. If bruises were kisses, he'd be a passionate bloke. At night sometimes, when he didn't have homework or school the next day—

Chander just had to be first in his class—he'd trail after while I graffed. He'd watch for coppers and help stow used stencils in my bin bag. He'd bask in my glory when photos of my work popped up on the web, in the news, or in café chat. Larking about with Chander was great; I'd never had a mate who was more fun.

Funnily enough, outside the cage Chander stopped touching me. No more brotherly arm around my shoulder or spontaneous reaching for my hand. For three years he kept space between us like it was a solid object. Then round about eight months ago he started to disappear for days in a row. I'd go by his parent's stall and Parul would wobble her head and say, "He's not here," in her precise, crisp way. Parul has a head like an unshelled peanut, dipping in at the temples and rounding out at her forehead and cheeks. Her warm brown skin shows off big beautiful teeth. She'd sit in a plastic chair, back of the stall, working and watching for shoplifters.

"Where's he gone to?" I asked one day, annoyed that I hadn't seen him but at the gym. It was a humid tea time last August, and the gummy heat made me cross.

"Studying." Parul kept char on the charcoal stove when she wasn't cooking cuzzer. It's half milk and primed with enough sugar to rot all your teeth in one go. She poured a cup and passed it.

I collapsed on a bale of cloth she hadn't yet sewn into skirts, and sipped her sugary char. "Why does he study so much?"

"Next June is A-Levels and he will have eight papers to sit. Such a blessing to have a smart brother. What do you want with him anyway? A girl should not be pursuing a boy. If I did such a thing I would fetch an earful from my mother."

Her hands were always busy: tagging bits and bobs with prices, hemming trousers, stringing bells on silken rope. This day she was putting the sleeves in a man's coat using flea-sized stitches.

"I don't want anything from him. I just popped round to say hello."

She kept her eyes on her work. "He's very important, you know, my brother. He has to bear up to a heavy load. He can't afford to keep wrong company."

I laughed at her. "Am I wrong company, then?" Poor Emma and George would be so insulted!

She glanced my way and pulled her eyebrows together, crinkling the dab of vermilion powder on her forehead. "No, so sorry, I didn't mean to offend. It's just that you know so little about his life." Her head wove back and forth, mesmerizing and friendly. She was mid-twenties at the most, with the saddest eyes I ever saw, like two cups of her too-sweet brown tea, about to spill over.

"What's about his life I don't know, then?"

It was hellish hot in the back of her stall in August, and sweat began to bead along my hairline. I swiped it away with a sleeve.

Parul rose and rummaged among boxes in the back, then returned with a small battery-operated fan. She clipped it to the flap of a box and pointed the breeze into my sweating chops.

"Ta," I said.

She cocked her head slightly, as if thanks were unnecessary. "We have another sister in Mumbai, working in a can recycling factory." Her hands went back to sewing miniscule stitches. "Our late father's best friend owns this factory, and when Chander returns to Mumbai with his British education, he will take over foreign accounts. My family will get half share of the factory as Gejra's dowry."

"The factory shares are your sister's dowry?"

"No, heavens no. If God had intended for Neha or I to marry, he would not have taken my father so soon. The shares will come from Chander's bride-to-be, Gejra."

The spittle in my mouth dried to a sticky lump. "Chander is getting *married*?"

"See? So much you don't know." She showed her exquisite teeth. "He has been engaged most of his life. Our father was best friends with Gejra's father, and both families have invested so much hope in the factory. It is small now, and barely feeds Gejra's family, but Chander will make it successful with international recycling. Then our mother will get proper medical care, Neha will not have to work long hours on her knees peeling labels off drums, and I will not have to strain my eyes sewing in a hot stall. With God's blessing we have a better life ahead of us, do you understand?"

Her smile stayed frozen after she'd done speaking, her pleading gaze not giving my face a rest.

"Let him be, no? There are lots of boys in London. With your good family name you can have your pick. I don't ask much."

"I'm not in love with Chander," I said.

But the moment I spoke the words, I knew they were a lie. Who was this Gejra, and why could she have him all to herself? The stall was insufferably close and I wanted to biff someone.

Parul looked miserably uncomfortable to have provoked an argument. She held up a palm, shook her head, and looked away. "Promise me you will let him be."

I set the teacup on the tarmac and stood up. "Make him promise to let me be," I said, "after all, he's the one who's bloody engaged." Then I legged it out of there.

I was so afflicted that I couldn't go home. I wandered about London until the wee hours, finally ending up back at the stall, everything folded now into storage, stowed away and still. I sat in the narrow space between metal containers and cried.

Love is stupid, isn't it, Maman? I'd been best mates with Chander for three years, and he'd never so much as given me a kiss. Had someone asked me the day before if I planned to marry him, I would have had a good laugh. Marry Chander, that gangly old galoot?

But now I felt stuck on him; we'd grown into one, like Siamese twins. He'd once told me that he would go home to India to pass his A-levels, then go to Mumbai University. Hmm, I'd thought, oh really? And I'd wondered what it must feel like to have University in one's future. But I hadn't considered separating from him, ever. And all along, he had known he would never be mine. The bastard, the bloody bastard. Engaged to Gejra.

~

Maman finds me a tissue and turns away to stare through the lace nets, out at the park, as I blow my nose. She waits until my weeping subsides, then gathers the spent, wet tissues into a ball which she holds delicately with the tips of her fingers.

"And the mirror?" she asks.

With all my crying, my eyes see brighter. Maman's face is bone china white, but a flush of high pink has made a run for it across her cheeks, like a deep fever bleeding through, and I wonder what she's feeling.

"Give us a breather, Maman, I'm done in."

"I'll go make supper." She leaves with dignity, my tissues cradled in one hand. I wonder for two ticks if she loves me, or merely suffers nostalgia from my resemblance to Xiao. She loved Xiao and he died. It crosses my mind that she feels responsible, never forgave herself, perhaps even loves him still. I want to believe that Chander and I will have a better ending.

# NINE

I n all of the months that I had inhabited Incir's hotel, I had never explored further than Apollo's Temple. Adventure made the hair on my cultured head stand up. I liked my travel in books, and in the tales told by government elite over cognac and sherry after the staff had cleared the dishes. Unlike you, *ma fille,* who travels the world with the confidence of your adoptive father, I had been just to Florence, once, to see Michelangelo's sculptures. I only abandoned Paris because I was hounded out.

~

It's the next morning, and Maman's Paris is gray and damp, dripping like a nose. Maman sliced a wodge of *baguette,* put a smear of butter on, and has spent the last thirty minutes nibbling its crust. She speaks to the window which she watches constantly now, eyes on the shadows under Square Barye's trees, and her hands have developed a slight tremor.

I am worn to silence by dejection over Chander. Relieved that she has not asked me to tell on this morning, I close my eyes and let Maman continue.

~

Once beyond the brush of the shore, a dirt road wandered through town. Toppled Roman columns, cracked and worn, lined the road. White rectangular houses of one or two rooms stood within shouting distance of each other, a few grazing goats staked out front. Crickets sang in kitchen gardens, grape vines leaned on wooden stakes, and patches of herbs bloomed, vibrating with bees in dusty front yards. Tomato plants sprawled out of rock retainers.

Women, dressed in traditional black *kara çarşaf,* watched us go by. Little children playing in the dry grass stood up, open-mouthed. The few men we saw turned away, then turned back again after we'd passed, observing our progress. I tied on Yurda's headscarf and rolled down my jeans cuffs. Self-conscious as a freak show, I lowered my eyes and scuffed down the dusty road.

Umut and I came upon the Roman arena from the side— the arena I had seen from Della's window. The road curved around a grove of black pine, ending at stone arches ten feet wide and soaring forty feet overhead. Crumbling, pecked apart by wind and rain, the arches still propped up the northern wall of a massive theater. Umut slid into the shade of the entrance and led me, crawling over fallen stone, to the theater's heart.

We stood in a circle of warm sand where gladiators once died. Row after row of stone benches fanned up, as big as Zeus' crown, twenty-six layers up to a vaulted platform, then another twenty layers beyond until the ragged stone edges blurred against the sky. The caws of crows pulsed in the hot afternoon.

I was gripped with wonder at old Incir, the grandeur that had once made this town famous for slave trading, shipping, and civilized living. The two thousand-year-old, perfectly aligned stone bleachers were made by the same Roman hands that invented concrete and conquered two and a quarter million square miles of the ancient world. Bleachers built to entertain people who had indoor plumbing, an easy sail to anywhere on the Mediterranean, and their own stamped gold coin. Architecture now surrounded by the hovels of poor fishermen.

Umut seized my hand and pointed up into the cavea. There, ten meters above me, sat a spot of a man, head bent over his work. Curious why Umut was prodding, I climbed a flight of steps that radiated from the center. As I came closer I could see that the man was Xiao Lian Chin.

Xiao gave a casual wave when he saw me, a calligraphy brush in hand. I froze, immobilized by the simultaneous desire to vanish back down the stairs, and catapult up them. I was too embarrassed to retreat, too shy to go forward. Umut, my bumbling cupid, put a hand in the small of my back and shoved. So I climbed.

I was winded and sweating in the humid air by the time I reached the hundredth step where Xiao Lian sat. I paused to catch my breath, glad that, for at least a moment, Xiao wouldn't expect me to explain myself. Then I glanced at his work and forgot all about my embarrassment. I dropped my knapsack and sunk to the stone bleachers, my eyes fixed on something I craved even more than Xiao: ink.

Xiao had ink: white, red, blue, green, black, yellow. Each ink was a work of art, dried into ten centimeter sticks and carved with bamboo leaves. He was using only the black, rubbing it on an inkstone, wetting it with drops from a water bottle, and working it with his brush. Several brushes with lacquered wood handles lay in an open box beside him. Their white goat hair brush tips flared wide, then came to a perfect point. I could paint with these: subtle wisps in the sky, heat drifting over the sea, dust in the black pines. The box also had inkstones, smooth and dark gray, polished to a dull sheen, clean and begging to be used.

"*Mon Dieu*," I said weakly. Overwhelmed with desire, I reached into the box and ran my fingers over the stiff ink, the warm stone, the soft goat hair tips.

Xiao rested his brush on his knee. "Do you do calligraphy?" he asked.

"No, I'm an artist. I draw, I paint…I…would you sell me your ink and brushes? I'll pay anything you ask."

If my desperate pleading tone was familiar to him from Mizou's table, he gave no hint of it. "You don't need to buy them. The set was a gift, and I only use the black. Here—" He closed the box and handed it to me. "Take the box as well. You'll need something to keep them in."

"Oh, Xiao! *Merci.* Thank you so much. You have no idea what this means to me." I sounded absurdly breathless and felt uncomfortably young under his pained gaze. To cover my racing heart, I clutched the box and pressed it against my chest.

Xiao smiled and just the left corner of his mouth lifted, raising his nose in a pleasing, asymmetric crinkle. He looked like my portrait. "I'm glad to give you something. Would you mind if I looked at your drawings?"

"They're crude and clumsy. I've had so little to work with." I balanced the box tenderly on the stone bleacher, and then reached into my knapsack. "You don't want to see my early attempts." I put aside the first *cahier*. "The angles and proportions got better about a month ago. *Voici—*" I handed over a stack of Apollo's temple, starting with perhaps the hundredth drawing where finally, despite charcoal and crayons, the shrine came to life.

Xiao leafed slowly through lined notebook pages, studying each sketch more thoroughly than they deserved. He paused particularly long at my silly rendition of a cricket, one that had crawled onto my drawing page and would not be frightened off by my moving pencil.

"You've captured it well. I can almost hear it singing."

"He wouldn't leave me alone. I think he was after the water of my sweat."

Xiao studied the whimsical stubby wings, fat thighs, and quizzical expression on the cricket's triangular face.

"*Cu Zhi*, encourage weaving. When fall comes they sneak into the house and sing as the weavers finish the winter clothes. My mother told me stories about crickets when I was a child, before I went to bed." His expression was soft and inviting, like his lower lip. "This one looks as though he's been in a fight. One antenna is bent."

"*Eh bien*, the world has knocked him around a little, but…he survives."

A few rows down, Umut let out a peep. With lanky leaps he hopped over the benches and shoved my portrait into Xiao's hands. It took Xiao a moment to recognize himself. Perhaps I had captured his dark undercurrent too well, or perhaps he took issue with the saintly radiance, but he flushed with an uncomfortable grimace and put the portrait down. His response wounded me, and I gazed into the arena, feeling raw and exposed.

He cleared his throat. "Sit down." He offered his water bottle. "You're so quiet at dinner, I almost forget you're there. You're from Paris aren't you?"

I took the water but didn't drink. Now that he was asking, I found I had nothing to say. I nodded mutely, trickles of sweat running down the back of my neck and adding to my shy misery. He couldn't have been more than twenty-two, but he seemed so much older. There were no lines on his face, no gray in his hair, but something about his expression and the slow way he moved gave the impression of days, weeks, years, piling into an insurmountable wall between us. I sat on the edge of the bench, fighting the urge to flee.

"Why are you in Incir?" he asked.

"*Eh alors*, it's cheap."

He laughed, his pleasure escaping from whatever had aged him and giving him a moment of youth. "Good reason."

"Why are you here?" I asked.

He smiled. "Incir is hard to find."

"Another good reason. Della says no one comes to Incir, they run from somewhere else. She would accuse us of having secrets."

Xiao sat very still, staring down at the gladiator's stage below as though some gripping fight took place there.

"Secrets are often things we keep because no one wants to hear them," he said.

"We have something in common, then," I said.

He swung his head around and studied me. Seeing through his eyes, I pictured a plain girl, withdrawn and sullen much of the time, pretentious and critical when she finally spoke. But he must have seen something better, because he confided, "I'm wanted by the Chinese government for sedition. They made it clear the last time we spoke that if the police pick me up again, I will die an unpleasant death." Far beyond him, islands of dark green pines spotted the rolling inland, breaking the long stretches of arid, harsh land. "Incir is a good place to rest," he said.

"Rest until…?"

"Until I am carried somewhere else."

"As if you were driftwood."

"Not driftwood." He lowered his eyes. "Dead wood. Tossed aside by my government. Hiding in a Mediterranean village because I am too stubborn to let them bury me."

Like the dissidents who plagued my father year after year: grim, conservatively dressed young men begging for funding and political support. But Xiao did not wear a suit, nor look so deferential.

"My father always said that China drove away her best and brightest—a culture dying of its own stupidity." I spoke with rasping Trotoskov authority.

Xiao stood up. "Don't you *ever* criticize my people."

The size, the seething fury of him caused me to shrink away. Umut squeaked with distress and leaped from his siesta on the bench, clamoring several levels down the bank of steps.

"A thousand years before Europeans wrote on cave walls, the Shang Dynasty had an economy, religion, astrology, geology, art, medicine—" Xiao mangled the French as he spit his words. "Chinese leaders gallop off in the wrong direction, but Chinese people have wisdom and spirit. They will never fall to the crass emptiness that rots your Western world."

Crows stopped screeching. For a moment the arena reverberated with a silence that boomeranged off the distant walls and returned to hit me in the face.

"Please excuse me," I whispered, sliding down the bench, away from Xiao's vehemence.

Xiao held his breath, long braid whipped over one shoulder, hand choking his calligraphy brush.

"Really, I'm very sorry. I spoke without thinking," I said.

He exhaled hard. "I've been told that you do a lot of that."

The heat of my blush was unbearable. I felt I might fry, right there on the Roman stone, sizzled in my own shame.

He gathered up his brush, black ink-stick, and papers. With a curt, cursory bow he strode down the steps. I watched him go: one hundred bounds to the bottom of the stairs, then a fast pace out the arched doorway.

When he was gone I pulled the headscarf off my head and buried my damp, overheated face in it. It smelled like Yurda's soap: the bitter, dry bite of lye. I wished I could cry. Cry for my loneliness, cry for my uselessness. But all I could do was ache unbearably. My father had made me a freak—unfit to go among people. Every time I opened my mouth, I collided with his prejudices and choked on his superiority. My art was my only quality of any worth.

For the next few days, I didn't speak unless forced to. At Mizou's table I faded from a decoration, to wallpaper. I picked at Yurda's food, ignoring her cheeky insistence that I take seconds. I no longer eavesdropped on what the men said. Xiao spoke so much Turkish by then that much of their conversation was beyond me anyway. My only moments of true companionship were found listening to Suat Bey's stories, leaning close to his licorice breath, watching the translucent rims of his eyes fill with tears at his own poignancy. Tears as clear and magical as a Vermeer painting of grapes.

If Xiao noticed my mood I wouldn't have known—I never looked at him. I still longed for him, but my iron Trotoskov will made my eyes glide over him as if he were invisible. At night as I fell asleep, every feature of Xiao's face would draw itself on the back of my eyelids. Shaded in black, gray, and white, the sketch was a Henri Cartier-Bresson portrait, catching Xiao at the decisive moment of his anger. I told myself a million times that I didn't even know this man, I should just forget him. But, *chérie*, when has the heart ever listened to the mind?

I spent my time in the temple, experimenting with Xiao's inks, while Umut wove grass into useless braids. From the moment a stick of color scraped an inkstone, the rest of the world vanished; it was just me and the ever lengthening days of perfect light. The sun rose every morning, and drips of brightness filtered through the net of laurel leaves. It tempered the Roman columns in the afternoon furnace until the marble melted to a pure erotic silver. It set at night in a bloody massacre of clouds. With the inks, I could catch more than the form and face of Apollo's temple: I could catch its ancient, mysterious core. I let Apollo possess me, make the heavenly visible, and I drank in his perfection with an unending thirst.

Then Umut disappeared. One morning in early April I sulked at Yurda's kitchen table, waiting for him. He was usually there before I rose in the morning, leaping about the yard on his long, jackrabbit legs, chasing crickets. Or sitting under the table eating Yurda's *Börek,* spinach sloughing from the flaky swirls of pastry and falling to the kitchen floor like so many droppings.

I waited an hour. To keep back boredom, I peeled the blanched tomatoes Yurda set in front of me. Finally I decided I would wait no longer; a chaperone was never my idea in the first place. I wiped the mealy red slime and scraps of tomato skin off my fingers, picked up Xiao's ink box, cinched down the knot of my headscarf, and walked out the door. Behind me I could hear Yurda clucking, no doubt tossing her head in that ubiquitous Turkish gesture for "no".

I had missed the sunrise, beyond the light that makes the world look newborn, but not yet into the afternoon that burned like fires of passion. Not an interesting light for structures, so I decided to do crickets. I put a jar lid of water on Apollo's altar and waited. It wasn't long before a little candidate hopped onto the smooth slab and inched towards the lid. Its feelers were twice as long as its body and as restless as a child's feet. In my loneliness I could see all sorts of emotions on its brown face: spunk, curiosity, *joie de vivre.* It became the cricket Xiao's mother told him folk tales about. I drew it to bring pleasure to Xiao, surrounded by spare oriental brush strokes of grass to remind him of home.

With each touch of the brush I poured out my longing to be kind, generous, and loved; perhaps Tatyana Trotoskov could reform? If only I were Tatyana Chin. Have you ever wished to be someone other than who you are, Jiè? *Enfin*, all of this blue you splash in your hair: a color of regret, *non*?

As I painted, I told myself the stories Xiao's mother might have told, about a little cricket who went out into the world with his mother's blessing and faced the terrors a cricket might face. His cleverness brought him home again, a wiser creature, safe once more in his mother's arms.

I never had a mother, my Little Cricket. It was inevitable, *je suppose*, that when Boris came of age, he decided that he liked to be obeyed. He lived in that time when men decided the direction and women decorated the path. His first decision was to marry the *magnifique* but vacuous Fleur de Leon. Fleur de Lyon, your grandmother, long dead now, *Dieu ait son âme*. I suspect you would not have liked her. She was, how would you say in your street English? An airhead. A dreamy woman, incapable of giving her daughters discipline. And you look like a girl who hopes for the occasional smack. Fleur de Lyon fled with Emma when I was two, leaving me to placate Boris. Emma grew up in Marseille with Fleur, a mother so overwhelmed by the world, she was hard pressed to provide any discipline at all. Is it any wonder that Emma flounders in the face of your Trotoskov will?

But I grew up inside Mme. Groseille's ever-correct propriety. When I was old enough to have instruction, Boris chose my tutors. And my hobbies, clothes, books, languages, and point of view. With Boris, there were skirmishes and détentes, treaties and hidden agendas, shows of force and surrenders, but I would not say that there was love. Beyond my thirteenth year, Mme. Groseille became my chaperone, the keeper of my manners, and my servant. Who knows if she loved me; I never thought about it.

But Xiao Lian Chin had a mother who told him bedtime stories. He left that mother in China. Though my stubborn Trotoskov gaze would not acknowledge him, my hands, somehow free from Boris' influence, drew what I knew Xiao longed for: his childhood.

All day I drew crickets, and the next day. Umut never came, but it didn't matter. The leap, the creep, the quiver of my crickets grew better and better, until I felt I could lay them on the altar and Apollo himself would descend to play among them. I was too absorbed to be afraid. Too engrossed to notice the snaps in the underbrush, until a shadow fell across my work.

There were five young men this time, and they were not smiling.

I set my brush down gently, not disturbing the thirty or so crickets that hopped boldly in and out of the wet coffee can lid. With my cold Trotoskov glare, I gauged the strength of what my adversaries had amassed. I recognized the original three: wiry and thin, so young they could not grow beards, but strong nonetheless. The leader had an ugly, festering wound, ripped through the side of his face. The new additions must have been younger brothers: one husky, one a whip of a child. My sole hope was to outrun them, but they stood in an arc blocking the path to the hotel. I could only run down the cliff path, into the sea.

They watched me with seething hatred. They would not run from a stick this time; they had prepared to fight the ferocious Trotoskov. "Victory requires bluff and might," my father used to say, but I could not win by might. Steeling myself, I dug fingers into the dirt by the slab of altar, grabbing big handfuls. Then I sat up suddenly to peer over their shoulders, as though someone were coming down the path. The split second it took them to follow my gaze was all I needed. When they turned back I was on my feet, throwing sand in their eyes. They cried out with surprise and flung up their hands. Startled crickets sprang in a black cloud and the boys leaped back, covered with insects.

I didn't wait to see what happened next: I ran. Behind Apollo's columns, slipping and stumbling down the zigzagging cliff trail cut barely wide enough for a toehold, and onto the beach. I turned at the water's edge to see if I was pursued. All five scampered, fleet as goats, down the path behind me. I could see the hotel with my bedroom window on the cliff above, inaccessible except by the path I'd just run. To the west was the high rock jetty, extending a quarter kilometer into the sea, embracing Incir and her fishing docks on its other side. To the east was endless beach, farther and farther from the hotel and safety. Refusing to panic, I ran towards the jetty.

The boys spread out when they hit the beach. Two ran behind me along the water's edge, and the others tried to outrun me inland, cut me off from the jetty's boulders. As they ran they waved like windmills, screaming who-knew-what in Turkish. They were fast enough that they would catch me on the rocks if I tried to climb the jetty. Tightening in around me, they drove me towards the sea. I had no choice but to wade in, shaking with cold and anger, bucking chest high waves that rolled and foamed to shore. Once beyond the surf, the water was only knee deep, but the boys were right behind me, screaming frantically. I thrust forward until it was deep enough to swim, then threw myself into the aquamarine blue and crawled with all of my strength, spitting out gritty mouthfuls of salt water.

Ten meters from shore I stopped and tread water, looking back. They had retreated and stood at the edge of the surf, calling to me. I was overwhelmed and outnumbered. It was early afternoon and hours before the fishing boats came in. A quarter kilometer: it didn't look that far. Certainly not a great distance for Boris Trotoskov's daughter. I would swim around the jetty and find a place to crawl onto the rocks. In the fishing port someone would help me. Turning toward the vast Mediterranean, I began to swim.

# TEN

As soon as Maman retires to prepare lunch I sling clothes in my rucksack and push off, sneaking closed the door behind me. It's not decent that she's T. Chin; it's a dirty trick that I won't stand for, worse than discovering she's my real mum. I almost leave *Little Cricket* behind I'm so cross, but at the last minute I stuff it in, unable to cast it off.

For the sake of an ideal I chucked school in the bin, wrote off George and Emma, and spent three years crawling London at night. I could have died in the ring, some bloke's fist on my temple as I earned dosh for paint. I believed in Little Cricket: clever bravery, unbridled future, loving arms to come home to. Hope, graffed over the grime and dinge of London. I made them believe, the ones who flocked with their kiddies. I thought T. Chin would notice, T. Chin would find me, somehow. And it was all a heap of effing drivel, written by a lovesick French aristocrat.

I head for Pont de Sully, rucksack swinging on my shoulder, trying to remember if the nearest Metro is at Boulevard Henri IV or Pont Marie. It's great to be moving again; I don't do well sitting so much. I'm in such a temper I'm knocking shoulders as I zigzag around the masses who stroll to lunch. They didn't set about to be bad parents, Emma and George, they just couldn't close hands around me, like protecting wings. Their hands were always open, so I fell out. All I wanted was walls not made of vapor. Solid walls, like Cozy Hole. The world is just too big, Mum and Dad, too freaking big.

Halfway across the bridge I look up and clock him watching me, sitting bang in the middle of the pavement, making it clear that I'm not going to cross the Seine. My heart leaps to my throat.

All six of his eyes look hungry, and his three tongues pant and drip. His serpent tail slaps the ground beside him. Now that I'm within throwing distance I see that he's a whopping creature, taller than me by three ugly heads and some meaty shoulders. He digs his claws into the tarmac and rises, heads sinking on their long necks, burnt breath blowing my way. One giant paw following the other, he slinks forward, closing the distance between us. Frenchmen in their black raincoats walk round him; bloody hell, they walk *through* him, blind as sots. But I back up, sweating and tingling, working out how fast he is. Is he faster than Pekelo?

"Stay back, Cricket."

Maman gives me a start and I whirl round. She's a pace off my right shoulder, sporting that black tarpaulin of a *kara çarşaf*, face hidden in her veil. Pint-sized as she is, she steps in front of me and keeps walking.

"Tell your master to come for us himself, *espèce de clébard*," she hisses through cloth. Mutt, she calls him. What the eff? She's going to belt him in the guts, so shrimpy he'll have to stoop to take off her head. Maybe she fancies he'll choke on her head covering.

"Leave off, Maman!" I shove through the rabble that's between us.

But she pushes on without a backward glance, a little black lump of walking sheets. "Scat! *Allez ouste!*" Flinging wide her hands as if a mongrel is in the rubbish. Her sleeves ripple and snap. The beast is just yards away now, snarling with sluggardly meanness. Blokes on the bridge stop to take a look, eyeing Maman like she's mental, standing in my way as I hotfoot it after her. I knock aside a few gawkers and grab for Maman's skinny arm. A monster head snakes forward to bite, the stench mortifying: wet, salty fur, and decay. Relentless death, laying claim to its own. His jaws that cold, deep cavern that yawns beneath our feet, scaring me witless.

Then Maman smacks him, *pow* on one nose with an open Trotoskov palm. He vanishes—*poof*—and Bob's your uncle! Struck dumb and shaking, I hang onto Maman's *çarşaf.*

"You!" she snaps, slapping my hands off her arm. "You run like a coward because the world does not give you what you want. I disappoint you? *Tant pis.* The world was not made to your order." She points a rigid finger toward her flat. "*Allons donc,* it is you he wants, after all. Come back and confess what you've done."

I stand there speechless, looking down on her little draped head, trying to remember the last time anyone ordered me about. Chander: only Chander had such brass. I could knock Maman around with my big toe, but she seizes me by the scruff of the neck and storms back across the bridge, dragging me as an ant might. Bystanders back away, exchanging cautious smiles over this *çarşaf*-clad madwoman. Hands fumble for cell phones in case she's dangerous. I could struggle but, bloody hell, it's her or the mutt with too many heads. So I stumble along peaceably enough, trying not to keel onto her as she yanks, watching over my shoulder to see if anything nasty sneaks from behind. The mongrel appears to have cleared off, but that doesn't put right my nerves; hairs on my arms prickle like something's creeping up.

Back in her flat she throws off her black coverings and points me toward the settee, lunch spread on the coffee table. "Sit and eat. Then you will tell me what you did to provoke Hades."

I slump into the settee and fold my arms over my chest, not sure what to make of this.

"I've had nothing to do with Hades, haven't even met the bloke."

Maman doesn't speak, just sits beside me and dabbles in her food: salad Niçoise with seared tuna. I don't disturb my serving. Finally she plonks her fork down and rounds on me.

"Tell me what you did, Jiè."

"I've done a shedload of things." I have no clue which of them might have irked a Greek god.

"How did you get hold of the mirror?"

Now, this is getting personal. She can order me back here, but she can't strong-arm me into having a cozy chat.

She stands, paces to the window. With her back to me she starts her sermon.

"You are a totally exasperating child. Poor, gentle Emma and George, jerked about by a Trotoskov terror. Had I known you were so much my child I would have raised you myself—

you deserved me." She turns round and there are tears, cutting a glassy path down her cheeks. "You will hear now, why I gave you away. If it is not sufficient reason, you may hate me as much as you like. But then you must tell me what you've done. I'm fed up with that mirror. *Fini.* Too many souls have been claimed before their time, I refuse to lose you, too. If Hades wants a fight, he need look no further, he's found one."

# ELEVEN

On the day I fled from the boys, the Mediterranean was so clear I could see to the depths where Poseidon lives.

Poseidon, god of sea and earthquakes. The one who dared violate Athena's temple by making love to Medusa on its floor, so inciting Athena that she turned Medusa into a snake-headed monster. When I looked into the fathoms underneath me, my throat clenched. Small, nervous shadows and larger ominous shadows waved below my belly, too distorted to identify. It seemed that anything, anything I might imagine waited below. I forced my eyes up to the familiar sky.

I was a strong swimmer and didn't feel tired until I tried to round the rocky point. Once beyond the protection of the wall, the sea was rough. All I could see over the tall, watery peaks was magnificent blue, extending forever. The jetty must have been to my right, but bobbing among the waves I could no longer find it. I wanted to go west, but no matter how hard I swam, I drifted east. Soon I had no idea where the jetty was, and I was losing sight of the land.

I panted, exhausted, my heavy clothes and shoes dragging. I flipped onto my back and floated, gasping in air. Water sloshed over my face and the depths sucked at my back. My self-control dissolved. Heartbeat loud in my ears, lungs burning, I thrashed against the tug of Poseidon's sea. Water closed over my head. Help me Apollo, please. All I create belongs to you.

Then the oddest calm possessed me. I heard Della's sugary voice, "You're such an arrogant little Napoleon," and I drifted into unconsciousness.

I woke in the safety of my father's library. A huge map of Eastern Europe lay spread over his desk. In June 1812, he was explaining, Napoleon attacked Russia with an army 800,000 strong, an overwhelming force, amassed to bring Russia to her knees. Faced with certain annihilation, the Russians did not play fair. They refused to fight, retreating and retreating until they had drawn Napoleon into the heart of Russia. They burned behind them, leaving nothing for Napoleon's men to eat or wear, nowhere to sleep, no forage for horses. Then they abandoned Moscow, which promptly blazed to the ground around Napoleon's ears. Outside their capital, they waited patiently for the cruel Russian winter to eat the occupying soldiers alive.

When Napoleon's army could stand no more, the Russians hounded Napoleon's retreat, forcing him back down the road they had already devastated, with no hope for supplies or shelter. They slaughtered deserters and picked off stragglers. In December 1812, Napoleon staggered out of Russia with only 70,000 men still alive. Barely alive: starving, ragged, frozen, and dying of Typhus.

Consider the Russian point of view, my father advised. When overwhelmed by force, it's wise to see your enemy's vector. Find in their chosen direction, some destination in common, and ride the enemy's strength to safety. My father knew his history, and he knew how to prevail.

But, as I lay drowning, I no longer cared about the clever strategies of brilliant generals. I floated in a quiet stupor, looking up at the white blue sky glistening though water, overwhelmed with the mute suffering of Napoleon's soldiers. They were carried to slaughter on a wave of grandiose hubris, battered, starved, and left to find their way home. Each had his own reasons for putting one foot in front of the other, for staying one step ahead of the snipers. Stubbornly, they refused to die.

With a kick, I broke through to air and lay on the surface, gasping.

I, too, refused to die, though I had no idea why. No one loved me. The only person I had ever loved despised me. I had given nothing back to the world, not even to the father who had at least fed and educated me. The force of my will was ridiculous; I could not think of one single person who would mourn my death.

Still, I kicked off my heavy shoes. Paddling with my nose at the waterline, I unbuttoned the shirt that dragged on my arms. I ripped off sodden jeans, no longer concerned about arriving in port naked. My clothes sank into Poseidon's realm, arms, legs, and shoestrings waving like Medusa's hair.

Dressed just in underwear I arched my back and studied the sun. When I was certain which way was north, I pointed in that direction and with tired, heavy arms, I swam. When I could swim no more I floated until I could swim again. I would wash in with the same tide that carried home the fishing boats. True to my father's lesson, the sea herself would deliver me from danger. Maybe someday I would know why I had bothered.

I vastly underestimated how long it would take. How achingly tired I would be. The toll extracted by trembling. The painful cramps that squeezed my feet and legs. The sunburn, thirst, and blurred vision from hours in salt water. I misjudged the eastward drift of the sea. But like Napoleon's men, I was desperately patient; no matter the depth of my suffering, I could do no other than die or go on. Around sunset I put my feet on sandy ground, rose out of the sea, and staggered onto shore.

I can only imagine how I appeared to the group on the beach: blonde hair ratted with sand and scraps of seaweed, almost naked, fair skin burnt to a lobster red, rising from the froth like a sea monster and reeling like the walking dead.

Through my swollen eyes they looked equally bizarre to me: dabs of pink, blue, and orange on yellow sand, like spots on a Seurat canvas. Colorful bumps, hunched in a circle, wind fluttering their brightly colored *çarşafs*. They faced a head, perhaps a marble bust? To my damaged vision it poked from the sand in a blur. They were laughing until they saw me, then they fell silent.

As I lurched forward, they rose as a unit, lifted to their feet with a gasp of horror. Muttering in Turkish they stepped back, head coverings whipped by the wind over their faces. Then, perhaps recognizing me as human after all, they rushed forward and caught me as I collapsed. Light, warm hands eased me onto the sand. Cloth fell aside and old women, young women bent over me, shielding me from what remained of the setting sun.

With my disturbed senses it was almost as if I could feel

their emotions: dismay, tenderness, protectiveness. Someone pushed through the group and held cold tea to my lips. Nothing had ever tasted better. I gulped the whole sugary thermos full, then lay in the sand. My burning eyes squeezed closed, I drifted in and out of their passionate debate—a babble in Turkish that my feverish brain felt I should understand and struggled, hopelessly, to make sense of.

Then I was lifted, a woman supporting each sunburned side. I stumbled, half carried, to the marble bust. As if in a dream, the statue shifted into focus and became an elderly woman, buried to her neck in the sand, white cloth draped over her hair. I saw the death of a child in her folding wrinkles, long hungry winters in her lean cheekbones, and years of companionship in her velvety eyes. Why had they buried her? My damaged logic could think of no reason.

She addressed me. I couldn't understand her words, but I could feel her desire to help.

"Incir," I croaked, pointing west.

"Incir." She nodded.

The sand around her quaked and two wrinkled hands sifted up. Onlookers held out their robes, fencing us in, as two others dug her free. The old woman heaved to her feet, stiff and slow. She pulled a white *çarşaf* over sandy bloomers and shirt, secured the cloth under her chin, and stepped into slippers. Women congealed around me; it was shocking, so much human mugginess against my raw skin. We moved off the beach as a lump and I was carried forward, weak and confused, in its center.

As we came into town the women pushed closer, hiding

my nakedness behind warm bodies. The village, big enough to have traffic, clanged and shrieked. I trembled uncontrollably, every sound too loud. Looking down to find myself, all I could see was bright cloth whipping around their socked ankles, and blurry sandals moving in unison with my bare feet.

I was borne into a backyard with a kitchen garden. Prickly cucumber vines and smooth eggplants grew from clay pots, the textures intense in the late afternoon sun. Three painfully hard concrete steps led to a kitchen that I barely glimpsed as I was herded into the bedroom. The smell of roasted pistachios was dizzying.

Hands on my belly, back, and shoulders, the women took what remained of my lace underwear as I stood shivering. Lace underwear, my dazed brain remembered, purchased in a forgotten world by Mme. Groseille during the June sales at Galleries Lafayette.

Someone brought a porcelain basin and drizzled water down my back, icy against my glowing skin, the sunburn excruciating as they patted me dry. Someone clasped a thick cotton bra around me, hiding my tender nipples in its padded, pointed lift. Someone steadied me, coaxing me into waist-high underwear and floral, gathered pants. Someone pulled the softest cotton blouse over my head. Someone led me to the kitchen sink and leaned me forward under the faucet. Strong fingernails dislodged sand from my scalp as cool water spiraled down the drain. Back in the bedroom, women combed at tangles until my hair fell straight and long.

I was too exhausted for the food they offered. It smelled of grilled lamb. I collapsed into bed and closed my eyes. Within seconds I spun towards sleep. As the whispers retreated and the door clicked closed, my heart flooded with wonder. Who nursed Napoleon's shattered soldiers when they finally made it home?

# TWELVE

I woke the next morning with a start, heart racing. Distressed, I sat up. I had no idea where I was. Blue gray light filtered through gauze curtains and barely lit the room. A coal stove waited for winter, resting in the corner. Rug lapped over rug on the floor, the colors garishly happy. Paperback novels in Turkish spiraled in a lopsided pile on the desk. I was in a woman's room, an unmarried woman by the size of her little bed. Then I remembered being lost at sea, and collapsed back onto the pillows. I was at the mercy of strangers. I lay there, gaze wandering uneasily around the privacy of another woman's bedroom.

A cotton *çarşaf* lay on a nearby chair, a blue tent that hung from the head to well below the waist, with full bloomers that flowed to the floor. The blue was the color of my eyes. The fine gold stitching at the hems matched streaks in my sea-bleached hair.

"Their hospitality borders on excessive," the British ambassador had said a lifetime ago, while our butler cleared the Chablis for the fish course and poured Pinot Noir to complement the roast. "A guest is a gift from God, they say. Such an odd notion." He had wiped his manicured fingers on a linen napkin. Eyes wide with consternation, he had exclaimed, "Their god expects them to go out of their way for perfect strangers!"

Strangers had gone out of their way for me my entire life. I had been waited on by dozens of Mme. Groseille's quiet, respectful servants. Despite them all, I had felt completely alone. Their duty was not done from kindness, and their competence was not tenderness. How far could I trust these Turkish strangers, whose duty was to God, and whose tenderness was so foreign?

I climbed out of bed and slipped on the blue *çarşaf*. It fit well over the white head cloth, blouse, and gathered pants I already wore. There was no mirror, but had there been one, I probably would not have recognized myself.

Barefooted, I opened the door and padded into the hall. Talking and the scraping of dishes murmured from the next room. The kitchen door stood ajar, and I hesitated in the doorway, hovering at the edge of their lives, peering into the intimacy of breakfast.

A slight girl of perhaps fifteen stood at the stove, steam drifting around her thin fingers as she poured water into a teapot. A middle aged man read the newspaper, plump belly stretching his business suit, the remains of bread on his plate. Two school-aged children, a boy and a girl, ate hard boiled eggs. They stopped mid bite and stared at me, mouths open around their wide, white eggs.

A woman in her forties looked up from her plate and saw me. She stood, speaking sharply to her children, who took down their eggs and whispered, *"Günaydin."* Good morning, I suppose. The woman dragged another chair to the already crowded table, waving me into the room with a smile and generous sweeps of her hand.

I shuffled across the wooden floor, trying to muster as much humility as a Trotoskov can. No matter what, I pleaded with myself, don't put down a heavy foot or exude an arrogant air. Sunburn stung my back, my stomach ached with hunger, nervous sweat ran under my arms. I was painfully aware in every fiber of my solitary soul, that I didn't belong.

I sat down. The businessman nodded once. The mother, holding back puffed sleeves so they wouldn't drag in the food, rearranged plates such that eggs, cucumbers, tomatoes, olives, feta, and bread were within my reach, then she sat back down. The girl brought me a tea glass with six lumps of sugar arranged in a pyramid on a plate. Her hands were patterned with henna, vines wandering from her fingertips and creeping across her palms to clutch a heart at her wrist. The henna was the same red brown as her headscarf, the same color as her eyes, deep as ripe chestnuts. She poured tea, then sneaking brief eye contact, she offered me a shy smile.

"*Merci.*" I said.

I sipped tea, bitter and thick, feeling ashamed; I'd lived here half a year and was completely ignorant. I couldn't ask their names, compliment the breakfast, or praise their kindness. I couldn't explain who I was, or inquire after the women who had saved my life. I couldn't even say, "Thank you" in a language they understood." If only I'd made some effort, all of these months, for someone other than myself.

Their eggs consumed, the little children hopped off their chairs and came to stand on either side of me, pressing uncomfortably close. With inquisitive fingers, they patted my shoulder, touched my face, and felt the gold filigree on my sleeve. I suffered their curiosity with as much good nature as I could find.

Whispering in Turkish, they grabbed up serving platters and forked enough food onto my plate to feed me several times over. Fortunately, I was ravenous. In my wealthy life I'd never experienced true hunger. That morning I quaked with the sheer need of it, trying not to gobble like a dog. My tea glass would no sooner be three-quarters empty than the girl would fill it again. Having been saved from Poseidon's sea for some unknown purpose, I was going to drown in Turkish generosity. But I gratefully drank every drop.

Breakfast over, the mother shooed the little ones away and stacked the dishes. I sat awkwardly in the way, aware that I was imposing, wondering if they had a telephone, wondering where I was, feeling very far—I had no idea how far—from home.

The kitchen door banged open and a heavy tank of a young man strode in. He kissed the father's hands and touched them to his forehead, did the same with the mother who was collecting silverware at the table, then smiled onto the head of the teenager who washed dishes at the sink. By her flush and downcast eyes I could tell that she liked him. He plopped into a vacant chair next to mine, and, to my relief, he began speaking in tortured English.

"You—American?" he asked.

"French. *Française.*"

"You speak English." It was not a question, it was a request.

"Yes, of course."

"You come, I take to Incir." He gestured toward the door with strong hands, dark from motor grease. On his youthful face I saw no hesitation, no worry that I would not follow.

I hadn't had much luck lately with young Turks. I looked nervously around the kitchen. The businessman smiled expectantly. The mother rinsed silverware. The girl kept her eyes on the suds in the sink.

"Incir," I said, fighting not to flash protective teeth, back stiff with ingrained mistrust.

He stood up. "You come."

I hesitated. Would they save me, just to deliver me to some horrible fate? I strained to remember any cautionary tales, told through cigar smoke by my father's friends. None came to me—all had been universally kind, in praising the Turks. It would be a slap in the face to refuse to go. I'd take the risk, rather than be insulting. I had no choice, after all they had done.

I stood up. "You tell them—" I spoke slowly, groping for a grateful tone, "—Tell them thank you. *Merci*. The sleep, the food, the robe—" I touched the gold embroidery on my sleeve. "Tell them, please."

The young man laughed, easy and confident. "The *çarşaf* is my wife." He gestured to the teen at the table.

"Your wife?" I looked at the girl, who blushed fiercely. "Tomorrow. My wife tomorrow."

"You're getting married tomorrow, with her?" I gestured towards the girl.

He gave one sharp, downward nod. "Her *çarşaf* for married."

"This robe? This is her wedding dress?"

"Yes." He beamed, uneven teeth giving his handsome face a charming humbleness. It was clear he thought this act of generosity very becoming in his future spouse.

I was stunned. Who were these people? I glanced at the delicate girl washing dishes, years younger than me, and felt an unflattering twist of envy. Eyes down to hide my shame, I thought of her charitable culture, her welcoming family, and her generous heart. And there I stood, rigid in her kitchen, barely able to master my mistrust. She had everything that eluded me, and I had nothing but steely defenses.

I pulled a corner of her wedding robes over my face, hearing my father's scoffing; this child was a poor uneducated waif who wouldn't amount to anything. But we all rocked together in the arms of her God; that was enough for her to give me her wedding dress. What would it take to teach us Trotoskovs such humanity?

"Please tell her thank you, she is very kind. You must be happy to marry this wife." I was too full of turmoil to raise my eyes again.

"*Maşallah,*" breathed the family in unison, when the complement was translated. May God preserve.

I nodded goodbye to the father. The children insisted on patting my fingers, calling out what I took to be blessings. The bride pinned a small string of glass beads to my *çarşaf,* muttering some sort of prayer. On the way out the door, the mother offered me her own embroidered slippers and pressed a wrapped package of food into my hands, then she threw a pitcher of water onto the bumper of the groom's old scooter.

"For safe trip," explained the groom as he dried the seat and turned the ignition. The rickety scooter puttered and stuttered to the corner, shaking our bones and throwing me uncomfortably close to him. If Incir was far away we might not make it.

But I was wrong in assuming we drove to Incir. He took me to a bus stop on a busy street. When the bus drove up, he had a prolonged conversation with the driver. I stood among waiting passengers, not at all happy that the young man was abandoning me, passing me hand to hand like a package. With a friendly wave he hopped on his scooter and drove off. I was to trust, and trust again, how many times? Which would I exhaust first: my limited faith, or Turkish hospitality?

The driver smiled, showing two golden teeth as I sized him up. He boisterously shooed away passengers in the front seat and placed me behind him with a flourish, where I sat, rigid and scared. An hour went by. Anxiety tightened my throat as the bus wandered all over the city, not going anywhere remotely resembling a road to Incir. One hour stretched into three. I churned inside, frantic, staring out the window as we passed the same market, the same mosque, the same elementary school over and over again. What was I doing on this local bus? This looping route was not going to take me home. It took everything I had not to stand up and demand, foot stomping and eyes blazing: Incir! I had no money, didn't even know which city I was lost in. No one gave me more than a compassionate smile when I attempted to ask them in French, English, German, or Spanish to help me. Around noon I could stand it no longer. I peered around the driver's seat when he stopped at a corner.

"Incir?" I asked, fighting to be polite, gesturing with the pleading shrug any Frenchman would understand as, "please, what's going on?"

"*Lütfen, lütfen,*" he answered, flashing his metal teeth and waving me back into my seat.

I had no idea what *lütfen* meant, but it was clear I was to stay put. I considered dashing off the bus and trying to find a telephone, but I had no money and couldn't read a Turkish phone book. I agonized over the notoriously corrupt small town police. "Hard to say which is worse," Suat Bey had muttered at dinner one night, "police on your side or police on your tail." I decided in the end not to throw myself on their mercy. Frightened and miserable, I hid in my *çarşaf.*

Then three girls got on, perhaps twelve years old, dressed in school uniforms. They were as giddy and silly as any schoolgirls, and except for their headscarves, they could have been Parisian. After paying, they bumped and jostled past me.

"*Parlez-vous français?*" I asked.

They giggled.

"English?"

"Yes," said one, her blue eyes pretty as cornflowers, framed by a grassy green scarf. "Good morning, class. Good morning, teacher," she said with pompous formality, then she and her friends burst into laughter.

"Please, I want to go to Incir," I persisted.

"Incir?" She looked confused. "One moment, Madame."

She consulted the driver—a brief conversation in Turkish.

"He take you there. You wait," she said when she came back. I wasn't a bit reassured by this scrap of a promise.

They shoved each other, still giggling, to the back of the bus, where they occupied the entire back seat, their arms linked. Pretty soon they started singing. The song wandered up and down the scale, circling around to a refrain every few minutes. To my amazement, other passengers began to sing along, bellowing the refrain like soccer fans or late night revelers, but more in tune.

It was well past noon now and, not knowing what else to do, I decided to eat the food the mother had pressed on me. Knowing that my rescuers expected me to need lunch was some solace. Pulling apart folds of white paper, I opened the package: a ripe stuffed tomato, a thick slice of minty eggplant, and a portion of flat, soft bread.

I was about to have a bite when a boy appeared at my elbow. He was four or five, with nervous mousey energy and mischievous eyes. He sat down next to me, wiggled until he had pushed close against my side, and squeaked something in Turkish. He looked at the food in my lap, up to my face, then down to my food. He glanced at his mother, slumped over, asleep in the seat across the aisle, her head supported by the window. His hair was clean, nails were cut, and clothes were neat. She obviously fed and cared for him; he was hardly a beggar child. Still, with quick fingers he tugged at a corner of my food wrapper.

Feeling his longing, I thought of the bride. She probably would have given him everything: slid the paper onto his lap and politely turned away as if she weren't hungry.

A Trotoskov would ignore him. No, first a Trotoskov would move a few centimeters to the left, so that the boy's leg was no longer brushing against his thigh, and then he would ignore him.

And I?

With a wave of sorrow I realized: I couldn't remember the last time anyone had asked me to give. A hug, a meal, a gift…. My whole life unrolled behind me, a long carpet that I had walked alone, carrying nothing anyone wanted. My loneliness, that wall that imprisoned me, suddenly turned transparent. And on the other side, this child, this beautiful little mouse, practically crawling into my lap. I thrust forward the paper wrapper and let him chose.

He chose the bread. Mouth stuffed full, he began to sing the refrain that half of the bus was now singing. He grinned at me and tucked his chin in that congenial Turkish gesture for agreement. Bread crumbs made a mess of his lap, falling into the pleats of his dark trousers and down the front of his white shirt.

I chose the tomato and took a bite. Juice spurted out the yielding side and dribbled, pooling in my cupped palm. The child thought this hilarious and he chuckled, waving a disapproving finger. Then he saw the crumbly debris in his own lap and thought this even funnier. His eyes rolled with delight, back and forth from my mess to his. Glancing at his sleeping mother, he giggled and squirmed, as if anticipating what she might think of our untidiness. The refrain came around again and he began to sing with gusto, elbowing me to sing along.

Singing in public: it's what drunks do. In all my life, I had never seen Boris sing. But the boy elbowed me again, mouth full of bread and grinning with enthusiasm. So I thrust aside ingrained dignity and warbled off-key. In a language that I didn't know, in the crowded bus of an unknown city, next to a little mouse whose name I'll never learn, I sang. And for a moment, for one pure and splendid moment, I was light with happiness. Tears of joy danced down my cheeks and were absorbed into the *çarşaf* under my chin.

We split the eggplant and ate it together, wiping our hands on the remains of the paper wrapper. Unable to speak to each other, we made childish sounds to express how much we liked the minty flavor. When the boy's mother woke and collected him a few stops later, he left under whiny protest, yanking on her hand as she tugged him off the bus. She carried him down a dusty street, him looking over her shoulder and yelling, "*Allahaısmarladık!*" at the departing bus.

*Allahaısmarladık.*

Goodbye? Probably with a blessing to keep me safe until we met again. I leaned out the window and stumbled over the pronunciation, trying to say it back. I waved until he was no longer in sight. Then I lay my head on the seat, missing him, rocking in the bus with soft singing still floating in the background. The girls were gone and one lone woman sang now, her voice barely louder than the hum of the engine. The foreign words, the minor scale, evoked melancholy, and emotions that I couldn't name. I closed my eyes. Totally lost and stripped of all I had, I gave up and let myself rest in the hands of my fellow man. I fell asleep.

When I awoke it was dusk and I was the only passenger on the bus. The light was golden—that embracing evening yellow that makes even a junk yard worthy. Out the window we passed lightly rolling hills, little houses like those in Incir, and children driving a flock of goats. I had been on the bus probably twelve hours. It would be dark soon.

I poked my head around the seat and the driver lowered his chin with two sharp nods, acknowledging me. Then he pointed. There, at the side of the road, were broken marble columns. Ahead I saw Incir's Roman theater: a slice of dark shadow cutting a circle out of the landscape.

"*Hôtel*," I said, pointing with mounting excitement down the road.

"*Otel*," said the driver.

He rattled the city bus off the pavement and onto dirt, past the village houses that lined the road to the theater. People poured out their front doors, no doubt interrupting their dinners, amazed at the unusual spectacle of a city bus, throwing dust up in their tiny town. As if we were the pied piper, they followed. When he could take the bus no further on the rutted road, the driver turned off the engine.

As dust settled, townsmen gathered by the front fender, silent. Women in their dark *kara çarşafs* flocked together at a respectful distance. The driver opened the door and stepped into the waiting group of men. Heads together, they mumbled in low, serious voices. Every now and then, one man or another glanced at me with curiosity.

Self-conscious and vulnerable, I looked away and covered my face with a corner of the wedding *çarşaf*. I could not imagine what they must think of me in this village, given all that had happened.

After a long conversation, one of the men called his wife, who came forward, several women trailing behind. The driver summoned me from the bus and delivered me, nervous and awkward, into the knot of women. The women closed around me, smelling of sweet herbs. All dressed in black with their faces covered, I couldn't tell one from the other. In the confines of their circle, one reached forward and tugged at the blue cloth over my nose and chin. The soft cotton fell aside.

*"Allaaaahhhh...."*

I startled, their piercing cries taking me by surprise. A wail rose from the group, a keening grief one might expect at a funeral. Women hit their chests and howled as if I were beloved and dead. Others grabbed and hugged me, passing me from distraught woman to distraught woman. Squeezed and gripped, I gasped for air. Their tears and kisses wet my cheeks. I was held so close in the knot of their emotion I could hardly breathe. Finally I was pushed into strong arms, and when she pulled aside the cloth covering her chin, I found Yurda. Yurda, face distorted with sobbing, holding me against her as if I was her child. Crying words that I could not translate but that were as clear in my heart as my native French: I was dead, and then miraculously returned to her. Praise Allah.

Arms around me, the group hustled me down the goat path. We passed through Apollo's temple, marble turned to amber by the setting sun. The women waited outside as

Yurda hurried into the kitchen of the *pension*, yelling loud enough to rouse the whole hotel.

Soon doors banged overhead and footsteps clattered on the stairs. Mizou, Suat Bey, Kemal, Damad, Della—everyone crowded through the kitchen door, taking up cries of praise and prayers of thanks. Hands pet my head, held my sweaty fingers, and patted my shoulder. Tears streamed down my cheeks, I was so overwhelmed by the joy they took from touching me.

And Xiao, Xiao stood with his back to the wall, face passive, saying nothing.

Yurda passed glasses of tea and a tray of pastries through the back door, into the hands of the waiting village women. Through the door I could see the townsmen gathered in a separate group outside, yakking and taking Yurda's refreshments from their wives' hands. I sat at the head of the kitchen table, comforted again by hot tea, too besieged by the outpouring of love to speak.

Eventually the villagers drifted away and the kitchen emptied except for family. Della sat down next to me and took one of my hands.

"Oh Lordy, but you are a sight for sore eyes. Where have you been, child?"

"*Alors*…I don't know."

"The bus was from Alanya." Mizou took a seat next to Della, for Yurda had a permanent place on my other side, which she refused to cede.

Della squeezed my hand. "Tell us what happened, hon. We're dying to know."

"It really wasn't *grand chose.* I was attacked by the same boys again, but this time there were five—"

"The little *espèces de salauds!*" Suat Bey leaped from his seat and pounded arthritic fists on the kitchen table. "If I had been able to get my hands on the puny bastards, they would have come crawling to you for forgiveness. Lucky for them they were locked up, *Princess*, the day you disappeared, or I would teach them that there *is* something worse than a Turkish jail."

"They're in jail?" I had never once considered what might happen to the boys.

"Of course! They are due to stand trial for murder." Suat Bey jutted his thin chin into the air and fiddled with the ends of his long moustache.

My heart seized with guilt. Had Napoleon ever felt guilty? War had terrible consequences; in my desire for revenge, I had forgotten.

Mizou took advantage of my shocked silence to translate for Yurda. Yurda reached out and took my other hand, murmuring in Turkish. Now I was pinned down on both sides with a grip of love.

"Go on, child," said Della, squeezing my fingers.

"I ran, and had nowhere to go except into the sea. I thought I could swim around the jetty, but once in the high waves I became lost. I eventually found my way to the beach, but far down the coast."

Mizou raised her hand and made a sign, a gesture that gathered then cut the air like a benediction, or a spell.

"Praise Allah that you didn't make it to the jetty. There are rip tides and whirlpools, nasty currents and God knows what else hiding in those rocks. It would have killed you for sure. You were blessed and lucky, child."

On the other side of Yurda, Suat Bey leaned into the conversation. "You swam all day, lost in the ocean, and fought your way to shore. Ah! Such bravery. I am so jealous, *Princess*, that I do not have such a tale to tell. Were there sharks?"

"*Non*, but I suppose I might invent some."

A grin snuck across Suat Bey's mouth, hiding roguishly under his yellow-stained mustache. Without a word, he winked at me.

"We want to know what *really* happened," said Mizou, glancing sideways at Suat Bey.

"I found a group of women—they had buried an old lady to her neck in the sand. Why do such a thing?"

"Arthritis treatment," said Mizou.

"Ah! Of course. They took me home and cared for me, then sent me home on the bus."

"They didn't *send* you on the bus, child," said Della. "No bus goes from Alanya to Incir. The driver drove you here after his shift was over, out of kindness."

"*Mon Dieu!*"

My God! All that way. Such a long day. Bless him, Apollo. And I, so inpatient and mistrustful, determined to make an idiot of myself.

"Yes. And thank God he did, for if you hadn't shown up the boys would have been tried for murder. The whole town had their suspenders in a twist." Della shook her head as I deciphered this piece of American slang. "You can't imagine how grief-struck we were to have lost you. To have let such a thing happen."

"You did not...*let*...this thing happen to me."

"Oh yes we did!" Della glared at Yurda, who lowered her eyes and began to cry. Plump, juicy tears hung off her chin, wobbling as she sobbed. "Yurda was having so much fun making the boys the laughing stock of Incir, that she didn't think what a few proud little roosters might do. They locked up Umut—poor little kid almost died before Xiao found him in the donkey shed—and then they went after you. Wound anything you want around here, child, but don't wound Turkish pride."

Yurda hung onto my hand as if it were a life raft. Between gasps and snivels she forced out some Turkish words.

"What is she saying?" I turned to Della.

Della shook her head and looked away.

"What is she saying?"

Mizou pressed her lips together.

"Suat Bey? Tell me." I begged.

"She...." Suat Bey cooed, as if speaking to some harem sweetheart over the garden wall. "She cannot express how much she is in your debt. The boys' mothers hate her for driving them to such an *extrême*. The whole village has been doing penance for your death, and she felt responsible. She is grateful that Allah has spared you, and that you have returned to us as a—" he cleared his throat, "—as a child who, er...loves God."

"Loves God?"

"Yes, she interprets your *çarşaf* as an acceptance of the laws of Islam, and your savior from the sea as a miracle, you might say."

"*Oh la!* But…this is no miracle. And I didn't choose these clothes. They were given to me when mine were lost."

"Don't tell her that, *Princess.* We all need illusions in order to live with ourselves. You cannot believe what our Yurda has suffered, and now you have made her, and the whole village, very happy. You are a living embodiment of God's compassion. A tiny lie will not kill you, *non*?"

"I don't know. It doesn't seem like such a little lie."

"Och!" scoffed Suat Bey, "I tell much bigger lies all the time." He raised his glistening blue eyes to mine. "Just cover up and wear a headscarf in the village, *ma jolie fille,* and walk around with a chaperone. That will be sufficient."

*Ma jolie fille.* He called me his pretty daughter. How could anyone refuse such a gallant old soldier?

"A chaperone? Umut?"

"*Non.* He is too ashamed of his failures, and perhaps too frightened, though there is no danger. The whole village would go to any lengths, now, to protect you." Suat Bey looked to the man standing against the wall. "I have spoken to Xiao, and he has agreed to escort you."

My heart stood still in my chest.

Xiao dropped his gaze to the floor, his expression dark and unreadable.

# THIRTEEN

I couldn't bring myself to leave my room the next morning. I told myself I needed time to ponder all that had happened, overwhelmed as I was by the love with which Incir had mourned my "death." In fact, I was mortally embarrassed, knowing that I had been dumped, a heavy package, into Xiao's lap.

I sat at my desk watching the sea, my head strangely empty for someone who had so much to think about. I stared at the jetty where I had become lost; it didn't look that far. I saw village fishing boats, slivers of color on a teal sea, making their way through the choppy texture toward the horizon.

Scenes from my childhood drifted over the waves. My father held no sway in this dreamy world; I watched him float by without fear or anger. He was a brilliant politician, I realized, adept at getting his way, and he would die horribly alone. For the first time in my life it occurred to me to feel sad for him.

When I didn't show up for lunch, Mizou knocked on the door.

"*Oui?*"

"May I come in?"

"*Bien sûr.*"

She opened the door and hesitated in the door frame, watching me quizzically. "Are you all right?"

"I think so."

She closed the door and stood by the bed. "Do you need anything?" She used the familiar *tu*, but this time it sounded of sisterhood.

"I...I don't know."

Looking around the bare room, she selected a patch of floor, and sat against the wall. I was in the only chair.

She gave a self-conscious cough. "I hesitate to raise this, Tatyana, but I think it must be discussed. I realize that Xiao is an awkward choice of a chaperone for you. Suat Bey, bless his heart, means well, but he is sometimes too wrapped up in himself to see what is right before his eyes."

I stiffened. "And what is this, that is right before everyone's eyes?"

Mizou looked at the three rings on her hands: a gold wedding band, a blood red garnet set in scrolled silver, and a black rock in an elaborately spiked setting. Her usual dinner time bracelets were gone. "Don't force me to embarrass you. Suffice it to say that I know love when I see it."

I turned back to the pounding waves, pulling my blonde hair over my face to cover my shame.

Mizou was silent for a minute, then she said, "May I tell you a story? It is not as amusing as one of Suat Bey's, but I think you would like to hear it."

"Go ahead."

She cleared her throat. "I was twenty when I first fell in love. I fell for Suat Bey, a dashing and decorated soldier many years my senior, a soldier any woman would have gladly married. My family is Roma: the hunted ones. We lived all over Europe and the east. You have already guessed that I am not really French, *n'est pas?*"

I nodded, still watching the rhythmic crash of the sea.

"Suat Bey was wealthy, charming, ran in the highest circles of society. I was poor. Beautiful, yes, but an ethnic outcast, a worthless belly dancer, called in to entertain the lusty. He would sleep with me, of that I was sure, but I had no hope that he would marry me. So I did something—," she paused, cleared her throat again, "—very dangerous. Something only youth could do, because youth do not understand how deeply, and for how many years, they could regret."

I turned around. The solemn chill on her face made my skin rise and shiver.

Her eyes locked on mine, and I could not look away.

"I stole from my grandmother an ancient mirror, passed down through generations and hidden from the young. The mirror, it was said, had been cursed with a spell that could bind lovers as if they were one. The lovers lived safe under the spell's protection, as untouchable and immortal as the gods." Her fingers unconsciously wandered to the black ring on her hand, spinning it around her finger. "Whomever I regarded in the glass would fall in love with me, and only me, into our long forever after. My famous soldier could not die on the battlefield. The renowned seducer would philander and whore no more."

"Why is this a curse?" My throat felt parched, tight.

"Because, this is Hades mirror, made to keep the fair Persephone true." Her voice dropped to a whisper. "You remember how he stole Persephone, and fed her pomegranates to trap her in the underworld, one month for each of the six seeds she ate? But what of the other six months? Such an ill-favored god as Hades couldn't trust his unwilling bride to be faithful. So he forged this mirror and bound her to him, and if she betrayed him, he had the power to drag her back into the underworld. There she would stand forever on the bank of the river Styx, longing for her life or the peace of death, unable to have either."

"And if I use the mirror?"

"Xiao is yours, for as long as neither of you betray your love. One betrayal, and you both belong to Hades."

I forced myself to breathe against a weight of fear. "There is no such magic. The Olympian gods are long forgotten. *C'est ridicule.*"

"No, Tatyana, magic that can kill is not ridiculous, and gods in their homeland do not die. I see you in Apollo's temple, I know you believe."

I struggled to look away. "I don't believe in magic."

Mizou reached to the hem of her orange robe. With a yank and a twist, she tore the fabric, ripping off a strip of shimmering orange. Then she reached behind her and pulled out something, wrapping it quickly in the swath of silk.

"Anyone who believes in true love, believes in magic. They are equally improbable, equally elusive, equally desirable." She put the package on the floor and slid it toward my chair. "You and Xiao would never come together. He is a man with a political destiny, devoted to his people, chaste as a monk and as self-sacrificing as a mother. You are an immature, wanton—"

"Wanton! I am a virgin!"

"You are wanton by Muslim standards. A spoiled but talented artist, who has thought of nothing but her tortured self all of her life. Still, if you want him—" she nudged the package closer, "—you may have him."

"Why are you doing this?"

Mizou stared into my eyes, as hypnotic as a snake.

"You are much like a young belly dancer I once knew. I look at your face at dinner and I remember what it is to crave a man so deeply. He will turn you into a generous woman, if you let him. And that is what you want, *n'est pas*? Don't fight him, Tatyana." She rose to her feet. "I will see you at dinner."

She left and closed the door.

I didn't have the nerve to touch the package. For all of my brave words about magic, the silken folds that concealed her gift might as well hold a viper.

~

That night, as Della wrapped me for dinner, she said, "Watch my hands, hon. I am leaving before long and you'll need to make these tucks yourself."

My heart sank. "Where do you go?"

"Back on the Silk Road. Look here—it's the natural curve of your hip that holds this drape in place. Do you see where I'm putting this?"

"Yes, but why do you go?"

"Sometime in June the tourists arrive, and this place loses its charm. Anyway, I have work to do. If you let the silk slide through your fingers, like this, you can mold it into three drapes for the front, you see?"

"Yes. You sell silk?"

"I sell whatever the market is buying." She tugged and the dress fell apart, drifting to the floor in a mass of burgundy folds. "Now, you do it."

She settled one hand onto her hip and leaned back, soft as a paint-on-velvet Southern Belle. With motherly concern she watched me fumble with the slippery fabric until I had formed a sort of dress.

"Not bad." She reached out and tugged the cloth off again. "Do it one more time."

I re-wrapped the dress. It did not hang as gracefully as Della's work, but it stayed on. Della knelt and lifted the fabric she'd pulled from her trunk, stretching to fold it.

"Where does this road go?"

"What road?" She bent over her work, her back a smooth curve of velvet gown.

"This Silk Road you speak of."

"Oh, it starts in Beijing, goes north through the Nei Mongol Plateau, to the ruins of Genghis Khan's Karakorum. I take the northern route to avoid winter on the Tibetan Plateau, then drop down into Samarkand in Uzbekistan. I circle the Caspian Sea to Tabriz, in North Iran, take a boat up to the lower Volga, then travel by train to Crimea, on to central Russia, and then to Erzurum in northeast Turkey. It takes about six months."

"Do you like this…this moving about all your days?"

Della looked up, soft brown eyes guarded. "Some people have to leave home to have a home. Do you understand?"

"*Oui.*" It was why I left Paris, why Xiao left China. I

wondered if the ghosts of Della's family followed her down the Silk Road, as Boris' specter followed me. "Will you come back to Incir?"

She slammed closed the trunk. "If tourists don't ruin it."

"Why ruin?"

She stood up. There is a statue in Paris called *La Defense de Paris*, sculpted by Louis-Ernest Barrias. The statue is a formidable woman standing in front of a cannon with a sword in her right hand. *La Defense* is as far from a Southern Belle as a woman can get, and it shocked me how fast Della transitioned from seductress into hardened soldier.

"You don't know much about the world, do you, little one?"

"I…er…I don't know."

"Do you think this business about the boys had anything to do with you?"

"Yes, it was my *erreur*. The feud would not have started if I had not—"

"Hogwash." Her tone was muddy with impatience. "This town is fighting for its life. The Arabs who live here can trace their families back to the seventh century. The *kara çarşaf* is more than religious respect, it's a political statement about who will govern this village. Incir's Roman aqueducts fell when the Arabs invaded. Incir's mosque shall fall to an invasion of European tourists."

"And who will the Western tourists fall to?"

And there was her slow smile, sauntering sensually across her mouth. I realized now that her smile was not the Nile crossing continents: it was her soul, traveling the Silk Road.

"You're sharper than I gave you credit for. Who do you think the West will fall to?"

I didn't hesitate. "Xiao's people."

"Why the Chinese?"

I repeated, verbatim, what my father had said to the German chancellor that fateful night Emma decided to marry George Galt. "If the Chinese ever stop killing their brightest and start following them, they will be unstoppable. You would be wise to ally yourself with them, *mein Herr*. Remember Genghis Khan."

The chancellor had put down his salad fork, looked condescendingly over my young head, and said to Boris, "The Chinese are no longer Mongols. In any event, I shall be dead by then. Most likely *mein Herr*, so will you."

Della drifted to her desk and opened a box. She lifted a carved coral necklace, the colors of a ripe peach, and sauntered back to where I stood.

"Here," she said, clasping the stones around my neck. "Wear this and look beautiful. And see if you can't repeat what you just said to our friend Xiao. It might help your boat get her tail out of the muck."

I flushed. Obviously, my insulting political pronouncements had been a topic of conversation during my stint as a dead girl.

"Mizou gave me a…a gift," I stammered as we left Della's room.

"Did she?"

Della stopped at the head of the stairs and stared down the long spiral, looking into the evening ahead. I wondered what she saw. To me, all I expected was humiliation as I faced Xiao.

"In that case, you'll have what you desire," she said. "Mizou's gifts work that way."

The men—Suat Bey, Kemal, and Xiao—rose when we came in. Suat Bey made an elaborate fuss of seating me next to him, pushing in my chair, pouring water, dragging the bread basket across the table.

"*Oh la la, Princess,* but it is good to have your lovely face back at our table again. And look! The wicked sea has sunburned you. Tonight before you go to bed, you must pass a tomato over your cheeks, so your delicate skin does not peel. Can I offer you a *dolma*? Yurda makes a *yaprak sarma* that would honor even the sultan's table. *Voici, Princess.* Take two, she has rolled them particularly small...."

He babbled on, hardly taking a breath, straining graciousness to its limit.

"Thank you." I wanted to kiss his impeccable Turkish hospitality on the tip of its red veined nose.

"You are our Odysseus, wandering to unnamed shores. Tell us, now. You have had an adventure, *non*? Surely there is more to say than that skinny cow of a tale you told last night. How did you survive, out there in the vast Mediterranean?"

He took a few grape leaves, and then reached for the Feta. Without asking, he slid a crumbling, moist hunk of cheese onto my plate. "Were you frightened, *chérie*?"

"*Oui.* I thought of Poseidon, and his lover Medusa. It was almost as though I could see them, deep below me, where the turquoise light fades."

"Medusa?" His bushy eyebrows shot up. "That monster that leads lost sailors to a stony death? We have lost several fishing boats this way."

"Papa!" warned Kemal, with a flick of his fork in Suat Bey's direction.

"Hush, son. Let the maiden tell her story."

From across the table, Xiao began to laugh, an uninhibited delight so unlike him that I looked up. For the first time in weeks, I met his gaze head on. He grinned at me, a sloppy layering of pleasure and stupidity.

My God, he was drunk! For a moment I was speechless, staring at the Raki glass he raised in a wobbly toast to Suat Bey.

"Go on, *Princess*, you are keeping an old man waiting. Much slower and I may die before the end of your tale," muttered Suat Bey.

"Ah, *oui*. So, I was very tired and I thought about Napoleon."

"Napoleon?" Suat Bey considered the pine nuts and rice that oozed from his *dolma*. "Why ponder a dead Emperor at this dreadful moment?"

"I thought about his soldiers, the 70,000 that survived the invasion of Russia in 1812."

"Very sad, yes. One war I cannot claim to have fought, praise Allah. And did this decimated army lead you to shore?"

"*Non*. I was trying to decide why. Why try so hard to survive?" I picked apart the *dolma* on my plate and stirred in some crumbles of cheese. With a glance at the sodden and smiling Xiao, I forced myself to go on. "Did you ever ask yourself, Suat Bey, when death was galloping down on you, why you wanted to live?"

"*Mais non, Princess!*" He threw his hands up with dismay. "There were always more women, more adventures, more chances for honor over the next hill. Why not get back on my horse and go on?" He gave a head wag in Xiao's direction. "Even when I had to crawl to the horse, I still wanted to ride."

"*Je vois.*" And I did understand, but it didn't help. I was nothing like Suat Bey. If I had his ability to love the world and all of its misguided inhabitants, I too, would hop on my horse and ride on. I emptied my glass of water and reached for the pitcher.

"I know why." Xiao's voice was slurred and his French hard to understand. He set down his Raki glass with a clumsy thump. "My prison was in the shape of a cross. *Shi*, the Chinese chess piece that signifies the bodyguard. My cell was a ten foot square painted blood red. Like a sunset. When they roped me up to the wall by my neck, I prepared to die. A bullet in the back of the head, an unmarked grave. I was ready. A month later, when I still hung on that wall, death seemed the kindest gift anyone could give."

He reached for the Raki bottle, but Kemal got there before him and shoved it out of his grasp. With an apologetic smile Kemal took the pitcher and poured Xiao water.

"One month later I could no longer think about life, or death. I couldn't think at all. When they cut me down and told me I had five days to get out of China, I was too weak to walk. I crawled out of Qincheng prison. A railroad worker took pity on me and pulled me home in a cart. A neighbor gave me soup, on the condition that I never tell who fed me. As soon as I could stagger I sold a pint of blood for 100 yen and took a train to Guangdong Province. There the local criminal element smuggled me out in exchange for the deed to my Beijing apartment."

Xiao put his face in his hands, causing hair to collapse forward in a cascade of jet black. "Do you know why you don't want to live?" I could barely hear him through the slits between his fingers. "Because you have already died. You wait in heaven." He looked up, weaving and unfocused. "You are just a spirit ghost, Tatyana. A slender, elusive, spirit ghost, come to entice me away from the land of the living."

With that, the Raki took him. If Kemal had not shoved aside Xiao's plate, Xiao would have dropped his head right in it.

We sat in shock. The gruesome story, his suffering—it was unbearable. And his description of me—I had no idea what it all meant.

Damad, who had finished his dinner and played under the table, popped his head up beside the slumped, unconscious man.

"Are you all right?" He shook Xiao's huge shoulder. "Papa, Xiao drank too much Raki."

"It happens even to saints, my little soldier," said Suat Bey.

Kemal couldn't lift Xiao alone, so Yurda came from the kitchen, and together they hauled him upstairs. I followed, carrying his feet. Smooth, well formed, dirty on the bottoms from his flip-flops. I fought the urge to rub my hands over them. I had never thought to ask what a warrior weighs, but I was grateful I only had to lift his feet. We laid him on the bed. Kemal opened the neck of his shirt, then left to find a blanket to throw over him. In order to avoid gazing at Xiao's beautiful, unconscious body, I glanced around the room.

Like all of Mizou's hotel rooms, it had a bed, a chair, and a desk. Moonlight streamed in from the window over his head, drawing a bent arrow across his scarred chest and down to the floor beside him. There, next to the cot where he slept, was my art. Lying on top of the pile was his face, his charcoal eyes open and alive in the silver light.

I picked up the portrait. Underneath were my painted crickets, springing joyfully from page to page, the ones I had abandoned the day I ran into the sea. I pushed them aside. Underneath the well-thumbed paintings lay my box of ink. His box of ink. Our box of ink.

Kemal returned with a blanket and I hastily left the room, not wanting to further my reputation as 'wanton'.

Back in the dining room, Della stretched across the table to hand me the chicken *kebab*. "If I interpret Chinese valor correctly, that gift from Mizou won't be necessary," she said under her breath as I took the plate.

*"Pardon?"*

But she didn't elaborate.

～

That night, before I went to bed, I lifted Mizou's gift and laid it on my desk. Cautiously, I pushed aside the orange silk. The same moonlight that caressed Xiao's face, two doors down the hall, fell onto the heart-shaped back of the mirror.

Oh Cricket, you know how seductive and dreadful that mirror is. The jeweled eyes that watch, jealously guarding the dead from the living. The skillfully placed mosaic pieces forming pink, lolling dog tongues: tongues that know the taste of eternity. You could hope he would growl a warning from his well-fed jaws, but his master is greedy. Impatient. We all travel eventually to misty death: the wicked to Tartarus where evil is quartered, us mortals to be ghosts in the Asphodel Meadows, and heroes to the beautiful Elysium Fields. But Hades prefers we die sooner rather than later, and he wants us all to himself. He loves the wars that Aries foments, welcoming the many subjects she sends him. And it's so easy to trust in love when you are young, so easy to give away the future.

Blue waves wash up the mirror's handle, washing around the gruesome dog. The curved cheeks of the heart accept the thrust of the handle as a woman accepts a man. Take what you want in life, because death comes for you, regardless.

Hades loved Persephone. He dragged her, screaming, into the underworld and made her his reluctant queen. And who can blame him? Love stands beyond reproach. No matter what evil love is capable of, it continues to sway our hearts. Even against our wills.

My hand was drawn to take the mirror from the folds of silk, and I turned it so I could see the glass. The reflection was clouded with mist and dread, and darkness looked back at me. In the ancient silver face I searched for Hades, but instead I saw eyes behind a sequined veil, blood on a curved sword, a hand sliding up a bejeweled belly. And then I saw Xiao's eyes, lifting toward mine in that second before the Raki possessed him, desire seeping from his dazed glance. I found the mirror pressed to my lips, locked in my first kiss. I knew in that moment that I would use the mirror, regardless of the consequences.

# FOURTEEN

I woke the next morning to a knock on the door. "Who is it?" I sat up, dazed from a profound sleep.

"Yurda."

I slipped on pants and a T-shirt and opened the door.

Yurda marched in. With one hand she swept up my abandoned jeans and underthings, and dumped them on the bed. With the other hand, she held out a package wrapped in brown paper. She dropped the package into my hands. Like the *Fêtes de Noël* in December, I was being showered with gifts.

When I had recovered from my surprise I said, "*Merci*," and lay a kiss on her downy cheek.

Ordinarily in Turkish etiquette—my father's dinner guest once explained—one does not open a gift in front of the giver. But Yurda stood there looking at the crinkled package, clearly waiting for me to open and admire. I tore the paper.

It was a black *kara çarşaf* like the ones worn by Incir's village women, the seams finely closed by hand. Not the *burqa* that shrouds even the eyes, worn by the most fundamentalist of Muslim women, but a dark cotton robe with the face as open as a moon. Underneath were black bloomers. It had been thirteen centuries since the Arabs had invaded Incir, and more lax Turkish ways had gradually prevailed. I was being welcomed into modern Incir.

With an impatient flick of her hands she gestured for me to try it on. I pulled the bloomers up to my waist. They fell to just above my bare toes, almost brushing the ground.

Yurda raised her eyebrows approvingly, tisking and tutting with satisfaction. She looked about my stark room and found the hairbrush on my desk. With swift, forceful pulls, she took the sleepy tangles out of my hair and brushed until it gleamed. She pulled the slippery strands into a loose bun at the back of my neck, and pinned it in place. She draped the black headpiece over me and stood back to see the effect. After a moment of quiet contemplation she took a corner of cloth and drew it over my mouth, covering everything but my eyes. With two sharp jerks of her chin she nodded her approval.

Letting the cloth fall aside she laid her palms on my cheeks and began to speak. I didn't understand a word. Her hands were warm, calloused but gentle. Her eyes brimmed with tenderness, her skin smelled of mint. The words went on and on, full of ks and zs and umlauted u's. Though I couldn't decipher so much as my name, her meaning flowed through the rhythm of the words and the softness of her eyes. She took me into her heart, kissing both my cheeks. I was her daughter now.

With a final pat on the side of my chin she turned to the bed and gathered my dirty laundry, stuffing it under her arm. No doubt, off to show the village women that I now wore proper underwear, not the scanty scraps of lace that revealed my erect nipples, or barely traversed the rounds of my buttocks.

After she left I sat on the edge of the bed, tingling with emotion. Parents come with a price. There would be expectations, plans, consents. I had run, once, from that price. But here was love. God knows why she loved me. I had mistaken her for a servant. I had offended and discounted her innumerable times. Still, like the little boy on the bus, she wanted to sidle close and revel in whatever mess we made. I felt wanted, needed. I would try not to disappoint her, I vowed. I went down to breakfast in the *kara çarşaf*.

My mind's eye had never drawn Xiao's complexion in greens, but that was his palette at breakfast. Yurda hovered over him like a dark-robed angel, offering a sacrament of foul smelling herbal tea and a sermon in Turkish. As usual the Turkish eluded me, but I caught Yurda's tone: charitable scolding.

Xiao drank the brown muck Yurda forced on him and smiled stoically, equally long-suffering in his ears and stomach. While muttering agreement in Turkish to all of Yurda's homilies, his glance escaped repeatedly to me, seeming to beg me silently to do something, anything. I grinned back sympathetically, but, as he could see by my outfit, I had already been conquered. Eventually, we escaped together out the back door, but only after eating every *Gözleme* she brought us, the hot grilled bread burning our fingers and the yoghurt dip icy cold.

Xiao offered to take my knapsack as soon as we were down the steps, and slung it over his shoulder.

"Where would you like to go?" He behaved as if we had done this every day, for years. The awkwardness I should have felt was swept away by his inelegant drunken stupor the night before; we were now brought equally low.

"I don't know." I thrilled, just to stand next to him.

"Have you seen the Roman baths?"

"*Non.*"

"*Et puis,* let's go. The ruins are not as beautiful as the temple, but the engineering in the heating chambers is impressive." He took off down the path ahead of me.

"Xiao wait, before we go—" I hurried to catch up with his long stride. "May I please have the inks back?"

He turned around. "Oh, of course. I'll get them."

Sparkling light hit Apollo's temple as I rounded the corner. Slick dew shone on marble, and glistening drops clung to the grass. Warm air drifted off the ocean and waved the tender new leaves of laurel. I sat down on the altar's slab and closed my eyes.

Thank you, Apollo, I breathed. Complete well-being glowed from my toes to my scalp. Spring in Incir, in the cradle where ancient man rocked. And Xiao, coming up behind me to spend the day by my side. I heard a faint scrape and opened my eyes. Xiao stood at the edge of the temple clearing, holding the inks.

"Would you rather stay here?" he asked. He looked so beautiful: strong legs slightly bowed beyond his shorts, as though he spent his days on a horse, and his denim shirt unbuttoned. I could imagine drawing the muscles in his arms. I wanted to just sit and look at him.

"*Non.* Let's see something new."

He turned away, his thick shoulders cut on one side by his

knapsack, and on the other by mine. Neither of us said anything as we followed the goat path. From far away came the second morning call to prayer, causing the donkey to take up his bray. Crows cawed, and the first cicadas of spring chirped, still timid and hushed.

We took several turns and forks, and eventually the path opened. The baths were a honeycomb of walls, eroded where Roman concrete no longer held. Snapped and worn columns stood where glorious porticos once welcomed bathers—the slave traders and olive oil merchants who kept the city fat. Arched doors let light into what would have been steamy inner chambers. Tunnels sank down to where water was heated. Carved into the wall were niches, taller than a man, to hold curly headed statues of naked beauty. The statues were gone and the niches were like eyes, watching what the world had become.

"Let me show you something." Xiao led us out of the intense sun and into the cool interior. Against the wall was a lone marble seat, carved smooth and swooping up to a rigidly straight back. Two eroded, indecipherable sea monsters formed the armrests, and chiseled lion paws supported the base.

"*Voila,* you can see into the courtyard, and draw in the shade so you don't worsen your sunburn."

He put down the knapsacks and took out the inks. With thick fingers he plucked up a black ink and inkstone, and then handed the rest of the box to me. Reaching in his knapsack he found a Beinfang watercolor pad, 21 x 27 cm, the thick absorbent pages rustling as he flipped through the book.

"This is new. I…I hope it's all right." He handed the pad to me.

"Where did you get this?" I was too stunned to remember to thank him.

He eased to the ground and leaned his back against the bench. "Manavgat. There's a small art store there. I bought it a while ago, but the time never seemed right to give it to you."

I flushed and looked away. "Because I was so snotty?"

Xiao laughed, gazing out the doorway, taking in the view across the courtyard littered with hunks of ancient marble.

"People have done worse than pointedly ignore me."

"I'm sorry, Xiao. I was insensitive about your country, and then I was such *un cochon* on top of it. I'm not very good at being nice."

There was that lopsided smile that I love, creeping up the corner of his left mouth, looking amused and poignant at the same time. "You're not a pig, Tatyana. You don't have to let your past tell you who to be."

He reached for his knapsack. With a little water from a plastic bottle he wet the stone, then he began scraping and mixing ink with deep concentration, as though he had forgotten me.

I opened the watercolor pad and ran my fingertips over the faintly bumpy surface. This wasn't Stephen Quiller paper, which, as Mme. Groseille used to complain, cost more for one sheet than a good plum tart, but it was levels above the thin, lined notebook pages I'd been struggling with. I opened the box of inks. I wanted to paint Xiao: his strong neck and scarred chest bent over his calligraphy, the crook of his substantial knuckles around the slender wooden brush, and his thick, soft lips pulled together in meditation. Feeling a little shy, I studied the colors of his skin and chose my inks. I could smell thyme, growing off in some patch somewhere, visited by humming bees. I could smell Xiao: faint hints of salt water with undertones of warm man. Slowly I let myself drift into seeing only him, every breath that expanded his chest, every strand of hair wafting with the breeze into his parted lips, every shift of his spine to accommodate the hard stone he leaned against. When I could feel him completely, I started to paint.

I did painting after painting. He wrote, sometimes lying on his belly in the dust. He wandered out into the courtyard in the sun, sat on a stone and leaned back on his locked arms, his face up into the noon glare. He napped, flat on his back with the crook of his elbow over his eyes, twitching with dreams. He lifted from his knapsack my old drawings of crickets, and studied them one by one. Then he wrote some more, calligraphy flowing down the page.

Around noon, he took a brown paper package from his sack and opened it. It was a thin, flat round of crust, spread with minced beef. He took a jar of tomatoes and cucumber out of his pack and spread it over this Turkish version of pizza, then squeezed on a half a lemon. "*Lahmacun?*" he asked, cutting it apart and offering half to me.

I put aside my drawings and took the messy slice. We ate together without speaking, listening to the drone of cicadas in the hot afternoon. Heat rose off sand and marble, making the air shimmer like the surface of a mirror.

When I had finished eating, I wiped my hands on a cloth

he offered, and then leaned back against the bench. "Tell me about your family," I said.

"*Qui?*" he asked, looking surprised. "My mom and dad?"

"Yes, and brothers and sisters."

"No brothers or sisters. I'm from China, remember: '*Deal resolute blows against excess birth guerrillas!*'" He laughed at his dramatization of Mao's pronouncement. "Our family could never afford the birth fine. Anyway, my parents were already in too much trouble to openly violate the law."

"Why were your mom and dad in trouble?"

Xiao looked down at his *Lahmacun*, which draped over his fingers as though it suffered from the heat.

"My father was the renowned Thuzong Chin. He came from a long line of China's revered gourmet chefs. Once upon a time, a chef in China was half poet, half magician."

He folded the remains of his thin bread, and stuffed meat, which had crept to the edges, back in between the folds.

"My father could blend flavors until they became sleight of hand, something completely unexpected. A perfectly baked chicken made of tofu, a roasted duck made of vegetables." Xiao finished his last bite and wiped his big hands carefully on a cloth. "He was from the Hangzhou line of chefs, and could put together a meal whose courses were like stanzas in a poem. For the poor, work meant eating: *jiao gu*, to have grains to chew. But for the rich eating is a cultural heritage, an intellectual pursuit, no less important than civilization itself. The Chinese arrogantly suppose that they alone see food this way, but I notice a parallel attitude in the French."

I laughed. "*Absolument.*" Absolutely.

"Chinese are no less proud, but we hide our best food from the unsuspecting world, so they think we eat sweet and sour pork chops." He laughed and folded the cloth, tucking it away. "Imperial China fell only nine years before my father was born. Nine years between centuries of emperors, and the modern world." He flicked an ant off his knee with his thumb and rubbed at the spot where it had bitten him.

"My family survived the Japanese occupation of Shanghai in 1937 by hiding in the French Concession. They had money, so my father was tutored in Confucian Analects, Tang dynasty poetry, and Chinese classics. Then he was sent to Hangzhou to his grandfather, to learn the family tradition of cooking. He came back to Shanghai a rising young chef, sought after by the rich."

Xiao's hand wandered to the scars on his chest and lightly passed over the damage. "My father was twenty-nine when Mao seized power. He woke one morning to the soldiers of the People's Liberation Army, sleeping on his front porch. As badly as the soldiers treated his friends—executions, re-education, personal political files—they never touched my father's family. The party leadership needed to eat, after all, and who better to serve them?" He didn't sound bitter, but his voice had an edge that made it sharp.

Xiao spread his hands wide, as though judging their large reach, then tightened them into a knot. "He was passed from party official to party official like a whore, until the Great Leap Forward. Then, because he spoke French, he was attached to the branch of government that managed the foreigners who poured in."

"My father was the French ambassador in Shanghai during that time."

"*Voila.* It's a small world, *n'est pas*?" Xiao's anger melted away and he gave me a sweet smile, as though he approved of this distant connection.

"What happened to your dad during the Cultural Revolution?"

"He died. He was sent to a labor camp in Manchuria to dig irrigation ditches and sow grain. He died in a mud and grass hut, of starvation." Xiao fastened the full darkness of his eyes on mine, not shielding me from his pain. "I don't think he died of physical starvation, I think he died because he could see nothing worth living for."

I swallowed and nodded. I understood. "And your mom?"

Xiao smiled, warm as Incir's noon sand. "My *maman*? She's a peasant girl who walked from Guangdong to Shanghai with a bag of old clothes over her shoulder, and sweet-talked her way into Dad's kitchen as a scullery maid. Because of her impeccable peasant pedigree, she was spared re-education and sent home."

"Guangdong? Isn't that where you went to escape?"

"*Oui.* It was uncles and cousins who smuggled me out."

Xiao raised his arms behind his head and stretched. I could see strong collar bones between the open buttons of his shirt. I wanted to run my fingertips over them.

"*Eh alors….*" I dragged my gaze to his face. "…Your relatives forced you to deed them your Beijing apartment, in exchange for escape?"

Xiao flushed. "Did I admit that? I must have been drunker

than I remember." Then he grinned. "*Oui*, they're ruthless."

"So your *maman* is still alive?"

"*Oui*. Alive and well protected. Guangdong is one of the few places where Party cadres are scared of the locals. My uncles are shady, with a reputation for vindictiveness. Without them, I could never have been so outspoken."

"What do you mean?"

Xiao blinked. "Well because of my mother, of course. I would never have endangered her, not even for my motherland."

"What did you do, anyway, to upset the officials so much?"

Xiao reached over and picked a painting off the stack. It was one of him, napping. His arm had fallen aside and his mythic face was in full sun, half bleached by the glare, looking like a warrior from an ancient dream.

"Why don't we talk about you for awhile?" He lay the drawing across one knee. "How is it that you paint so well? Did you have instruction?"

I stared uncomfortably at the pitted, ancient Roman wall across the courtyard. It was only fair that I be as honest as he had been.

"*Oui*, but I was inattentive. I feel sorry for my teachers. The classes were just an excuse for me to draw in peace, and my teachers mostly irritated me."

The intense noon sun made the shadows on the concrete bricks look unreal, as if they'd been shaded with black pencil.

"Your art is amazing." Xiao turned his eyes to the ground, as though suddenly shy of me. "It is not just that things look alive, it's as if they are about to speak, or just moved. You capture how it feels to *be* that thing."

The compliment took me by surprise, and I flushed hot, struggling for a response.

Sitting cross-legged, Xiao laid his palms together and rested them in his lap. "I realize that this may be awkward for you, but, may I speak my mind?"

"*Bien sûr,*" I whispered.

"When you died...I mean," he laughed, "...when we thought that you had died, Umut came to my room looking for the portrait that you had done of me." He shifted his weight over crossed legs and leaned forward, filling the space between us. "Umut shoved the portrait into my hands. For the first time I dared to really look at it. I had seen it before, of course, the day we argued in the arena. That day I saw only my scars and how furious they were, carved in red across my chest. I try to forget them, you see. And in your drawing they were so...fresh."

He grimaced, as he had that day in the arena.

"I...I'm sorry," I stammered.

"No! Don't be." Xiao met my gaze, and I flushed again and turned away from the intensity of his warmth. "Umut made me look at the portrait. I couldn't believe that you knew me so well. Here I thought you never looked at me, had nothing to say. That you only sat in judgment, but did not participate in the world. And all the while you took in the essence of all you saw. Even that nasty scar, you drew with such compassion and sensitivity. I completely misjudged you. I apologize." He bowed his head. "I apologize for mistaking you for a bourgeois piece of intellectual fluff. I truly saw you that way. I was no more capable of seeing your worth, than The Party was capable of understanding my father. Forgive me."

Speechless, I reached a hand and gripped the hardened strength of his shoulder. Touching him sent a pulse, shooting down my center, hot and wet. I took a quick breath.

"Please, Xiao." I leaned forward and slid my hand along his smooth skin, up to his chin, raising his face to mine. "I am an awful person, not worth the space I occupy. You read me correctly the first time. My drawing is a fluke—an idiot doing calculus. Don't suffer on my account."

For a moment I was within centimeters of him, his mouth ample and soft, his eyes looking into mine. The early afternoon light turned the skin on his cheeks to polished bronze.

I'll never know what would have happened next, because Umut burst onto the scene, dashing as fast as jackrabbit legs could propel him. Xiao stumbled to a stand and backed away, his posture denying how close we'd been. Umut grunted and babbled in Turkish, which Xiao appeared to understand, and he answered hesitantly, the language equally awkward in both of their mouths.

"He says the boys are coming." Xiao stooped and gathered up his calligraphy and ink stick, as though looking for something other than me to occupy him.

Surging and glowing inside, uncomfortably aware of Xiao's heat only a meter away, I stood and brushed dust off my *çarşaf*. I tucked escaping hairs into my head covering, trying to look proper. "The boys?"

"Kazim, İbrahim, and Hüseyin—the three who attacked you. They want to apologize for their behavior." Xiao appeared to have recovered his composure, and he gave an amused smile. "Yurda apparently told you about it this morning. She somehow can't believe that you don't understand every word she says."

"Do you know them?"

"Of course, I know everyone in Incir. I fish with these boys."

I gathered up my portraits of Xiao's half-naked beauty and shoved them into my knapsack. "They aren't in jail?"

"*Non.* There was no murder. The police have taken their bribes and washed their hands of the affair."

"Why are they apologizing? Can't we just leave well enough alone?"

Xiao stood too close to me, too far from me, his heat stronger than the smell of the lavender and making me a bit light-headed.

"I'm sure their *imam* insisted on it. The community has been harmed, and good will must be restored. Have you ever lived in a small town?"

"*Non.*"

"Next to a good harvest, relationships are our most important resource." Xiao winked at me. His smile had a mocking sweetness. "Just ask my uncle Zhao, from Guangdong."

Sweaty harvest aside, Uncle Zhao would have done well in diplomatic circles. I backed away and sat on the marble bench, half concealed in the deep shade. Umut sidled over and squatted at my feet as though he were my guardian rabbit.

The boys arrived a few minutes later, shuffling up a dust cloud that gave thickness to the stark sunlight. The two younger ones walked in front, looking humiliated beyond endurance, every attempt at honor or pride scoured from their faces. They were children, I realized, racked with guilt. Thank God they had not died for our foolishness.

The leader still had a festering scar on his cheek. In contrast to the other two, he looked tougher and broader today, more like a man. He put a hand on one friend's shoulder, pushing the boy forward. The boy stumbled to a stop in front of Xiao and stared at the sand, trembling.

He muttered something in Turkish.

"This is Kazim," said Xiao. "With his deepest respect he asks that you forgive him. He has asked his *imam* to show him the path to correct behavior."

Kazim had a cowlick on the crown of his head that made his hair stand up like a wave from the sea—a talisman Suat Bey claimed could protect a child from drowning. That cowlick was now bowed towards me, and I had to fight the sisterly urge to pat the curl back down.

Kazim backed away, eyes down, and the next boy slunk forward, avoiding all eyes by fixing his gaze on the claws of the lion's foot that supported my bench.

"This is İbrahim. He will regret forever his part in harming you, and he praises God that you are well."

İbrahim's eyes were too sad for a boy so young. The thought of him huddled, shivering and terrified in the dreaded Turkish jail, was too much for me. I turned away to hide my tears.

The leader pushed between his two comrades. "This is Hüseyin." The young man stood rigid, as if he intended to take a beating without flinching. "He asks that…." Xiao paused and blinked. "He asks that you forgive him for letting desire mislead him. He sees now that what he does affects more than himself."

There was a long silence, during which cicadas droned. *What he does affects more than himself.* A crow fluttered down and hopped a few steps towards Xiao's open water bottle, forgotten in the center of the courtyard. With a jab of its beak, it knocked the bottle over and drank as the liquid spilled into the yellow sand.

Finally Xiao said to me, "Do you have anything to say?"

I closed my eyes. I could feel Umut, his back pressing lightly against my legs as he breathed. I wished I was miles away. But I wasn't. I was getting too old to run from my mistakes.

"I was disrespectful to your village, your religion, and your customs. Please forgive me for being such an arrogant fool," I said.

Xiao translated, articulating the words carefully with polite deference, and it occurred to me that, as he knew and fished with these boys, he was probably a reluctant witness to their humiliation.

The younger boys looked visibly relieved that it was over. They turned and hurried away by the goat path. Hüseyin lingered in the clearing, shifting awkwardly from foot to foot as he mustered the courage to speak. Finally he looked me full in the face, and smiled.

"He asks if it is true that you have accepted Islam as your faith," said Xiao.

I could barely convince myself to speak. With a prayer for Yurda's pardon and Suat Bey's understanding, I whispered the truth. "*Non*."

Xiao did not translate my answer. His deep-set gaze bored into his leather flip-flops as if he were very uncomfortable.

"He wonders if you are available for marriage," he said.

Like a bucket of water in the face, I gave an involuntary gasp. What did Hüseyin see that so fascinated him? Xiao described me as slender and elusive. I suspected that Hüseyin focused instead on my curves, curves that had once appeared quite accessible.

"Tell him, I...I am honored that he asked, but I do not intend to marry," I stuttered.

"Then he asks you to remember him if you change your mind. Praise Allah," said Xiao softly. With a slight bow of his head, Hüseyin strode out of the clearing and disappeared into the brush.

I hastily gathered my things. "I'm going back to my room," I said, slinging my knapsack over a shoulder. I stepped around Umut and hurried through the brush. If Xiao followed me, he stayed out of sight.

In my room I locked the door and yanked off the *çarşaf*, exposing my jeans and sweaty T-shirt.

*What we do affects more than ourselves.*

I went to the desk and lifted the mirror, peering into its

reflection. The glass was dark with my eyes, and with a shadow of Xiao's eyes. I wanted to be worthy of love. I'd been sarcastic and gruff with the none-too-bright Mme. Groseille, jealously cold to my sister Emma, and had needled my controlling father mercilessly. For the first time it dawned on me, that they may suffer over my disappearance. Perhaps I had not simply faded like a stain out of a dress. Perhaps I had torn a rent in their lives. Perhaps much of my loneliness was of my own making.

I put down the mirror and went to my bed. Trembling, belly pressed into the mattress, I propped myself on one elbow, picked a charcoal and sheet of *cahier* paper off the floor, and began to draw.

It took a minute to recognize the face: the deep furrow between his eyebrows; a crop of dark, thick hair barely tamed by scissors; the lips pursed tight over a biting insight. In my drawing he held his head high and back, as if to make a man of normal stature, taller. But he looked down, down onto the heads of his two daughters, and in the folds around his eyes was a wavering cringe, as if despite all appearances, he doubted himself. My father had been at a loss, I realized, a complete loss as to how to raise a child. Every step of the way, he had stumbled.

I put aside the drawing and picked up another lined, hole-punched page. This time I drew the head of an alluring young woman. Straight, long nose sliding down her slender oblong face. Masses of dark hair piled on her head and held in place with diamond hairpins. Soft, bare shoulders restrained by yards of white voile and satin. And her eyes, shadowed and dark, watching like a cornered animal. Even on the night of her debutante ball, as all of upper crust Paris admired her, Emma was desperate to escape. Wretched, trapped, awaiting her chance. I knew it well. We had struggled with the same fate.

I laid that drawing on my pillow and took another blank page. This time I drew a whole body: the matronly weight made chic by haute couture; the shoes as polished as her decorum; the hands clutching a purse that held her small salary; the eyes worn to dull gray by years of thankless service. She had no children of her own, no husband, no lover. She would have cared for me as a daughter, if I had let her. I did nothing but add to Mme. Groseille's unhappiness, and to her list of chores.

I tore a fourth blank page into thirds. On each I wrote, "I am well, please don't worry. Tatyana." Taking three envelopes, I addressed to each their own drawing: Boris Trotoskov, Emma Galt, and Mme. Claire Groseille. That night I gave the letters to Della, to mail when she was far, far away.

# FIFTEEN

The next day, Xiao and I walked down the cliff path to the sea. Yellow sand stretched into the waves, both sand and water rippled from the constant breeze. I stopped to absorb one more time the blue of the Mediterranean, so luminescent that it took my breath away.

Xiao stood beside me, carrying our knapsacks. "If we go east down the beach, there is a small cove where locals never go. We could swim there."

"I can't swim in a *çarşaf.*"

"*Non.*" Xiao laughed.

"You won't tell Yurda if I take it off?"

"Yurda's still after me for drinking too much Raki. She reminds me of the prep chef in my dad's kitchen. Every time he wanted something from me, he'd recall the time I stole a Hami melon from the pantry. Then he'd ask me to scrub the pots."

Xiao turned, walking backwards down the beach, the wind blowing his long hair forward over his face, brushing his wonderful lips that smiled and smiled. He had been so serious before, so devout. That day he looked positively playful.

"I worry about disappointing Yurda," I yelled after him.

"You will disappoint Yurda, but if you're not a little trouble now and then, mothers have nothing to do." He slung the knapsacks further up his shoulders. "*Viens,* can you run in that thing?"

"I don't know."

"You want to try?"

I hoisted thick cotton to my knees and gathered handfuls in a firm grip. "On your mark, get set...."

But he didn't wait. He took off, galloping down the beach like a camel, two humps of knapsack swinging wildly on his huge back. I raced after him, catching him finally when the weight of our sacks slowed him down. We crawled over a rock promontory, the cuffs of my bloomers damp from splashing waves. When we reached the top I stopped, entranced.

We stood above a cove of baking beach that ended against a tall cliff. Rocks closed the semicircle at the other end. Gulls, used to having this piece of heaven all to themselves, napped in the sun, one orange foot pulled into the downy fluff of their bellies.

"Does it please you?" asked Xiao, glancing shyly at my face.

"It's perfect." I scrambled down rocks, startling gulls, who squawked and waddled down the beach.

I surveyed the cove, and seeing no one I could offend, I shrugged off the *çarşaf* and shook out my hair. In shorts and a T-shirt, I danced towards the water. "Do you swim?" I asked.

Xiao lifted his shirt over his head. "I was raised in Shanghai, on the East China Sea. I know how to swim." He laughed his lopsided smile, ironic. "But mostly I've ridden waves of political reform."

His brown skin had a soft matt sheen. His chest was sculpted with broad, bold sweeps, and was much more desirable than any of the models who sat for me at École des

Beaux-Arts. I wondered if it was a woman's name, written above his breast, and then dismissed this as silly jealousy. I turned my face toward the sea and took a deep breath of cool wind.

Staggering into the rough water, I dove into the curl. Giving myself over to the torrent, I closed my eyes and washed towards the beach. When the wave retreated it left me flat and happy in the sand. Xiao and I threw ourselves into the sea again and again, tumbling over and over and spitting out sand on the beach. Xiao's long, black hair became as knotted and full of seaweed as mine. His brown skin turned pink over the swell of his shoulders. He laughed until the somber pain melted from his eyes, and their darkness took on a honey warmth.

The current had pulled us gradually toward the rocks, so we climbed a boulder and sat, my leg not quite touching his. Though he was centimeters away, I could feel his skin. I thought of the mirror, and wondered what it would be like to be bound to Xiao by a spell. In the bright sunshine, the curse seemed an alluring fantasy.

I pushed knotted hair out of my eyes and said, "You grow your hair so long."

Across the cove, a flock of seagulls fought over a dead creature in the sand. Xiao watched, half distracted by the raucous scuffle.

"I grow it in honor of my friend, Bao."

"Why, in honor of Bao?"

He turned his full attention to me, eyes traveling the length of me from my sandy toes to my riotous matt of blonde tangles. Not like men in Paris look at women— picking the parts they approve of and staring with bold appreciation. It was more a reading, as if I were a book. He must have decided that I was a good read, because he said, "Bao was a railroad worker, like me. He tried to organize us into a labor union and disappeared one day. When he came back the police had shaved off all of his hair. I don't know what else happened to him because he refused to speak about it."

"So…you don't cut your hair?"

"Actually, our whole railroad crew shaved ourselves as bald as Bao, when he returned." He spread a hand on the rock, the black and brown a pleasing contrast, like a sepia photograph. "Then when his hair grew out, he wouldn't let anyone cut it. So I don't cut mine either."

"I'm not sure I understand. Why would Bao care?"

Xiao's hand slowly closed, like an anemone pulling in.

"Face. You know—pride. If a friend is publicly humiliated, it's what others do—share the humiliation." He reached up and pulled back his mess of hair, almost brushing my cheek with his flexed biceps. I felt the tingling across my face.

And then it dawned on me.

"Is that why you got drunk, to share in my humiliation?"

Xiao looked away. In profile, the roundness of his nose looked flatter, making his eyes and mouth even more prominent.

"*Eh bien*, you understand." He stood up.

I sat dumb. What an amazing thing to do—to take on another's dishonor. Not something I had ever encountered, in the diplomatic dog fight of Boris' world.

"Thank you, Xiao."

He had his back to me. "Don't mention it." He climbed over the rocks, heading toward the beach. "What will you paint today?"

I rose, too, and we made our way back to the sandy cove.

"Water."

"Why water?"

"I want to get the color right. I never want to forget. It's a color that could feed me forever, like loaves and fishes." I sat down by the knapsacks and took out the box of inks.

Xiao watched as I set up my inkstone palette. "I never thought of colors as feeding anyone."

I chose the white ink stick, the green, blue, yellow, red, even the black; I needed them all. "What will you do?"

"I want to write my mother, so she doesn't worry. She can't read, but the monk down the road will read it to her."

He reached into our box and took out the black ink stick.

"Tell me about your mother."

"There's not much to say. You'd like her smile, very soft. I think it was her smile that my father fell for."

A soft mouth, a sweet smile. Like Xiao's. And like yours, my Little Cricket.

"What's her name?"

"Jiè. Her name is Jiè Wanhua Wang."

And so now you know, my little one, how you got your name.

I scraped the white ink stick on the stone and added another drop of water. Green was the trickiest part, because water isn't really green, it just looked green when the gold of the sun passed through blue waves.

"Tell me how you got into so much trouble."

Xiao put down his brush. "I can't write a letter with all of this chatter."

"You don't want to tell me."

"*Non.* I don't like to think about it."

"I guess I'll have to wait until you've had too much Raki."

Xiao flushed, laughing, and the scar on his chest turned a dusky, violaceous hue. He picked up his brush and dipped it in ink.

"Why don't you tell me something about you?" With steady, swift strokes he formed boxy Chinese characters.

"What do you want to know?"

"Why did you leave Paris?"

"It doesn't matter."

Xiao put down his brush and stretched his legs into the sand, digging a trench where they slid. "Are we friends?" he asked.

"I hope so."

"Then you need to give back. You can't just take all the time."

For a second the world stood still. Of course. One gave to people by telling them your story, like Suat Bey, only perhaps less…embellished. It had never before occurred to me that intimacy was a gift.

"I'm sorry. I'll tell you. Give me a moment to think."

I mixed in green, watching it darken the white until I had just the shade of foam's translucency. I put blue on a separate inkstone, scraping it carefully.

"I was accepted full time at École des Beaux-Arts. I was to

study under Marie Creusault. Do you know her work? She's one of France's best contemporary painters. Less abstract. She doesn't lose herself in the theoretical, she goes more for emotion and beauty. You understand?"

"I think so. And what happened?"

"My father said no. He enrolled me in the Sorbonne, to study law and political science. If I was not content to be merely a diplomat's wife, I could be a politician. With his influence, he could guide me to the top. Perhaps someday France would accept a woman president."

Xiao's lips parted slowly, and his eyes widened with disbelief. "And that's why you left? Because he wanted to help you...." He snapped his jaw closed and turned away.

"It was not what I wanted."

Xiao shook his head. "I would die, almost did die, for the chance to influence China's government. I can't believe you turned that down."

"I'd make an awful president, and an even worse president's wife."

His eyes bored into mine, restraining anger behind his stony countenance. "Don't you have any sense of responsibility? How can you turn away, when the chance to touch so many lives is practically handed to you?"

His anger stabbed a spiky wound into what was most fundamental about me. Searing pain shot through my center.

"It wasn't right for me. The only peace I find in life is through art. Art is all I'm good at, and all I want to do."

*"Merde alors."*

I'd never heard Xiao swear. He looked away.

"I need to take a walk. I'll be back in a while." He stood up, dropping globs of sand over his calligraphy. Grains congealed on the wet inkstones, and a fine layer dusted the wooden box. Head down, he walked away. His bare back blurred as I watched him wander down the beach.

Mizou was right, we not only came from different worlds, we sought different worlds. It would be best, really, if I did not love him. But these are not things we choose, are they, my little Jiè?

A tear dripped into the blue on the inkstone, diluting it to the watery wash I needed. Picking up my brush, I forced my thoughts away from Xiao, away from his eyes in the mirror, that glass looming behind us like a crouched beast. I thought instead about being lost in the Mediterranean, kilometers of blue water all around me, dying in that color that I love so much. With all my heart, I painted the sea.

Xiao came back some while later. I was too absorbed in my work to be aware of the passage of time, but I felt him, still hot with emotion, beside me. He picked up his calligraphy brush and wrote a long letter, painting each character with passion. I found myself surreptitiously watching him, my concentration *gâché* by his brooding and my pain. I had the urge to apologize, but…for what? Because I didn't long to save the world? Because I didn't have either the charisma, or the stamina, to sway a regime?

I began to burn with anger. He missed the value of my art. He admitted that I was good, but gave it no value. As though I painted window dressings for the Bon Marché. I wasn't Picasso, but looking at the sea gripped in my hands, the washed and blended foam of it crashing over the page, I knew I was good. Better than good.

I gathered up my inkstones, brushed off the sand, and rinsed them with painty fingers at the edge of the sea. I collected my ink sticks and arranged them in the box. I wiped my hands on my shorts and slipped on the pants of the *çarşaf*.

"I'm going home."

Chucking my painting into Xiao's lap, I reached in my knapsack for the top half of the *çarşaf*. With surprising proficiency I pinned it closed under my chin.

Xiao picked up the page and stared at my work. Then he must have realized that I really was leaving, because he scrambled to put away his calligraphy brush, ink, and stone. Hastily, he dusted himself off.

"You don't have to leave just because I'm leaving." I grabbed my knapsack and started down the beach.

"Yes, I do." With the box under one arm and his knapsack over the other, he came after me. He caught me in five quick strides. "I promised Suat Bey I'd look after you."

"I'm sorry he placed such a burden on you."

I shook his hand off my shoulder and advanced down the beach, sand weighing down the damp cuffs of my *çarşaf*.

Xiao said nothing.

I clamored over rocks and down to the hotel beach, then took off walking as fast as I could, my baggy pants snapping as they whipped around my shoes. It didn't matter how fast I strode, I couldn't leave him behind. With big, easy lopes he stayed alongside me.

"Tatyana, wait a minute."

I didn't even look at him. Trotoskovs know when to gather the army and retreat.

"Tatyana, stop, I have something very important to confess." He reached for my elbow, but I slid my arm across my chest, out of his reach.

By this time I was practically jogging. I reached the narrow path up the cliff to the temple, and climbed it in such a huff that I was out of breath at the top. The sinking sun was perfect on the marble of Apollo's columns, burning them rosy, but I didn't stay. I swept into the hotel, up the stairs and into my room, closing the door smartly behind me. Such was the nature of my stupidity. If only I had stopped and let him speak. If only I had listened.

I went straight to my desk and dumped the knapsack.

"Go to hell, Xiao," I whispered into the mirror's glass. "I refuse to love you anymore. You can just go to hell."

# SIXTEEN

I slept poorly; Yue Fei galloped around, bloodying up my dreams, and Xiao's scar pulsed urgently before me, a gory message that I couldn't decipher. I woke to discover the mirror beside me in bed. Sometime during the night I must have put it there. I dressed for breakfast and went down in my *çarşaf*.

The dining room was in an uproar. Damad had found a puppy, a mutt with the long nose and slender eyes of an Egyptian Golden Jackal, but the more stoutly muscled body of a shepherd. For a half-feral animal, he was quite friendly. He wiggled among the folds of my clothes, putting warm paws first on my lap, then on Della's. He had the instinct to avoid Mizou. He licked cheese off Xiao's fingers, and then chewed on Suat Bey's laces, causing Suat Bey to tell the story of the time he almost froze to death in the Küre Mountains and had to eat his shoes. The puppy dragged the greasy lamb bone Kemal gave him across Mizou's rug, and when he squatted to widdle, Mizou swept him up roughly and dumped him out the back door.

"I don't want a dog in the house." Mizou looked lethal as she came back from the kitchen, slamming the dining room door behind her.

"Oh, what's the harm? Just a little puppy." Suat Bey sopped up honey with a hunk of bread and used it to gesture towards Damad. "A boy needs something to wrestle."

"They spread diseases and tear up the furniture." Mizou lowered herself rigidly into her chair, regal and furious.

Xiao, Della, and I studied our plates, observers, not family, when it came to a domestic squabble.

"Really, there's no harm in the *petit chien*." Suat Bey took a swig of tea and stared down his wife as though she were an advancing army. "He stays, and that's final."

Yurda came in with a bowl of steaming boiled eggs, muttering into the folds of her headpiece. If I didn't know her better, I'd have thought she was swearing. She bypassed Suat Bey's outstretched hand and plunked the food in front of Mizou, making it clear where her allegiance lay.

"*Pardon, je m'excuse.*" I rose from the table and escaped out the back door, Xiao following. The sun was already hot, and cicadas buzzed a monotonous drone, making the air quiver. I slung my sack over my shoulder and took off down the path towards the temple, determined to put distance between myself and Xiao. Xiao's footsteps thudded behind me in the sand.

As I arrived at the temple, I decided it was beneath me to try and out-run him, so I tossed aside my sack and threw myself onto the altar, feeling the cool damp on my back. Xiao scooped up my sack and held it, drooping on one crooked finger as if it weighed nothing. He rested against one of Apollo's columns, his back to the sea. I looked past him to the far horizon, where waves melted into sky. Gulls drifted overhead like flakes of white. Neither of us said anything for a long time. I certainly had no intention of breaking the silence.

Finally Xiao said, "I know somewhere special I would like to take you."

I shielded my pupils from the sun so I could see the dark of his eyes. "You don't have to do this, Xiao. When they are done arguing in there I'll ask Mizou to find me another chaperone."

"I like to be with you." He said it simply, with such flat emotion that it sounded merely of loyalty. Loyalty to Suat Bey, no doubt.

I rolled onto my side, tucking my feet into the drapes of my *çarşaf*. With my head propped in one hand, I stared at him. I couldn't read his expression. He looked stony, far away, as remote as his father's prison camp.

"What does it say on your chest?" I asked.

This broke his aloofness. Startled and confused, he met my gaze. For three beats of my heart he appeared to consider whether to answer. Then he dropped the knapsacks and sunk onto his heels in a squat. I could hear his breath, coming in short, sharp exhales.

"It says, 'serve the country loyally'. It's what Yue Fei's mother tattooed on his back." He put his fingers to the sand and dug them in.

"You know that you look like Yue Fei?"

Xiao snorted. "Of course."

"Did your mother cut that into you?"

"My mother? *Non.* My mother is so soft hearted she cries when she wrings the neck of a chicken. She could never take a knife to me."

I sat up. "Who then?" I asked out of spite, peeve, wounded

adoration. It was no sooner out of my mouth than I regretted my cruelty.

He didn't answer. He looked like a man humbled by a great burden, his head bowed, his braid a heavy black snake wrapped around his neck, his fingers now dug six centimeters in the soil. He said nothing.

Too ashamed to just sit there, I went to crouch beside him. I put my hands on his cheeks, warm and a little rough where he shaved, and I lifted his face to mine. We were only centimeters apart, the softness of his lips so close that his breath made me tingle.

"I'm sorry, Xiao. Forgive me. My little *souffrances* are nothing compared to what you have endured."

"*Tais-toi*," he said. Shut-up.

And he kissed me, pressing warmth and breath, cracking open a door, and I was flooded with want. For a brief moment we flowed together into desire. Then he pulled back, clearly as surprised by the kiss as I had been.

His eyes on mine, his lips still a breath away, he whispered, "They cut me down after two months, and the policeman said—" Xiao leaned forward and touched his lips to mine, a tingling, restrained brush. "—'I mark your chest so you can never come home, scum. China doesn't want you!'" His voice was gruff, barely audible. "I was so dead to the world by then, the knife slices hardly hurt. Why are you crying, Tatyana? I survived, and here I am, with you."

And he kissed me again, the sweetness overwhelming and salty from my tears.

It was the *kara çarşaf* that saved you, my little Jiè.

Squatting in its voluminous folds I couldn't get my arms around him. I stood to untangle myself, wiping away tears, and the puppy danced into Apollo's clearing, chased by Damad, Umut, and Yurda.

The puppy pranced between us, mangling Yurda's wooden spatula in baby teeth. Yurda roared after the mutt, one hand gripping her pants and the other flailing furiously, practically bowling us over. The boys spun around us like sprites as I stumbled, emotions reeling, frantically backing away from our compromised position. Had Yurda seen what we were drawing toward, I might have lost my chaperone there and then. Perhaps you would never have been conceived. As it was, we went to Manavgat instead.

Manavgat. A dusty, long hitchhike to Serik, followed by a crowded bus ride. More singing on the bus. It was hot. I pulled folds of the *çarşaf* over my face against the dust and sat as close to Xiao as I dared, neither of us speaking. I think both of us had been frightened by the levy that the kisses had broken, and neither of us were ready to drown.

When we arrived, he led me through a maze of streets to the market. Behind a stall that sold brass pots, crowded by another stall that sold cinnamon sticks and garlic, was the door to the art shop. Inside it was cool and quiet.

The owner rushed forward when he saw Xiao, exclaiming in Turkish. They jabbered together like old friends, perched on stools that the owner dragged from the back. After a polite hello and a glass of tea, I excused myself and explored. Lefranc & Bourgeois oils, Italian painting knives, pre-stretched canvas panels, Gouache watercolors, Canson acrylic pads…I was possessed by gluttony. While they drank tea, I amassed a pile that even Xiao would struggle to carry home. I drank another glass of tea, nodding at the owner's sociable attempts to speak English.

We left in the late afternoon, wandering through the streets, sweating under the weight of my avarice. Women shook rugs out the windows as they do in Paris. Coffeehouses overflowed with men. Shopkeepers called from doorways, pleading with us to buy, or at least stop and socialize. Xiao found a taxi stand and raised his arm. The taxi stopped and they bargained over price as I wilted in the heat. Finally we put everything in the trunk and settled into the back, the windows rolled down and a sticky breeze in our faces. I leaned my head against the seat, my throat to the peeling cloth of the ceiling. I could smell old cigarettes in the taxi's ash tray.

"What will you paint first?" Xiao asked, eyes closed and shirt front open to the rush of air from the window.

"The hotel. I want to make a painting for Mizou. Do you realize that there is not a single painting in the whole *pension*?"

"I hadn't noticed."

"I want to paint one for every room, with the view from that room."

"My room, too?"

"Of course."

Xiao smiled and turned his head away, as if suddenly shy.

"From my room I can see Apollo's Temple. You've already painted that."

"Which makes me eminently qualified to paint it again."

"You, painting in my room," he breathed. Xiao had his face to the scenery flowing by the window, so I couldn't see his expression, but he sounded as though he were awed with wonder.

"With a chaperone," I added, "to protect my reputation."

He turned back to me. He gave a quick glance to the front to see that the driver was not watching, then brushed my throat with his fingertip. "I am your chaperone."

I caught his hand in mine and set its thick heat back in his lap. "Xiao we have to be careful. We can't put the dragon to guard the treasure, *n'est pas*?"

"In China, dragons are good luck."

"Luck?" I asked. The taxi driver lit a cigarette and noxious blue fumes wove towards Xiao's open window.

"My father doesn't believe in luck. Everything is diplomacy and cunning. Calculate correctly, and you always win."

"Perhaps your father is right."

"I don't know." I watched the stream of smoke disappear in the wind. "Do you believe in magic?"

"Of course. Chinese are very superstitious. We have charms, sayings, and rituals for all important things. We are at heart a rural people, and all rural people are superstitious."

"You were raised in Shanghai. That's hardly a rice field."

"I was raised in Shanghai, with a kitchen god in the kitchen altar, spirit money on my grandmother's tomb, and ten thousand other daily rituals to appease my ancestors. My father's grave is sited on a hill that looks like the wings of a goose in flight. Very auspicious." He raised his dark eyebrows. "And you?"

"The only magic in my country was Joan of Arc. My father said she wasn't a witch, she was merely a nuisance. If she'd been a witch the English couldn't have hanged her so easily, and she would have been of more use."

Xiao gave a gracious smile. "I'm afraid the French were battered into rational thinking by The Enlightenment. Such a loss to French offspring." He checked the driver's attention again, and then reached for my hand. "But you haven't told me if you believe."

"Sometimes I believe, and sometimes I don't," I said, accepting his thick, ink-stained fingers into my cupped palms. "Sometimes I wish magic could change our destiny."

You see, Little Cricket, how we get what we wish for? I was too insecure in our budding love. Or perhaps too wise, having looked so long and hard at the Mona Lisa. Perhaps I suspected, even then, the truth. Or perhaps it was Hades mirror, eating away at my heart.

~

For the next ten days I painted at my new easel, set in front of the hotel. Ordinarily the hotel was a drab view, with its square, whitewashed face and regimented windows, topped by an ugly metal water barrel that filled the showers by gravity. But with Suat Bey's poetic license I distorted the angle so that Apollo's Temple stood boldly to the South of its real location, making a hotel garden. The beach swung around as though the *pension* were on a point, surrounded by the sea.

It took me three tries in water color and two tries in oil to get it right, but finally I created a canvas that made Mizou catch her breath, and we hung it together in the dining room, over the cedar table.

Painting outdoors brought me an audience, and soon I had townspeople dropping by, trying to look picturesque. I succumbed to their hints and began to paint portraits. I painted Turgut, the produce vendor, pulling his donkey cart full of tomatoes. I painted Kemal's fisherman friend Boya and his new bride Rüya, sitting with the tea set Kemal gave them as a wedding gift. I painted Damad and Umut, frolicking with the puppy. I painted Yurda's whole family, upright and satisfied, little ones crawling on their feet. I painted the three boys, Kazim, İbrahim, and Hüseyin, leaning proudly over Kazim's goat. I smoothed the scar I'd scratched on Hüseyin's cheek, and I painted him as handsome as the day that he lay on Apollo's altar. Before long I had painted at least one person from every family in Incir. I had something to give that everyone wanted; I had never known such heaven.

Gifts arrived. Turkish Lokum, sticky when bitten and smothered with powdered sugar, too sweet to eat. Chocolate. Late tulips from someone's garden. A basket of tomatoes, so ripe that they split when I touched them. Every morning there was something new in front of my bedroom door. There were no notes, no explanations. My room, once so bare and empty, was filled with color and enticing smells. I left the windows open to avoid being overwhelmed by the scent of flowers. I no longer screamed when I woke with crickets in my bed.

And every night, though I went to sleep with the mirror

on my desk, I woke with it beside me, sometimes even lying on my chest. I did not try to explain this, and I tried not to let it frighten me.

Xiao, who didn't feel obligated to chaperone as I sat in the shade of the pension, left every morning to fish with Kemal. He came back at night and took his place, smiling at me from across the table. Neither of us acknowledged the three kisses, or made any attempt to repeat them. Perhaps we were both aware of how flimsy a *çarşaf* is, when confronted with passion.

Now that the weather was hot, Mizou moved dinner to the patio north of the pension, and we ate outdoors under a corrugated iron roof. The conversation was lively, skipping from French, to English, to Turkish. Suat Bey told story after story and consumed enough Raki to kill a god. Della loaned me earrings and put my hair up. Mizou watched me with quiet, uneasy eyes. The puppy chewed. Yurda found a hundred things to scold me about, but I didn't understand a word of it, so I merely smiled and let her kiss me on both cheeks when she was done. It was, without a doubt, the happiest time of my life.

And then the puppy began to stagger.

# SEVENTEEN

It was subtle at first, a slight incoordination that caused the puppy to trip over his big paws and tumble over his nose. Damad and Umut thought it comical, and imitated it with somersaults. Within a day or two he stopped eating, and rapidly grew thin. Damad and Umut tried to comfort him, force him to eat, but he was irritable and wandered off into the brush alone. Then, three nights later as we all sat at dinner, he wobbled onto the patio. Whining piteously, he lurched towards Damad. Damad leaped from his chair to welcome him, but Mizou was faster. She swooped her little son into her arms and dumped him in Kemal's lap.

"Get up! Everyone, get up and go to the kitchen. Hurry!" hissed Mizou.

We rose uncertainly, knocking over chairs in our haste.

"Let me do this, Mizou," said Xiao quietly. He picked up the carving knife.

"*Non!* All of you leave. Now." She snatched up a cloth napkin and inched towards the dog.

In response to the noise and movement, the puppy began to snarl. Vicious, spine shaking growls lifted his upper lip as foam seeped from the corners of his mouth. Focusing on Mizou's moving feet, he lunged.

Xiao flung the carving knife, and though it hit the dog square in the neck it didn't stop his forward momentum.

Mizou grabbed the dog behind the ears just as it reached her ankle. Whispering a curse in a language I had never heard, she yanked the dog off her flesh and held it up, frothing and fighting at the end of her braceletted arm. She dangled a corner of the napkin in front of the puppy's nose. He snapped at the cloth, catching it in his teeth. Mizou wrapped the napkin tight, tying closed his snarling jaws. Then she drew out the knife Xiao had so accurately thrown, and stabbed the puppy in the heart.

Damad screamed. Pinned in the strong arms of his brother, he shrieked and shrieked. Kemal threw him over one shoulder and carried him, his little arms and legs thrashing, into the *pension,* away from the sight of his mother with her hands dripping foam and blood. The rest of us stood, frozen in horror.

Xiao was the first to recover. "Mizou, *viens vite*, we need to wash your wounds. Quickly." He pushed aside chairs and stunned observers and grabbed Mizou by the shoulders.

She dropped the dog.

"Yurda, bring me your strongest soap," Xiao commanded. Yurda stared blankly until Xiao repeated the request in Turkish, then she bustled off as Xiao dragged a protesting Mizou to the bathroom.

Kemal came back empty handed, scratched on the arms from Damad's fury and briskly slapping tears off his hardened, tanned cheeks. He sat down and poured himself a Raki.

"Well," said Della, "I guess we ladies had better clean up. Come on, hon." She took me by the elbow. "Let's get this dog buried. Don't touch it. We'll wrap it in the tablecloth."

Suat Bey set his Raki glass down with a thump. "A rabid dog," he mused. "I haven't seen one of those since 1942. It reminds me of the time…."

I whirled around. "How can you tell stories, Suat Bey? Mizou might die."

"Die?" Suat Bey laughed, a bark like a painful wound. "*Non.* A good Roma knows how she'll die. Mizou told me what's coming for her in the end, and it isn't a rabid dog. There are nights that she wishes it were a mere rabid dog, I'm sure." He reached for Kemal's Raki bottle and poured himself another drink. "Kemal, go help Della and *La Princess* bury the dog. Delicate flowers in silk saris shouldn't be hefting shovels."

Kemal got up and followed us, dragging the dead puppy wrapped in Mizou's tablecloth. Della and I watched as Kemal, stripped to the waist and browned muscles glistening sweat, dug a deep hole by a column of Apollo's Temple. We slipped in the dog, and then watched Kemal cover the hole.

"Should we say a prayer?" I asked.

"Over a mad dog? Honey, I don't think so."

Della left arm in arm with Kemal, the faint crunch of their footsteps fading into the evening air.

I couldn't tolerate the void, aching in my chest. I returned to the *pension* and found my charcoal and a piece of Damad's lined notebook paper. Back at the temple I drew the little dog over and over, leaping, rolling, crouching, sleeping. In the center I drew Damad, his arms thrown wide among all the puppies.

Umut crept up behind me and sat, shivering though the

night was warm, watching me draw. When the work was finished he took it from my hands and sniffed it. I put an arm around him as he studied the sketch, wiping away the reluctant tears that kept sneaking from my eyes.

"Damad," he said, "Damad."

It was the only word he ever spoke that I understood. Then he bounded off towards the hotel, the drawing held to his heart.

I gathered lavender and mint, and lay them over the grave. When I turned around Xiao stood on the path, hesitating at the entrance to the temple.

"Thank you," he said.

"For what?"

"For the drawing you made Damad. He was hysterical, inconsolable. The drawing seems to have calmed him. Umut's with him now. I think he's going to be okay."

"I did it for myself," I said.

Four long strides covered the temple's sand floor and brought Xiao to the altar. "Tatyana, most of us who do good things for others, really do them for ourselves. You truly are a kind person."

I turned away and looked south, out to sea. I could feel him coming closer. Not hear him, for he walked very quietly in the sand. Not see him, as my eyes looked far away to the harsh clouds gathering over Egypt, rolling north, Poseidon's wind blowing at their heels. Not smell him, as the lavender at my feet filled the whole temple. I could feel him as though our skins were one. Feel him move to stand behind me, lift strong arms and slip them around my waist. He pulled me into his heat and laid his lips on my neck. Such a pleasure, I forgot to breathe.

"A storm is coming. I have to help Kemal secure the boats," he whispered, but he made no effort to leave.

I could hardly think beyond his breath on my skin. "Is Mizou going to be okay?"

"She's stubborn. I offered to go to Manavgat tomorrow and call for the vaccines she needs, but she is adamant that she's not in danger."

"Did the puppy bite her?"

"*Oui*, on the ankle."

"Then you must go."

I turned around. Now I was in his arms facing him. It was a big mistake. His lips were on mine without hesitation. I was pulled into him, off balance. All I wanted to do is fall into his warmth and melt away, but he held me upright. He held us both upright. After a moment he pulled away.

"I shouldn't be alone with you. We don't do these things in China, sex before marriage. It's not acceptable." He stepped back with a slight bow. "I'm so sorry." He took another step away from me, achingly formal in his attempt at distance. With every step backwards I wanted him more.

"I would go for the vaccines, but they are expensive. I can't afford them," he said.

"I'll give you money." I would have given him anything.

"What will you live on?"

"I have a lot of money, don't worry. My family is rich."

"But you and your father are estranged, *n'est pas*?"

"I'll pay for the vaccines, Xiao. Come by my room tonight,

after Kemal's boats are secure. I'll give you Traveler's Checks." I reached for him, but he took another step backwards.

"*Non.* You mistake me for Yue Fei. I am weaker than you think, and less honorable. You should run from me." And he fled, leaving me confused with desire.

~

I woke to a terrible storm. Wind bashed at my shutters and shrieked through the curved roofing tiles. Waves broke: explosions on the beach shaking the hotel with their weight and power. The mirror, lying on the mattress next to me, quaked with each strike of the surf. In the glass' smoky interior, a veiled, jeweled woman glided over the sea, troubled and ghostly. Her solitary drifting made the little hairs stand up on my skin. I pushed away the mirror, leapt out of bed, and pulled on a T-shirt. Tugging open the windows, I pulled wide the glass panes and reached for the shutter latch. Crickets, hiding from the wind, flew out from between the wooden slats and fluttered into my room. I pounded on the latch with my fist, finally forcing it down. The shutters banged open against the wet stucco wall.

The waves were monstrous. If we had not been so high on a cliff, I might have feared they would take the whole hotel. I peered into the fury, rain stinging my face, unsure what I looked for. Something had woken me. Something was out there. I stood shivering, frightened, quickly wet through, staring into the storm and thinking that I must have lost my mind.

Then I saw her, standing on the beach in her orange robe stained with dog's blood. She had her arms bent over her head as though to ward off a blow, her rings turned to the sky. Wet silk whipped around her like a shroud. And as she stood, it rose from the sea: a monstrous three headed hound, gray as tarnished iron. It twisted three long necks, heads howling, mouths the gates to hell. Cerberus, the terrifying hound of Hades, keeper of the dead. Its snake of a tail whipped in the waves. But this was not a myth, read in my father's book as I sat by the library window. This was eternal death, come to devour us.

Mizou didn't move: a frail twig before the jaws of terror.

She didn't move.

Mizou!" I screamed. "Mizou!"

The monster crashed into the ocean and a huge wave rose in its wake. A tsunami flooded over her and washed up the barrier of the cliff wall, sending water to the very foot of the *pension*. Suat Bey's lawn chair, Yurda's flower pots, Damad's deflated soccer ball—all retreated with the water and tumbled over the cliff.

I gripped the windowsill in terror, sure that I would see only empty beach as the wave withdrew. Water foamed and churned, pulling back with a powerful suck. Mizou was still standing, impossibly stubborn and spindly. Her arms were raised, clothes soaked and clinging.

I whirled around and looked at the room. My bed was there, now hopping with crickets. Rain water pooled on the floor. My jeans lay in a crumpled heap. I was not dreaming.

I yanked on my pants and ran downstairs, barefooted. I

jammed open the lock on the *pension* door and dashed across the flattened humps of grass. Foamy seawater still bubbled in the bent blades. Broken seashells jabbed my feet.

Trembling violently, peering over the edge of the cliff, I cried, "Mizou! Mizou!" But she was gone. The beach was empty. "Mizou!" I stood screaming, hysterical. Around me, wind howled. Rain pounded on my head in slaps and belts.

"*Princess, ma Princess*, what are you doing?" Suat Bey's bony hands gripped my upper arms. He weaved unsteadily, smelling heavily of Raki. "Come inside. What's wrong with you, *ben*? Have you lost your mind? Come in, now."

Staggering in his drunkenness, he dragged me away from the edge of the cliff.

"Mizou was on the beach, washed away by a wave. We have to help her." I struggled against his strong clasp, trying to turn back to the sea.

"*Mais non,* the sea dares not touch her. Come in before you catch a chill." He hauled me through the front door. "Yurda!" he called, "Yurda!" The cook appeared at the bottom of the stairs, eyes half open and hair falling out of her hastily applied scarf. He thrust my trembling, soaked body against her plump warmth. "I have gotten so old, a woman must guard me," he muttered as he bolted the front door. "Would that the sea could swallow us both."

Scolding in Turkish and brushing tangled hair from my forehead, Yurda forced me into a kitchen chair. She put a pot of tea on to boil, insisting on four lumps of sugar, though one was too much, and she wouldn't let me thin the tea. I sipped her potent, syrupy drink and worried about Mizou as Yurda ruffled my hair with a dish towel. She threw a blanket over my shoulders and rubbed my stiff hands in her strong hot ones until my fingertips could feel again. As I began to recover she gave me a lecture, clucking and sighing, nodding and throwing back her head with feverish emotion. Before she would let me leave she had me throw salt into the flames of the stove. The crystals flared and sparkled.

When Yurda was finally reassured enough to release me, I went to my room. Suat Bey had latched the shutters, closed the windows, and mopped up the puddles. With the addition of crickets, who had taken over the bed and clearly planned to sleep with me, the room was as it had been before the storm.

I went to my bed and picked up the mirror. The glass was quiet now, resting as though asleep. All I could see on its surface were my own frightened eyes.

You see, my precious Jiè, I had plenty of warning. I knew that I was in over my head. But we don't listen, do we, when we have our heart set on something? We forge ahead, like Napoleon, as if we could rule the world.

# EIGHTEEN

iao said nothing as he took my signed checks and left the next morning for Manavgat. Mizou didn't come to breakfast, but Suat Bey reassured me that she was fine. He appeared unperturbed by my description of what I had seen rising from the sea, hanging over Mizou's head. He had told too many lies, I guess, for the fantastic to disturb him.

"You underestimate her, child." He placidly sipped his coffee. "There is little in this world that can harm her."

"*Mon Dieu*, Suat Bey, you have to at least admit that she was bitten by a rabid dog."

Della came down the stairs, overhearing the last of our conversation. She sauntered into the room. "Let it drop, hon. Xiao will order the vaccines and that will be the end of it."

Damad crept in, climbed into my lap, and stole an olive off my plate. Folded with boneless flexibility into the crook of my arm, he chewed and sucked the olive pit noisily. I sat in silence, feeling his wiggly little boy warmth as we shared my breakfast. Recurring glimpses of last night's terror confused and exhausted me, and I ached for Xiao.

Hoping to shake off my dread, I decided to spend the day painting. I started with the view from Della's room, gazing down into the gladiator arena that crows now owned, though this time of year their caws competed with the numbing drone of cicadas. From the height of the pension I could see into the concentric rings of benches, half lit from the east, deeply shadowed from the west. I used oils and an impressionist style: my tiny dabs of color gave the effect of a vast crowd cheering the fight in the sand below. I painted the sky—streaks of clouds still bruised from last night's battle. The effect was of ancient, epic drama. Della loved it.

"I'll take this room from now on, every time I visit. Makes me feel as though the modern world has up and gone away."

I no longer needed Della to wrap me, but I stayed in her room to dress, borrowing a blue silk and her Lapis Lazuli earrings from Afghanistan. As I tugged and tucked the silk, Della stood by the window, admiring the view I'd painted.

"Will you be here when I return?" she asked.

"Are you leaving so soon?"

"Any day now. As soon as the first tourist sucks down a *café au lait* on Mizou's terrace."

"I don't know how long I'll be here. I haven't thought about it." But where could I go? This was the closest to a home I'd ever had.

"Well, I hope you're here when I get back. Your intellectual snobbism has grown on me." She turned around and appraised me, head to toe. "You're worthy of him, child. That's saying a lot when it comes to a man like Yue Fei."

"He's not Yue Fei."

"He's more Yue Fei than he lets on. You make him happy, and I don't think he ever knew happiness, 'til he met you. Don't let him die a martyr's death."

"I have no control over what he does."

Della sauntered forward and straightened an earring that had tangled in my hair. Her touch was light and sure, her voice low. "You do, sister. More than you know." She let the blond strand fall, and ambled to the door.

"Della?"

"Yes?" Hand on the door handle, she turned around. I wished I could paint her, leaning there on one hip, the look on her face so sensuous, so disillusioned.

"Is Mizou a witch?"

"Witch?" Della laughed, her head thrown back, her bare throat long and soft. "Why do you say that, child?"

"Last night during the storm, I saw her—"

"Hush!" Della shook her head. "Don't meddle with Gypsies, little sister. They don't answer to the same gods the rest of us do. Come on, let's see if your man's back from Manavgat."

He wasn't.

At dinner, he was the topic everyone avoided. Suat Bey hung over me like a hen, pecking about to find tender morsels to put on my plate. Mizou was subdued and depleted, her complexion as sallow as her folds of yellow silk. Damad had regained the confidence to play under the table at my feet and no longer crawled from lap to lap. Della and Kemal spoke Turkish, turned toward each other in an intimate stoop that shut out the rest of the world. Yurda was preoccupied with fussing over Mizou, so for once she didn't try to overfeed me. I escaped from the table as soon as it was polite.

I went to bed. I had given up moving the mirror back to my desk every morning. It stayed by my pillow, peaceful in the moonlight, the face of it reflecting nothing but white ceiling. I turned it over. The hound's gems of eyes were dark and empty. Enamel waves washed around the handle, wrapping me to Incir. My love for Xiao, my place in the village, Mizou's magic, my awe of the mirror: all of it was right, all of it was wrong, all of it held me in its grip. I fell asleep clutching the handle, the raised mosaic dog pressed to my cheek.

I woke several hours later and knew he was home. No knock, no creak, no voice revealed him: his presence alone seeped into my sleep and permeated my dreams. I slipped on my *çarşaf* and opened the door. He squatted against the wall, hunched over his knees, long hair unbraided and drifting to below his waist. Such a big man, I barely stooped when I reached for his shoulder.

"Xiao," I whispered. "Are you okay?"

He looked up with a start. "Tatyana. I have to talk to you."

"Now, in the middle of the night?"

"*Oui.* Come walk with me, we can't talk here."

"Come into my room."

"*Non*, please no. Let's go to the beach. Please, Tatyana."

"As you wish. Let me put on warmer clothes."

I closed the door and added jeans and a shirt under my *çarşaf*, plus socks and shoes. When I reopened the door he was standing, back against the wall, a newspaper under his arm. He had re-braided his hair and his posture was upright and tense.

We crept down the spiral staircase. Xiao pulled the bolts on the kitchen door, and then closed it carefully behind us.

We didn't speak as we crossed Apollo's temple, bright in the full moon. We threaded the cliff path to the shore. The sea had an uneasy calm, splashing lightly at the shoreline. We picked our way over rocks, around sleeping gulls, and down into our cove. Sheltered, observed only by drowsy birds, Xiao sat cross-legged in the sand. I gathered up the folds of my clothes and eased onto my knees in front of him.

"Did you get Mizou's shots?"

I could barely make out his face in the moonlight.

"They're coming by refrigerator truck in three days. The doctor showed me how to give them. How is she?"

"She looks terrible. Xiao, I have to tell you what happened last night."

"Wait, Tatyana, please let me speak." He unrolled the newspaper. "Look!" He pointed to a page in Chinese. I strained in the dim light. The only thing I could read was yesterday's date in the lower right corner—June 5th, 1989.

"Xiao, I can't read Chinese."

"*Je m'excuse*, I'm not thinking straight. It says that 600 were killed in Tiananmen Square: workers, students, citizens of Beijing. Bulldozers flattened people, machine guns mowed them down. My friend Bao was re-arrested. I have to go, Tatyana. I can't stay here." Anguish wrenched his face. "The railway workers need me. Bao needs me. My country is rising and I'm not there, I'm not there...." He took my hands, clasping them completely inside his big fists until they disappeared. "Tatyana, the people will follow me—"

"Xiao, they'll kill you," I interrupted.

"If I die in the end it doesn't matter—China will change."

"It does matter." I yanked free my hands and grabbed his shoulders. With a violent shake I hissed, "You can't give something to China if you're dead."

"Yes, I can. Yue Fei—"

"To hell with Yue Fei. You are Xiao Lian Chin, the hunted dissident. Revolution takes more than throwing your body onto a pile of corpses."

Xiao caught his breath. "You're stronger than I thought." He stared at the sand. "What should I do, my little Trotoskov?"

"We'll have to work it through. Rushing chest first into a furious political backlash won't accomplish anything."

"I suppose you're right."

The diplomat in me spoke before I could censor her. "I know many important people. The European embassies are the place to start."

He looked up, smiling as though savoring a victory. For a minute I thought he might tell me that he loved me, but he didn't speak. I waited, hoping, but he didn't speak. Finally I said, "Xiao, you need to survive, come back to me when this is over."

"I hope…." He lay my small hand face up in his huge one. With the lightest touch he stroked my palm, sending quivers over the crease lines. "I hope we'll be more than simply reunited. When the revolution is over, I hope to marry you."

He would have kissed me, I think, if I had not looked away. Looked away from what I had always wanted, now in my reach, now about to be snatched away. The future towered over us like a tsunami, unlikely to end well.

"What did you need to tell me, Tatyana?"

"Last night during the storm I saw…." I stopped. My vision of Mizou seemed histrionic, outrageous, a child's nightmare compared to the real dangers Xiao faced.

This is the first thing you must forgive me for, Jiè; I never warned him. He never knew what stalked him. He would have believed, I'm sure, with his superstitious mind, perhaps would have told me the truth to prevent our downfall. But I'm so poor at giving of myself, I didn't share my fears.

"It was nothing, I guess." I stood up. "We should go. It's cold, and very late."

He stood too, and helped me dust sand off my clothes. We didn't speak again until we were at the top of the cliff path, both of us sweating from the climb.

"You're right, you know, about China," he said.

"What do you mean?" We walked side by side between Apollo's pillars.

"Driving away her best and brightest."

"Oh, that."

"You're right about a lot of the insulting things you say. That's why they're so insulting."

Moving ahead of him, I walked toward the altar. "Being right isn't as wonderful as it sounds. Sometimes, I'd rather be loved."

He slipped a hand around my waist and stopped me from stepping forward. I turned to face him and found his mouth.

It wasn't at all what either of us intended, but there was that moment when intent faded and urge surged forward, drawing us down together onto the marble altar. I don't know how we separated enough to get our clothes unfastened, or at what point the *çarşaf* became our blanket. But you were conceived there, my child. And I can honestly say that your father loved me. Despite all that followed, I always knew that he loved me, because no man could be that tender, without love.

# NINETEEN

sing names I supplied, Xiao went into a frenzy of letter writing. Every day there were several thick packets for Europe. Della went to Manavgat on business and brought back more black ink. Within a week, answers began to return. I turned away from the sight of them, letters sitting in the hall basket, waiting to whisk him away. They made my heart rise to an unnatural position in my throat.

Mizou recovered quickly, the color back in her cheeks within a day or two, even before the glass vials arrived on ice from Istanbul. Xiao threatened to hold her down for the first shot, and though she did not curse him, her glower would have wilted anyone but a warrior. But she took the shots, first from Xiao's hands, and then every three days after, from mine. After each shot, I threw my arms around her and held her close, praying to Apollo to protect her until the shots were complete.

I painted to forget Xiao's preparations to leave. I painted from Mizou and Suat Bey's room, spare and cold, located on the top floor with a view of the fishing boats in the harbor. Then Damad's room, looking out over Yurda's herb garden, his bookshelves full of the things he'd collected on the beach. Next my own room, facing south and the ocean. In the sky I painted Cerberus, then dabbed him out with tumultuous clouds to hide him from the unsuspecting.

At night as everyone slept, Xiao came, opening my unlocked door and stealthily closing it behind him, putting the chain in place, lifting his shirt in the waning moonlight, dropping his pants. The mirror stayed on the desk as we slept, wrapped so close that we melted together. The glass seemed to have lost its power to move in the middle night.

Though we made love over and over, he never entered me again. He was afraid of shaming me, he said. If we were to make a child, it would be as man and wife. But would I get the chance to marry a man, so wedded to his cause?

The night that I completed the painting of my view, Xiao came in very late. I had been sitting for an hour wondering over Cerberus, the room lit only by a luminous sliver of moon. In my painting, the horror of the creature lay hidden between sky and sea. Such a fantastical thing could only exist in my imagination, and yet, alone at night in the dark, there were moments I felt Apollo at my shoulder, saw Hades' face against the sky, and smelled dog fur in the sea breeze.

Xiao closed the door. "You're still awake?" he whispered. "I thought you'd be asleep."

"No, I waited. I finished the painting."

He snapped on the light and came to stand behind me. "It's sinister. I've never seen you paint sinister before."

I ran my hands up under his shirt to where his warm ribs spread wide. "It suits me, don't you think? Maybe I should just do Gothic abstractions from now on." I tugged at his shirt, to laugh with him at my joke, but he winced and pulled away.

"What's the matter?"

"Nothing." He turned his back. "I sleep alone tonight."

"Why?"

He didn't answer.

"What's the matter with you?" I walked around in front of him and planted myself between his body and the door.

"I didn't want to tell you, but…I took the scars off."

My stomach clenched. "You what?"

"I took the scars off, or rather, Kemal did, with a hot iron poker."

"Are you mad? What did you do to yourself?"

I yanked up his shirt. The brief glimpse made me dizzy: a palm-breadth strip of skin, burnt to smooth white and black, oozing silky water. The characters were gone. He pulled his shirt down and caught me as my vision faded to black, bringing the world to a spinning, buzzing point. He held me in his arms and guided me to the bed. Kneeling beside me, he stroked my hair. Sobs burst from my throat.

"I had no choice. I'll be leaving soon. Branded as I was, I could never hide." His hand on my forehead was as hot as a fever. "I'll have to scar my face, too, when I get to China, otherwise I'll be recognized. Could you love me, if I no longer looked like Yue Fei?"

"I don't care what you look like." My words gagged and stumbled. "I just want you alive, here, with me. Please don't go. Please. You'll be ground up like so much meat. Please." Crying took my breath away.

Xiao cupped my wet face in his hands, kissed me, kissed me again. Every time I tried to beg him, his mouth closed over mine, suffocating my protests, driving down my anguish with his tender desire. We made love, him holding me away from his wounds. Afterwards I cried. He was lost to me, and I feared he was lost to the world as well. He lay grim as a clay warrior, guarding his realm with unshakable determination.

Then, restless and tortured, I got out of bed and wandered the room, staring at my painting, handling my ink brushes, flipping through my old *cahiers.* I circled and backtracked, torn apart, directionless, compass broken. Finally I stood with my swollen face in my hands and silently prayed.

Apollo, help me to stop this man. He goes to a senseless death. Don't let him die, hanging by the neck in some dark cell. I will give you anything, Apollo. Just save him from cruelty and inhumanity. He is too good, too good, to be delivered into the hands of butchers.

Standing before my desk, I stared at what remained of the moon. Without thinking about it, my hand went to the mirror.

This is the second thing for which you must forgive me, my daughter. Later I found much to blame on Boris, but it was I who lifted the mirror, turning the surface to catch my devastated face. It was I who twisted the glass again, until it reflected Xiao's bowed head, such agony in his strength, such courage in his resolve. But it wasn't I who raised Xiao's head. Something else, some murky evil lifted his gaze with wonder and terror, shook him like a punch when his eyes caught mine in the glass.

"Tatyana?" he whispered, as though his throat had been burned.

"You must come back to me. No matter what else happens, you must come back to me. We belong together."

Our reflected gazes locked, inseparable.

"I will," he said. As though in a trance, he rose to his feet. Standing before me, he laced fingers through my hair.

I barely remember that kiss. Not like the first three in Apollo's temple, or the hundreds in my small, narrow bed. That kiss was captured by the mirror, the dark glass swirling with mist and whirlpools.

I woke alone the next morning, exhausted, nauseated, retching. I knew immediately what was wrong. The mirror lay next to me, a ghost of Xiao still looking from its depths. I dragged myself out of bed and pulled on my *çarşaf* to go after him.

~

Xiao was not at breakfast. As Della had predicted, tourists had arrived overnight. I stood in the doorway staring at the strangers on the terrace, feeling as though I might vomit, fingering the rough black fabric that enveloped me.

"Sit down," said Mizou. "The man you are looking for has gone to Manavgat for the day."

Next to Mizou sat a young lady who was unfortunately beautiful, over six feet tall with a face I'd seen in airbrushed photos somewhere, perhaps selling perfume on Metro billboards. She was dressed in a blouse that I could almost see through. The boyfriend by her side leaned on her tanned arm, and on her every word. They spoke French. I blinked, as though to wash them away, but they were still there when I opened my eyes. I collapsed into the open seat on the other side of Mizou, and poured myself some tea.

"This is the model, Nina Blanche, from Paris." Mizou's gracious smile barely hid her distaste. "And this is her photographer, Johannes."

The woman smiled as though she expected me to be *enchantée*. Then she babbled on about the photo shoot they planned to do in the ruins, dressed in Grecian toga. Johannes gushed over his lenses and what they could do to improve the light. They had already trampled all over Apollo's Temple and had decided it was just the spot. I clamped down my teeth so hard I could feel a headache, pounding with what I ached to say. I looked to Mizou, but she looked away; did I think she could live on my meager monthly payments alone?

Yurda came in with a heavy tray of freshly baked *Bőrek* and I stood to help her lower it to the table.

"Pastry is not something that I eat," announced the model.

At least she said it in a language Yurda didn't understand. She rose with a flutter. "Let's go exploring." I watched her drift off the patio, Johannes with his cameras bobbing after her.

I poured myself more tea, trying to settle the fury in my chest and the queasiness in my stomach.

"God, how do you stand it, Mizou?"

Mizou rolled her eyes to the patio's corrugated iron roof and sighed with restraint. "I have two months of hell, and ten months of heaven a year."

"I suppose that's a better deal than Persephone got."

"Persephone?"

"Hades wife, condemned to the underworld six months a year."

Mizou shuddered at the mention of Hades name. "Oh, yes, Persephone. How could I forget?" She lay a hand over mine. Her fingers were cold, almost icy. "Please don't leave when Xiao goes. I'd miss your educated conversation, *ma fille*."

I felt a wave of nausea, and cringed at the urge to vomit. "I don't know what to do."

"*Eh bien*, you have a home here, if you want."

A home: Yurda to mother me, Suat Bey to adore me, Mizou to guide me, Apollo to protect me. I stared at the tea leaves in my glass, imagining a home safe from Boris. It was more than I'd ever hoped for.

"Mizou? Are you frightened of the future?"

She withdrew her hand. A light breeze from off the sea lifted her gray hair, tickling her face with wisps of trepidation. "We are all pawns, Tatyana. But now and then a pawn can master a king and pretend for a moment that she is important. You used the mirror, didn't you?" Her eyes met mine. All I could see in their dark depths was resignation. "Without it I would have become a whore, tossed from man to man like a dirty joke. That was a future I could not bear. Until I break the mirror, I am mistress of my life. What waits beyond, is at least a hell I chose."

"You have to break the mirror?"

"*Mais oui.* It is a wicked thing that I should have destroyed years ago, but I could not bear to part with Suat Bey, could not bear to see him die."

"The mirror protects him?"

"Yes, child." She laughed, bitter and tired. "From all of that poisonous Raki, if from nothing else. And it will protect

Xiao. As long as he is true to you, he is safe under its spell. Let's hope he finishes this nonsense of revolution and sends for you before my strength runs out."

"What will happen to you?"

She shook her head. From the kitchen, Suat Bey bellowed for coffee, followed by Yurda's indignant scolding. Mizou picked up her tea glass and closed her eyes. Steam from the tea skittered lightly across her face as if it were afraid.

"And if I break the mirror for you, when the time comes?" I whispered.

"*Oh la!*" She laughed into her glass. "You? Don't even try, child. You are but an instant's reflection. Better that the eyes of Hades stay on me." She stood up. "If you see Nina and Johannes in the Temple, remind them not to leave their garbage about, would you?"

But I didn't go to the Temple. I went to Xiao's room, which he never locked, and pushed open the door. My drawings hung by dressmaker's pins on every surface of the walls, wrapped like a blanket around the room. Over his bed leaped my inky crickets, joyful and unpredictable. On the ceiling, placed so it could be seen from the pillow, was the bold little cricket with the broken antenna, the drawing I had handed him, high on the steps of the Roman Arena so many months ago. Xiao had written something in calligraphy, Chinese characters that I could not read, down the left side of the page.

I went to the window and looked out at Apollo's temple. Nina was there, spread over the altar like a sacrifice. A shocking pulse of light from Johannes' camera bleached her image for a moment, as if to erase her away. But she reappeared. With luck they would make love there and Apollo, in his fury, would ask Athena to give her snakes for hair.

I went back to my room for paint. I would start with the sky, which Johannes' flash bulbs could not touch, and hope they were gone by the time I painted the arc of columns.

Late in the afternoon there was a knock on Xiao's door.

"*Entrez.*" I didn't look up from my painting, assuming it was Yurda with food.

"I came to say goodbye," I knew the voice, the smeared southern twang, but it had a gravely pitch that made me turn around.

A heavy man with a black beard stood in the doorway, dressed in a red quilted robe, a blue scarf tucked around his neck. Perhaps from Central Asia: a Turkmen, or Tajik. He carried a tray of bread, honey, and goat cheese. "Well, how do you like the foot soldiers of western civilization, hon?" The stranger gave me a barely perceptible wink.

"Della?"

The man laughed, guttural and grating. "You recognized me. I thought I was going to have to ask for a mint julep."

"Why are you…?" In my shock the English wouldn't come. There was nothing about the rough-edged, weathered stranger that could fit into a velvet evening gown.

"You think I lead a caravan over the Altai Mountains dressed as a woman?"

"You sell silk."

"Yes, honeychild, I travel the Silk Road." She closed the door and stood with the tray. Her feminine shoulders were lost in yards of quilted cloth, her considerable bust now blended into a paunch. "Clothes make the man." Her voice lifted into its feminine register, and she gestured towards my *çarşaf*. "I think you're wearing what suits you." Della set the tray on Xiao's desk and sat down on the unmade bed. "You going to be all right, hon?

I didn't know. I couldn't answer.

"Eat something. You're so thin. I worry about you, child." She stood and came to the desk, pouring strong tea from the small brass pot. "I'll be in China by October. I'll look for Xiao in Beijing. Here—"

"*Merci.*" I took the glass, but I couldn't feel its warmth in my numb hands. I felt empty, so sick to my stomach I couldn't bear the sight of the pasty cheese. "Della?"

"Yes."

"I missed my *menstruation* last week." "Your period?"

I nodded.

She slumped down on my bed. "You have great timing, you know that? You're like a country western song. Is it his?"

"Who else? I am not really a wanton woman, *en effet.*"

Della frowned. "Well, unwed mothers aren't too popular in this town. You'll have to tell him. He can delay his political madness long enough for you two to get married."

"I can't ask him to stay only for me."

The scowl on Della's face could have shaken a mountain.

"Why in the hell not? What is it with women and sending men off to war? You think the only people with rights are the brave, dead ones? Tell him to put the one billion people of China on hold and stay to take care of his lover and his baby."

I didn't say anything. He wouldn't stay, that was the truth of it. At least, I feared he wouldn't. For him to walk away from me I could somehow understand, even if I could hardly bear it. But if he walked away from you, little daughter, what kind of a man would he be then?

This is the third thing you must forgive me for: I didn't trust myself enough to tell him. Or more likely, I didn't trust him enough. You against the one billion people of China. Hardly a fair match for an unborn child.

"Well," said Della, getting up. "You'll do what you do. If you don't make him marry you, get out of town before the pregnancy shows. For Yurda's sake, if not for your own."

Yurda. With typical selfishness I had not considered what my unwed pregnancy would do to Yurda. This was not a fault she could scold and fuss away. I dropped my head, flooded with guilt and sorrow. Unless I forced Xiao to marry me immediately, I could not live in Incir.

"Eat, now. You have responsibilities." She kissed me on the head. "I'll be on the road."

"You and Xiao are both leaving." I felt flat, deadened beyond protest.

"I leave and come back, regular as a flock of geese. You're the one who's unpredictable." She squeezed my shoulder, and closed the door behind her.

I stared at my easel. Filmy clouds slept in a bed of soft blue across the top of the otherwise blank canvas. I looked down at the temple where Nina and Johannes drank cola, side by side in the shade of a column. I wiped my hands on a rag and stood up. I wandered around Xiao's room. I touched his pillow. I touched my crickets. I went to his desk and rubbed my fingers over his smooth inkstone, smearing black onto my fingertips. He was going to China to make a revolution. I would stay and hide, unwed and soon unwanted.

In a fit of frustration I swept all of his correspondence off his desk, scattering letters with my forearm and sending them fluttering through the air. One letter separated from the chaos of pages, and landed at my feet.

I've asked myself a thousand times if he would have lived, had I not read that letter. If we do not know of a betrayal, is it a betrayal? I might have someday gone to him in China, oblivious, and lived as his wife, you, my little sweetheart, at our side. What would his betrayal have mattered, these sixteen years later, and Boris long dead?

But I picked up the letter. I recognized the language: French. Leaving my black fingerprints all over it, I unfolded the pages. It was a draft, addressed to Boris Trotoskov in Xiao's upright script, edited and re-edited until the French was articulate and correct.

*June 8th, 1989*

*Cher Monsieur,*

> *I am pleased that we have come to an agreement. I leave within two weeks for China, and feel confident that the people will rise with me and usher in a new day for our beloved country. I look forward to meeting you again*

*when I am head of state.*

*I have had ample time to evaluate your daughter; she will make an excellent wife. The dowry arrived safely in my uncle's account. When your daughter is first lady of China, I promise to remember what France has done for me. China and Europe both stand to benefit from closer ties between East and West.*

*My mother's people are satisfied with this arrangement and will give you no further trouble. The payment they recently received should be the last, and your life is no longer in danger. Forgive them for the years of threats and harassment, and they, in turn, might forgive you for abandoning my father.*

*As for your concubines, what you have done to bring down the regime that killed them is ample recompense for your cowardly behavior. Though it is not within my power to absolve you of their horrible deaths, I will ask at their graves that they show you mercy.*

*Stay well, Sir, we have much work to do together. Tatyana is beloved in Incir, and will be safe here until you come for her. Come soon: her funds are almost depleted.*

*Respectfully,*

*Xiao Lian Chin*

At the bottom of the page it said "Final draft mailed June 8th, 1989."

My father's famous chef, left to die when my father fled China, had been Xiao's father. It was Xiao's relatives who visited, extorting blood money all those years. And I was the final prize, sold to erase Boris' shameful debt. Ever the able diplomat, Boris had ridden Xiao's filial piety, anger, and ambition like a wave, and set me up to be the next first lady of China.

# TWENTY

G et out!" I'm not sure how my feet carried me there, but I found myself in Apollo's ruins, insane with fury. I snatched up a dead laurel branch and advanced on Nina and Johannes, who sat surrounded by discarded wrappers and pop cans. "This is a temple, not a picnic grounds. Fuck off."

The couple scrambled off the altar, hastily collecting gear. "She's nuts," said Nina, as they hurried away.

I was so angry at Xiao and my father, I wanted to slit their throats. I slammed the broken laurel branch against the slab of marble and howled. "Go to hell, Boris Trotoskov. I hope you die miserable and alone." It barely hurt as I fell to my knees in the rocky sand. "I am not a pawn, you bastards. I won't be tricked, sold, and tampered with." Oblivious to bruises and scrapes, I beat on the altar, lost in a darkness that I could neither see through, nor walk through.

A fierce hand grabbed my arm and I whirled to see Mizou, glaring at me. "What is the matter with you?"

I thrust out the letter, crumpled into a ball.

Still gripping me, she shook the page with her free hand and read the letter.

"*Mon Dieu.*" Her brown face blanched, white as Raki. "Where is he?"

"Manavgat."

"No, he's back. He needed to send word home, because he leaves tonight." She dropped my arm and hurried around felled hunks of marble. I followed as she rushed to the cliff edge.

From the sandy, crumbling cliff, I saw Umut run out the jetty, looking for the boats. He stood in the breeze, hand shading his eyes, looking west into the sunset. If only time could have stopped there, at the moment he saw the black masts, his hands thrown wide with joy.

Xiao sat on the jetty rocks. He knew that I watched him; I could feel it in his posture, in the curl of his hand around the brush, in the fullness of his lips, wet from his water bottle. Even as he betrayed me, he loved me. Even as I hated him, I wanted no one else.

Mizou ran down the goat path toward the beach, impeded by the current of laughing children who dashed and scrambled up the trail against her. The waves reached. Gulls screamed. Xiao waved to Umut, and I heard Cerberus growl. A low, vibrant rumble that no one could mistake for the surf. And Umut was gone.

My soul dove with Xiao. Salt burned fiercely into his raw scars, and he gasped. Water rushed down his throat. It took everything he had to boost the child up, not pull him under with the desperate clasp of drowning. His last thoughts were for Umut. I know, because night after night the mirror brings his drowning struggle into my dreams, relentlessly. And I feel the teeth clamp onto his foot.

One week later I lay, eyes wide in the middle of the night, staring at the ceiling. There was no one to forgive what I had done. Nothing kept me breathing but you, Jiè. Somehow I staggered forward, maimed by sorrow and guilt. Alive only because of you, my little girl, one bleak step dragged behind the other. Had I been alone, I would have laid down on the devastated ground, and died.

There was a soft knock on my door. "Tatyana, are you awake?"

"*Oui.*"

"Let me in."

I unlocked the chain. Mizou shivered in her bathrobe and slippers. She stepped around me and closed the door behind her. "I have come for the mirror."

She shook so violently that I reached to hug her.

"*Non.*" She pulled away. "This is something I do alone. Give me the mirror."

"You're going to break it."

She didn't answer.

"Why, Mizou? What harm can it do now? Xiao's already dead."

She gripped her fingers together in a knot. "And you? Do you think Apollo will protect you forever? Gods lose interest in us mortals, Tatyana, when we cease to amuse. It's time that this ended." She held out a shaking hand. "Give it to me."

"And Suat Bey?"

"He is an old soldier; he never was afraid to die." Mizou flipped the light switch, and the bulb overhead glared. "Where did you put it?"

From across the room our gazes took in the scratched, bare desktop.

"Maybe it hid itself in your bed," said Mizou. The mirror's autonomous wandering didn't seem to surprise her. She walked to the bed and threw aside covers. "*Merde.*" She punctuated her foul French with curses in a language I didn't know. She looked under the bed and kicked at my dirty clothes. "I'll have to search the whole hotel."

"Wait, Mizou," I grabbed her arm, thin and steely. Sorrow rushed up my throat, too heavy to bear. "Don't break it. Wait for Suat Bey to die, please."

"*Non, ma petite.* It's over."

"What will happen to you?" I squeezed desperately, refusing to let go.

She leaned down and kissed me on the cheek. "Goodbye Tatyana." Her voice was soft with love. "I will watch for you in my dreams. Call for me if you need me, and pray for me at Apollo's altar. Perhaps he will intervene for me, too, just a little, *non*?" She pulled out of my grip and disappeared down the unlit staircase.

"Mizou!" I called after her, whispering as loud as I dared.

She didn't answer. I padded after her in the dark. I turned on lights in the dining room, the kitchen, the terrace. I searched the cliff overlooking the sea. She had vanished. Exhausted, I went back to bed where I shivered all night, unable to sleep, listening to the growling sea.

~

The next morning I woke to Mizou's voice. Gulping back my morning sickness, I yanked on my *çarşaf* and threw open the door. Yes, that was Mizou downstairs, talking to a guest. She must not have found the mirror! Weak with relief, I leaned against the door frame.

Guests were arriving in clumps now, like jelly fish, filling the *pension* with the sting of the modern world. With stoic graciousness, Mizou was explaining the taxi system in French to some man. This is how one gets to Manavgat. No, there is no phone here. Then the man spoke again and my heart clenched like a fist.

Boris Trotoskov.

I had been warned that he was coming: Xiao's letter. In my grief, so profound that I had forgotten even Boris, I had made no preparations. He was here. Here to take me.

I flung myself into my room and snatched up the bride's *çarşaf.* I folded it carefully and packed it in the bottom of my knapsack. I grabbed Xiao's ink box and my charcoal pencil. I found my passport and the few remaining traveler's checks, stuffing it all on top of the blue and gold cloth. For the second time in a year, I weighed in my hands heavy oils, water colors, and vellum, and abandoned them. I pinned on my head covering and pulled the bottom corner over my nose and chin. Cautiously, tingling with terror, I snuck down the hall to Xiao's room, slipped inside, and locked the door behind me.

Mizou had refused to rent the room, even though the hotel was now crowded. Nothing had been touched since Xiao's death. My drawings hung like butterfly wings from their pins on the wall, moving slightly in the breeze from the open window. His bed was unmade. I put my face in his pillow and breathed in his faint scent. My longing for him was a pain so deep I thought it might kill me. I clung to his pillow, unable to let go. Only my father's voice, patronizing and impatient, drifting up the stairs and mixed with Suat Bey's grumbling French, brought me to my senses.

I yanked the pillow case off Xiao's pillow and filled it with my drawings. I took even the cricket that hung on the ceiling above his bed. I had to empty the jeans, shorts, and shirts from my knapsack in order to fit the bundle in. I kept only my sweater. I turned the knapsack around and hung it against my chest, under the folds of my upper robe. It bulged and the contents strained the zipper, refusing to close. I tossed away the sweater and forced the zipper closed, then pulled down the *kara çarşaf*, covering the sack like a huge belly. With sweaty fingers I tugged at the head piece and pinned it over my face.

I closed my eyes, hot with tears. Goodbye Incir, I whispered. Protect them, Apollo.

Shuffling like an old servant, head down, back bent, I picked up the tea and bread Della brought me so long ago, dried to a crust now and rattling on the tray from my trembling. I unlocked the door and, holding it open with one hip, slid out of the room to the top of the stairs.

He stood. These were not chairs, fit for a Trotoskov, that Mizou offered. In his impeccably tailored suit he looked funereal, obscenely grim among the family I loved. He did not look up when I crept, scarcely daring to breathe, down the stairs. Since when does a Trotoskov take note of a servant? And thank God they don't.

"The police station?" Boris asked.

Suat Bey bristled. Toe-to-toe with my father, Suat Bey

looked like a whippet against a bull. But he leaned forward until my father was forced to step backwards.

"There is no need to go to the police. We are cooperating. Perhaps the young lady does not wish to be found," Suat Bey growled. He looked ferocious. For the first time, I understood why Suat Bey was considered such a terror on the battle field.

My father put his head back to better look down his nose. "Old man, I am not here for a philosophical discussion on the rights of women. Hand over my daughter, or give me directions to the police station." He used *tu*.

I shuffled across the room and out the door, too frightened for even furtive eye contact with Mizou. In the kitchen I put down the tray. Yurda buzzed around the kitchen in a terrible lather, hands waving and hips swaying, muttering to herself. No doubt my father had, in the short time he'd been here, managed to exceed the limits of Turkish hospitality. All of this, despite his ignorance of the Ottoman language. I put a hand on Yurda's arm and turned her around.

"Manavgat," I begged in a whisper. "Manavgat, Istanbul, *aéroport*."

She pointed a weapon of a finger towards the dining room door. With a hissed tirade of Turkish she spit out a lecture that would fry anyone's ears, even those who didn't understand her.

"*Mon papa*." I gestured towards the sound of Boris' authoritative French, and then patted my chest. "Papa."

"*Papaz?*" At first she looked incredulous, as though I confessed genetic ties to a swine. Then she tossed back her head and clicked her tongue in livid disgust. "Istanbul," she said. Yanking black cotton over her face, she led me out the back door.

Her brother-in-law arranged a taxi to Alanya, then a bus to Istanbul. Her sister gave me a parcel of food for the trip. Her husband accompanied me to make sure I would not get lost. Twelve hours later, still dressed in *kara çarşaf* with Yurda's string of evil-eye beads around my neck, I boarded the plane for Paris.

# TWENTY-ONE

I fared well for a while, living alone, drawing in my little window overlooking Paris. I never went out unless shrouded by my *kara çarşaf.* If Boris knew where to look, he was blind to me. Of course, that is the nature of the *çarşaf.* Its dark privacy enfolded me, held close by those in Incir who I loved. And I felt safe.

Even being frugal, I cashed the last traveler's check two months before you were born. By February I had spent my last *centime.* One day mid-February, cold sleet fell on Paris, stinging my skin and dragging at my wet *çarşaf.* I knelt in front of a bakery, back to the warm wall and hands cupped towards the morning shoppers. The scent of fresh bread, pumped into the street by fans in the kitchen, was an overwhelming perfume, waking you up, Little Cricket, so that you kicked and squirmed in my womb. Morning commuters poured from the Metro, surging up the stairs with each arriving train, warm coats buttoned tight and scarves over their faces. I begged for coins from each new wave, silent, black cloth covering all but my pleading eyes.

Everything I owned lay in my knapsack, resting beside me in the grime of Paris. I would be on the street tonight, the last of my landlady's goodwill depleted, if I didn't pay at least forty of the *francs* I owed her. And you, my precious unborn baby? I had bought you the last meal I could afford. We had eaten less and less for the last few weeks, making do with two meals a day, then one, then one every other day. We would eat from the *poubelle* tonight, digging through the discarded wrappers and cigarette butts until we found something edible among the trash.

All morning I knelt, until the ache in my knees had become a numbness, reaching up my legs and gripping the womb where you kicked so restlessly. When I stood up at noon, clutching the three *francs* and the loaf of bread given by my fellow Parisians, my legs would not support me. I collapsed in a black cloud of cloth, the baguette bouncing into the mud and the *francs* scattering. As the commuters poured around me, indifferent in their busy importance, I wished with all my heart for Turkish generosity.

"*Eh bien*, are you all right, Mademoiselle?" A man leaned over me. The folds of his colorful North African robe made a rainbow blur in my vision. His skin was as dark as my *çarşaf*.

"*Oui*. I sat too long. I'll be okay."

"I would lift you, but…." He gestured with respect toward the *kara çarşaf*, and quickly dropped his hand again. "Let me call an ambulance. You are very pale."

"*Non*. Really, it isn't necessary." I struggled to stand, and passed out.

～

"Alors," said the doctor the next day. "Your baby is still alive. *Dieu sait pourquoi*." God knows why.

In particular, I thanked the god Apollo.

He put down the Doppler probe and pulled the sheet back

over my belly. "How long had it been since you had a proper meal?" He jerked his chin towards the empty tray, littered with the debris of my hospital lunch. "Was this your first in two days? Three days?"

I looked away from his critical tone, out the window to the icy rain that dripped off the lead colored eaves and flowed down the ashen stone. Gray, like my mood. Paris was a city of a hundred grays. Watered down from black despair, like a stroke from Xiao's black ink stick.

"Where is my knapsack?" I asked, still looking out the window. I didn't need his criticism; I knew how poorly I managed.

"To hell with your knapsack. Look at me."

Reluctantly I turned in his direction. He was a little man, features sharp as pinched clay. His white coat hung almost to his ankles, as though it had been intended for bigger things. White flecks twisted through his brown curls, reminding me of Della's hair.

"I have called your father," he said. "He should be arriving soon."

"*Non!*" Some tenuous grip inside me snapped. I sat up, stiff as fury.

The little doctor took a step back. "I cannot in good conscience send you out into the street. If you can give me an address, I'll let you go. Otherwise, you will wait for him to collect you."

"How did you get my name?"

"You carry a passport in your knapsack, Mademoiselle. And despite the dark, dramatic clothes, I was informed by your father's housekeeper that you are not Muslim. So you can take off that inappropriate outfit and start facing your responsibilities."

"How dare you order me about, you skinny little snail." I grabbed the wires that were plugged to plastic discs on my belly and yanked. The doctor would get even worse treatment when Boris arrived, but this bossy little do-gooder would get his first taste of Trotoskov from me.

"Get out." I spat the words. "I'm dressing, and you violate my privacy." I pointed to the door, IV line dangling from my arm like a loose thread, meant to tie down a giant.

"*Votre bébé….*"

"My baby is fine. You said so yourself. You overstep your authority." I snatched the IV needle out and watched his eyes go instinctively to the sight of blood, trickling down my forearm. Turning my back to him, I packed Yurda's *çarşaf* and tugged on jeans that no longer closed in the front, wiggled into the sweater I had found abandoned in the subway, and jammed swollen feet into socks and shoes. When I turned around, to his credit, he was still there. Shaken, but trying to hold his ground.

"Where will you go?" he asked.

I narrowed my eyes and took a step towards him. "To hell," I said, lowering my voice to a gravely whisper, "and I'll drag anyone who follows down with me."

He blinked. "You are crazy, Mademoiselle. I should call Mental Health to detain you."

"Call Mental Health, you're going to need them when my father gets here." I shouldered him aside and left as fast as I could carry my pendulous belly.

Out in the hall, I found the front desk. The receptionist was a good ten years older than I, but she had never seen Hades' hound, Xiao's scars, or Poseidon's depths. And she was not related to Boris Trotoskov. When I demanded my knapsack in the tone used to command servants, she produced it without argument or hesitation. When I leaned across the desk, glowering, and asked for a *franc* to ride the Metro, she produced that, too, avoiding eye contact as she dropped the money into my grimy hand.

I hurried to a public WC as soon as I was out of the hospital. Locking the door of the stall, I zipped open my sack and took out everything, reaching to the very bottom. There, carefully folded and preserved, was the blue wedding *çarşaf*. Somewhere, the pretty bride scrubbed her laundry with her mother-in-law, or took tea with her friends. "Apollo protect her," I whispered.

I pulled the robe from my sack and looked at its crisp, unspoiled beauty. I could slip it over my ragged jeans. In its blue folds I would feel safe and loved, as though women pressed around me, hiding my nakedness. Boris would look for a girl in jeans, or *kara çarşaf*; he would not find me. But I could not bear to soil it. With shaky hands I put on the black *kara çarşaf* instead, then grabbed my things to stuff them back into my sack.

It was then that I saw it. At the very bottom of the worn canvas, lying like a snake. The silk of Mizou's robe, orange in some light, red in others. I didn't need to unwrap it to know. Silk folded around a heart. The glass impaled forever on the handle. Tangled over with waves that looked so wet, it was a wonder the fiendish dog did not drown.

I flattened closed my knapsack and squeezed shut my eyes. For whatever reason, the mirror had chosen to travel with me.

What had been fear, hunger, and desperation, now congealed into madness. Pressed against the white metal bathroom stall, I was overwhelmed with panic. The grays of Paris, waiting outside, became watching shadows. The creaks in the room beyond the stall door were the sounds of predators. The smell of my fear marked my whereabouts for all who hunted. And he watched the streets—a merciless immortal, more relentless than my father. Watched the streets, seeking me.

For the first time, Boris' door beaconed; more than heat, a soft bed, and a hot meal lay enticingly within the steel jaws of his apartment. Boris would stand against Hades. He, with his great barrier of a will, vast ego, and snarling ability to survive, could protect me. For one moment, I considered giving up everything—you my little love, my art, my future, all that remained to me—just to put a wall between myself and terror. I was insane with fear, the jaws rising over me, threatening to strike.

Over the thousands of kilometers that separated us, I screamed for Mizou. Locked in that small bathroom stall, I shrieked her name over and over. I yelled until my voice was gone, the mirror pressed underneath me as I sank onto my knapsack, my heart empty of everything but fear.

Save me, save me Apollo. I cannot fight a god.

And in the darkness behind my closed lids I saw a figure, galloping toward me: red cape, spear as tall as a man, blazing armor. I thought at first it was Suat Bey, dressed for war. But as he came closer I could see deep set eyes and full lips. Yue Fei, or perhaps Xiao. In my confused state I couldn't tell. His horse reared before me, putting nine centuries of ferocious loyalty between us, my little baby, and the hound of hell.

The terror retreated. Gradually tile and metal, a bathroom stall, emerged from the mist around me. I lay curled on the floor, holding my belly, our hearts beating against my hands.

As soon as I could walk, I left the WC. Hidden in black, I slunk along the walls into the hole of the Metro, and took the next train to Pont Neuf.

Pont Neuf, the bridge where the insane and homeless sleep.

Sergei Chepik painted it once, adding huge, crouching gargoyles and a watchman on the topmost bell tower of Saint-Germain l'Auxerrois. The painting looks down across Pont Neuf to a mysterious and bony rendition of Notre Dame. An orange tint seeps over ashen blue Paris like a fog. A thin Paris: fat buildings shriveled to skeletons in the eerie orange light. You can't see, in his painting, the concrete quay under the bridge where I huddled with the other *clochards*. But you can see the stature of Henry IV, looking deceptively benign with his smile, his perky horse, and his pigeons. I wasn't fooled: I knew I was hunted. Even Henry IV watched for me. That painting expressed my madness as though Chepik had seen into my soul.

For three days I neither ate nor drank. I retreated far under the arches of the three hundred-year-old bridge, flattening myself into the darkest, deepest corner, clutching my knees around my huge belly, rocking. My mind was possessed by terror. Hades was after me. He had abandoned Mizou and come for me. Time passed in a haze of hallucinations: the storm, rising over Mizou's *pension*, washed the lavender off the puppy's grave and dragged down the remaining columns of Apollo's temple; Xiao's scars, white and stiff, howled with agony like burnt lips; Suat Bey covered in blood, hacked off heads, surrounded by a hundred Bulgarians; my father raised his hand to slap aside Yurda's head covering as she backed against a wall. I could see nothing of the *clochards* who came and went around me. All of Paris vanished before my nightmares.

We would have died there, child. We almost did. But on the third day a voice called my name.

"Tatyana, Tatyana…." Pounding like a fist on the door of my insanity. I don't know how long the voice hammered before I finally looked up, squinting into the dim light. "Tatyana, holy Jesus honeychild, have I found you?"

The edges of his robe caught the light: red. I knew the color. I knew the beard. I knew the softly smeared accent on American English. "Della!" I thought she was another hallucination, but such a welcome one! I reached out a hand.

"Child. Oh my God, I found you. Come here," she knelt down and held out her arms, beckoning me from the cramped corner.

"Della." I uncurled, crawled towards her.

"Oh my sweet girl, what's become of you?" She held me against her, so tight, so safe. "Let's get you out of here. Can you walk?"

"I can't leave. The mirror. King Henry's pigeons will see and they'll tell the hound. Xiao can't fight it forever, and Suat Bey fell to the Bulgarians. Help me Della. Even Apollo's temple cannot stand against it…." I babbled nonsense into the coarse fabric of her robe as she stroked my head.

"Oh, hon. Mizou said it was bad, but she didn't see the half of it. Come on now, let me take you somewhere safe." She pulled me to my feet. "Is your baby still moving?"

"*Oui.* She kicks and fights every time it rises from the sea. Such a brave little girl."

She reached for my knapsack and slung it over one shoulder. "Come on." I closed my eyes against the daylight, cowering into Della's side. She carried me against her up the stairs. "Taxi!" One hand clutching me, she waved down a car. "Take us to La Varenne."

"*Je ne parle pas Anglais, Monsieur.*" The taxi driver looked annoyed to be ordered about in English.

She ignored his surliness. "La Varenne. You understand La Varenne, don't you?" She opened the door and helped me into the back seat, climbing in after me. "Here is the address." She shoved paper into the driver's hand. I slumped against her, smelling lamb, lavender, and the glue of her artificial beard.

～

And so you were born in a two story box of a house, not unlike Mizou's hotel, but damp, drafty, and surrounded by a stone wall. Broken bottles poked from the wall's cement, and the iron gate closed with an old rusty padlock. In the back was a garden with crooked almond trees, pears, and plums, and a laurel left for wild, branches making a heavy canopy over tangled grass. Your birth certificate says you were born Marie Rose Trotoskov, and that you died ten minutes after you were born. The Armenian midwife who delivered you asked no questions. After bathing and swaddling you, she put you to my breast, and signed the paperwork declaring you dead as you suckled. It must have cost Della a fortune.

For three weeks after your birth I rested. Then one day, with you in a sling across my chest, I sat on the back porch in a scrap of spring sunshine and drew the almond flowers. I was weak from loss of blood and the defeat of reality, but in the sunshine, with a charcoal pencil in my hand, I felt threads, fine as the frost on the porch, weaving closed the holes in my mind.

Della came to sit beside me.

"I have to go soon, child. The mountain passes are clearing and I have work to do." She didn't dress as a man, now that the midwife was gone, and her softness was contained in a knit dress. Hair fell like rough water over her shoulders. With a fingertip she stroked your pudgy pink cheek. "She looks like her father."

Thank you, Apollo.

"I need to have another birth certificate made. What will you name her?"

I said without thinking, "Jiè, like her Chinese grand-mother."

Della lifted you from the sling. "Lordy, that's a short name for such a glorious face. She's going to be a pretty one." She patted you and lay you over a shoulder. "And her last name?"

I looked down at the flower lying next to my sketch, rosy, with a deeper pink in the center like your tiny full lips. The only time I had seen Xiao's last name written had been on the letter to Boris. Jiè Chin. I couldn't do it. Chin would remind me forever of betrayal: my father's betrayal of Xiao's father, Xiao's betrayal of me.

I looked up at you, sleeping against the roundness of Della's shoulder. Your skin was so white. It was the only feature of mine you inherited: my skin. Jiè Trotoskov. No. That, I would never do. Never.

Della leaned her back against the porch railing and sighed. "I've asked someone to come see you."

"*Qui?*"

"Go see for yourself, hon. She's in the living room."

Yurda was my first thought, and my heart leaped. Then I realized that Paris was too far from the dust and gossip of Incir for Yurda. Mizou? Of course, she had come for the mirror. I hurried into the living room, expecting bracelets, rings, and a braid of gray hair.

A slender form stood looking out the window, thick, dark curls pulled back in an Italian leather clip. Her pants were tight and her shoes were French high heels.

"Emma."

She turned around, every lovely hair in place, her turning graceful as a brush stroke. "Tate." She stepped forward, and then stopped, struggling to read my face. Unsure of her welcome.

"What are you doing here, Emma?" I thought I'd forgiven her, but the hatred was as strong as ever.

"I've come to help. I hear you have *un bébé*...." The sister that was to conqueror kings and guide nations stuttered to a halt in the face of my Trotoskov glare.

"Does Papa know where I am?"

"*Non.* And I won't tell him, I promise." She crossed to the couch. It looked shabby beside her, the cloth aging, worn thin next to her beauty. She sat down. "Tate, I received your drawing in the post." Her hands wandered nervously through her hair. "You could never have drawn so well if you didn't understand. I thought, *peut-être*, we could be friends—" When I didn't say anything, she looked at her hands, so slender and small against the folds of her black cashmere sweater. "George and I have money. Please let us help." The pleading look on her face could have won concessions from princes. But I was her abandoned sister; they ran to Marseille knowing full well whose hands they left me in.

I turned away. To be helped by strangers when I washed out of the sea was one thing. To be helped by the sister who should have rescued me years ago, was another.

"Della says the lease is out in two weeks. You'll be back on the street." She cleared her throat, the delicate sound a hummingbird might make. "She says you are not sleeping well, and you're haunted by some...some *miroir* that followed you from Turkey. For the sake of the baby, at least accept cash for a flat. We could support you until you find work."

"*Non.*" I faced her, reinforcing my answer with another glare.

"What are you going to do?" Only a slight rise in volume told me she was losing patience.

I stood staring at her. I was Napoleon's soldier, home from the war; I only knew how to put one foot in front of the other. When I thought about the future, a hound rose from the waves, driving me into a state of terror. I couldn't think about it. I couldn't think.

She stood up, balanced on very high heels as though they were extensions of her little feet. "Here is our address on Rue Balzac. George and I will be staying for another few days. Please ring me. I'd do anything for you, really I would." She pressed a card into my hand, and then kissed the air beside my cheeks four times, twice on each side: affection without any intrusive touching.

When she had gone I sank to the couch. Wisps of insanity drifted with dust on the floor, rifled the curtains by the heat vent, bent orchard branches and scattered the petals. I would be on the street again, hiding from Boris, from Hades. And you, my precious Cricket? If they found me, they found you.

That night, when I went to tuck in the covers of your bassinet, I found the mirror lying next to your little fist. I gasped, almost shrieked. Wrestling it from your crib, I seized it in both hands and lay in bed with it under my chest. I would close my eyes, my grip would loosen, and I'd awaken, terrified that it would get away.

I threw off the covers and padded barefoot in my nightgown into the cold night, down the stairs and to the back door. Slipping the lock, I stepped into the moonlight. With the mirror's handle still squeezed in one hand, I crossed the lawn and pulled a handful of laurel leaves off a low-lying branch. Intoxicating laurel, chewed by Apollo's priestesses for divine hallucination. "Guide me, Apollo," I whispered.

The leaves were tough to chew and bitter, numbing my tongue, juice pooling because my throat gagged and refused it. I spit out fibrous veins and stems and tried to swallow the pulp. My head buzzed and my stomach heaved. I vomited and vomited, down on my knees in the frozen grass. Finally I folded on the ground. The night roared closer, loud as the sea, then faded back, roared closer and faded back, and I was a part of the darkness, rocking, sinking to the very bottom where mysteries lie.

Michelangelo's statue of David let his raised arm fall. He stepped from his pedestal, perfect in limb and muscle, and walked that long museum hall in Florence, past the unfinished statues fighting to be released from stone. He appeared in Apollo's temple where I knelt, prostrate. He lifted the mirror out of my hands and dashed it to the ground by the laurel. A crack opened in the earth, deep enough for an anvil to fall for nine days.

"All that you make its mine." His voice poured like liquid.

You, my baby, lying on the altar, so near to that yawing crack. So calm, brave, tiny.

A woman in a silver robe took you up in her arms and walked to the cliff. Agony seared me; I could not watch you go and I could not look away. As she stepped off the edge, feet suspended in Incir's warm air, she turned to me.

Emma.

"Come for her, Tate. She'll be waiting."

Emma disappeared, blown away by the Mediterranean wind.

"Paint," whispered Apollo. "Paint, and I will protect you and that child you love so well."

~

When I woke in the morning, all was Apollo's pristine peace: ice melting, frost retreating, the earth deep and wet. The light glared with freshness. I heaved my shaking, painful body off the ground and went to take a bath.

Apollo owned me, as truly as he claimed you. Every stroke from my brush must appease him. I gathered you in your little bassinet, hid myself in the *kara çarşaf* and took the Metro to Emma's.

If she was surprised to see me, she didn't show it. She stepped aside and let me pass without a word. George sat in the drawing room, looking solid—a man who handles people's fortunes. He stood up, nodded, and then excused himself. I could see why Emma risked all to elope with him.

I set your basket on the coffee table, the honey weave of rattan reflected in the glass. You were awake, dark eyes wandering, trying to focus on this new and shocking world.

"Take her to London." I blurted it out as quickly as I could, terrified that I would lose heart and snatch you out of the basket.

Emma pressed her lips together, looking pale.

"Raise her as your daughter and never tell who her mother is. I don't want her to grow up thinking her mother was insane, an immoral slut who had her out of wedlock and killed her father—"

"Stop, Tate." Emma took a step toward me, holding out her hands, shadows of pain dark on her face.

I gripped my collapsing shoulders, wracked with sobs, praying for the stamina to go on. "If the story must be told, let me tell her."

Emma kicked off her shoes, and in few paces stood in front of me. She lifted strands of blonde hair from my eyes, fingers as soft as feathers. "I'll never tell her a thing." She swept tears off my face. "I'll send her back when you're ready. I will love her as my own."

I tore free of her touch and pulled the mirror from my knapsack. I bound the heart and handle tight in Mizou's silk.

"Lock this up. Never let anyone touch it or look at it."

"It will go in George's wall safe." Emma took the silky package, and then put an arm around me, pressing me to her chest. We are the same height, Emma and I, when she wears no heels. She smelled of Italian leather and Chanel. Holding her close, I could feel how frail she was under her well-cut clothes. She would not have survived, had we changed places as children. She would have been crushed by Boris, like Fleur: folded up, mangled and bent, nothing left but a sweet scent. I had protected her. Throughout those long and empty years, I had given a profound gift.

"Tate?"

"*Oui?*"

"Forgive me." She clutched me closer. "I was as frightened of you as I was of Papa. I couldn't see how you differed, you were so much alike. I never thought about how you suffered."

She said this into my shoulder, her tears making vague circles on dark cloth. "Forgive us for not taking you with us."

I kissed her cheek, hot and salty, powdery with rouge.

"Take care of my little Jiè, and I will forgive you anything."

~

When I returned to La Varenne, Della was dressed as a man, her monstrous suitcase packed and by the door. She sat on the couch with a glass of wine, reading the paper and scratching her beard.

"Well?" she asked, as I collapsed into the seat next to her.

"I have a last name for Jiè."

"Hallelujah."

"Jiè Galt."

She put down the wine and turned to me. I had seen Della fierce, seductive, and annoyed, but I had never seen Della exhausted.

"Praise the Lord. You made the right choice little sister, for you, and for the baby." She took my hand, and love traveled up my cold arm, seeped through my empty heart, and flowed into my hollow soul. "Now you need to put yourself back together, hon. You're splintered as an axed log."

# TWENTY-TWO

o what happened to you, Maman?" I ask. I've sat in her drawing room all these hours, clobbered by her tale, listening as she once did to Suat Bey.

Hard to suss out what's real or fanciful, and perhaps there's a bit of mental in there, too. But every time she meets my eyes—so like my dad's, she claims—I can see she's tangled in pain and guilt. And love. Tied up with aching ribbons of love.

"What happened to me, my Cricket?" Maman's knackered, collapsed back in her chair with those sea blue eyes pinched closed.

"Yes, after you kissed me goodbye and gave me up. You did kiss me goodbye then, right?"

Emma raised me to expect kisses. It makes my heart knock about in my chest when I think about it. I have to get out of this spot of bother, get back to London, and maybe do a hint of apologizing.

"Yes, *bien sûr* I kissed you. Your little head was as round as a melon, and your hair stuck up like a fluffy baby chick's."

I laugh because I like this. It reminds me of being tickled as a child, chased about the house, and read to before I was sent to bed. I never meant to run from that. It was the crack, you see, gaping underneath me. I didn't know how to win through to solid ground. Even as a little one, there was this feeling of something reaching up to snatch me. And I did things it's a dead cert I'm sorry for.

"So, then?"

"There's not much to tell."

"Then it won't take but a minute. Please, Maman, where did you go when you left La Varenne?"

She opens her eyes and stares: not much like herself these last few hours. She trembles as if old nightmares have returned. She clocks the pigeons on the balcony with a jaded eye. She sniffs at shadows in the corners, as though they had a wet dog's pong. "All right, I'll tell you. But it's late, don't you want a rest?"

"No, Maman. I can't rest, not knowing."

~

Those were the days that I will always see in gray, a hundred nuances of gray, like my beloved Paris. Gray, like the ghost I had become, trying to find something solid in my mind to hold on to.

Della gave me twenty *francs*, nearly all she had left, and her pair of Lapis Lazuli earrings. Yes, my Cricket, the same earrings you gave to Pekelo. Don't look so crushed, child. They were to be a gift for your twentieth birthday; to give a gift, one must open the hand and let it go.

Della departed by train from the Gare de L'Est.

I decided to live in the Metro, so all my coins could buy food.

Seven trains meet at the center of Paris. Between Châtelet les Halles and Châtelet winds a maze of corridors, too tangled to secure, too busy to patrol. Hidden in the *kara çarşaf*, I found all of the corners where the *gardien* never swept, and learned the hours when the begging was best. Even during the best hours I made practically nothing, and soon Della's money was gone.

The dreams and illusions were relentless at first, a wedge in reality through which The Furies poured. I wrapped myself, sometimes even my eyes, in the *çarşaf*, hoping like a child that what I could not see, would not see me. As the mirror was transported away, I could feel the horror ease.

Then one day, George locked the mirror in his safe. I know, because the visions abruptly stopped. I sat up that afternoon and saw thousands of commuters, rushing into their lives with heels clicking and coats fluttering, and I knew by the fact that I could see them, that I was safe.

I took my charcoal pencil out of my knapsack and drew the first face I saw: a child, watching over his shoulder as his mother yanked him down the corridor. So like the little mouse I loved. *Allahaısmarladık!*

Within a few days I had sketched an arc of faces on the concrete passageway where I slept: people stilled mid-flight, a moment recorded from their frantic lives. When the pencil was nothing but a nubbins, and I knew it was time to rejoin the world. I could live without food, a home, or sanity, but I could not live without a charcoal pencil. I left the Metro and walked to the Marais.

"You again," said the old *juif*. "Have you stolen from the same horrible man who came looking for the last jewels?"

"These are not stolen. They were a gift." I held out Della's

Lapis Lazuli earrings, a deeper blue than the Mediterranean, warm from my hand as though they had baked in the sun. I ached to hang them in my ears again and go down to dinner, you, my baby girl, on my hip. A story from Suat Bey, a lecture from Yurda, a kiss on the cheek from little Damad; if I could only have bought these things. I would have paid anything. I would have sold anything.

The man turned away. His hand-knit sweater stretched over his broad back, making fine holes that showed dots of white shirt. Like light from the baskets over Mizou's dining room table.

"I'm done with charity to you. I'll lose my license, buying stolen goods. Take your earrings elsewhere."

"Please. I have nothing to eat. Nothing else to sell. My father won't come looking for these, I promise."

"Your promises are *bon á rien*. Scat, before I call the police."

Dropping onto a stool, he pointedly picked up a book and began to read. His white hair fell forward like Suat Bey's. His old hands looked strong. Xiao's hands would have looked like that someday: loose skin over long bones, ropey veins over dogged muscles. I thought of Yurda's plump hands, how they smelled of mint when she arranged my *başörtüsü*.

"Could I draw you?" I asked.

"What?" My question startled him, and he turned around, hostile voice contradicting the curiosity in his eyes.

"A portrait. I'll only charge you six *francs*."

"And why would I want a portrait, drawn by *tu*?" He had grand, square cheekbones and a long single eyebrow, pulled down in the middle with contempt.

I dug in my knapsack and pulled out Xiao's pillowcase. My hands looked painfully sallow as I reached into the white cotton softness and found my work.

He took the pages. Adjusting his thick glasses, he thumbed through them, now and then giving a brief glare in my direction as if to remind me that we were not on good terms.

"You steal from artists, as well as your father?" He rested my work on the counter and did not offer the drawings back.

"Those are mine."

"I don't think so, Mademoiselle. You don't look like a girl with that kind of talent." He flicked a hand towards my ragged robe, dirt ground into the fabric.

"Let me draw you. I'll prove it."

"For six *francs*? Ha!"

I tucked in a strand of hair, slipping from my *çarşaf.* "I'll draw you for nothing. If you like it, you will pay me ten *francs* to keep it."

He hesitated, long enough to let me know that he was interested, short enough to let me see that he was bargaining. "I'm too busy." He pushed the art in my direction over the counter.

"No you're not. I'm the only one in here. You have nothing to do. Nothing to lose." I used *vous.* I reached in the pouch of my knapsack and pulled out my charcoal pencil. "Sit down and read your book, this won't take long."

"Four *francs.*"

"*D'accord.* Four *francs*, and you will also buy one of my other drawings for ten *francs.* But only if you like the portrait."

The old man paused, then nodded slightly, and his thin smile surprised us both. "*Marché conclu.* You're clever. If you weren't so dishonest I'd hire you to run my store." He sat down and picked up his book. "Put the photo of my wife in the background," he said.

I moved my art aside to clear a surface on the glass counter. The scrap of charcoal pencil was dull, so I spent a moment sharpening the little stub with my pen knife.

The store owner bent over his book, trying to look absorbed. After a few minutes he let fascination get the better of him. "Well?" he asked, looking up. "What are you waiting for?"

"Do you have paper?"

"You're an artist and you don't have paper?"

"*Non.*"

"What makes you think I have any?"

"Any kind of paper will do. I can draw on anything."

He frowned, as I remembered Yurda frowning when I asked for paper in her kitchen, then I took from her precious hands a blue lined *cahier.* Here, I was handed a thin sheet of onion correspondence paper.

"*Voila.* Get to work now, and stop wasting my time."

Having nowhere to sit, I stood at the counter and watched the man read. Worries rested in the corners of his mouth, pulling them down, and I wondered if he had children raking up trouble. His eyebrows, so severe as he ignored my scrutiny, couldn't hide his gruff humor. His wife rested in the photo on the shelf over his shoulder, a lovely lady of seventy or more, with dense white hair and a coy expression. I drew her first.

I drew her huge, hanging over his shoulder in a gilded frame, occupying the whole wall behind him as she clearly occupied his heart. I drew him scholarly, considering the words faintly scratched on the page as one might consider the universe, his thick brow slightly raised in wonder. I drew his hands on the book with the love I would have drawn Xiao's.

When I was finished I cleared my throat. "For you, Monsieur." I held out the translucent page.

He put aside his book and took the portrait. For a moment I thought I had insulted him. He stepped back and dropped the onion skin on the counter, face contorted.

Then I realized that he was fighting the urge to cry. "Who are you?" he asked.

"No one. Just an artist."

He reached to his cash register and rang it open. With strong, old fingers he took out a fifty *franc* note and laid it between us. "Take your drawings of crickets to Qianlong on the quay by Notre Dame. Tell him Meir Resnick sent you."

~

Qianlong. You will never know him, *ma fille*, as he died a few years ago. Tuberculosis, I believe, or lung cancer. But years before he coughed himself into the grave, he took this half crazed, destitute artist off the streets and made her famous. Fame can be an ugly thing, chaining humans to a stone and displaying them naked for the hungry world. But I did not have the luxury of painting for the world; I labored to satisfy Apollo. You lay on his altar, my Jiè, his knife forever at your precious throat.

In any other hands, as young as I was, my style could have been chiseled and chipped into a cliché, my art as mediocre as the critics who praised it, and Apollo would have abandoned us both. But not with Qianlong by my side. He raised Chinese crickets: fighting insects that tore each other in half when they fought, and singing insects whose voices were as sweet as Suat Bey's harem tulip. He was not afraid of ancient gods, hunting beasts, or dead heroes. And he had no patience for the mediocre.

The first time I met Qianlong on the quay, he lounged under the flapping awning of a curbside stall. He was perhaps fifty at the time, legs so long that he sprawled over two folding chairs, muscled arms tattooed with fighting cranes, a burning cigarette between two fingers, a newspaper covering his face. Spread on the table before him were cages made by his own hands: hollow gourds with fitted wooden lids, clay jars with etched elaborate doors, woven bamboo baskets. Hanging behind him were slatted boxes, curved to hold a prized insect against the hip. Each cage contained a cricket. Their creaks and trills crooned down the sidewalk where tourists strolled towards Notre Dame.

I cleared my throat once with nervousness, then cleared my throat again for his attention. He snored. Finally I said, *"Pardon, Monsieur."*

He threw off the newspaper and stood up. "What?"

It took all I had not to run. His face was one hideous scar, razed so badly by old burns that his features melted together. I dropped my gaze from his disfigurement and cautiously inched my drawings forward. "Meir Resnick sent me."

He glanced down at the leaping, joyful paintings of crickets. All of his intense energy congealed into a knot. With practiced swiftness he pounced on my art as though catching a living creature. He rifled through my drawings, scrutinizing them with lidless eyes, every back and forth of his eyeballs visible under tight skin. I stood, wishing I could flee but not willing to abandon my work.

"Where did you get these?"

"I drew them." I found it impossible to look him in the eye.

"And who wrote the Chinese characters?" He passed a finger, blessedly unscarred, down the column of Xiao's writing.

"A friend."

He leaned forward and stuck the stiff, flat sheet of his face into mine. "These are love poems to a blonde. To you, Mademoiselle?"

"A—a," I stammered, backing away from him, "a lover wrote them."

Love poems. The enormity of my ignorance hit me in the gut. How little I had known about Xiao's deep and complex loves: his political alliances and patriotism, his filial duty to his betrayed father, and his tender passion for me.

I looked into Qianlong's eyes, the raw unrelenting pain of them, and I teared up. "He died," I whispered.

Qianlong leaned back, still clutching my work. If my sadness touched him, his rigid face didn't show it. "The poems are good, but the drawings are exquisite."

Nothing about Xiao was merely good, I wanted to say, but I didn't argue.

"What do you plan to do with these?" he asked.

"Sell them, so I can eat."

"*Non.*" He set them carefully on the table. "That would be very foolish. We can do much better than that. Give me a few days to reach my contacts in Hong Kong."

He stretched a hand under his counter and took out two pieces of cardboard. With an X-Acto knife, he fashioned a neatly folded and trimmed portfolio, and tucked the drawings inside. His arms were bare despite the cold spring weather, and the cranes on his biceps writhed in a perpetual fight—more alive than his face, which he could hardly move. His hands were the least frightening thing about him, so I watched those.

He put what he had made on the counter. "Where are you staying?"

"I live in the Metro tunnel, Châtelet les Halles."

"Homeless?" He reached for one of his insects, singing in its cage on the table beside him. He nudged the cage into a ray of sunshine. "You may sleep on my couch," he said.

I snatched up the portfolio and backed away. "*Non, merci.* I'll come back in a few days."

He laughed, his lips mere faint lines, the sound muffled by what remained of his nose. "I wouldn't touch you, *ma fille.* I'm offering you a place to stay, not *un micheton.*"

"I only sell my drawings."

"Understood."

～

We sit cozy on the settee, Maman's thinness up against me, barely padded by that horrible wool dress she wears. I lace my fingers through her cold ones and squeeze, urging her on with it. "So you went to live with him, Maman?"

"*Oui.* When I stopped being afraid, we became friends. We were never lovers. I think, in fact, he preferred men, though I never pried into that part of his life."

"And you wrote *Little Cricket*?"

Tears flow freely, wetting her chalky cheeks. "Because I longed for you so. As I drew, curled in the window seat of Qianlong's flat, I told myself the stories I had once imagined your grandma Jiè telling Xiao. But now, it was me tucking you in at night, dreaming of kissing you on the forehead, wishing to see your eyes drift closed as the story ended. Every year, photos of you arrived—birthday parties, football teams, giggling groups of friends. Emma sent them as regularly as the spring until you turned thirteen. And then…they stopped coming."

This stabs me worse than Pekelo's knuckles in my ribs, and now I'm crying, too, aching more than any kicking I ever took. "I'm sorry Maman. You've every right to go spare. I've been rubbish as a daughter."

"I'm not angry at you, Cricket." She reaches a thin hand and combs her fingers through my fringe, the roots growing out black now that I have no blue dye to wash through them.

"Enough for tonight." She kisses me on the forehead. "Sleep now, for in the morning we must find the strength to face our troubles."

# TWENTY-THREE

I wake to a low snarl, ripping into my sleep, making my pulse run for it. I sit bolt upright and account for every shadow in the room, ready to swing a fist.

Nothing. No stink of wet dog. No panting. Outside, then? I stare at Maman's lacy nets that hinder the view of Square Barye. Paris is unnaturally still, as though the inhuman sound shushed the wavering sirens and roaring autos.

Fear's got me plastered to Maman's settee. It takes a bit to dredge up courage and swing my bare feet onto the floor. But that's the first thing Pekelo taught me: look your opponent in the eye. I creep across the drawing room and push aside the nets. Square Barye's trees stand black and thick, the dirt underneath all shadows. I can barely make out the rail between the grass and the Seine. Nothing moves. I shiver, watching. Sometimes in the ring, it's best just to wait: sniff and taste the air, know what your opponent smells like. But all I can smell is my fear, sweating out of me in icy-cold drips.

Something creaks behind me. I whirl around, fists up, and almost snap kick Maman in the frigging chin. It's a devil of a habit, this sneaking up every time the dog raises his snout.

"Bloody hell, Maman, I almost clobbered you!"

"*Pardon, chérie.*" She snaps on the light, clutching a jersey over her nightdress. Her face is lined and peaky, and I wonder if she's slept. She takes my hand and pulls me down beside her on the settee. "It's time now, Cricket. I need to understand who's at risk before I break the mirror. Tell me what happened."

~

Where to start, Maman, with the folly of my jealousy?

How could I take hold of a competitor who wasn't there? Gejra had no neck I could sling an arm around, pressing into that soft indent below her throat. She had no knee I could snap backwards, no ears I could stun by quick slaps to the sides of her head. She floated, untouchable and faultless in my imagination, always just beyond my pathetic attacks.

So it was Chander who took the brunt of it. I punished him in every way I could: holding him down in the ring, joints strained seconds beyond his taps for mercy, hitting too hard in bony unprotected parts, leaving bruises. In Pekelo's class we had always been brutal, but now I was brutal and angry.

I didn't tell him why. For all of September I left in a hurry after sparring, pushing off before I gave Chander the time of day. I grieved between the polished wood shelves of Charing Cross Library, assured he'd never ferret me out: who'd look for Jiè among books? I graffed lonely new territory—City and Southwark—well-guarded tourist areas where Chander would never think I'd go.

But his eyes still lit up when he saw me, voice patient and steady as a bloody saint. His sweetness was going to drive me round the bend. And I wondered; had Parul told him we'd bickered over him, like two wrinklys at a bargain bin? Given

Parul's dislike of quarreling she'd like as not kept mum about it. So nothing had changed for him. He was still engaged, and I was still his best mate. Only now I was in love, and I couldn't help but speculate if he was in love, too.

So I searched for hints, compiling a mental list: the stiffy pressed against my leg—he'd always had one—when he pinned me to the ground; the way his eyebrows shot up the moment he saw me, as if a leaping heart had startled him; the way he called my name, then unconsciously ran one finger over his lips, watching me walk toward him.

Instead of asking, "*Had* I won his love?" I'd have done better to ask, "*Should* I win his love?" Was love really called for, given his engagement? But I'd grown up confusing right and wrong with getting-out-of-a-tight-spot or getting collared. I was far too clever (I decided) to get collared in love alone. Which meant, when all's said and done, that if I could wiggle his love out of this one tight spot, all would be cushdy.

I started doing little things to nudge his love along. I took my bra off before we sparred and let my Bristols hang soft and free. I smiled at him, great thumping grins with extended eye to eye resuscitation. I tried to chat him up, asking about his studies and walking him home while he griped over A-levels, standing for long good-byes under his family's window. But he was as good as blind; he kept his hands to himself and his focus on his future. After about a month of being left on the doorstep, instead of being invited up—we'd been best mates for almost four years and I had yet to see his parent's flat—I felt a bit desperate.

"Right, then," I said one day, as he was about to scoot into his foyer, "I'm going to graff the London Eye. Want to muck in with me?"

Did you ever take a flight of fancy, Maman, hoping to dazzle somebody, then realize there is no retreat? My cheeks pinked up, thinking what a prat I was. Graff the London Eye? Not likely.

Chander grinned, his smile wide and wobbly. "You're a wonder." For a second his eyes met mine and he gazed through my sockets, down my throat, and all the way to my sweet cup of tea. "Why the London Eye?"

Now that it was out, the idea glowed in brilliant color, and it occurred to me—"Millions of tourists a day," I said. And such a curious three dimensional space. What could I piece there? Whatever, it would not be like any graff ever seen. Maybe not a half-witted idea, after all. I flung my arms overhead with the sudden thrill of it, and his gaze slid for a tick to my jugs. Then he turned his eyes to the street and retreated a few paces.

"I'm off. Here comes my mum." He slid into the doorway and hesitated, frowning, smiling, frowning: a fight between his lips and the devil. Finally he added, "Meet me at the storage container after closing."

I beat down the biggest smile in love history. "Seven or so?"

He nodded and slammed the entry door.

I backed up against the brick wall and stood there, enjoying my victory. Enjoying the people rushing round each other on the narrow pavement, cheeks red in the cool

October afternoon. Enjoying the flow of his mum's sari as she hobbled toward me. Ashra swung a string grocery sack with carrot greens poking out, and every time she dragged that dead left foot, the sack bumped her in the bum. Whoosh clomp whack, whoosh clomp whack went her sari, foot, and bag. She didn't speak English, Chander's mum, so she just nodded when she opened the flat door, her eyes crinkled slits as if she were trying to like me.

I could have wondered, Maman, about Ashra's bravery, facing the world every day with that left arm and leg that refused to go along. I could have asked myself how her life would be different if Chander made the family's fortune. But I was enjoying the fantasy of paint, streaming from a can and fanning up the A-frame legs of The Eye, an explosion of crickets scattering over one of the world's biggest Ferris Wheels. And most of all, I was enjoying my victory over Gejra, love's heat in my stomach, cozying up to my cup of tea.

There wasn't yards of leg room in the storage container, but Chander made it nice by rolling a rug over his sister's bolts of cotton—a homemade futon of sorts. Neither of us could stand without whacking the metal ceiling, but with a few torches hung from above, it was snug. The only bit missing was a loo.

I was bright-eyed and bushy-tailed, waiting as he rolled out the rug that first evening. I reckoned that he was going to make a play for me, and though I wasn't ready to bunk up, I looked forward to a kiss or two.

But Chander stretched out on his stomach, dug a notebook from his slicker pocket, and laid down the serious facts: Lambeth has the tightest security in all London. One hundred and sixty council owned CCTVs, plus relocatable police cameras, Transport of London cameras, and spots on the underground. Talking cameras even tell you where the bin is if you leave rubbish on the park bench. Graffing the London Eye and not getting nicked was practically out of the question.

"How much time you going to need, luv?" he asked.

Bloody hell, I didn't know. I'd just suggested this on a lark, to turn his head. And now the idea had legs and a heartbeat.

"Half an hour?"

"Half an hour—take CCTV down for half an hour; are you daft?"

"The Eye is friggin' *big*, Chander."

He rolled over and lay on his back, gorgeous eyes searching the wavy metal ceiling only three feet from his nose. "Can you climb in the dark, no torch? I can probably think of a way to get the cameras off—not for long, mind you. But we can't have you visible from below."

"Fair enough, I'll climb in the dark."

I hadn't sorted that bit either. Somehow I'd have to go up a slippery metal leg and hang on while I graffed. I reached and poked a finger in his ribs. They had more muscle on them than I remembered; he was less the bony boy now, more the lean man. "Lighten up, heavyweight. This is fun, remember?"

Chander closed his eyes and lay there for too long, face grim and miserable. I squirmed inside, wishing we'd get off security and on to kissing. Finally he said, "I shouldn't be doing this. It's all frolic and sport for you, and your parents will bail you out if you get banged up. If I go to jail, I'll rot there. Then, what would become of my family?" His eyes snapped open. "I swear I get brain dead around you." He rolled over and propped his elbows on the rug, heavy head in his hands, the sleeve of his woolly close enough to brush my nose.

And it just popped out of me. "Do you love her?"

"Who?" He turned his face to me.

"Gejra."

You'd expect a bloke to cringe when you clump him with a surprise, but not Chander. He just kept burning into me with those melty brown eyes.

"I've been engaged since I was five, Jiè. That's why we moved here—to keep our father's promises. I'll go back to Mumbai, and when Gejra turns eighteen we'll marry. I'll spend the rest of my life supporting the whole bloody lot of them. It's what I have to do."

I felt like a total doughnut, a hole where I should have had a middle. "Don't you want to?"

He blinked, rolled his gaze to the ceiling. "Does it matter what I want? I'm not going to leave my sisters to wrestle it out alone."

"But do you love her?" I asked.

The storage container was quiet, his breath slow and tight. The side of his face lay in an edge of torchlight, a slice of a circle shining on just one eyeful of his pain.

"I don't know. I haven't seen her since I was a kid. She's a bit of all right, I suppose."

I couldn't leave well enough alone, even though I could see

how I battered him. We're two of a kind, Maman. We can't take what we've been given, and be content.

"But you're going to marry her," I insisted.

"Absolutely."

Suddenly the smells around me seemed very foreign; the curry hurt my head, the cotton dust made my eyes water. I needed to clear off before I started gagging. It was hot, unbearably hot in there. I rose to a crouch, the flippin' container only five feet tall.

"Where are you going?" he asked.

"I need air."

He grabbed my hand. "Wait, Jiè."

"Wait for what? For your wedding? For you to go back to your dolly in Mumbai? Don't be a dickhead."

He got to his knees. "I'm sorry."

He crawled closer. I turned to go but he pressed up, the bones of his pelvis against the round of my arse, his long rake of ribs draped over my back, his hands cupping the softness of my chest. "Give me this gift," he whispered. "I love you, Jiè. Please, stay."

I hunched there, enveloped by him. When has the heart ever listened to the mind, Maman? If only I'd thought of our future, perhaps I would have sorted it out a bit better. But I was too selfish by half. All I could see was that Chander wanted me. I hadn't the strength to turn away. I turned round instead and opened my mouth, my heart, and my knickers.

～

We spent all winter and into spring preparing. That was our excuse for meeting in the storage container after the market closed, running hands over each other, using as many condoms as we did reams of note paper. We fit together. Not just two long bodies whose groins and lips aligned, but minds that swelled where the other dipped. Do you understand, Maman? Any bump in the road, he lifted me over. Any wall in his path, I found a way round. Graffing The Eye became our labor of love.

Chander took on the headache of security, photographing CCTV placements, calling up videos on the library computer and studying which camera saw where. I suggested a black paintball gun for the peskiest lenses, he figured out which wires to snip.

That left me with what to paint. I must have done a thousand sketches, and nothing came within a mile. I wanted something brilliant, unforgettable. A deep upwelling of wildness, rising from the ground and escaping over London. The turning wheel making the painted crickets flutter to life. A news clipping Chander would take from his wallet and stare at when he was Gejra's, and know that he was, in fact, still mine.

Maybe he would be mine; we'd bolt from London after it was pieced and live somewhere hot and sandy. Or he'd forgo his family and enroll at University of London. We'd get a flat together, someday he'd marry me. I created better fanciful futures than I did sketches for The Eye. Everything that came off my pen frustrated me. The effect wasn't right, the crickets didn't fit, the concept wouldn't suit the space.

Not only was my art floundering, but I had to be upstanding: going to school, pressing my uniform, even doing some bloody homework. Otherwise George would take my pocket money away. And I needed dosh because paint was pricey. Thirty-six- to forty-square-feet of ground, plus eighty or more feet up the A-frame legs—that was thirty cans at least. At three and a half pounds a can, that was over a hundred pounds just to piece the base. And I'd not even figured in the capsules that hung round the wheel, carrying passengers high over London. Then add exchange into Euros and posting from *Deutschland,* because I wouldn't settle for anything less than the best paint. I sneaked to Emma's dressing table one night and found she'd impounded her jewelry box; the dressing table was bare but for a hairbrush. So I nicked everything George hadn't bolted down, bargaining hard with Alton to drive up my cut. Coins accumulated slowly, too slowly; the letter came in March that Chander was accepted into Mumbai University, pending passing his A-levels in June. His term in London was nearly done.

So I was as cross as two sticks on my nightly tramp to The Eye two weeks ago. That time of evening the promenade along the Thames has only late commuters, who hardly looked at a girl in school uniform with a rucksack full of books. I stood alone under the thrusting arms of the base, scuppered. Thirty-two capsules, barely silver in the darkness, hung locked by a circle of spokes. The capsules trembled in the breeze as if they fancied taking flight. But I couldn't paint the burst of crickets I wanted; the spokes were too thin to piece. The turning wheel was too symmetric, mechanical, inevitable. There was no freedom, for all my hoping, no flying away with youthful power and vigor. We were trapped, Chander and I, and deep in my hollow I knew it. He would not turn aside from love for his family, no matter how he loved me. And I was wrong to ask.

I walked home in the spring rain across Waterloo Bridge, looking down over the rail at the silver Thames. A flickering sheen of city light hid cold, sullied currents below. Both our love and The Eye were entirely hopeless. But I could not stand, Maman, to go back to painting little corners of dark, pissed-on walls. I wanted the extraordinary, and I wanted every bit of Chander's love; I didn't want to relinquish even a bite until the whole was consumed. So I would order paint, cut stencils, and hold out hope.

I was twenty pounds short, that's why I took the mirror. I didn't know squat about it; it simply looked like something Alton could sell.

One day Mum's dressing table was barren. That next evening the mirror lay next to her hairbrush, orange silk falling open to show its face. I snatched it so fast I hardly looked at it, scampering off to catch Alton before he shut up shop for the night. I needed to get my paint order in the post, and what a lucky little sod I was to have something to offer for sale.

Alton was rolling down blinds as I sped round the corner.

"Wait!" I huffed up to the door.

"What ya got, little lady?" Alton is from Arizona or New Mexico—I can never keep them sorted—and for all appearances he thinks he's a cattle rustler, complete with slicked-back hair, turquoise belt clasp, and dusty, pointed boots. But then he ruins the effect with ever-so-expensive cigars dangling from the pocket of his tailored tweed coat.

"Sell," I panted, reaching in my rucksack and pulling out the silk and mirror.

"Hmm. Bring it inside."

He slam-locked the metal blinds and led me into the store. Since he'd shut for the night only one dingy bulb was burning. The untidy pile-up on his shelves was beyond the glow, and the only visible things were his little square cash desk, two high bar stools for customers, and his old laptop. Alton never procures a thing without searching the net. His keyboard is grotty with fingerprints and crumbs and makes sticky little sounds when he taps.

He powered up his computer. When he put aside the silk and turned the glass over, he whistled.

"Nasty thing," he murmured, and he quickly set it down.

He lifted his gaze to me, soft bags sagging under his eyes, his tanned wrinkles drawn back in a grimace, taking me in for a long moment. He wanted to ask where I'd nicked it from, I could see it in his eyes, but he made his living from not asking, so he looked away instead. His hand hovered over the mirror, clearly reluctant to touch, and I saw the mosaic back for the first time: a three-headed dog, one head snarling right in my face, one alert, stalking something in the distance, one asleep as though horribly sated. Fear gripped me in the chest, held me to the spot. I might be nuts, but I could swear that dog hunted me, circled and sniffed, closing in as I stood. No rational reason— pure instinct made my pins tremble with the urge to run.

"Must be off." I backed toward the door. Alton stopped tapping on his grimy keyboard, grinning as I shied away. I didn't care. "Give us a price tomorrow," I said, and I bolted.

I fled Soho like a rabbit, darting and panicked, blind to traffic and pedestrians. I was almost flattened, leaping the center railing on Shaftesbury when a lorry swung off of Earlham and caught me in the road. But I didn't let up.

I arrived at the storage just as Parul finished her prayers. I ducked round the corner, heart pounding, and spied through the door as she knelt before her portable altar, dusting every speck off the painting of Krishna, refilling bowls of colored powder, and closing the incense burner. Spot on in the center of the altar was Chander's university acceptance letter.

I hadn't looked Parul in the eye since Chander and I started shagging, and it's a dead cert I wasn't up for it then. So I stayed hidden as she kissed her father's photo, pressed her palms together in a bow, and closed the doors of the little wooden shrine. Then she got up off her knees, straightened leaning bolts of cotton, and inspected her neatly arranged goods before she locked the container door. She walked off, leaving behind the mystic scent of charcoal incense. She prayed relentlessly now, four times a day Chander had said, by way of explaining how incense now overpowered all other smells in the container. I crouched down between metal walls and waited, hanging onto my knees, shaking. It was daft to hide there, like a kid with a monster under her bed.

I wish I could say I felt guilty as I shivered—regretted all the wayward things I'd done, and was about to do. But my craving for Chander was made of sterner stuff than my morals. So I huddled, frightened, missing him, resenting that he'd found something to delay our nightly rendezvous.

And I tried to suss out how Emma had come by that horrid mirror, and why she'd left it about so conveniently when she'd locked the rest up tight. Eventually I convinced myself that it was just a stupid bloody mirror, and that Chander truly had stood me up. It took until the small hours to dredge up enough courage to slink home. I made my way to my parent's flat by the broadest, best lit roads, and scrambled up the rope dangling from my dormer window.

The next day after school I dropped by Alton's eBay and poked among the shelves, waiting for his punters to finish their business and clear out. All sorts of things crowded Alton's shop: a heaping muddle, offered for sale, none of it ever dusted, and your guess is as good as mine how Alton ever found things.

Finally the shoppers cleared out and I had Alton to myself. He pulled a lock-box from under his cash desk and keyed it open. The silk had been wrapped tight to hide every inch of the back and glass. I plopped my rucksack on the counter—a wall between myself and the dogs.

"Three hundred pounds," he said.

Bloody hell! Alton studied me, obviously keen for some hint as to where the mirror came from. It took a minute to pull round from my shock. "For the both of us, or just my cut?"

"You get a fifth," he said.

"No effin' way!" Alton had never given less than a quarter, and I wasn't about to let him prey on me now. "Half."

"A quarter."

"A third, and you owe me a favor."

Alton narrowed his teeny blue eyes. "You don't want this thing, little lady, it's cursed. I'm doing you a favor by getting rid of it."

"Get stuffed, Alton. It's worth a packet."

He drummed his fingers on the counter. Was the bit about a curse just a way to beat down my cut? No—I knew in my trembling guts, and from Alton's unease, that it wasn't.

"Fair enough: a third and I'll tell you where I got it," I said, "and you'll explain about the curse."

He rocked back on the heels of his boots, pulled a cigar from his tweedy pocket, and bit off the end. For Alton, this meant we had a done deal.

"This puppy here," he wiggled a knobby finger over the mirror, "has the markings of witchcraft. We Anglos don't truck much with the supernatural, but Hispanos believe in all kinds of creepy shit. Some folks in New Mexico might claim this glass is love charmed."

I laughed, on edge. Maybe a love charm could untangle my muddle with Chander, but then again, winning his love wasn't the hitch. "So that's the curse, is it? Seems to me that would make it more valuable."

Alton stretched over his cash desk, close enough that I could smell the bitter, gnawed cigar clenched in his teeth. "You lookin' for a free lunch? You want to fill your cute little belly and not pay the piper? 'Cause I've never seen it, not in all my horse-tradin' years. Nice things *always* come with a high price tag."

I had that taped; that mirror was no blessing. It scared the liver out of me, and I was absofrigging-not going to touch it again, love charm or no.

"Just hawk it," I said.

Alton lit his cigar and blew reeky smoke toward the ceiling . He had a strict rule about asking, but that didn't mean I wasn't to tell.

"Right then, so I nicked it off my mum's dressing table."

He narrowed his eyes, like he tasted a big meaty slice of porky pie.

"It's true, I swear. I've no clue where she got it." I held out my hand. "One hundred quid, if you please."

Still scowling, he stubbed out his burning cigar tip, then dug in his cash box and laid ten crisp tenners on my palm. I snatched up my rucksack and legged it out of there before he could change his mind. I put an order in the post that afternoon, rush delivery. We could graff The Eye next week.

# TWENTY-FOUR

That night, Chander finally deigned to bring his arse to the storage. I'd been waiting for twenty minutes between the walls, and I was seriously shirty.

"As a matter of interest, where were you?"

"My mum's doing poorly." He was crumpled and mussed, as if he'd slept fully clothed. He slumped as he shook out the rug, then he threw himself onto our little bed and held out his arms. "Give us a kiss," he said as I plunked myself down beside him.

His bad news slapped the face off my plan to give him what for, but resentment still ricocheted about inside—I didn't fancy being second place. But I told myself to grow up and get on with it.

"Worse, is she?"

"It comes and goes. Can we talk about something else?"

"Righto, sorry." I sat up and dug in my rucksack, finding our plans. I cringe to think about how quickly, and with such relief, I put aside his family. "I ordered paint today. Should arrive early next week." I breathed deep, sucking in excitement. "Shall we piece The Eye on Wednesday?"

Chander propped himself on two elbows. "So soon?"

"When do you leave for Mumbai, Chander?"

We both knew it was two weeks, so he didn't answer. He swept aside the papers, pulled me over on top of him, and fiddled with my blouse buttons. He was so hungry—his mouth, his gaze, his hand sliding into my knickers. Everything about him thrust into me, desperate. We rolled over and I lay under him, too rushed by his desire to feel much more than tenderness. His suffering pulsed into me, overwhelming. When he was spent we held on, chests rising up and down like one set of ribs. We lay there, hopeless; our love squeezed into a narrower and narrower time, and soon it would be gone.

Chander rose to a crouch and pulled on his trousers. "I'm going to the loo," he said, and he left. I sat up and wiped his tears off my neck.

It might be, Maman, that we would never have been trapped if it wasn't for the photo. I was resigning myself, bit by bit, to letting him go—did I have a choice? I couldn't really pull down so many lives. I was dishonest, thieving, and disgraceful, but I had some shabby remnant of a conscience. I knew I could stand without Chander. With all of that Galt money backing me, nothing could really topple my world. But Parul, Ashra, Neha, Gejra…Chander was their legs, feet, and shoes, and only with him could they walk out of hell. We'd do this last wild lark together, and then I'd let him go. I promised myself, I'd let him go.

Then I saw his wallet lying by my rucksack. It must have fallen from his trousers when he yanked them on. It lay open, and her little face frowned from a photo in the plastic window.

I reached to dig the photo from its pouch. It said on the back, "Gejra, nine years old." Taken years ago but still crisp and clean, as though he looked but didn't touch. She leaned against a yellow stone wall, a blinding pink scarf about her neck. The pretty triangle of her face was shadowed with sullenness, and her eyes studied the photographer with doubt.

How could a tyke so young look so disillusioned? She would not make Chander happy, I realized. This was not a love they could grow into after years of living side by side. She had already given up on the world. She would shrew him to death and he would endure it, because he carried his burdens like a man.

The storage door opened and Chander saw me, photo in hand. He kicked off his shoes and knelt beside me. "Sorry, luv," he said, reaching for the photo. But I hung onto it.

"You can't do this, Chander."

He knelt, silent, eyes on mine, so calm, a smudge of tears still on his cheek.

I tossed the photo and it fluttered to rest by my rucksack. "You will come back to me. Go to Mumbai if you must, but don't marry her. Make your bloody fortune, then find a way back to London. I'll wait."

He didn't move. Frustration pressed up my throat. I couldn't read his thoughts. "Swear you won't marry her. Swear it, Chander."

His gaze dropped. He wouldn't do it. Nothing, no one, not ever would convince Chander to shrug off his responsibilities. I snorted with vexation and snatched for the photo, determined to rip it into scraps. My hand knocked aside the rucksack and there lay the mirror, face up, the glass shimmering with torchlight.

It moves of its own will, doesn't it, Maman? At the time I just blinked, incredulous, trying to suss out how I'd lifted it at Alton's. Misplaced it in my rucksack, somehow.

Amazed, I wrapped fingers round the handle, half to see if it was real. I owed Alton a hundred pounds, I thought. He'd never believe I hadn't pinched it from him. He was going to be hopping mad.

My hand rose, showing a face in the glass: my own eyes, folded at the corners, full mouth, and dramatic brow. I looked… different than I expected. Fiercer, less generous.

Was I really such a formidable biffa? All of that overbearing will that crushed everyone; it was a miracle anyone loved me at all. I caught my breath and angled the glass away. And there were Chander's eyes, filled with love. Our gazes met in the glass and his tenderness poured into me, growing round my soul.

We are bound together he and I. Is that a curse, Maman? If it is, it's a tangle worth dying for.

That was the last night I slept with him. He didn't return to the storage. He bunked off Pekelo's class. I watched from the alley across from his family's flat, but never saw him. Was it his mum? I didn't have the nerve to knock on their door and ask, face Parul and my qualms.

The paint arrived. I posted him a note: *Are you all right? We're set for Wednesday night.* Chander didn't answer. Wednesday morning I prepared my black clobber—hoodie, trainers, gloves, and face paint. I sorted the ropes and harness I'd rigged to get me up a smooth leg. I counted my stencils, bound the paint cans into threes with tape so I'd find colors quickly, and stored what I couldn't carry on my back in a rubbish bag. I filled the paint ball gun and nicked Dad's wire cutters. I studied the CCTV plan.

Then I sat alone in my room, heart full of Chander, and cried. I was worse than no use to him. He'd been wrong; our love wasn't a gift that would pull him through hard years to come. It was a glaring light, exposing life's misery. Without me, perhaps he could at least make peace with his future. I had spoiled his chance for happiness, just as much as Gejra had.

Night came, and I still hadn't a clue what to graff. I felt reckless; with Chander out of the project there was nothing to lose. I would paint on instinct, abandon myself to no borders. The mirror had vanished. I couldn't find it anywhere. I gave up on returning it to Alton, figuring I'd find some way to make it up, or deal, Pekelo-style, with whomever he sent after me.

At two am I waited by the storage. This was when we always left to graff. Much earlier, and the piss-heads weren't sloshed enough to ignore us, much later and dawn caught us still out. I figured Chander wouldn't come. He'd made his choice; it was all that I deserved for having forced myself in where I didn't belong. But I waited an hour, then sneaked out alone, brokenhearted, across Waterloo Bridge.

Jubilee Gardens lay black and deserted. The massive white A-frame of The Eye jutted from the earth, holding the fragile ring of dangling capsules high against London's skyline.

It was sheer boastfulness to try to graff it. Boastfulness, and desperation. I steadied my shaking hand and took aim at the camera monitoring the leg of the A-frame, closest to County Hall. With two tries, I blackened the lens. Some plod at a CCTV screen was likely muttering, "Damn it all, the camera's gone haywire." Hopefully he wouldn't rewind and see me aiming my can.

I kept expecting lights and sirens while I strapped on the harness and circled ropes about one fat metal frame leg. Even with my Pekelo-hardened leg muscles, it was a bother shimmying up, and fighting boots aren't the best foot gear for slippery metal. When I'd climbed the leg, nearly eighty feet to level with the rim, I started painting downwards, layering colors as fast as my heart was pumping, throwing my weight recklessly against the harness as I slapped up stencils with whacking hunks of tape, sometimes spraying myself in my mad rush. I checked my work for only seconds with the torch; crickets, crawling from the ground, headed up a leg, looking grim and determined.

Despite my rush, it took twenty minutes to work my way to the pavement. But the rozzers didn't come, so I blessed my luck and pieced the crack from which crickets crawled, splitting the earth like a dark melon. Then I tossed aside spent cans and stored the remainders in my rucksack.

Now was the roughest bit—clip three wires, shoot two paint balls. Too many lenses would go out at once. They were bound to investigate. Every second counted as I heaved myself over the wire fence. It was go hell for leather; I needed to finish the capsules below, then climb too high for rozzers to interfere. I yanked out my stencil with three crickets on a yard-wide page, these with eyes turning up from the ground and wings tensed for takeoff. I didn't want to cover the mid-capsule windows, as tourists had a right to the view, but fast as I could I pieced lower windows and silver siding. On the roof, insects took flight, up, always facing the sky, wings spread with joy. I didn't bother with safety lines. I slung my gear on my back and used long legs, far reach, and strong arms to climb free hand to the next capsule. I belted myself to whatever handle or pull I found and struggled to flatten the stencils in the breeze.

How would it look? I didn't know. But I knew how it *felt*: exhilaration, escape from despair. Chander would wake in the morning and know how he was loved.

I was fifteen capsules up, at the crest of The Eye, when I saw him. A teeny speck below, the vertigo of looking down making him swim and waver. It was dark, but I didn't need light to know him; we were tied as two threads in a knot. He gazed at me, up the impossible height, and my heart fell to him, four hundred feet to where he held out his arms. I couldn't bear the finality of his goodbye, the clutch of never again, of choices, and of no choice.

"Come back to London. Don't marry her," I yelled.

He yelled back, but I didn't hear because spotlights came on and police rushed in. Chander stood gazing up, unwilling to turn away as they gathered round. Then they closed ranks.

For a moment there was a black lump, churning. Then bodies flew as water scatters off a fan. Chander, the feet and legs of his family, resisting arrest. Chander in the center of a whirling ruck, losing it all for one last look at me.

I searched, frantic, for a way to lend a hand. There was no

climbing blindly backwards; that was not nearly fast enough. He'd come to grief long before my boots hit the ground. I looked round for something, anything I could do. Paint, I had paint! Reaching over my shoulder I pulled bound together cans from my rucksack, threw back an arm, and lobbed. They landed with a *pop, pop, pop*, colors spraying in frenzied arcs, blokes hitting the ground as though they heard gunfire. I threw another, and another.

And Chander was off and running, past Queen Elizabeth Hall, headed for the necklace of lights that marked Waterloo Bridge. Below was chaos: wavering spotlights and a slippery rainbow of painted people, teeming in Jubilee Park. I felt Chander's feet cross the river.

Run, you diamond, run.

He turned for one last look, and was gone.

I gazed through blurry tears, out over London, brilliant with little lights. Gusting breezes tugged at my trembling grip, my gut wobbled when I looked at a world-full of tiny things. I closed my eyes, listening to the music of sirens and megaphones, feeling the tight, sweet night. I leaned out away from the capsule and felt wind lift under my back. I cinched down my rucksack, took one last breath, and let go.

I wasn't falling, I was soaring, rising above pain and loss, flying to a better future.

⁓

I hit the Thames with enough force to knock the sense out of me. By rights I should have died. I don't know how long I was out. I can't say, Maman, how I came to lie, wet through and practically frozen to Victoria Embankment, tucked far under the north end of Waterloo Bridge.

At the time it seemed an unfortunate miracle: a cursed bit of good luck. I'd like to pretend Chander pulled me from the water. But he never would have left me, shivering and unconscious, propped against a rubbish bin.

Perhaps your Apollo saved me. Has he been that chuffed, Maman, with your beautiful offerings? Or was it the mirror, that unbreakable bond holding us to love and life until one of us betrays? Then it's to the dogs for both of us. Or maybe I was saved by some wandering sot.

I opened dazed eyes, sore everywhere, mind dragging its heels and senses slow off the mark. Nothing felt broken. I knew I should move, but couldn't: I was too battered.

Waiting for inspiration, I listened to police whistles—a road block on the bridge above me. Puttering boats dragged the river looking for my body, no doubt. I had one consolation for being alive: perhaps I could find Chander.

I pulled myself to my knees, rucksack wet and heavy. With unsteady hands I peeled off my hoodie, used it to wipe away the last smudges of black face paint, and stuffed it in the rubbish bin. I loosened the drawstring on my tracky bottoms and dumped them as well. Dressed in jeans and a wet jumper I sauntered west, trying to be as causal as you please but shaking with the effort, heading for Carting. At the next bin I disposed of my remaining cans and stencils, peeled off the gloves, and checked for dabs of paint. I was clean. I fluffed out my hair. The sun was rising. No one gave a girl a look, walking fast up Carting Lane's steps, trying to get warm.

The storage was empty, the door swinging on its hinge.

By the clutter left behind, they'd closed shop in a hurry. Only the scent of charcoal incense lingered. I went round to his flat; the blinds were up and the windows blank. No one answered the bell.

He wasn't gone: I couldn't credit it. I couldn't still be alive and him forever out of reach; I couldn't bear it. I refused to get all trembly inside, cry in his foyer, make a silly bugger of myself. He hadn't left town, not without telling me he'd come back. Not without standing beside me and watching The Eye come alive.

Having nowhere else to go, I walked home. I knew there was trouble when my window was shut and my escape rope gone, so I crept in the front door. I could hear George and Emma having a chat in the drawing room. Dad was serious round-the-clock, and he was congenitally incapable of yelling, so it was often hard to suss when he was angry. But this time, I had no doubt.

"…Can't imagine what she's done to bring the police knocking at all hours. I say, enough is enough. Let her mother raise her!"

I stood, back to the door, heart rate climbing, listening through the open crack. A mother? Fancies of T. Chin returned from far-off childhood. Little Cricket leaping home, Cozy Hole and Mum waiting.

"Calm down, George." Emma's voice shimmied like she was near tears. "I promised her mum I'd keep her 'til she was sent for, so there's no shipping her off to Paris. Perhaps a boarding school—"

Paris? You can't imagine, Maman, how stunned I was, both to know that they knew you, and that you were so near, so reachable. Maybe you waited with open arms for me to *crackle clickity-sproing* in the door. I was filled with so many pressing questions that I flung aside the door.

Emma gasped, George scowled. They both looked me up and down, likely finding me damp and smelling of river.

"Jiè!" Emma turned white, livid. I'd never seen her so steamed up. "What on earth have you done?" Though Emma had never cuffed me and was too small to make a dent besides, I instinctively backed out of striking range.

"Where were you last night? The police are looking for you," said George.

So much for my feeble attempts to disable CCTV. Should I lie, or scare the effing shit out of them? I chose neither.

"Who is my mother?"

Emma blinked, still capable of surprise at my insolence.

George levered himself up to full height, which put him about even with my nose. "You're not asking the questions here, young lady, we are. Did you take that godforsaken mirror from my safe?"

A lot of good the truth would do me; they'd never believe it. So I didn't answer.

Emma collapsed onto the couch. "Why in bloody hell did you go and steal your mother's mirror? Why not just take the best silver?"

It was Emma's face that did it: her beauty waxen, her eyes back and forth across the floor as if afraid to light on something, her trembling fingers gripping thick hair. It put a chill up my shirt, as if those dogs panted on me. I backed toward the coat tree. That mirror was witched, and something bad was about to come of it. Chander. I needed to find Chander.

"Tell me. I need to know," I said.

Emma raised her eyes. She sussed me too well not to know what I would do. "We can't. And please don't go looking for her, either. Just bring the mirror back and we'll lock it up tight again."

And here was what had always been true: that crack in the foundation underneath me. The secret that followed me, getting in free punches, dodging, invisible, out of reach of my fists and feet. We'd been shadow boxing all my life, that secret and I.

Now, somehow, I'd dragged Chander into the ring with me. What was the price Alton had warned about? It wasn't fair if Chander had to pay.

"Tell me the truth," I said.

"You're a funny one to ask about truth," said George.

My mother's mirror, with some absofrigging horrible curse. I backed into the hall.

My mother would know—what it was, what to do. Alton could find her. He might try to slap me about a bit, but when push came to shove he'd lose if he took me on. I'd make him find her, even if he put a few goons on my tail afterwards. I stepped backwards and hit the coat tree, knocking into Dad's mackintosh, making the tree wobble on its wooden prongs. I slid a hand in his coat pocket, gripped his wallet, and then turned for the door.

"Where are you going?" George stormed after me. "Jiè, come back here this minute."

But I was, and always will be, a much faster runner than George.

~

Empty storage shed, empty flat. On second look, it was even more obvious that they'd gone. I stood in their silent foyer, cut deep with fear, sadness, and guilt. Maybe they huddled at Heathrow, awaiting the next flight, or hung in the sky over Italy. Would we all lose Chander, when the mirror's price was paid? Whatever the curse, I had to get to my Chinese mum before any witchery found him.

When I came round the corner to Alton's eBay, there sat the mutt from the back of the mirror, half hidden in a doorway across the road.

It was creepy, bizarre, made my hair rise at the roots and wiggle with fear. That first time I saw it, I couldn't wrap my mind around it. It wasn't much bigger than a normal dog, three necks twisted about each other, three heads watching in different directions.

I'd knocked my head too hard, I thought, and I looked again. It was as though I couldn't see the three heads, but somehow concluded they were there. Blokes just sauntered by, Maman. I don't understand how only you and I are bothered by it. I'm not absolutely certain it's real, mind you, but then, two can't share the same madness, can they?

I kept it in sight, not willing to turn my back until I came to Alton's stoop, then I cautiously ducked in the doorway, one middle knuckle out for fast striking. The place was empty except for Alton, who slumped on a bar stool, tapping at his keyboard. I stood right in front of him, close enough to snap him into a headlock if needed.

He looked up. "Hey, Jiè." He gave his grin of tobacco-stained teeth. "Back with more?"

"No…I…."

So he didn't know the mirror was missing. Brilliant! Not likely that I was going to clue him in. I relaxed my fist and stance. "I'm looking for my mum. My real mum. I think she's in Paris. Could you find her?"

Alton licked dry lips. "Maybe. What's her name?"

"Don't know for certain. Could be T. Chin."

He tapped about a bit, glanced at his screen, then tapped some more. "There's about thirty T. Chins in Paris. Any other clues?"

Wasn't much else Emma and George had said. "No, sorry."

"Well what are you hopin' for, little lady, a miracle?"

He reached under his cash desk and drew out his lock box. Adrenaline shot through me as he inserted the key. Bloody hell, he was about to discover that the mirror was missing. I'd have to take him down, hope I didn't damage him so much, he couldn't tap tap on his gummy keys. Buzzing for a fight, I set my feet and clocked the spot that would paralyze his punching arm.

"I've been lookin' into this here, and I feel I need a better explanation as to where it came from."

Alton, asking questions? That mirror must have scared

him from his cigar tip to his horse-prodding toes. I wasn't breathing as he turned the key. He lifted the lid and I nearly keeled over; there lay the mirror, bound in orange silk. He tilted the lock box, and the horrid thing banged the side like a wasp in a jar.

"This ain't the kind of thing left lying around the house. How about you tell me the truth, for once? Then we'll talk about finding your mom."

I was so gobsmacked I couldn't speak.

Had I *imagined* holding it in my hand? Chander hadn't commented when he saw it; maybe it was never there. But I was certain I'd felt the bond, twisting us into one, and I knew that Chander had, too.

I stared down into Alton's eyes, little and mean as a snake's, and him likely wondering what lie I schemed up as I stood there with my gob open.

Well, a lie is as good as the truth, sometimes.

"I stole it from an armored safe."

"That's closer." He snapped the lid closed. "I'd consider it a personal favor if the owner never got wind of where it went." His snaky eyes bore into mine. "And a major wrong worth rectifying if he shows up here, lookin' for it."

He was threatening me, as if I weren't just a trivial seller. He must value that mirror at well over the three hundred quid we'd negotiated, likely ten times that much, which meant he'd cheated me royally. That pissed me off, but first things first.

"Let's find my mum," I said.

Alton dragged his gaze off me and back to his screen. "What's your birthday?"

"April 1, 1990."

It only took him ten minutes, Maman, to find record of my French birth certificate (and early death), uncover your name, and nose out a current address. Cozy Hole, I thought as he scribbled the address. This is terrific, Mum, I'm coming home!

"Tatyana Trotoskov. Whoa baby, *she's* your mom? Her stuff sells for a hot dollar. Maybe with a little luck, some of it will come my way…?" He offered me the paper scrap. "Who'd a thought you're the brat of the most sought-after artist in Paris."

Brilliant, I thought, he doesn't think I have wits *or* talent.

As I took the note, I locked his tap-happy fingers in my fist. "I'd say this address is worth fifty quid." I grabbed the lapels of his tweed coat with my free hand. "So you only owe me eight hundred and fifty more for that mirror, considering my thirty percent." I twisted the cloth, putting knuckles into his trachea. "But seeing as we're mates, I'll let you pay me later." I released him before he blacked out, leaving him coughing and choking at his cash desk.

Don't look so rattled, Maman, it's basic self defense; I can't afford to have Alton thinking I'm a target. As Pekelo taught me: give them a peek at what's underneath and maybe they won't request the full monty.

It was a long ramble to St. Pancras station, and I spent it grieving over Chander. Is marriage to Gejra a betrayal, Maman? Of course, I didn't know yet what the curse was, but I'm a fighter and I know when I'm in the ring. I worried over every bloke who got within six feet of me. I shied clear of dogs. At the train station I leaned my back to the wall. Eurostar took me from St. Pancras to Gare du Nord, and yes, Maman, I mailed George's wallet back after paying for the ticket.

Then halfway to Paris, I looked in my rucksack for my jumper and found the mirror, solid enough to tent the rucksack's side. Jesus bloody hell. My guts turned cold as ice. Who was I up against?

After one experimental poke, I didn't touch it again. I sweated through the second half of the ride, wondering: what is the going price for eternal love?

~

Dawn is coming, and Paris' gray light seeps through Maman's lacy nets. She sits post-upright on the settee, that aristocratic bearing never tiring, even though her face is pale milk. I can feel her slight tremor where she presses against my side. I ask myself, what is she worrying over? And by the way she listens toward Square Barye, I fancy it's Hades and his mutt.

Then she says, "And The Eye?"

I'm astounded. I should know better by now; it's all about art for Maman. Could anything ever possess me with such devotion? Xiao and his China, Chander and his family....What did I have that meant so much? Fair enough, my crickets rose as I imagined. But that's all impact, statement, message to Chander and the world. Rise, love, be free—not driven by a need for beauty, but by the need to scream. My wild attempts seem immature beside Maman's skilled discipline.

"I saw it in the Eurostar terminal, on the waiting room telly," I say reluctantly.

Her thin, blonde eyebrows shoot up. "*Eh alors?*"

I take her ink-stained fingers in mine. "They come from the earth, up the leg in swarms as I'd hoped. As they reach the rim, wings twitch open, and the urge to fly presses them on top of each other." I squeeze, and she squeezes back. "A thin trail of them rise with the capsules, seeming to escape to the sky as they come to the crest of the turn. It's beautiful, Maman. The newsreader said it was amazing, uplifting. All of London is entranced. But—" Sadness wells up, filling me to bursting.

"*Chérie!*" says Maman, widening her eyes with alarm.

"—But the wheel keeps turning, and they fall again. They have boundaries, Maman, do you understand? They can't get away from the loss and grief and disappointment. They have to stay, and it isn't fair. It isn't fair."

My throat closes, choked with tears. Maman guides my head into her lap, that old gray wool dress smelling of almond soap. She strokes my head, and I can't stop sobbing into the warmth of her soft wool lap, against the belly where I was made.

"Sweet, sweet Cricket. You're so young, so much ahead of you." She kisses my burning cheek. "*Eh bien*, all that passion inside and nowhere for it to go. Don't give up." Her voice soothes, gentle as her hands. "Your Chander is a strong young man. Perhaps he can meet his family's needs, then learn to draw some boundaries of his own, *n'est pas*? In the meantime, you must find something to give your heart to." She smiles down at me, blue eyes deep as the Mediterranean.

"I want to be an artist, Maman, not just a show off."

She laughs. "And you are not?"

I sit up, swipe back my soggy hair. "No. I'm just a child with a beautiful voice, shrieking at the world."

"Well!" She takes a deep breath, studies me closely. "Then we shall put you in École des Beaux-Arts, see if perhaps they can't bring the volume down a bit, sharpen your skill."

My heart leaps, gingered up like bubbles. "Shall we? Really? Do you reckon I could be as good as you?"

"Oh, much better than me. I've had no training, and worked all of these years under a curse."

She stands and goes to the bureau against the wall. Under the writing surface are two drawers, and she slides one open. Her hand brings forth the mirror, which she lays on the coffee table.

My heart sinks. "What shall we do with it?"

"We? No, Cricket. I alone." She spreads apart the silk and stares at the dog's hideous faces. "I am going to Incir to destroy it. It's folly for Chander to marry Gejra, but if he does, he shouldn't die of it." She turns to me. "And you're going to art school to grow up, without Apollo's unreliable protection."

I jump to my feet, towering over her. "I'm coming with you, Maman, and you can't stop me."

She stares, a steel rod of a look, and I wonder how her delicate bones bear up under that unbending will. Then she chuckles, a little wheeze at first, then with such force she bends over, holding bony ribs. And I am fed up with her having a laugh without me.

"Belt up, Maman. I can crush a neck with one hand. Whatever you're facing, you'd do well to have me along. I'm coming, and that's final."

She wipes tears from her eyes, gasping for breath. Then a long silence stands between us as we eyeball each other, neither of us capable of losing.

"Is this a Trotoskov, asserting herself?" she says finally. "Or is this from your warrior father? Maybe it's Jiè Wanhua Wang, who walked alone eight hundred kilometers to Shanghai." She rises to her toes and places a brushing peck on my cheek. "I'm proud of you, my fighting cricket, and your father and grandparents would be, too." She sighs, her eyes still wet and glistening. "*D'accord*, tickets for both of us. And may Apollo show us mercy."

# TWENTY-FIVE

Incir. It's nothing like Maman described it. We lodge in a yellow Marriott Inn with a candy pink indoor swimming pool, as if we're in Mayfair or South Bank. Maman looks done in as she pulls back the bedspread in our crisp hotel room. When I give her a peck good-night I slip *Little Cricket* into her hands, wishing there was more to be done for her.

The next day, we walk to the old town on hot, paved city roads, past rows of fresh stucco buildings. In the heart of old Incir, wooden shops sport colorful awnings, and signs advertise bars, souvenirs, and a discotheque. Some women wear headscarves, but I see no one but Maman in *kara çarşaf*. There are no goat paths, wandering through brush to the *pension*, so we follow the pavement.

Apollo's Temple is fenced with barbed wire, and a fee is required to see it. The huge columns are lit at the bases with rainbow colored lights. Ragwort, with its farty smell, has driven out the lavender. It's too early in the morning for the ticket collector to be on duty, so I leap the concrete barrier that blocks the way to Yurda's kitchen and hoist Maman over by her armpits. We come to the ruins of the old hotel from the back.

Yurda's kitchen door swings and clumps in the April breeze. Mint sprouts and blooms, smelling sweet from cracks in the doorstep. Nothing bubbles on the rusty hunk that was

Yurda's stove. Tiles have gone missing from the kitchen floor. Doors creak, hanging off their hinges. There is a dent in the bare wood floor, where the heavy dining room table once stood. A sorrowful feeling blows in with the salty wind. Maman floats room to room, silent, and I stick close, feeling uneasy.

Maman mounts the winding stairs. She goes first to her room, bare except for the view of the sea, dead crickets caught in the shutter slats. Maman is so right; the Mediterranean is a staggering blue. So like her eyes, that blue, one struggles not to drown in the color.

Then she wanders to Della's room and studies the Roman arena. She doesn't speak, taking in rings of bleachers, thrusting to the sky. I fancy she sees Xiao in the cavea, his hands round a brush and an inkstone on his knee. She doesn't say. Despite all we've been through, Maman is solitary, not given to tagging the walls with her feelings. But it's obvious that she's knocked sideways by grief and loss, so I stand behind her, hands on her shoulders, hoping she susses my love.

Xiao's room she avoids until the last. She spins about uncertainly where his bed once lay, as if not sure what to do. She clocks the temple out the window, surrounded by ugly wire, but cringes at the sight and turns away. She traces fingers over tiny holes where cricket sketches once hung by pins, then she turns to me.

"*Allons*, we will go find Yurda."

"Are you all right, Maman?"

"*Ma petite*, I don't think I will ever be all right. But life goes on now, doesn't it?"

I take her hand, and we walk downstairs together.

Yurda must live where she always did, as Maman has no trouble finding her house. But Yurda's breathing space is gone, her garden shaded by neighbor's houses, built in a tight-fisted block. Satellite discs and TV antennas slice her view of the sea. Maman smooths her black bloomers and messes about with her head covering, tucking and straightening, then she knocks on Yurda's door.

"*Bonjour*, Yurda *Hanin*," she says to the stocky old matron who pokes her head out.

It takes Yurda a tick, then she throws up her hands, and Maman is pulled into her pillowy bosom. Yurda babbles in Turkish, swamping Maman with more kisses and pats than an aristocrat should have to bear. She squeezes Maman's hands, neither of them able to let go. She pulls Maman into her foyer and on to the drawing room. I follow unnoticed, feeling beside the point.

"Umut," calls Yurda. "Umut!"

There's a clatter from the stairs, and a man in his twenties lopes into the room. He still looks like a rabbit; Maman was spot on. Those long legs and that floppy gait, the nose too teeny for his face. He, too, recognizes Maman, and presses hands together, bowing in front of her over and over. All I can make of his guttural speech is the word *Maşallah*, repeated like a skipping CD. Then Umut sees me.

He squeaks and freezes, as though I were a flash of light, catching him on the hop. Yurda turns to look at me, and gasps. For the first time it grips me that I am illegitimate: a bastard child conceived in a decidedly conservative village. I grin like a nitwit, flustered.

"Xiao," Umut says. He lifts my hair, strands of it spreading, falling over my eyes. He doesn't stroke my face, but waves a hand slowly, as though feeling my features from an inch away. I stand all awkward as he sniffs me, as if he's wondering whether I'm real.

Yurda shoves him aside and hobbles circles round me: tugging at my shirt hem, squeezing my sizable shoulders, running fingers over the scar above my eye and my damaged ear.

I glance all edgy at Maman. She must have known this was coming when she brought me to Yurda. Maman maintains her erect Trotoskov bearing, and it hits me in the heart how proud she is of me. I may have been illegitimate, I may have been given away, but no child was ever more loved.

After Yurda pokes every part she can reach without tiptoes, she stands back and nods a sharp downward jerk of her chin. I gather that I've passed muster, because she puts both hands about mine and pulls them to her heart, exclaiming passionately in Turkish. With tremendous relief, I kiss the cheek she offers. She's the closest to a granny I'll ever know, and I'm chuffed that she likes me. Maman looks near to weeping with happiness.

Despite the fact that we're unexpected, Yurda feeds us, and feeds us, and feeds us: minty yoghurt, roasted lamb, stuffed tomatoes, zucchini pickles with garlic and dill, then pastry—layer upon layer of fluff pastry, tasting of rose water and honey. Bloody hell, I'm stuffed to my earlobes. With tears in her eyes she insists that I could do with another serving. Maman eats lightly, nursing a glass of tea that she readily lets Yurda refill, but managing to fend off second and third servings. I'm not so deft a negotiator, so by the end of the meal I fear I will be sick.

After we help Yurda clear the table, Maman pulls the mirror from her leather bag. She lays it on the lap of her black robes, leaving the orange silk wrapped tight.

"Mizou?" she asks, patting Yurda's hand.

Yurda sticks out her lower lip, a curl of grief. She turns to Umut and instructs him in Turkish, and he dashes out the door. Then she natters earnestly to Maman, on and on as if Maman understands perfectly. Maman listens, smiling, clearly not following a word, but going in for the attention like a spoiled kid. A few minutes later, Umut returns with a leathery old geezer who is close to seventy.

Maman rises, mirror in hand. "*Bonjour*, Kemal. Do you recognize me?"

"Of course." He's stocky and strong, and I suspect still dragging sharks from the sea, but his French is musical and soft. "What a pleasure to see you again, Mademoiselle. If only Suat Bey were here to share it." He turns to me, and his eyes widen as though I'm a vision. "And this is—?" He stops, the answer impossible.

Maman takes a breath and blurts it out. "This is Xiao's and my daughter, Jiè."

If he's shocked by the implications, Kemal covers it well. With frank appreciation, his eyes travel once from my loaf to my toes, and then he nods politely. "You bestow honor upon our poverty stricken house," he says with a formal bow.

"*Enchantée.*" I nod, trying not to be stiff-upper-lip in the face of his graciousness.

Maman sits down, and Yurda cedes her seat to Kemal and plops her round arse between me and Maman. Yurda's hand idly pats my shoulder and plays with my blue hair as Kemal and Maman prattle in French. Every once in a while, Yurda flashes a toothless grin, and I can't resist the urge to put an arm round her, making her grin even wider.

"Where is Mizou?" Maman asks finally.

Kemal shudders and looks away. "Tell me of your trip, was it comfortable?" he asks.

"*Oui*. We were kindly treated as always." Maman pours Kemal tea, and then sips her own. "*Allahaşkina*, Kemal, I want to know of Mizou."

Kemal clucks and raises a bushy eyebrow, still staring at the worn rug.

"Please, I wouldn't ask if it were not important."

Kemal doesn't respond. He picks up his tea glass, tanned and calloused old hands trembling.

"*Beni seviyorsan*," says Maman.

I have no idea what this bit of Turkish means, but it has the desired effect. All of the brown wrinkles on Kemal's weathered face bunch into a grimace.

"She disappeared last November," he says quietly. "Vanished. She went to bed one night and was gone in the morning. It happened about two weeks after Suat Bey died."

Kemal and Maman lock eyes. Even shark fishermen can look spooked. Maman looks pained.

Yurda pushes herself to her feet, muttering mysteriously. She hobbles out of the room, then returns with a salt shaker. She pours a whacking big handful of salt into her palm and waves it over our heads. Then she totters across the room, opens the grate of the coal stove and chucks the salt into the flames. It flares into green and blue fire.

"What the bloody hell?" I whisper to Maman.

"Driving off the evil eye." She turns to Kemal. "We need to get into the temple tonight. How do we arrange that?"

"If you ask my worthless opinion, you should stay out of the temple. Since they put a fence around it, it's been sullen with anger."

"Angry or no, I have business with Apollo."

Kemal sighs. "Umut is keeper of the temple gates. I'll tell him to let you in."

~

Maman can't tolerate what the town has become: twee tourist gift shops painted bright colors, clothing stores selling plunging necklines, billboards of westernized models. She insists on staying in our hotel room while I wander about in a blue funk, drinking water from a plastic bottle, trying to distract myself.

I dread the coming confrontation. I could never say this to Maman, but in my heart I fear that between Boris' cruelty and Xiao's death, she's a bit touched. But then I've seen the dog myself, so have we both gone round the twist? Wouldn't it be pleasant if nothing came of tonight, and we smash that nasty mirror and traipse home. But deep down I'm preparing for a fight, guts and muscles settling into total commitment. After all, the mutt is just a pet, and we have yet to meet his master. At least Maman won't go into the ring alone.

Neither of us is hungry, so after I return to the hotel room we rest, side by side on the bed. Maman closes her eyes like she's having a kip, but I can tell by her shallow breathing that she's awake. I lie on my side and study her profile. With a stab of sadness, I realize that she has the same nose as Emma: that long swoop down her face, and delicate nostrils. But unlike Emma, Maman's knocked off center; one half struggling to align with the other. I can see what Xiao loved: brilliance, talent, impatience with life's failings. She saw the same in him. They passed a double dose of their impatience on to me. Poor Emma and George, so tolerant of it all.

"How did Emma get away?" I ask.

"From Boris' grand marriage plans?"

"Right."

Maman smiles, imp-like in her pleasure. "She's such a clever one. She and George eloped, then when the marriage was a *fait accompli*, she wrote a note to Boris, announcing a grand ball in London, all the heads of state invited to the wedding reception, of course. As displeased as he was with the marriage, he could not refuse to come—such a scandal it would have caused!" Maman's laugh tinkles. "She had him over a barrel, and he never forgave her." She sighs and falls quiet again. "Did you like Incir?" Maman asks finally, whispering into the gloom.

"No. I prefer your memories of Incir."

Maman squeezes tight her shadowed eyelids. "Della was so right, bless her wandering soul. She died in a snowstorm in Kazan, winter of 1997. I cried for a month after receiving Mizou's letter."

"Sorry, Maman." We lie in the air-conditioned stillness. "And what became of Grandpa Boris?"

She's silent for two ticks, then, eyes still closed, she says, "There's painful memory: Boris' end. But all of my memories of Boris are painful. Why would he be any different in death, than he was in life?" She raises stringy eyebrows and flares her nose, as though sucking in resolve. "He found me, eventually, but I was well past twenty-one and too famous for him to do much damage. I saw him only once, in my gallery. He studied my paintings—temple, crickets, Xiao, Incir's villagers, and my more recent work of Paris and her street people. His tour around the exhibit was cold and methodical. It took him hours and left me exhausted watching him. Then he dropped his business card in the donation box for homeless children. No money, just his card. I didn't see him again until his death."

I wait. Chander taught me that; there is a time to shut your gob and just let it be. If only I had done more shutting and less running on, more listening to him and less asking for me, perhaps he would have chosen me over Gejra.

Evening fades into night, and our faces became indistinct. Is it me, or do I hear eerie creaks in the hall? Is the streetlight orange, like dead goldfish? I take Maman's fingers in mine and they are ice.

"Boris called me to his deathbed," she says finally, about the time I've forgotten the topic. "But when I arrived, a stroke had left him unable to speak. He handed me his will, kissed my hand, and closed his eyes." It doesn't take a genius to see that she doesn't want to cry, but tears choke her anyway.

There's a long silence before she's on with it. "In his will, he said, 'Forgive me, I mistook you for a colony, and you were a sovereign state.' Even until death, he couldn't see me as a person."

How dreadful. What a blessing that I've had Emma and George, whose failures were exceeded by their steadfast effort, and nothing was greater than their love.

"So he didn't die alone, after all."

"*Non.* I stayed by him. I couldn't have lived with myself otherwise." She turns towards me and I can better see her exhaustion. "It's important to forgive, Jiè, starting with yourself."

I've a long way to go; there's such a massive pile to work on.

Maman rises and takes the bride's blue robes from her suitcase. Gold embroidery gleams at the hem. "Take this. If you ever marry, I'd be honored if you wore it." She puts the beautiful cloth in my hands.

"Ta. I'll wear it." I can't imagine how I'd look in it, but what's the difference? I'd do anything for her.

She lifts off Yurda's *kara çarşaf*, her golden hair making a run for it down her back. "Thank you for everything, Yurda," she whispers, as she tenderly tucks the robe and scarf away in her bag.

She straightens her plain gray wool dress, then turns about, and for a moment the full measure of her sadness and fear grip me. Her face, normally so composed and distant, shows raw emotion: an agony of love, loss, and frail courage.

"*Au revoir, ma petite.*" She lays her cheek against mine.

Not the aristocratic kiss she's so disdainful of, but a kiss meant to be remembered.

Holding her close, I whisper, "I am coming with you."

"*Non.*" She pulls away. "You have come far enough. The rest belongs to me."

I pursue her, grabbing her sleeve. "You've no choice, Maman. If you leave me, I'll just follow you. I won't let you go alone."

Tears spring into her eyes. "Please stay. Hades has taken enough from me."

"I'm coming, and you can't stop me." And given our size difference, this is verifiably true.

Instead of anger or pleading, she pulls the silk-shrouded mirror from her bag and walks, head up and back straight, out the door.

# TWENTY-SIX

It's dark, a wodge of moon half hidden behind clouds and hinting at light. The sea is a thumping black pool behind the temple columns. A few spring crickets shrill in the ragwort. The place makes me fidgety. Umut meets us at the gate. He releases lock and chain, and scrapes aside a stretch of metal fencing. Then he stands uncertainly in the gap he's opened, watching us pass and creep toward the altar.

Maman turns round. "*Allez,*" she yells at him, "go home." She flings up her hands as though scaring off a crow.

He stands staring, like he doesn't think well of this project, then finally turns and lopes off with his ring of keys jangling. Maman closes the gate. Apollo's columns stand above us like ginormous legs and I'm insignificant, shivering at their feet.

Maman pads through sand to the center of the half circle. Tucking her dress under her, she kneels at Apollo's altar.

Seeing her at the square marble slab, I realize what's gone missing: the laurel's canopy. Dead branches lay ripped off the tree and strewn about, and the trunk's a bare post. I prickle with warning, sliding into fighting stance, feeling the sharp edges of something angry.

Maman unwraps the mirror and tosses aside the silk. The goldfish orange has taken on its freakish red in the darkness. The silk lies on the ground for a tick, then trembles in a faint breeze. Grabbed by a sudden blow, it rises and skitters over sand and pebbles, wrapping about my feet.

I reach for it, a scrap of Mizou's robe, frayed where she tore it. Did Hades heave her, struggling like Persephone, onto his shoulder? What a ruck that must have been. And where is she now?

I find I can't stop shaking; I don't fancy an eternity on the banks of the river Styx. I scrunch the silk in my fist and press against a marble column, minding my feet where the cracks might form.

Maman lays the mirror on the altar, calm as if she has a clue what she's about. She gropes in the sand at her feet, her skinny back bent like an old servant. She finds what she's hunting and lifts it to the sky: a hand-sized hunk of Apollo's marble.

"Apollo!" Her voice quivers, perhaps as much from the effort of being subservient, as with fear. She pauses as though considering her words, then says, "I've served you well, faithful and devoted. My best work—given all to you. Now I entreat you to help me."

A cold draft blows off the ocean, picking up folds of her gray dress and twisting it about her thinness, ruffling her pale hair. I've an urge to edge closer where I can react quickly, but find myself pinned, like as if some invisible hand has me up against the ropes.

Bloody hell, this isn't a proper fight; the gods are cheating already! Almost as if the sods were afraid of a fair match. I shift the only thing still moving—my eyes—watching for the first punch.

Maman's still got that wedge of marble suspended over the mirror's face. "I stand against your greedy uncle," she yells, "to demand he give back what's mine. Don't let him take your loyal servant, Apollo. I call him forth now, and if you love me, save us all." With that she smashes the marble scrap down on the mirror's glass.

There's a plink, as though a pebble clipped a metal door. I'm unable to take my next breath, my throat's so tight. Crickets are no longer chirping. The wind abruptly ceases and it's gone way too frigging calm.

Maman waits.

When nothing follows, she lifts the marble again. "Break, you hideous glass," she whispers, hammering it another one.

This time the blow results in a faint crack, shivering the air and crawling up my spine. I pant, my shaking torso still pasted against the column. Then silence, except for the muttering sea.

One more time, Maman heaves the marble. "I, Tatyana Trotoskov, command you to break." With all the high and mighty resolve of Boris' daughter, she clobbers the mirror: ferocious, furious, deadly.

Glass shatters, slivers exploding like a flock of birds, flapping about, weightless on dark wings. They flutter in the moonlight, then settle in the sand around her. On her knees, arms stretched and fingers clinging to the altar, forehead in the dirt, Maman waits.

Nothing.

No splits in the earth, no ancient gods or monsters.

I give a tentative wiggle of my fingers and find I can step

away from the column, easy as pie. It's over. I let go a weary breath, closing my eyes, tears stinging. Let her suffering end now: guilt washed clean, duty done. Chander and all future Chanders, safe: that's the vital thing. And her slavery to Apollo released, our lives no longer hanging over Hades' gaping crevice. I'm done in with relief.

Then, in the sensitive darkness, I hear a mounting hiss from the sea. A pulse of thunder rumbles toward shore. Icy breeze crawls over my face, lifting my hair and fingering my skin. My eyes snap open and my heart leaps to my throat, pounding as though to escape out my gob. I whirl about, staring round the column at the full face of the Mediterranean.

Gentle rings spread like a pebble's wake. Shimmers of phosphorescence light the circles with a delicate green. The rings tremble and widen. The center dips, a soft sucking sound, and water swirls down a funnel, spinning into murky depths. The hole's edges skip lightly outward, running wider and wider until the dark funnel engulfs Incir's bay. A vast, black cone, sinking impossibly deep.

And from this hole rises Hades' guardian.

Cerberus is absofrigging huge, an effing mountain. Against him we are tiny souls, barely felt, passing down his throat. Thick necks untangle. Dog snouts lift slowly, sniffing the breeze. Six eyes wander left, then right, searching. I beat a retreat into a column's shadow.

"Maman," I try to whisper, but the warning's too horror-struck to leave my throat. I'm scared witless, paralyzed; *no one* goes to the matt with this creature. Nothing Pekelo has taught me could be a jot use. I've been preparing forever, I realize, to fight for my life. I always knew this was coming. And now I see that it's futile.

One low growl leaks from a throat, merciless and hungry. I sweat and tremble against the column, peering over my shoulder. Maman lies unmoving in her position of supplicant prayer, forehead in the sand, half hidden in the altar's shadow. I'm not for cert that she's alive. We've got to leg it, now, before he clocks us.

The creature snaps back a head, and three dripping gobs open, teeth to the moon. With all of death's agony, he roars.

Dirt vibrates under my feet, edges crumble, and earth falls away in whacking sheets. Cliff path and footprints of a hundred generations rumble into the sea. Now at the lip of a precipice, Apollo's columns quake and rock, my pillar gripping impossibly to the cliff's edge. I cling on in a panic, arms about cold marble.

Cerberus snuffles and casts about, then goes ominously still. Three snouts point, spot on in our direction. He's sussed us out, and like any dog in a fight he's taking our measure.

I'm desperate to run, but my pins won't support me. I'm suffocating in screams but my gob won't open. A ghastly calm possesses me, and I know we are going to die. Without even throwing a punch, without one kick of protest. We broke Hades' favorite toy, his pet has come for us, and there's nothing to be done about it. Had I known I was bound for this, I would have been kinder, softer, more forgiving. I would never have scarred myself, and those who love me.

Behind the beast, fog rolls in, heavy across the sunken bay.

Edges of it reach my face and cling to the sweat and tears. The wet air congeals into gray phantoms, hazy forms passing around the beast and winging toward me and Maman. My hair prickles on end.

In the mist, the beast hesitates. One massive dog head twists east, and one swivels west, as if uncertain. The phantoms are coming on fast now, and I can make them out; two galloping horsemen. One is a big man, hair streaming to below his waist, a spear the length of two men across his saddle and a massive bow over one shoulder. I know the bones of his face, those folded deep-set eyes, that sturdy mouth. Even in the midst of such fright, I'd know my dad. My heart leaps as I rise from my cowering crouch.

Beside Xiao rides a man, a sword in each hand, an unstoppable whirlwind. His Kiliji is a length of molten silver, thrust before him, the golden prayer at the handle blazing. His Yataghan whistles as he whirls it overhead. He stands in the saddle, a blade thin geezer, tough as iron. Suat Bey.

"Look!" I yell.

I turn to see Maman unfold from her bow. Eyes wide, she studies the approaching riders. Her thin fingers sift through sand, finding two shards of mirror. As the horsemen gallop down upon us, she rises and stumbles to the cliff's unstable edge.

"Xiao," she whispers, soft with longing, and she snaps a scrap of glass in her hand. Blood drips from her fingers.

"Suat Bey!" And she crushes the other sliver.

Then she juts her hands, wide open to the sky, flinging blood and mirror shards. "Do you love me, Xiao Lian Chin?" she cries.

Dad's horse rears, yards from our cliff, and the rider locks eyes with my Maman.

"Will you save your *Princess,* my Turkish hero?" she yells.

The other horse spins a circle before us and stops dead, the rider balanced, toes in the stirrups and swords raised.

How magnificent they are! Better than anything I dreamed up, listening to Maman's tales. For a moment they look down on us, and I know what it is to be loved.

Slowly they turn about, standing between us and the monster. In the horrid quiet, horses paw and snort. Xiao raises his spear. Then, with wolfish instinct, a dog head lunges.

Open jaws scorch through the mist, hot salt and decayed breath blowing over us. We're staring into his dripping maw of teeth, wide as forever. Xiao heaves his spear into the dark throat, then spurs his horse and gallops in after.

The creature shrieks and snaps closed his teeth, tossing his head up to the sky. Arrow tips breaks through the crest of the snout, and blood pours from a nostril. The head writhes, flopping on its neck, whipping back and forth with Dad trapped inside. Jowls weave down, slapping the water with a stunning whack.

I lean over the cliff edge to see, guts twisting as I scream, "Dad!"

Maman's steely grip holds me from tumbling, head-long into the sea. The dying head floats on choppy waves, then sinks. My dad is gone.

Another hulking head lunges, teeth snarling. Maman yanks me out of reach and we're falling over each other. But

Suat Bey kicks his horse and collides with the outstretched neck. As though possessed, he hacks with his shimmering Kiliji. His Yataghan swings like a scythe. Fur flies.

The beast twists and bites, seizing Suat Bey's horse out from under him and flinging it heavenward. But the hero leaps and thrusts, burying both swords to the hilt in the hide. As the neck whips up, Suat Bey holds on, letting swords slice down in a long glide. The throat flays open, sinew and ripped windpipe spread wide.

Then the neck collapses, thrashing up a bloody froth. The swirling vortex hisses, and sinks deeper. Cerberus is sucked in: chest, necks, then the final living head. Suat Bey, still clinging to his swords, is dragged under in the beast's wake.

The vortex collapses on itself and is gone, leaving only dark, choppy water.

I crouch, holding up my quivering Maman, or perhaps she supports me. Tears spill down our faces.

"Are they dead, Maman?" I force words from a sick-dry throat.

I don't know if she has no answer, or if she refuses to speak it. "Xiao, my love," she whispers. "*Eh alors,* Suat Bey?"

She relaxes her grip on me and wipes blood off her hands, then tears off her face, leaving two red streaks down the front of her dress and a bit on her cheeks. In a few swift paces she crosses the clearing. Grabbing a laurel branch, she snaps off a jagged end, then strides to the altar.

"I'm ready for you, Hades. *Allons-y,*" she bellows.

No frigging way.

"Let's leg it!" I hotfoot it toward her.

She stands like a spike, stabbed into the ground.

"There is nowhere to run, Cricket." She raises the stick and smacks the altar. "Come for me, you evil pig," she calls. "See if you can drag a Trotoskov into Hell."

Then she waits, branch raised.

She doesn't wait long.

Underfoot, the ground rumbles. A shaking, then the sand rises and rolls, waves of fluid earth reeling underneath us. The altar splits with a thunderous *crack*, knocking Maman backwards.

I leap to grab hold of her, but she shoves me aside and staggers to her feet, wool dress ripped at the hem. She steadies herself and grips the laurel stick.

"*Bâtard,*" she swears. "Enough with the theatrics."

Out of the crack in the alter, comes a finger.

One finger, as large as a wrist, silver and ethereal, glowing with slippery light that slides down the skin like steam. The light meets ground and shimmers over the sand, creeping into dark clumps of ragwort.

The fingertip searches the edge of the crack, then hooks the broken edge of the altar. With a flick, it flings the thousand pound fragment aside. The altar crashes into the cyclone fence, flattening it. Other fingers slide from the crevice, until a whole hand rests in dirt.

I back up and ease into a fighting stance.

"Maman, let me have a go at this one." It's thicker than two of me, but it has hands, so it might have soft places. And here, finally, is something I can do. Something I trained for. A fight where I, too, can be unsportsmanlike. And I plan to be.

Maman ignores me, shifting the stick in her hands, rigid in her awkward pose. Not a thing in her posture betrays fear, but she's daft to try this; she doesn't even stand right for a ruck. Arm raised as though she wields a deadly blade, she waits with a frigging twig in her hands.

"Back up, Maman!"

She's too bloody close; you can't size up a bloke from that distance. Once a wall of muscle has a grip on you, the fight's over. In and out fast, that's the only ticket, change range with every attack. But Maman stands within a yard of him, as if begging to be trounced.

Another hand extends from the crevice. He's taking his bloody time, slow as a champ no one dares to challenge. Both hands grub for purchase in the soil, and one of them finds the dead laurel trunk. With a grunt, Hades hauls himself from the underworld.

I'm too awed to speak. Gods are beautiful. Beautiful. He's twice my size and built as only the ancients could imagine. He stands naked, buff and perfect, his rod dangling like a thick rope. His crown of curls, his gleaming muscles, his omnipotent bearing: he could snatch up Maman with his little finger.

He glowers down on her—tiny, skinny, battered—and doesn't even bother to sneer. There are strike points on that thick chest, I'm sure of it, but my knuckle could never sink that deep. I'd have to leap ten feet to hit that flawless throat. "He'll expect you under him. Never give a man what he expects," Pekelo would say. Then he would whisper in that strained, high voice, "Now we'll see how fast our Cricket is."

Maman glares up, like he's a naughty boy and she's about

to teach him a lesson. I'm not sure which one has more icy arrogance. He flexes silver fingers, and reaches a massive hand to seize Maman's head.

And it doesn't matter who he is, he's not roughing up my Maman.

I jam Mizou's silk, still gripped in my fist, into a trouser pocket. Backing up for a running start, I fly in with an upraised elbow, hoping to get deep in an eye socket and follow through with claws to the other eye. But he raises a forearm and I bounce off like a spit ball.

He turns to see what puny insignificance dares to challenge him. His eyes—what other world do they see? I barely register, as if I were dust—they consider me briefly, then turn back to Maman.

She's nose to his knee and craning her neck up, all her Trotoskov fury buzzing like fly wings.

He must have a weakness: a gap, heel, or tenderness. I need something that will force him to the ground. As he raises his hand again, I smack, full power of my spinning kick into his low back. He whirls about, annoyed, but I'm too fast to snatch hold of, and in that second, Maman strikes.

With all her force, she plunges her broken laurel branch into the back of his knee. It passes deep into silver flesh and sticks there. Like Suat Bey's harem eunuch, Hades buckles.

But this is not a mortal, to be brought down with one crippling blow. This is an Olympian, one of three who defeated the Titans. His beautiful face scrunches into a hideous snarl. As he falls, he twists about and grabs Maman by the waist, locking fingers round her and crushing.

Her head snaps back and masses of blonde hair tumble over Hades' silver skin. Maman gasps, kicking and squirming. Hades, down on one knee with the stick still poking like a thorn, heaves her onto his shoulder. He struggles to a stand. With a growl he limps toward the crack in the underworld.

He will take her. I frantically search for anything big enough to stop him. There's nothing I can lift, hurl, or heave that would make an impact. My body, for once, is too small. I must leap high again and hope that his face is tender.

I back up for a good running start, and Mizou's scrap of silk wriggles from my pocket. As I run it spreads in the wind, darting before me like a Fury. It reaches Hades before I do and wraps round his neck, tightening. I land a back-fist in the center of his face and he stumbles. He drops Maman and grabs his bruised nose, claws at the cloth. The silk cinches tighter.

Maman lies crumpled, panting. Stiffly, she rises to her knees. As the god fights to breathe, she reaches for the stick that juts from his flesh. Yanking it free, she teeters upright. He is choking, face swelling, silver lips turning dusky.

Maman raises the branch, dripping with his silver blood, and aims high overhead, to his chest.

"Give back what you have taken from me," she whispers.

He turns bulging eyes to her face. Eye to eye, god to Trotoskov, they consider one another. Will she stab him in the heart? *Ah, such piety. Such charity. You will do the same yourself, Princess, if you are ever forced to threaten a life.*

Maman steps back. "*Allez-y!*" She points to the crack in the earth, voice steady as a sovereign's. "Release them."

The god coughs, breath a luminous haze. With both hands, he rips the scrap of silk from his neck, shredding it. For a brief second he smiles down on the tiny mortal who glowers at him.

Then his fist comes down, a solid ball of muscle, as big as her head, falling to squash her flat. And I am ready to die with her as I hurl myself onto his shoulders.

I'm spinning, he's turning about, trying to shake me off. I grope for that dip under the jaw that will kill a man, but even bearing down with all my force doesn't worry him. So I jam all my fingers into an eye. He howls and hurls me.

"Apollo, help us!" shrieks Maman.

I smack hard ground, the wind knocked out of me. Apollo's Temple quakes. Heaving marble columns lift off their foundations, toppling with thunderous booms, crashing around god and mortal. One falls onto Hades' chest, his gorgeous ribs pinned flat.

The earth shifts, and the furious, heaving god slides into his crevice. With a creak and rumble, the crevice starts to close.

"*Non!*" screams Maman. She falls to her knees and crawls to the crack. Cheek flat in the dirt, she thrusts her arm and shoulder into the gap. "Give them back, you son of a bitch! Xiao, Mizou, Suat Bey!"

The earth groans, and she snatches out her arm as the crevice snaps closed.

Maman rolls over and lies in a heap, the temple collapsed around her, her face as white as death.

"Maman!" I scramble over broken marble and slip in loose earth. "Are you hurt?"

She doesn't answer. Her eyes close.

"No, you have to live. I need you."

I gather her up in my arms. She's insubstantial, as though the fight took the last of her scant weight. Her face is filthy, chin cut, blonde hair grotty with blood and sweat.

"I couldn't save them," she whispers. I hug her, pressed to me like a child. She gives a spent smile. "But Boris would be proud, *n'est pas?*"

"Absolutely." I kiss her cool forehead. "Only a Trotoskov could give a god a good drubbing."

She giggles like the girl she never got to be, and then tears fill her eyes. "Did you see Xiao?"

"Of course."

"I miss him, Jiè, more than I can stand."

And she closes her eyes, and stops breathing.

"Maman!" I shake her. "No! No!"

Distraught, I lift her, rock her, grip her to my heart. She lies limp and yielding, all color drained from her face. No breath, no pulse, no life.

Crouched over her body I wail, inconsolable. I've lost her.

Maman, who longed to be loved. I love you, Maman. You are more than I ever dreamed you could be. Don't leave me again. Don't leave me, Maman. My heart's about to break.

And I love Xiao, who lost his dreams, and lonely Boris. Poor Fleur, who came and went without a sound, and Emma with her unshakable loyalty. I even love dear George, who accepted me as his own and got nothing but trouble for it.

And my tender Chander. He will betray love no matter what he chooses. I was so unfair to you, Chander.

And then I'm crying for myself, the sea washing behind me, for somehow I must live without them. Live to be worthy of them.

When I can cry no more, I stand and lift Maman from between the fallen pillars, to raise her body toward the sea. As I turn to the bare horizon where the temple once stood, I see the Mediterranean. Dawn is coming; the sea glows soft as a kiss. A blue like no other, anywhere in the world.

Over those exquisite aquamarine waves, a shadow rides toward me. A vision more of hope than of flesh: two horses, walking side by side. One carries a Turkish soldier, lean and tough, hugging a Roma dancer draped in sequined veils. On the other horse sits a powerful warrior, behind him a *Princess* in a gray wool dress, her hands round his waist and her cheek on his broad back.

The horses stop before me, and Maman leans down, running thin fingers through my blue black hair.

"Go on now, Jiè," she says. "We will wait for you in the Elysium Fields." With a kiss on the cheek, she whispers, "And wherever you go, my Cricket, I will always love you."

# EPILOGUE

11 August, 2007

Dear Jiè,

The battle still rages over whether or not to scour *The Eye of your mischief*, and so far your admirers are winning. I don't recommend, however, that you come back to London any time soon. I'm delighted that you're so chuffed with art school, and that you don't find living in Tate's old flat depressing. Paris is rather gray isn't it? It takes a stout heart to live there.

George and I are looking forward to your show in September, but we won't be a bother and stay with you, so don't fuss over getting paint and canvas off the floor.

Oh, and a chap named Alton came looking for you. He seemed a rough sort, so I told him he had the wrong address. Did I do the right thing? Take heed, in any case, as he may show up in Paris. I know you are capable of defending yourself, but please don't hesitate to call the police. I'm not sure our hearts can bear any more sorrow.

Enclosed is a note from Mumbai, India. Do you know someone there? Someday, my child, we will have to get acquainted.

I love you,
Emma

~

*30 July, 2007*

*Dear Jiè,*


*It may take ten years. Can you wait? She's married herself off to someone else, someone much more to her liking, I'm afraid.*

*I am happy, thinking of you.*

*Chander*

# ABOUT THE AUTHOR

**DR. LISA MURPHY** has been a practicing physician for over twenty-five years. She is the author of two published novels, *The Turkish Mirror* and *The Wyrmstone*, both works of Magical Realism. She has also written a book of humorous short stories, available in English and German editions: *In My Father's Garden* and *Im Garten Meines Vaters*. She is currently working on a four-volume series of historical fiction that extends from 1832 to 1865, encompassing the Civil War. She says of her work: "I am particularly fond of language: ancient, modern, ethnic, upper class, gutter slang, the language of thieves or the idioms of doctors, the words a mother might choose, or a wizard. I collect vocabularies and marvel at speech patterns. We have delightful ways of expressing ourselves, we humans."

# The Wyrmstone

---

I, Mimi Jovel, inherited The Wyrmstone. Too magnificent to give away, too deadly to keep. I thought I had enough troubles: my parents dead, two brothers to raise, Child Protective Service on our backs, adult-sized bills to pay … Now we're haunted by an eight-hundred-year-old sorcerer who has decided to entangle us in a dragon war. Dragons, in case you were wondering, are wily, conniving, nasty creatures.

But there's hope. My brother Justin is an obsessed Age of Dragons player who makes all of his decisions by rolling twenty-sided dice. My little brother Nicholi will only listen to his stuffed bear. Three kids, a stuffed bear, and some twenty-sided dice; we'll survive, just you see.

# *Prologue*

My brother was a goodhearted fool who lived and died by the stupid things fools do. As the eldest, I was entitled to the succulent lands of Tuscany that my father had civilized, one bloody war at a time. But my father's will allotted his vast estates to my bland-tempered brother, and I inherited nothing but a sorcerer's staff.

Having no resources with which to correct this slight, I stayed my tongue, biding my time. Then in 1201 my lord brother decided to marry. He was showered with gifts, and came into possession of an amethyst.

The gem was the size of a snake egg and as purple as a bruise. Skilled fingers had cut it flat on the back, and carved its face into the six facets favored by Yvess, the Highland dragon empress. My brother brought it to me that I might charm it, to bring his flushed and delicious wife many offspring. He did not know the legend of the gem. But I did.

So I indulged him. I bound the gem in a tangle of golden roots as grasping as the sweet fig of a girl who had captured his heart. Into that gold I carved a spell to grant pregnancy and powerful sons. Then, I indulged myself.

Since my father's death I had secretly watched the dragon, but had not dared to approach him. Even a young dragon of a thousand years can dominate an unwary sorcerer, and this was the ancient Lowland King, a Great Wyrm of the swamps. I was cautious not to alert him to my interest, admiring only from afar the impressive swath of crushed villages that trailed behind him, undeterred by my brother's army. Adrikhedon, they called him: Dark Destroyer. A fit implement to relieve me of the brother who chafed against my skin. This dragon would be mine.

While my brother wasted his last days planning a wedding feast, and his final nights dreaming of his bride's maidenhead, I read my father's sorcery texts. On the wedding night I retreated to the dungeon. In a cauldron of pounded lead I sacrificed our family's most potent relics: the legendary sword Deathwish, proven against the Highland Emperor Wyrm; a cinnabar vial of the lethal Night Veil, stolen from Arabic alchemists; and a black drop of dragon's blood, dripped from the vial concealed in my father's staff. Drawing on all I had learned from moldy books, I melded these into a Mist of Forging.

*Bring me Adrikhedon to do my will.* Deep in the dungeon I sucked in the searing hot vapor, and blew the acid breath of my soul's desire into the tangle of gold that gripped the stone.

Out from the stone flew Yvess' dragon guards, roaring with protest, frenzied for slaughter. Huge ghostly horrors, they swirled above in the dusty rafters, shrieking with lust to get tooth and claw into me. I trembled, shielded by my thin cloak, cursing my father for having taught me so little. I had known the stone was strong; legend said it was enchanted by Yvess herself, and she is the sovereign of magical illusion. But I had not foreseen such powerful resistance. I had but seconds to dominate, or die.

There is an abyss where lives the soul of man; half beast, half human, the soul crouches, forever twisting, now toward heaven, now toward hell. A sorcerer can reach but once into this darkness, and whatever he grabs to sacrifice will never be his again. With clawed hands I ripped from this abyss the human I had so little use for, and thrust this scrap of myself into the gold.

"Go," I panted, holding aloft my father's staff. "Crumble to dust wyrms of Yvess, for I, Pancrizio Sovrani, claim the power of this stone."

With screams of ire the creatures lunged. Mist of dragon breath on my neck. The prick of talons over my heart. But my staff prevailed; inches from my throat they folded, drifting like so many cobwebs in the dungeon dampness. And then they dissolved into ash.

Dawn of my brother's first wedded day, and a lone rooster croaked at the timid sunrise. Soaked in sweat and vigorous with my mastery, I held up my prize: the Wyrmstone was complete.

"Adrikhedon," I whispered. I climbed the twisted staircase from dungeon to tower, arriving at the bridal chamber. "Adrikhedon."

The dragon came immediately, green and terrible. Lords, guards, and riffraff alike slept off the wedding wine as it hovered. It exhaled once on the thick walls of the tower, searing a gap through which it poked barbed jaws. In one slobbering bite it seized my brother by the neck and lifted him skyward as he thrashed.

I tossed aside his screaming wife and stood in the mangled hole. My father's staff poured forth foul darkness from my right hand, and the Wyrmstone streamed a milky light from my left.

*"Adrikhedon, proch mandatum niss calx sna rŭ gethrix, draŭtox."*

My Draconic was mispronounced and far too softly spoken. The dragon hovered, turning his golden gaze on me. He shuddered with such a violent retch of hatred I thought he might drop my brother's corpse. For what seemed an eternity he hung aloft, wings flapping foul air over my head, short swords of teeth bared. His glare ate at my will, probing the power of the stone. His contempt pounded like blows from his tail. I shook, but dared not cower. Had I shown a rag end of fear or a flicker in self-command, had the stone been anything short of its legend, he would have devoured me. But I overmastered, and with loathing and reluctance the dragon turned aside and did my hest, carrying my brother's mangled body back to his swamp. And thus Adrikhedon became my slave: untrustworthy and disagreeable, but obedient.

In time, the girl my brother loved was also subdued. Women, it appears, are as difficult as dragons. I never knew if the first son she bore was mine, or if he was sired by my craven brother. The boy fled me as soon as he could run. No matter, he was one of twelve sons, each bigger and more powerful than the last. Together we scraped scars into

Tuscany that would have made my father howl. Maimed and starving, his subjects begged for mercy. In the jaws of Adrikhedon's dragon army I ground up all that my father had done and spit it out, bloody and ruined, on his grave. Sweet redress for how little faith he had in me.

And then Yvess was revenged; my twelfth son was so brawny he slew my body soon after the first wisps of hair sprouted on his chin. But I am not so easily destroyed. What remained of my soul retreated into the gold that grips Yvess' jewel. My son was too frightened to use me, too greedy in his dotage to pass me on to his heir. So he hid me.

We are trapped now, the jewel and I, in a world that no longer believes in dragons. For eight hundred years I have waited, my hatred fettered, my fury impotent. Now is the hour to seize fate by the throat. She comes, a mere girl who cannot resist, the one destined to wield the Wyrmstone.

# Chapter 1

The blade hit with enough force to jab zings through my head. I raised the hatchet in the pouring rain and hacked at the roots of Mom's dead fig tree, slamming blindly into the muddy hole, sure that my butter-loving heart would collapse. Barely visible in the filthy mess, the wood didn't even splinter.

Exhausted, my fingers let go. The blade dropped, driving several inches into the goo. Mom planted this fig, and she should have dug it out. It's absurd to plant a fig in the Pacific Northwest. It made hundreds of tiny green fruits that grew all winter long. They got fatter and fatter through the summer until you could almost taste how sweet they were going to be. Then, just as the first heavy rains began in September, they fell off. Thud. Dry and stringy with tough skins, coated with fine hairs, bitter. Not even the squirrels would eat them.

My mother grew up in Tuscany, the northern part of Italy, where I guess figs are friendlier. Maybe when she planted this tree she didn't know any better. But Mom was from the root-hog-or-die school of gardening. More erudite gardeners might give you a lecture on "the right plant for the right place." Mom never talked about it, she just ripped out anything that didn't thrive. Roses have blackspot? Yank them up by the roots. Columbine infested with caterpillars? Throw the whole wiggling mess into the clean green container. After years of intolerance she'd made a magnificent garden that admirers drove miles to visit. "How do you do it?" they'd ask. She wouldn't say. It was ruthless mass murder. She is, or rather *was*, a serial plant killer.

But not the fig. The fig could do no wrong. Green fruit beetles ate the leaves. Phomopsis canker killed branches. Nematodes knotted the roots. Mom battled these deformities as though the fig were a sacred trust. Diligently, Mom pruned, dug in worm compost, and swept away aborted fruit before we were overrun by ants. That repulsive fig took as much fussing as the whole rest of her third acre.

Then it died. Two weeks before her plane exploded, the trunk cracked and the black, dry remains of the cambium fell out of the gap like ash. It was left to me to finally dig the tree out. I put it off, and put it off, and put it off, inert with sorrow whenever I thought about pulling on her gloves and lifting her garden tools. Now here I was, unfit and unwilling.

I took off soaked gloves and wiped mud off my forehead. I hated sweaty tasks, and Mom and Dad left behind a lot of them. My brother, Justin, had more than enough muscle for this excavation, but he refused. Since our parents' funeral Justin made all of his decisions by throwing a twenty-sided die. In the case of the fig, Justin rolled a two, claimed the dead stump sat on "unhallowed ground," and avoided the courtyard, carefully entering and exiting by the driveway.

Fantasy could be annoyingly convenient.

Justin is totally obsessed with the roll-playing game Age of Dragons. He advises me, "When all else fails, consult a dragon." No doubt a dragon could easily rip out Mom's dead fig stump, or even put a talon on why I chose to dig it up today, in the pouring rain. But dragons rarely ally with humans (Justin claims), and always for devious purposes, so good luck. That's probably for the best (Justin would warn), because dragons are risky business, cold hearted and cunning. They spend centuries lying in caves, plotting, and when they emerge they are formidable, outwitting even the sharpest hoard thieves and wyrm slayers. I guess that's why one waits until all else has failed. And there was another significant drawback: dragons don't exist. So, forget dragons. Since Justin's dice had instructed him not to help me, I was on my own.

Well, not quite. Because as fate arranged it, Mom and Dad left behind another opinionated kid, Nicholi, who won't listen to anyone but Didoo, his stuffed bear. Nicholi is only six; he can't hit with enough force to dent a daffodil. But Nicholi and Didoo are full of advice. They would cite Wikipedia: a hatchet has to have a head that weighs less than three pounds, or it isn't a hatchet. Three pounds was useless, they'd point out. This task needed one of Justin's Dwarven battleaxes. Lacking any magically forged weapons, I yanked the puny blade free and slung it aside. Wiping my filthy gloves down the front of Mom's raggedy garden coat, I went to find a pickax.

Mom's garden shed is just like Mom. *Was.* Just like she *was*: weird, but prepared. The dusty metal shelves were crammed to sagging with every strange thing she thought the family might need. A shed-full of her paranoia: her small hands bundling, sealing in baggies, wrapping together with wire, tucking things neatly into drawers as if someday our branch of the Sovrani family might be called upon to do something extraordinary. But all we ever needed were mundane things. That polished bamboo pole, honed to an impressive point and leaning beside the rake? Made for a squirrel nest high in the boiler chimney. That sledgehammer, handle thick as a troll's wrist and its head five pounds of deadly bludgeon? Used to pound in rebar for staking the dahlias. That mysterious clear tube of green liquid, sealed in a glass jar on the highest shelf? Instant bonding, indestructible, invisible drying glue for when Nicholi accidentally breaks Justin's Swamp Dragon miniature, which he isn't supposed to even look at much less play with, and Justin will be home in fifteen minutes and does she have anything that dries fast?

Since her death we rummage in here daily. Inside the doorway I stepped around the coiled Bonsai wire that Justin used yesterday to make a Skeletal Hand of Power. No doubt this was something to wield as his Age of Dragons friends rolled dice and leaned toward the center of the table, calculating hit points. This reminded me that said Hand still hung by the wrist, copper claws tightly flexed against the wall opposite Justin's bed, arched like a Tarantula about to spring. Mom and Dad didn't agree on much when it came to parenting, but about weapons they took a united stance; only Justin's Age of Dragons miniatures could brandish swords and hurl axes. No full-sized weapons, even homemade imaginary ones, in the house. For Mom's and Dad's sake, I'd have to do something about The Hand. Given the mood Justin had been in the last few days, the politics of removing The Hand were tricky. Something I wasn't looking forward to. I sucked in a deep breath of resignation and winter mold.

In the spring Mom's shed smelled like alfalfa pellets for the roses, and then WD40 in the fall for the pruning sheer hinges. Mom's odor changed too; you could tell her state of mind by her scent. On boisterous days she wore the sensuous Italian perfume Flora, filling the room with sweet, pollinating flowers. On bad days, when she folded into herself as quiet as a secret, she left behind whiffs of pungent, bittersweet Night Veil. Every morning the scent of her perfume hung over the coffee pot like news from afar. Despite all of my efforts, I'd never been able to wrap my head around her bizarre ways, her fears, not even her smell. No matter how heavy my regret, I would never understand.

I grabbed the worn handle of Mom's pickax. Mom had only been dead for two months, and already her pickax was nicked and stained with rust; one more thing that suffered without her. But it was still sharp—Mom asked Dad to keep her tools lethally sharp. And it was heavy. I hauled it out of the garden shed and attacked mud, roots, and sawed-off trunk indiscriminately, flinging crud ten feet in an effort to demolish something, anything, my misery.

At least I only had to contend with the stump. Our neighbor, Marty, who was deeply in love with his chain saw, sauntered over the day after the funeral and offered to cut the dead fig down. I guess this was his equivalent of bringing a casserole. At the time I was too numb and overwhelmed to think it through. Whistling and waving his blade, Marty sectioning the rotten tree, easy as slicing a Twinkie, then shoved the chunks into the belly of his covered pickup truck. He left a bare smudge right in the center of the courtyard where the tree's canopy had intimidated other plants. A mini wasteland in Mom's beautiful garden, with a hacked up root ball slimed in mud and an excavation hole rapidly filling with rain. And I stood in that hole, icy water rising over the top of Mom's steelshank boots and pooling in my wrinkled socks. Gritting my teeth against the exercise, I raised the heavy pickaxe, cursed, shivered, and chopped.

I was about to give up when on my last weary swing, I heard a chink. Not the jarring crack of hitting a rock. Not the dampened thud of something organic. A metallic chink that quivered up my spine and made my ears ring with alarm. I froze, axe poised, breath held.

What the heck?

Cautiously, I stuck a gloved hand into the goo. A menacing heat diffused through my glove. Holy moly. I snatched back my hand. Dropping the pickax, I leaned above the pool of icy water, and peered into the slimy recess.

A small rectangular box lay wedged in the very heart of the roots, dented by their squeezing. Faint light seeped from box's seams, a milky glow that lit the roots, creeping onto my face. Warmth tingled through me, a glimmer of awe and fear. I felt a pull as binding as a rope, tied around my neck. This was it. This was what I'd been digging for.

That was ridiculous; I was here to dig the stump out.

I sat back on my heels and squinted into the hole. Mom must have put this here; no one else dared to work in her garden. But what was it?

My heart leapt, puppyish with excitement. Calm down, Mimi. Hanging out with Justin and his Age of Dragons friends had warped my brain. This was not from Justin's *Book of Legendary Treasure.* The odd glow was an illusion of twilight, or my head, buzzing with that awful physical labor. I took a few deep breaths. Mom did mysterious things, but with ordinary objects. Given the ups and downs in Mom's stability, the box could hold anything from an umbilical cord to a gold brick. I could badly use a gold brick. Best case scenario: this would help pay the rent. Worst case scenario: the contents would be gross and senseless and I wouldn't be able to throw it away fast enough.

With semi-frozen hands, I clawed aside clay. The roots didn't yield to my tug, but hung on with a death grip. So I retrieved Mom's long-handled pruners from the shed. Straining and grunting, I snipped the roots one by one. They didn't spring back as I had expected; they curled around the box as though nothing short of chipping and shredding could destroy them. I had to pry off the fingers and snap them into little chunks at their knuckles.

Finally, I freed one face of the box. I wedged my hands around the metal sides and pulled. Hard. I braced myself with a foot and put my aching back into it. My grip slipped and I staggered backwards, falling to the bottom of the hole, wallowing, soaking wet in soggy boots.

Taking off a dripping glove, I shoved Mom's wool night watchman's cap out of my face. That fig was supernatural in its determination, as though it had a will of its own. But the box was mine. I could feel it yanking at my heart. I wanted it with a passion that overwhelmed common sense. So, despite a nagging thought that this was hella-stupid, I was going to free it.

I threw aside Mom's gloves and knelt in the muddy water. Wedging both hands into the cranny above the lid, I rammed my fingers through the tangle of roots and hooked the back of the box with my fingertips. Bracing my legs against a knot of wood, I groaned under my breath and heaved. Slowly the box moved. With creaks of protest the roots released their prisoner, scraping two deep gashes into the backs of my hands. I gasped from stinging pain as the container slid into my lap, heavy and warm as a living heart.

It was a stout, battered toolbox, six inches deep and one handbreadth square. A slender handle twisted, bent on the top. Dirt caked the seams and rust ate at the dents. The hinge pins were corroded, and the color had long ago chipped off the box's metal surface. In the front, a scruffy combination lock secured the tongue and loop of the catch. The numbers were long ago worn away and the dial was rusted. The box had the hopeful weight of gold bricks. I shifted it on my lap and its dense contents dragged from side to side.

I stood up, hefting my prize, cheeks so numb with cold that the drops barely stung. Rain trickled off my cap and into my open collar. The cuts on my hands burned, and my soaking wet jeans clung to my calves. I ached all the way to my soul. The loneliness of a funeral is nothing compared to what hits after the mourners leave. I had to bear this somehow, grow up fast for Justin and Nicholi. As Judge Burrows had reminded me at the custody hearing, I was only eighteen and couldn't afford to screw up. The court's supervisory stare was on me like a red laser dot trained on my forehead. One summer at the South Sound Culinary Institute didn't make me an adult. Partying with my boyfriend Duke was an education, but not in parenting. I'd had to leave college while I was still a dishpig, cleaning up after the master chefs. I'd better keep my head on straight or my two brothers wouldn't be in my custody for long. And as difficult as they were, I adored my brothers. They were not going to foster care. Not as long as I was alive.

I looked down at the damaged box. My mother buried this. I didn't know what it was or why she hid it. So much about her life, even her death, made no sense at all. But whatever was in this box was unmistakably mine. I knew it from the end of my frost-frozen nose to my feet, marinating in mud. Please, I begged, please—may it give me the strength to carry us through.